A. R. Horvath
*presents*

# Birth Pangs:
# SPERO

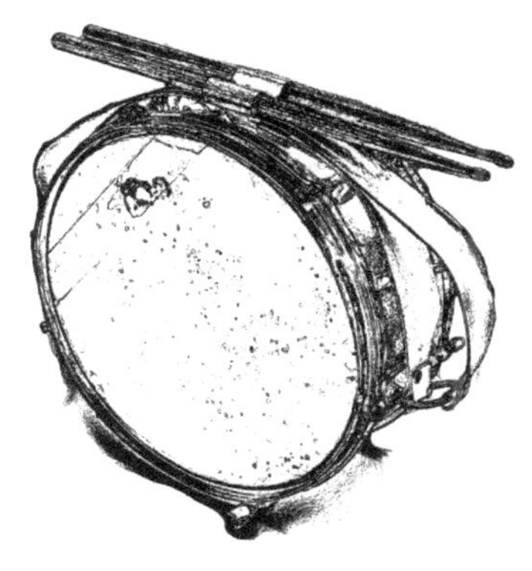

A.R. HORVATH PRESENTS

# BIRTHPANGS

## *THE SERIES*

"I consider that our present sufferings are not worth comparing with the glory that will be revealed in us. The creation waits in eager expectation for the sons of God to be revealed. For the creation was subjected to frustration, not by its own choice, but by the one that subjected it, in hope that the creation itself will be liberated from its bondage to decay and brought into the glorious freedom of the children of God. *We know that the whole creation has been groaning as in the pains of childbirth right up to the present time…*"

Book 2

# SPERO

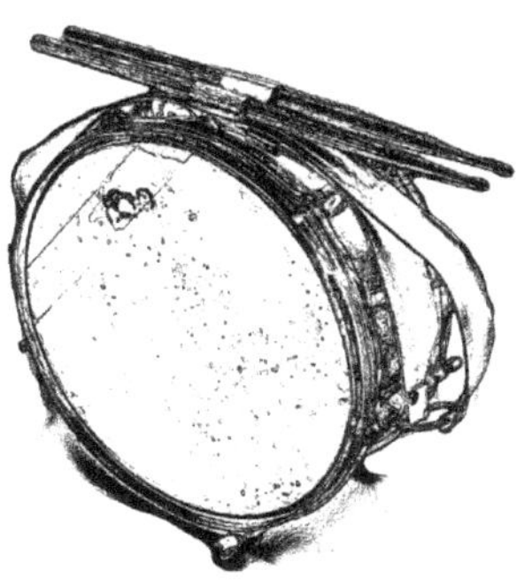

www.birthpangs.com

Published by Suzeteo Enterprises
www.suzeteo.com

Part of the Athanatos Pulishing Company
www.athanatosministries.org

Cover and interior graphics by Luke Thompson
www.sojournerdesign.org

Illustrations by Kelley Kaffenberger
www.kaffenberger.info



ISBN-9# 0-9791276-3-7
ISBN -13# 978-0-9791276-3-2
Printed in the United States of America.

Thanks especially to my wife,
whose steadfastness makes projects like *Spero* possible.

Most of all, thanks to *the* One who Broods and Wills and Quickens; the Dream Fulfiller…

This book is dedicated to my children.

Brothers, we do not want you to be ignorant about those who fall asleep, or to grieve like the rest of men, who have no hope… But since we belong to the *day*, let us be self-controlled, putting on faith and love as a breastplate, and the hope of salvation as a *helmet*.

-1 Thessalonians, the Bible.

Mrs. Schachter had lost her mind… on the third night [in the cattle car] … a piercing cry broke the silence: "Fire! I see a fire! I see a fire!" … She was howling, pointing through the window: "Look! Look at this fire!" … Some pressed against the bars to see. There was nothing. Only the darkness of *night*. "She is mad, poor woman…" … "Jews, listen to me," she cried. "I see a fire! I see flames, huge flames!" It was as though she were possessed by some evil spirit. We tried to reason with her, more to calm ourselves, to catch our breath, than to soothe her: "She is hallucinating because she is thirsty, poor woman… that is why she speaks of flames devouring her…" … [Finally, much later] we were pulling into a station. Someone near a window read to us: "Auschwitz." … And as the train stopped, this time we saw flames rising from a tall chimney into a black sky… In the air, the smell of burning flesh.

-Elie Wiesel, *Night*.

# == Chapter 1 ==

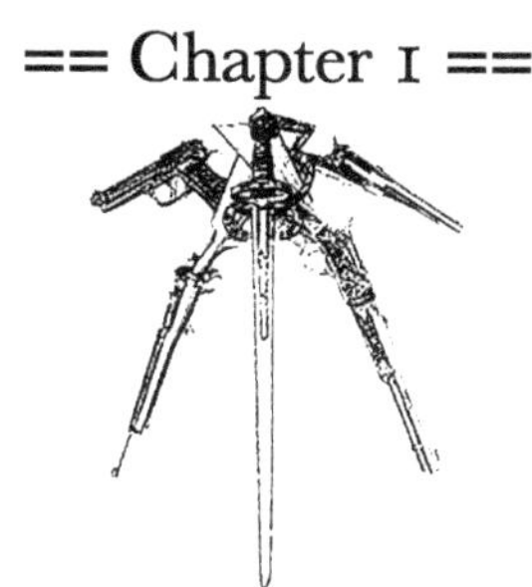

"Do not despair, my child," the woman exhaled soothingly. She reached her hand through the fallen beams and pieces of window to touch his. He was miraculously untouched by the fallen debris; nonetheless, he was imprisoned beneath it. With the boy's safety momentarily assured, the woman appraised the situation.

The evening had been proceeding normally enough. She had been preparing to enter the marketplace when things had gone awry. The market was a collection of vendors gathered in the remains of one of the "supermarts" of old, its owners long gone now. In many areas, these buildings had been stripped for materials leaving virtually no remains. In places like this one, most of the building still existed, even if in disrepair, and served as shelter for various merchants. Such a building had its hazards, but generally served its purpose well. Even in its prime, however, it had been inadequate to endure the calamity she and the boy now found themselves in.

A light had flashed to the east, followed by a rumbling. All eyes were drawn to the horizon to find a sun where there ought not to have been a sun. Then the building began to shake and tremble. The woman had only a moment to notice the boy near the entrance to the marketplace, and then to notice the walls buckling. She had jumped towards him and shoved him away from the danger, but alas, she had been too far to rescue him completely; debris fell all around him, trapping him. The boy was lying, frightened, under a heap, and she was not strong enough to create an opening.

"Do not despair," she repeated. A confusion of sound emanated from the building—a mixture of continuing collapse and human cries. People were running in all directions around them. Some were running past her out of the ruins, but some were running in. Others, outside, were hurrying by to some unknown destination. The woman remained hunched over with her arm extended into the heap to touch the young one's trembling hand. She heard a disconcerting shout nearby and turned her head to see that the speaker had spoken truly: a fire had broken out. She noticed now, too, that there were other bodies under the heap. These did not appear to be as fortunate as the boy. She averted her eyes.

"Help me!" The boy strained to call to her. He was on his belly with his head turned out towards the open plain, which was once parking lot. He could not lift his body even an inch. A steel beam was nestled across his back, though it did not apply pressure to him.

"Yes, I will," she replied firmly and calmly. She sat up and shouted at some of the people who were running around her, but none of them stopped. They all had someone else on their minds, someone else to save. Or worse, they were cowards looking after their own safety. The woman graciously discarded this possibility, but could not keep from being annoyed that no one was coming to her aid. She bowed low again so she could look into his face. "I will get us help," she assured him.

"No one will believe what I have sing," the boy replied. The woman looked at him with surprise.

"I don't understand," she said, studying the boy's predicament again to see if maybe he'd sustained a head injury she couldn't see.

"Look," the boy instructed her. He said it, but he could not point. She followed his eyes instead, and this meant turning around to glance behind her.

Coming towards them was a man. There was something extraordinary about the man. He seemed to be fantastically beautiful. His clothing seemed to belong to his being so that one could not be sure he was clothed at all. Rainbow colors flitted about the ground around him as though he were a prism dividing the light that passed through his utterly substantial body. He had a sword. It sprayed light about just as the man did. Remarkably, none of the people running around them seemed to notice.

The woman gasped. She fell backwards ignominiously, but quickly regained her composure. She fell at his feet in a manner that suggested to the boy that she was worshipping the man.

"My Lord!" she exclaimed. "I would not have expected this in a million years!"

"No eyes shall see, no mind shall conceive," he laughed in reply. "Arise, woman." The woman leapt up and meant to embrace him, but he stopped her with a solemn gesture.

"The boy ..." she said.

"Yes, the boy," the man reminded her.

"He's trapped under the weight of these things. The building has fallen apart all over the place, but he is in a pocket of safety," she informed the man.

The man placed his sword on the ground and bent low to look into the rubble. "Hello, boy," the man greeted him.

The boy was certain that there were colors dancing around him that he had never seen before. He searched his mind for some label to attach to this remarkable thing he was witnessing. One possibility seemed obvious. He ventured, "Are you an angel?"

The man threw his head back and laughed. The boy found this to be an unexpected and unnerving response to his question. He felt embarrassed and driven to try to think of any thing at all that might explain the man better. Lying there immobile, he grasped for other explanations until finally thinking of one. It seemed a long shot. He had heard both searching statements and derisive statements about this possibility out of the same mouth—his father's. Because his father never seemed to have made up his mind on the matter, the boy was hesitant to say anything, especially after hearing this man's response to his question. Still, he could think of no other possibility.

"Are you ... Jesus?" the boy stammered. The woman shrieked.

"Forgive him his blasphemy, my Lord!" she exclaimed, throwing her body between the man and the rubble that was the boy. "He does not know any better!"

The man sat up and looked at her sternly, "Is that not the tragedy of this generation, this race?"

"Pardon him, please, my Lord!" she insisted.

"Surely you know that there is mercy for the ignorant," he chided her. "Full-throated justice and full-blooded mercy dance together with ease within *him*. Surely you know."

The woman's face reddened slightly. Of course, she knew. The boy, on the other hand, still had no answer to his question. Despite his position of peril, he couldn't help but stare at the marvelous man and consider what he might be. But the man was doing something, now.

The woman was gently moved aside, and the man had produced what seemed to be a sash. He wrapped it around his waist, once again making it difficult to discern what was garment and what was skin. All this while, people still rushed to and fro about them without any awareness of the marvel among them. The man was on his hands and knees. He passed out of the boy's sight, presumably working down by the boy's legs. Suddenly the claustrophobic cave expanded. The heap spread up and out, away from the boy, and he was able to turn his head. The boy rolled to his side and, to his amazement, the man seemed immensely larger. The man was actually above him, supporting the fallen debris on his back. The man seemed to have passed through the building's remains and lifted them right up. The boy looked up into the man's crystalline eyes.

He saw what seemed to be liquid light streaming down the man's torso. It was the man's blood. The boy was sure of it. The man looked down on the boy kindly with his oversized arms to either side of the boy, like pillars holding up a temple ceiling. The boy was in awe as he considered that the drops of light falling on him were the man's blood; this man was enduring pain for his sake. Though the man was suffering, no hint of it could be seen on his face.

Realizing that the initiative had shifted to him, the boy turned all the way around so that he could crawl out of his brief prison. But when he turned he caught sight of some of the other bodies that were nearby, one of which had been under the same pile of wreckage with him. It was his mother. Nearby was his brother. The boy froze there on his hands and knees and stared at the gruesome scene. His arms gave out, his knees slid back. The boy slumped back to his belly, still in danger, his eyes transfixed at the sight of his mangled family.

Something inside the boy snapped right then. Something broke, and the man and the woman both knew it when it happened. The boy's eyes went dark, and they knew it without seeing it. The man and the woman both began to tremble, but not because of the after effects of the explosion to the east or the movement of the building still settling around them. They wept. Their bodies heaved with their sobs. The boy lay there, still and broken on the inside.

Gathering her wits, the woman reached in and grabbed the boy from underneath his shoulders. She dragged him out, and he remained motionless the entire time. When the boy was out from under the heap, the man let the pile drop with a crash. He wiped the blood from his sides with his sash and reclaimed his sword. They wept for the boy a little longer.

"The saying that is written will come true," the woman said at last, gathering the boy into her arms. His head was in her lap, and she stroked his hair. The boy's lifeless eyes stared into the darkening sky.

"*Marana tha*," the man returned with conviction. He used his sash now to wipe his own eyes.

The two slowly regained their composure. The evening had progressed since the explosion had set these events in motion, but a great setting sun to the west and to the east still granted them a little light. The man stood over the woman, who was still sitting and comforting the boy. The sword was in his hand.

"Are you prepared to receive your charge?" the man asked her.

"I am," she replied, choking up slightly.

"Then receive it," he replied, touching her on each shoulder with his sword before returning it to its sheath, which belonged somehow to his body. There was a moment's silence. She looked at the boy.

"You can ease his pain," she offered hesitantly.

"I could, but such easing means dulling his memories. A man needs his memories in order to overcome them. Is it better that he feels no pain but is no stronger?" he replied.

"And yet some will not overcome," she asserted.

The man sighed. "Such is the weight of the dignity of choice set upon this race. Some will overcome. Some will not. The pain is not theirs alone, though, and neither is the joy that results. Yet, I can help heal this wound," he said, reaching down and placing his hands on the boy's head. He left them there for a moment with his eyes closed. He opened them and looked at the boy's eyes.

"It is nearly dark in there," the man winced as though he had been struck. "I will bear some of his burden, but I have also seared the wound closed. It will take time for the scar to fade away. I have acted carefully. I cannot remove the wound altogether, and by the inexorable way of things it will reopen. Pray that he is strong enough then to endure it."

"Will I see you again, my Lord?" she asked the man as he stood to leave.

"Are you still a child that you would ask such a question?" he responded gently. "You know that such questions cannot be answered by us. No eye has seen, no mind has conceived. Do your duty; that is *your* task. Do my duty; that is *my* task. His grace is sufficient for us, but I too long that we might yet dine together at the great table. Now, go. The times are yet dangerous and deadly, but do not despair. Do not despair, my Lady, do not despair."

With that, the man melted into the night before her eyes, leaving her to carry out the ordinary business of escorting her charge from this place of danger. But she knew that she was not alone.

\+ + + +

It had been late in the afternoon when the explosion had occurred. By the time the woman had gathered up the boy and carried him away from the ruined building it was nearly dark. She calculated that it was more dangerous to move in the pitch dark than it would be to endure the coming and goings of refugees. Having scanned for shelter, she settled into a hollow alongside the main road and held the boy close to her breast. She could feel him breathing; except for that, there was hardly a sign of life about him. She passed the night sleeplessly. She watched as the sun made its appointed appearance. A pall of ash in the sky in that direction made it seem as though the sun was making its arc through a sandstorm. It was beautiful in its own terrible way.

She didn't waste any time. Concealing the boy, she quickly scoured the area for some way to transport him. Though stronger than many men, even she could not carry a boy of this size for long. She found a piece of plywood that had worked itself loose from a house. She put two pieces of lumber underneath it and secured it with a length of rope she had found. To complete the task, she put a blanket on the plywood to soften where she would lay the boy. Then, she tied another length of rope to the ends of the two pieces of lumber and put the rope over her shoulders. Using her arms and back, she would be able to pull the child down the road. If she had been a different kind of woman, she'd have grumbled about the fact that there was hardly any gain for all the effort expended. It was only a temporary accommodation, anyway. As soon as she found something better she would certainly use it. Perhaps the boy would start walking again.

She trudged west. Naturally, everyone had the same idea. The sound of her lumber and siding scraping on the road was muffled by the sounds of people scurrying past her. Those who were healthy enough passed by quickly. After a couple of days, most of the people on the road were those burdened by injured loved moving at about the same pace as she.. A few days later, anyone uninjured in the calamities was gone. What remained was a train of the tortured making its way along a modern day trail of tears.

After about a week, she came to a bridge over a large river. She knew it was near the border of Indiana and Illinois. The boy had yet to make so much as a single noise and had made no signs that he would soon walk. The woman took this in stride. She couldn't help but wonder, though, if she might need to talk to the boy to try to ease him out of his shock. She could not carry him in this fashion indefinitely.

They had come to a crossroads. Refugees were passing through here to continue westward, but some were turning to the north. Others were arriving from the south. She decided she needed some information in order to determine her path.

"Hello there!" She called out to a man breaking camp near her own. The man eyed her warily initially, but then gave in. She had given him a winning smile.

"Alo," he replied.

"Which way are you going? Have you heard where we ought to go?" she asked him.

"Who would tell us? We're all just guessing, aren't we?" he chuckled.

"I think so. But I don't want to guess forever and end up in a worse place than I am now," she returned.

"Well," he said thoughtfully, "Many of those traveling south are saying that Chicago was nuked, and that makes a whole lot of sense to me. Why take out Indianapolis but not Chicago? But ash has been falling on us, blown in from the west. That makes me think St. Louis was hit. If that is the case, I would like to try—and I admit it may be for nothing—to get out of the path of that poison. I'm going to head north to Danville and take a left. I don't know if it will do any good, but I'm doing the best I can with the wits I have."

"That is a plan at least," she offered, "and that is more than it seems most have right now."

"No doubt about that," he frowned. "You'll pardon me, please, ma'am, but I'm going to get going. I figure my chances for survival improve the sooner I get out of this ash-wind. Between deadly diseases and nuclear explosions, I don't know if it matters where we go, I guess. It was a pleasure talking to you. Well, talking to anyone really. I'll look out for you." Then, before she could offer her own parting words, he had turned his back and was heading north just as fast as he could go.

"I say go west," a woman said from another site. "If Chicago is gone why would you want to be closer to it? Besides, even if St. Louis was nuked we're a long way from there. Can we really escape this foul atmosphere by jogging a bit north? I say get away from Indy just as fast as you can and if you head north you won't be heading away from it until you get well to Danville. On foot, that is another week at least."

"That is true," she replied. "But the problem is that both choices are cloaked in the unknown, yet I must choose between them. If your reasons are good and that man's reasons are good, I'm left to make up my own mind, come what may."

The woman shrugged, "I'm just giving you my opinion."

She hastened to ease her mind, "No, I welcome it. I just feel the weight of responsibility around my shoulders, and I would prefer to make a decision believing I have made it on facts."

"More facts I cannot offer," the woman replied curtly. Now, she too left abruptly. The woman and the boy were alone for a bit. People were coming and going, but she could not make up her mind. She confessed to herself that it was good to take a little break: that boy was heavy.

Shortly after noon, a larger party with a mixture of men, women, and children, came and rested near them. They struck up a conversation with her and kindly did not stare at the boy. It was clear that the party was an assembly of friends with a smattering of relations within it.

"Ma'am? Are you ok?" one man asked her.

She smiled kindly in response. "I am, thank you. Tired is all. The boy cannot walk, and I'm carrying him. But I don't know where to go. I'm thinking of sitting here for a spell until I decide," she laughed.

"There is no reason you couldn't come with us," another man informed her.

"I would be happy to help you bear your burden," the first man offered. She wanted to leap up at the offer, but didn't want to endanger the boy by putting him in bad company merely because her arms and back were sore.

"That is very kind of you," she smiled again.

"My name is Joshua," the first man said.

"And I'm Steve," the second man added.

"Pleased to meet you," she replied. "My name is Tasha. To be honest, though, I don't know the name of the boy."

The boy was lying on the makeshift stretcher, staring blankly into space.

"It is not your child?" Steve inquired.

"No," Tasha sighed. "I helped rescue him from a wreck of a building. I think his family is dead. But I'll take care of him. I'm happy to."

The men looked at her carefully and quietly. At last Steve spoke.

"I respect that, Tasha," he said softly. "Please, join us. We won't make promises we can't keep, but we will help you as long as you see fit to join us."

"Absolutely," Joshua agreed. Some of the women nearby nodded, too. It took some time, but eventually Tasha allowed the people in the group to tend to her and the boy. She hadn't quite realized until then that the rope had carved deep, dark, cuts into her shoulders. It wasn't that she had ignored the problem. She had covered her shoulders with a thick cloth but it had worn through very quickly, and when it did, she had reasoned that she may as well allow herself to get scarred up sooner rather than later. It made a telling testimony to Steve and Joshua, though. They felt they had the measure of the woman all in a glance.

Tasha soon discovered that this group had already made up its mind to head north to Danville and then head west to Champaign, Bloomington, and perhaps north into Wisconsin after that. While she could not possibly identify the various problems associated with heading north versus traveling west, she decided that traveling north with a supportive community was a much greater advantage than traveling west on her own. Well, not quite alone. Towing a boy.

The group set up camp for a few days. They scavenged the town of Terre Haute, which was the name of the city they were in, looking for anything that might be useful. Steve and Joshua had something specific in mind that they were looking for. Most of the town had been picked over pretty well, but they returned to Tasha jubilantly announcing that they had found a shed out in the woods a bit away from most of the houses; in that shed they had found an oversized children's wagon, which still had all of its wheels. They joked that the house they'd found it near was more like a fortress, for it had defied all their attempts to gain entrance into it. When they presented the wagon to Tasha, she couldn't help but be relieved. They worked hard to clean it up and managed to find some grease so the wheels would turn.

At the end of their time in Terre Haute, Tasha knew enough about this group of travelers to justify praising providence for dispatching such fine people to help her. Carrying the boy was still laborious. The wagon was difficult to pull on the run down state highways. At least there were others who would help pull him. They went north about a day's trip. It struck Tasha as they were setting up camp that it was high time she gave the boy a name, until he was able to talk on his own.

The weight of responsibility had never pressed down on her shoulders as it did that night when she closed her eyes to sleep. He was not her child to name, but name him she must. She would sleep on it and do her best. When she awoke in the morning, she had made a decision.

She put a cup of water on the boy's lips, carefully tipping it back so he would drink. His eyes were still lifeless, but she spoke to him anyway. "I will call you Coal, boy. But I'll spell it C-O-L-E so people don't think I've given you a silly nickname. Why Coal, you ask? Yes, I know you didn't say anything. I will answer you anyway, this time don't interrupt, alright? I will call you Coal because I see that you're under great pressure, and when that happens to coal what do you get? A diamond. You're hard pressed now, but some day you'll be a better man for it—if only you don't crack now. And I will make sure you don't."

She studied him as she finished giving him the water, but there was no hint of recognition. She sighed, fighting off the urge to be annoyed. She had hoped, for some reason, that trying to give him a name would rattle him out of his stupor, but alas, it seemed that she would have to pull him again. Steve, who wandered over as the camp was being packed up, spared her from this, however. He offered to pull the boy's wagon, and she smiled back her thanks.

"He'll talk in due time, Tasha. Don't you worry about it," he consoled her.

"I'd be happy if only he'd walk at this point," she replied, feeling badly even as she said it. It was not the boy's fault, after all.

"In due time," he repeated. Steve lifted the boy into the wagon and pulled it towards the place where the majority of the camp was finishing chores. Tasha followed them over and said good morning to Joshua.

"Did you sleep well, Tasha?" Joshua grinned at her.

"Yes, I did. I thought I should tell you all," and here Steve and others nearby perked up, "I have given the boy a name, since I don't know what his name really is."

"Alright?" Steve prodded her.

"Coal. Call him Coal," she told them.

"That's a fine name," Steve said.

Tasha wasn't too confident, "Do you think?"

"What's to worry about?" a nearby woman comforted her. "It is only a name."

"Oh," objected Joshua, "names can be quite important. Especially poorly picked names. I think Cole is just fine, too." The woman shrugged.

A woman whom Tasha had come to know as Mary came over, bending over Coal and brushing his hair out of his eyes. She stood up and wished them all a good morning. She had a potato bag over her shoulder and looked ready to go. The bag, no doubt, was the best she could find to carry her possessions.

"I was wondering if you would tell us the story as we travel today of how you found Cole," Mary asked Tasha conversationally.

"Quite a bit of it was a blur," Tasha replied, hoping it wasn't obvious that she was concealing details already, "but I would be glad to tell the story. It isn't too long, but it is quite sad."

So, as the group of travelers started north again, Tasha recounted the story. She didn't mention the extraordinary details about the man who helped save Coal, but did make it clear that without him Coal would not have made it. When she got to the part where Coal saw his mother and brother lying dead, Mary gasped and others nearby shuddered.

"That is so sad," Mary intoned quietly. Tasha didn't say anything for a moment.

"You had to take over, then, didn't you?" Steven pondered, mainly to himself. "You knew the boy had nobody. The right thing to do could not have been more clear."

"Probably more than you realize," Tasha responded cryptically.

"But what of the man?" Joshua interjected, frowning.

"Yes, what of the man?" Steve agreed. They both looked angry, jumping to the conclusion that he had saved the boy only to abandon him. She hastened to correct them of this assumption.

"No, you must not think ill of him. The man had other duties and obligations. He helped when no one else would or could. I hold nothing against the man. I don't want you to, either," she pleaded with them.

Mary looked at her inquisitively, "You seem to know more about this man than you've let on. Was he someone you knew?"

Tasha had no desire to lie, but was in no mood to explain herself fully. Trying to sound casual, she finally offered, "Only what I saw. There were plenty of people who needed help. Really, you'll just have to trust me."

Steve and Joshua seemed slightly appeased. Tasha wondered how much it really mattered, given that it was extremely unlikely that the two would ever meet the Radiant Man. Still, she couldn't help but be encouraged about the character of these two men. Mary continued to watch Tasha for a time, but eventually the matter was dropped. There wasn't much more to the story after that, and Tasha had it finished within five or ten minutes. The story telling and conversation surrounding it had managed to consume a good two hours of travel, however, so the group came to a stop to have a rest. Tasha was pleased to have an occasion to change the subject.

After the rest, the group of thirty or so men and women and some children trudged north on a road Tasha identified from signs as Route 63. They made it as far as Clinton that day before stopping for the night. Tasha learned more about the group of old friends as she went. Besides Steve and Joshua and Mary, Tasha met Randy, Jeremy, Karl, and many others. After the next day of travel, they had nearly arrived at Alta, Indiana, and Tasha had had enough time to conclude that this group would surely take care of her and her charge for as long as it was in their power to do so.

On the sixth day of travel, the road signs indicated that the cities of Cayuga and Silverwood were nearby. Joshua informed them that they would be passing over a small river just past Cayuga and urged them on, with the intent to camp near the river that very night. In order to move more quickly, several people ganged up on Coal's wagon. The sun was low in the sky when Joshua told them that the buildings they had recently passed some distance off to their left were the outer edges of Cayuga, and their campsite for the evening was only a little farther. The divided highway remained divided, but it could be seen spreading out into a V. Joshua quickly led them to the western side, explaining to the children among them that, in the old days, cars would have been hurtling at them in the opposite direction and explaining to the adults that it would be easier to access the river from this side of the road. Joshua appeared to know his Indiana geography.

Tasha was happy walking alongside the wagon enjoying the evening air and was looking forward to dipping into the river. The summer had been relatively mild, but without a constant supply of water these travels were quite tedious, even in more comfortable weather. On several days it had been too hot around midday to travel at all, and on several evenings, even when there was plenty of time left in the day to travel, they had stopped and camped anyway because water was available. Her reverie was disturbed by the sound of an argument breaking out among some of the men of the group. Even though the group treated her as one of its own, she still felt like she was eavesdropping and tried to block the conversation out. She could not help overhearing, however.

"Look," one voice stabbed, "think about all the cities we will have to go through. Big cities, mind you. Danville, Bloomington, Rockford, Madison. For all we know, any one of these cities might have been destroyed in the nuclear attacks, too, and we could be walking right into danger."

"Like I keep saying, it isn't only the nuclear attacks we have to factor in here," another voice rejoined impatiently. "It looks like this Disease is the real thing. How many people had already cleared out of the bigger towns even before the attacks just to seclude themselves against the Disease?"

A third voice interjected, "We should have started for Wisconsin right then."

"Well, we didn't. Here we are," the second voice snapped.

"I'm just saying ..."

"Never mind that," the first voice blurted out exasperated. "Like *I* have been saying, it isn't even the Disease we have to factor in. We've got the International Force to deal with, too. We're heading into the unknown based on the hope that there is a plot of land in Wisconsin we can find safety in. What if we're stopped and detained? What if our path is blocked by a nuclear wasteland?"

A fourth voice now spoke, "We could go around if it came to that."

The first man was silent for a moment, and the rest of them followed suit. Tasha was walking next to Mary, who was merely shaking her head. Finally, the first man spoke again.

"I don't understand the difference between a piece of undeveloped land in Wisconsin where we hole up for a time and a piece of undeveloped land either in Indiana or Illinois where we hole up for a time," he said.

"Because my family owns the land in Wisconsin, like I've been saying," the third man groaned.

"With all this empty land we're walking past, I don't see why that's important. Especially given current circumstances," the first man complained.

Joshua strode past Tasha and the women and children separating Tasha from the arguing men. She heard him address them.

"Alright, let's just stop talking about it for now," Joshua commanded. "We're only a few hundred yards from where a path breaks off to the right and takes us to the river." After a pause, Joshua added, "Good men can disagree and still remain friends." This was greeted with silence.

As if to get the last word in, the first speaker tossed in, "It is the middle of summer. Do we really think we can get to Wisconsin before cold weather sets in?" Mary shook her head again.

As Joshua promised, a sandy path appeared, sloping down ahead of them to where Tasha presumed was a river. Here, the wagon was of little use, and Ted and Karl dropped back to take turns carrying Coal. The sun had barely begun dipping below the horizon when Tasha spotted the river through the foliage. The foliage opened into a wide sandy area which promised soft sleeping arrangements.

They had only gone a little ways onto the bank of sand when Joshua put up his hand to stop everyone. A few of the men and women had already gotten to the river's edge and were lapping up water, but stopped when they noticed the silence that resulted from Joshua's warning sign. Steve was also standing in a guarded pose, scanning the area. As Joshua and Steve reached for their weapons, the rest of the group did as well. Soon, long metal rods and broken baseball bats and a few knives were produced.

Joshua must have realized that an explanation was required, because he said, "For as many travelers as there are on the road and the popularity, as I remember it, of this spot, there aren't very many people here." Joshua had never said a truer word: the area was devoid of travelers. Steve made a few signals to some of the men. Tasha realized what the signals meant as the men broke off into groups of three and began scouting out the area for obvious signs of danger. The women and children waited nervously on the sand bank, where they had sat down. Joshua stood still among them, listening carefully.

After a few minutes, the groups of men returned from poking around the area and reported seeing nothing.

"We'll set a double-watch tonight," Joshua said. "No, make that a triple-watch," he changed his mind. "Let's put two on the river bank and one up a little ways toward the road to watch for anyone coming down the road."

A watch for the group normally constituted of three men or women, but usually men because they much preferred letting the women sleep through the night. This wasn't for any particularly noble reason. Most of the men readily confessed with sheepish smiles that they just didn't want to get up with the children. A triple-watch meant nine men staying up throughout portions of the night. Of the three persons in the watch, two would remain awake and on duty, while one would sleep for three or four hours. In this way, though each of the men would be tired the next day, all three will have gotten some sleep; additionally, with two people awake at a time, it was less likely that someone would fall asleep on duty. Though it meant that almost half the men would be groggy and crabby the next day Joshua's judgment was never questioned, so it was quickly decided who would be setting the watches for the night. The group set about establishing camp.

As night fell, Tasha listened to the river meandering past and remembered for the first time in a long time how intensely she enjoyed listening to the songs of rivers.

## == Chapter 2 ==

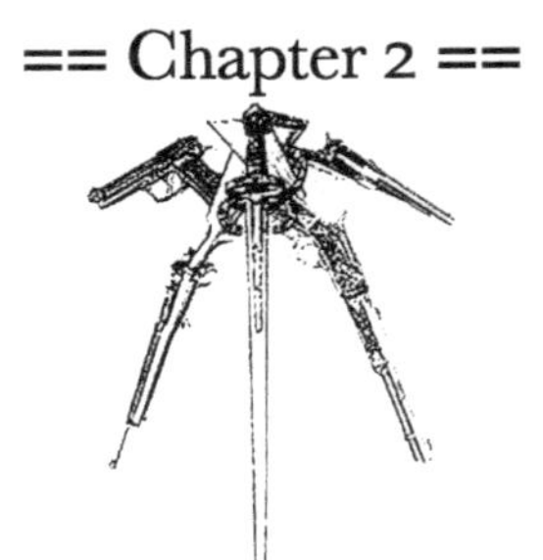

Tasha awoke with a start. There had been a loud noise. Now she heard a shout, and she deduced that one like it had woken her. Joshua forbade the making of a fire that night, so she was reduced to starlight and a half moon to try to make out what was happening. There was a flurry of activity. Men and women—dark shapes, more than anything—were darting in different directions. There was more shouting and then a single gun shot and then yells of panic.

"Women, too! These will fetch a fair price!" shouted a voice Tasha hadn't heard yet. Realizing that they were in trouble, and that she had not yet procured a weapon for herself, Tasha grabbed Coal under the shoulders and dragged him towards the underbrush.

She had pulled Coal a few feet in and was turning to return to help the group when she heard Joshua shout, "Smugglers! Slave traders! Everyone run! That's an order!" Tasha had a moment of hesitation to decide whether or not she should obey the order, and decided she ought to. She continued pulling Coal into the woods. She was not one to panic, but she found herself deeply regretting that she had never acquired so much as a sharpened stick during her travels. She threw Coal into a little valley formed by the thick roots of two trees and realized with a start that instead of being dozens of yards away from the river, she could still hear the river as though it was quite near. Tasha bit her lip as she pondered the problem.

The tree roots rose up in mounds so that Coal could lie down between them and not be seen. By listening to the shouting, she was able to determine that they were downstream forty or fifty feet from the campsite where the attack had begun. In the faint starlight, she was barely able to make out a number of small boats, some of them manned, near the sandbar they had originally descended upon. Meanwhile, there were tremendous crashing noises in the woods in all directions as members of the group fled and the bandits pursued. She began looking for a rock or heavy stick to use as a weapon if it came to it; further flight did not seem practical or prudent.

Indeed, even as she crawled around in the dark looking for a sturdy object, she could hear talking and crunching noises making their way down the coastline in her direction. She found herself on the narrow beach, her hands clawing at the sandy ground, searching ... searching. Her eyes found something before her hands did. A dark shape caught her attention. It looked like a broken chest or wooden box. Hoping to find some sturdy plank, preferably with a nail or two sticking out of it, she pulled herself towards the box. The voices were getting closer.

To her astonishment, when she put her hand down to brace herself as she began tugging at the planks of the chest, she felt a hard, metallic object with her fingers. Packing material seemed to have spilled out of the box, and she could slightly make out other bits of shiny metal buried in the material that remained. Rather than explore the contents of the box, however, she examined the object her hands had discovered. Realizing at once that her hands were on a sharp blade, she worked out which end was the handle and grabbed it. The voices and sounds of vegetation being crushed were even closer. She had a passing thought to investigate the chest a little more, but decided suddenly that she really must return to where Coal lay, only a few feet away inside the tree line.

She quietly crawled back, listening carefully to the sounds of the conflict around her. She took a moment to examine her blade. It appeared to be very well crafted with peculiar markings that she couldn't make out in the blackness. She estimated the length of the blade to be a little less than a foot long. It was sharp. Very sharp. It would certainly do. Actually, judging by the fact that there had only been the single gunshot heard early on, Tasha thought it very possible that she would be better armed than the searching rascals.

"Bless it," she whispered to herself. "Elijah's ravens must have just been here, and I missed them. Exactly what I needed: a fine weapon."

With the sounds of searching men nearly upon them, Tasha slipped behind one of the trees to keep in the shadows—not even the starlight illuminated her. She couldn't help conceal Coal any better without giving themselves away more. She would have to hope that the men would pass through and overlook them both. She thought ruefully that this hope was as much for the well being of the men as it was for her and Coal.

But the men saw Coal right away, and let out a whooping noise of victory.

"Hey, we've got one!" one shouted to another. Tasha let them descend upon Coal. She wanted to know how many she was dealing with.

"Hey, you there! Get up! Let's go, the game is up!" said another man. The two dark silhouettes were clearly contrasted against the sparkling night sky. The moon, Tasha noticed, was no longer hanging within sight. She twitched, preparing to speak to the men when she heard another grunt, suggesting the presence of a third man. She decided to wait. Sure enough, a twig snapped and a third man raised himself up.

"He's not moving," the third man stated.

"Is he dead?"

"Come on, get up!"

"It looks like a child."

"Is it a boy or a girl?"

"Catch a fair price for either."

"For different reasons," the third man said, a hint in his voice of the smirk he clearly was wearing on his face.

"It's a boy, and he's alive! But ... he doesn't seem responsive."

"He's faking."

"Get up, boy!"

"Just grab him."

Tasha had thought maybe that if they saw Coal was still they'd presume him either to be dead or simply not worth their time, but now that their intent was clear, she was ready to act.

"You will leave the boy alone," Tasha said coolly, hidden yet in the dark.

"There *is* a woman here! The mother, maybe. Fantastic!" one of the men scoffed.

Tasha wanted the point of decision to come earlier rather than later, so she quickly laid out her terms, "Gentlemen—and yes, I realize I use the word loosely—turn back now, leave the boy, and you will live. You have three seconds to decide. Then you will be dead, it is simple as that."

"HA!" yelled one man.

"One!" Tasha declared boldly.

"One woman against three men?" chortled another man.

"Two!" Tasha continued.

"She's by that tree, just grab her!" the last man shouted.

"Three!" Tasha stated with finality. The three men were converging on her even as she said her last. She felt one hand on her and slashed firmly towards the arm. There was a howl in pain and rage. Thrusting the blade towards the source of the sound, she plunged the knife through the man's throat. His shrieking abruptly stopped, and the man fell to the ground with a thud.

Another hand fell on her shoulder. The assailant had circled behind the tree. The other remaining attacker had stooped to see about his friend and, blurting out an expletive, lunged for her in the same instant that a second hand fell on her shoulder. She ducked down and spun away from the one grasping her shoulders and, in the concealing darkness, heard the two men collide. She didn't wait for them to sort out what was going on. She hurtled herself onto the men, slashing one man's face with her first strike and driving the blade into the other man's chest with her next one. She pulled the blade out as quickly as she had thrust it in and parried the oncoming blow of the other man, who stumbled backwards. The man she had impaled crumpled to the ground. She strode over him towards the final man, who stumbled backwards before her in the dark. Finally, he could fall back no farther, and he was sitting with his back to a tree, one hand holding his face together. She stood before him, her outline against the night clearly feminine: long hair soaking up the glistening sky, slender form, appropriately shaped. The rest of her features were hidden in the dark.

"I .... I have a gun," the man blubbered.

Tasha sighed, "You shouldn't have said that." An abrupt, overhand throw propelled the blade towards the speaker's chest, into the man's heart. He was dead before she arrived at his body to reclaim her blade. The man's hand had fallen away from his face, and Tasha saw with sadness the gaping gash in his face, which had driven him into fearful panic. She felt pity, but not remorse. She wiped the blood on the man's pants then stepped over the second attacker's body as she returned to Coal. Now she had to think.

It would probably be only a matter of time before the men were missed, and judging by the sounds of the night, there were still plenty of people being hunted in the woods. She could try to escape, but probably wouldn't succeed. She guessed that there were fifty or more slave traders in the melee. On the other hand, now that she was appropriately armed, and she could take a moment to hide Coal with more care, she might be able to turn the tide of the fight and rescue the people who had been so kind to her. She remembered the charge that had been given to her to protect the boy and then, after a moment, she said quietly under her breath, "And yet, also do good as you have opportunity." The decision was made. She must help the rest of the group.

Taking a moment to cover up Coal with grass and sticks, she listened intently to the night to decide her first move. She realized that the crashing noises in the woods were generally heading back towards the riverbank. Probably, all of those trying to flee had been rounded up and were being herded back to the boats to be shuttled to a better location for sorting. Tasha realized with horror that this was probably a very common event. Individuals and groups were lured down to the river by the nice sandy beach and the sparkling water. The bandits swooped down on them in the night, taking them away and then returning the beach to near pristine conditions so the next group would not suspect anything. Tasha boiled with rage, but she mastered her emotions so that she could devise a plan. She knew almost immediately what she must do: she could take the bandits on in small numbers, but if there were many together she stood little chance. And there was at least one gun out there.

Moving lightly through the woods, she made her way towards the nearest returning group. She made as little noise as possible. She had positioned herself perfectly for this returning group. Three men were poking and prodding a man, woman, and child ahead of them in the night back towards the riverbank. Tasha let them get past her. Before anyone realized what was going on, the three men were dead. She grabbed the arm of the husband and whispered a hoarse command, "Sit down, here, and don't move until I call you next. By God, don't make even the smallest noise."

Then she moved on to the next group. She managed to subdue six such groups, each time warning the ones she'd saved to sit still, until at last there were no other noises in the woods. Everyone else had made it back to the riverbank. Her friends were herded into a circle and surrounded by the bandits. Tasha took up a position upstream, well hidden in the darkness of the woods but with excellent visibility of the scene on the sandbank, and pondered the situation. In the darkness, she noticed that at least two men seemed to have long sticks in their hands.

"Guns," she whispered to herself. "Rifles," she clarified to herself. There were very few guns left in the region these days, most of them confiscated during and after the last war. It struck her as possible that these men were working alongside the new (relatively speaking) government. It would explain the presence of the guns and would support her theory that this sandbank was a constantly sprung trap. The International Force had often vowed to stamp down these sorts of practices, but it was believed by many that the IF itself was involved in them. If her theory was correct in this instance, there could very well be even more guns present. She would have to tread carefully. She would be no use to Coal if she were dead.

It didn't take very much longer before the scoundrels realized that less than half of their original number had returned to the beach; more than that, there were no longer the sounds in the woods of any more returning groups. Tasha overheard some of the men arguing.

"Where is Blaise?"

"We should go look for them."

"Why the hell would we do that? They'll be back when they're ready. We've got to guard the prisoners we've already got."

"It never takes us this long!"

"Our blocking force probably just let some through by accident, and they're rounding them up!"

"I'm *in* the blocking force, you ass," snarled the man in return.

"Watch who you're talking to!"

"Someone count us. How many of us are missing?"

Tasha heard them go on for a little while, but after a time, when still no one else had returned to the beach, clear sounds of panic could be detected. Tasha knew that there were close to twenty-five dead men in the woods and another twenty or so hiding men, women, and children, who were listening to the same thing and waiting for her call.

Finally, she heard someone give a command.

"Ok, Chuck, Ripper, Freighthouse. You three take the pistol and wander up the path to the blocking force staging point. See if maybe for some reason we've got prisoners being held there as well."

Tasha heard grunts and cursing and, after a moment, three men began cautiously and carefully walking up the very same path that Tasha and her group of friends had traveled down. Though it was still quite dark, Tasha knew that there wasn't a lot of time. The sun would be coming up in only two hours, and her advantage would surely be lost. She quickly darted up the slope, through the woods, towards the men. She made no sound.

The man with the pistol got off a shot, but that was all. One man did yell in agony—briefly—but only those two sounds made it back to the riverbed. Tasha kicked the gun into the brush and repositioned herself so she could see down on the bank. She could hear shouted inquiries and demands to know what was going on. Tasha reckoned that the bandits were down to perhaps eighteen men. When the scouting group gave no answer, she heard cursing and swearing from below and a lot of arguing and yelling. The essence of the argument seemed to be that the leader wanted to send another three men up, but none of the men wanted to venture into the night.

Tasha half hoped that the bandits would decide to stay and fight and investigate the matter so that she could remove the threat to later groups, but on the other hand, if the event served to change the survivors' behavior she'd prefer mercy. She ran her hands up and down her clothes. She was soaked from head to foot in the blood of their enemies. She decided that whether the rest lived or died depended on the decisions of the men themselves. If they fled and left the prisoners behind, they would live. She waited.

It seemed that the leader had lost the argument. No more men would enter the woods, and they were hastily making arrangements for the extra boats they had with them. The decision seemed to be that they were going to take the prisoners they had and tow the empty boats. Tasha could hear the note of relief in their voices as they made their preparations, untying boats, binding prisoners, cursing one another. They had made their decision. Tasha made hers.

She descended upon them in a blur. She had already identified who was friend and who was foe before she launched her assault, so she moved from man to man without hesitation. The prisoners were all standing, surrounded by guards, and she dashed in and out between them all inflicting instant death. Only after the sixth man had died was the alarm raised. He had made a noise of alarm before going down. Tasha darted into the pack of twenty or so prisoners, tripping over a body as she did. She fell down on the body and looked into its eyes. The blinking eyes of Joshua met her own. She looked away, choking back despair. His hands were clutched around a broken stick or spear protruding from his chest. She didn't have time now to help. The remaining dozen or so men were now dashing to and fro outside the gaggle of prisoners, finding their fallen friends and blurting out expletives and howling at one another in rage and fear as they looked for the culprit.

Tasha got another three before, finally, she heard the leader shout out in panic, "Leave the prisoners! Get to the boats! Save yourselves!" The bandits were falling pell-mell into the water, towards the boat. Tasha darted in among them. Another two fell headfirst into the water. The rest could now see the threat among them. At least, they could see the blackened outline of a man or woman rushing back and forth through the water, leaping with ease onto boats and launching himself or herself at the next victim, one or two of whom managed to howl in pain before going down. Mostly they only had an opportunity to shout in panic before being struck down. There were only six or seven men left, now, and they were occupying a measly two boats, paddling like mad to get downstream.

Tasha paused a moment and shouted back towards the now freed visitors in a very deep bellow: "Return to camp!" Then she clenched the blade in her teeth and dove into the water towards the men making their getaway. They saw her swimming towards them, and even though they were pulling away, she could hear their shouts of fear and even the sounds of some of them weeping in terror. She pursued them until they were well out of sight, and then she returned to shore. She sat on the beach, exhausted, catching her breath. Her bloody garments stuck to her; the river could not wash all that blood away.

After a time, she used her blade to dig a deep hole in the bank. She stripped until she was naked and buried her clothes in the hole. Conscious that her hair remained matted in blood, she returned to the river and washed it out. When she felt that she had cleaned herself off as well as she could, she worked her way back up the riverbank until she found the trees amidst which she had hidden Coal. She searched around for and found her bag, which she had abandoned, and put on some of her other garments. Hoisting Coal up into her arms, she half-carried, half-dragged him back towards the riverbed encampment. She was not the last to arrive, but pretty close. Her friends were mainly quiet, but some of the men were whispering to one another, and Tasha heard them. They were wondering if the Angel of the Lord had rescued them.

When Mary recognized Tasha, she called out to her and helped with Coal. She was weeping, "Joshua ...He's hurt, he's dying." Tasha remembered locking eyes briefly with Joshua during the ordeal and hastened over to him. He was breathing with great difficulty, but had a determined look in his eye. When he saw Tasha again, he let go of the spear protruding from his chest and reached up and pulled her towards him with both hands, leaving fresh blood prints on her.

"Your ... name ... isn't ... Tasha ... is it?" he gasped at her, holding her firmly. Tasha looked down on him with tears in her eyes, but said nothing. "Thank you," he said firmly. Then he died. Tasha sat up, wiping tears from her eyes.

"Why did he thank you?"

"Did you know each other before we met?"

"Why—"

"So sad, he was hallucinating …"

But Tasha said nothing.

Though it was still dark, no one could sleep. The sun poked its way over the horizon in little more than an hour, and the group was able to start seeing the scope of the situation around them. They started pulling the dead men away from the sand bar towards the edge of the woods, and as the sun rose higher, the men made their way into the woods to fetch the other bodies, which they knew were there. When they had completed this grisly task, there stood a pile of forty-five bloodied but cleanly killed men. As they realized the scope of their salvation, many of them began to cry, Tasha included.

There was considerable discussion about what to do next. Only Joshua had died. Leadership fell to Steve, but even Steve could not think of what to do with such a mound of bodies. Burning them or burying them seemed the best solution, but they had little experience with such things and digging a mass grave would require tools that they did not have. Quite at a loss, they decided to commit the bodies to the river. They heaped the bodies into the remaining boats and nudged the boats away from shore. They watched until the boats were out of sight, and then set about cleaning themselves up as many of them had become quite messy.

During the course of the search, four guns had been found. The group was now armed with a pistol and three rifles and a small but reasonable amount of ammunition for their use. There was discussion about how to best manage the weapons and the matter still wasn't settled when, an hour later, they set off from the spot.

There was yet more discussion about the placing of a plaque. It was agreed by all that something should be left to commemorate the event, but suggestions that it was the "Angel of the Lord" were dismissed. A compromise was eventually met. A thick plank was found, and someone produced a knife. They carved in the message and the date and found a way to secure it to the trunk of a tree where the path emptied into the sandbar.

Despite their elation at being saved, they were all quite ready to get away from the spot just as soon as they could. They moved Joshua's body up closer to the road where there was less threat of the river washing away the grave and buried it, leaving a cross for a headstone. Again helping with Coal, the group moved hastily away from the spot. They set up camp well off the road after only about five miles and quickly went to sleep, exhausted. The next morning, they were all still desperate to get away from the area. They broke camp very early and now, with a little rest in them, practically jogged their way north.

They didn't stop until they arrived on the outskirts of Perryville, which they learned was not far from I-74. The campsite was thick with travelers, many of whom had similar plans as their own, but some were fleeing south, away from Chicago. The group could not help but share in whispered and reverent tones what had happened to them near Cayuga with some of the other southbound travelers. Those who believed them and still wanted to head south were told to look for the plaque commemorating the night when the Angel of the Night rescued them from the hands of their enemies. Some chose on the spot to head in a different direction, while still others simply scoffed.

Still very much interested in getting as far away from the area as possible, the following morning they broke camp very early and pushed forward to I-74. Bands of IF soldiers were moving hastily on foot towards the east. There were many dead bodies on the ground along the road. They had died from radiation poison or fallen at the hands of the Disease. The look of terror on the faces of the IF soldiers told the travelers that something grave was amiss, but none of the soldiers stopped them or even talked to them. Two days later, the group arrived in Danville thanking and praising God that they had made it that far, that they were away from the scene of their gruesome rescue, and glad to find a little warm food and water that didn't require a trip to the river.

The group was not interested in lingering in Danville, even though the city had made many efforts to accommodate fleeing refugees and travelers and it would have been a comfortable stay for them. They still occasionally shared their story about the Angel of the Night, but it only came up when talking with someone seeking information about traveling back in the direction they had came. The most important thing to come out of their stay in Danville was learning that Rockford and Madison were intact, even if likely decimated by the Disease by now. This seemed to resolve the argument among the men of the group in favor of heading to Wisconsin as soon as possible, and it was for this reason that they restocked and left the town as quickly as they could.

For safety's sake, they stuck to I-74. Though weather and age had attacked the road, it was still much easier to travel along than some of the other roads they had been on. There were many other travelers on the road as well, but groups of travelers tended to be wary of one another. One couldn't know who might have the Disease, and there were plenty of bodies lying away from the highway to remind them that it was a constant threat.

Nearly two weeks of travel brought them to Champaign. Though not as accommodating as Danville, the group was still able to find people and businesses that could resupply them. Like everyone else, Tasha and her friends cautiously talked to people they came into contact with to learn about what was in front of them or possibly coming behind them. It was in Champaign that they first realized that they had not seen a soldier of the International Force for some time. They also learned that Bloomington had begun fortifying itself to resist the IF, if it chose to return. Bloomington also had a family registry where people could leave notes for one another to try to reconnect with family members who had been separated by the past wars, the nuclear attacks, and the dispersing Disease. Once again eager to leave quickly, the group was soon on the road, heading for Bloomington.

About a week later, they set up camp at a rest area that was roughly halfway between Champaign and Bloomington. They arrived late in the evening and did not have time to properly set up camp before night fell. A watch was set, and Tasha joined the rest in quickly falling asleep. She had one arm over Coal, keeping his tiny body warm, and her blade was comfortably nestled in her other arm.

The following morning, Tasha sat up to greet the mid-August sunrise. As she was about to stand up to go about her business, someone grabbed her arm. She instinctively reached for her blade and turned her head to perceive the attacker, then gasped: the boy was clutching her arm.

Most of the camp was still sleeping, but some men and women were awake and turned when they heard Tasha gasp. Those who were close enough to realize that the boy was the cause of the surprise stood up to see more clearly. Tasha sat back down and looked at the boy intently. His eyes still seemed vacant, but there was a glimmer there that she had not previously seen.

"What is it Coal?" she asked him tenderly.

To her great surprise, he answered her: "I see a man and a lizard, but the lizard has become the man. He didn't put it to death when he had the chance, and now it is the man who sits on the shoulder of the lizard, and the man gets smaller and smaller. Beware. Behold, he rests beneath the divided tree."

The statement was so unexpected that Tasha couldn't help but fall back in shock.

"He's mad," one of the men nearby said under his breath.

Tasha had recovered and once again was at the boy's side, "I don't understand," she told him. "What about a lizard and a man?" The boy was staring intently at her, but Tasha felt that in some sense it wasn't the boy at all. Then there was a new expression on Coal's face, and he spoke again, but this time in a different tone.

"My name is *King*," Coal said matter-of-factly. Once again,

Tasha gasped, and so did the others who were watching. In fact, the size of the group of observers had grown as more people had woken up.

"This child is speaking gibberish," a woman said. "It's the heat. It's gone to his head."

But Tasha, who was studying the boy, felt differently. "No, I think something else is going on here. I think he's coming out of it." Even as she spoke, however, the new expression faded, and he had returned to his initial, trance-like expression. She had a hunch he had something more to say, and she was right.

"The Lizard-Man sits beneath a tree and waits for his prey, not satisfied with what he has already captured. He is a white-washed tomb. Beware."

And here, finally, the boy went back to his comatose state. Tasha rocked back and forth in contemplation. Some things had occurred to her in rapid succession. She promptly shooed away the gawking members of the group while patting her blade to make sure it was still safely concealed in her garments, and her eyes darted back and forth around the rest area.

To anyone who asked about the event, all she said was, "His name is not Cole; it is King."

## == Chapter 3 ==

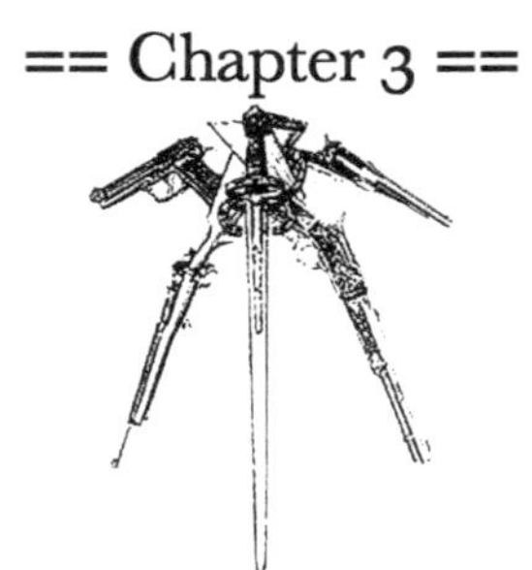

The group that Tasha had been traveling with found the whole event odd, but this did not affect their relationship with Tasha and King. There had been people from other groups around when King had spoken, though, and some of these were clearly unnerved and hastily packed up and left, throwing uneasy glances behind them. Superstition was rampant. For her part, Tasha couldn't stop double checking the location of her blade, and her eyes were constantly searching the landscape for potential threats. If anyone noticed this curious behavior, they didn't say anything. Shortly after lunch, the group made off for Bloomington.

Besides constantly scouring the countryside for anything worrisome, Tasha also watched King with increasing interest. She was certain that on occasion his eyes would become more alert. These were passing episodes, but she welcomed them as signs that the boy was thawing. She took to letting the men pull King whenever she could so that she could glance at the boy more often and keep better apprised of dangers. After a couple of days of this, however, she dropped her guard. When they were about two days out from Bloomington, there was a noticeable increase in foot traffic in the area, and Tasha knew that they must not be far. Remembering King's warning and understanding that there were going to be far more people around than before, Tasha resumed her vigilant scrutiny of her surroundings.

After a mere hour of their morning's travel, they could begin to discern the outlines of buildings on the distant horizon. The old Interstate was now positively crowded with people coming from all directions making for the intact city. Their group had trouble staying together the closer they got to the city. By the time high noon had arrived, they were somewhat scattered. They stopped for a meal near a grove of trees and gathered each other up. One of the men pulled King's wagon over to Tasha and left to aid in rounding up the stragglers.

"Hello there!" called out a booming voice. Tasha jumped and automatically put her hand beneath her cloak.

"Don't frighten the woman," a woman said meekly. Tasha noticed now that they had sat down near a family resting from their travels. They had cut branches of leaves to use as a roof, made possible by the fact that their particular tree had been struck by lightening recently and half of it had split and fallen to the ground, providing a shelter of sorts. There had still been leaves on the branches of the tree, so all they had to do was reinforce it somewhat to make a perfect shield from the arching sun. It was easy to see now why she hadn't noticed them, because the branches also helped shield them from view from the road.

"Elise, don't be silly. I didn't frighten her one bit!" the man boomed out again, emerging from underneath the shelter to introduce himself. "Welcome to our stand of trees. I'm Jim Parson, Reverend Parson, if you will, or Pastor if you like. Pastor Parson works, too." Pastor Parson was grinning widely at Tasha, offering his hand for a friendly handshake.

Instinctively, Tasha's hand grabbed his, and they shook hands. The man had a warm, winning smile, and Tasha's unease passed.

"My name is Tasha, and this is my charge, King," Tasha said by way of introduction.

"Fine, fine," he bellowed happily. "This is my wife Elise, and back here somewhere, here ... come on now, come out, be civil now, are my daughters. Left to right and almost by age are Sonja, Jennifer, and Tory." Hesitantly, the three teenaged girls emerged from the shelter and Tasha shook their hands after first shaking hands with the wife, Elise. Almost immediately, the three daughters withdrew back into the shelter.

"I hope you don't mind," Tasha apologized, "I'm going to have a bite to eat."

"Not at all!" he bellowed. "I'll talk, you eat!"

Tasha wasn't so sure she liked that arrangement. Granted, she was happy for conversation, and the man was friendly enough and thankfully also a man that had devoted himself to God, but she had been looking forward to thinking and eating without distraction. He seemed like the kind of man who wouldn't be deterred, however, so she nodded and gave a weak smile. As if on cue, he began talking in his loud and boisterous manner.

"I don't think we'll be staying in Bloomington," he began. "No, I think we'll be moving on to Iowa or even Nebraska. We have relatives all along that way, and we think there is less chance of the Disease posing a problem—and let's face it, we can't be sure that the nuclear strikes are completely over, can we? That's what we think, isn't it, Elise? So, we'll stock up in Bloomington. We think they have lots of resources, and I think I have what is needed to trade for it, and hopefully it will get us all the way to a major city in Iowa. But we really don't know yet what has been destroyed in that direction, do we? We just know that it's too crowded around here, and with Chicago and St. Louis and Indianapolis destroyed, everyone seems to be rushing to the middle. Well that is just too many people for our tastes, isn't it Elise? No, we'll be going on ..."

And on he went for a full twenty minutes, smiling gregariously at Tasha and glancing back at his wife on occasion when he'd say her name. Elise, in turn would smile weakly back at him and nod, and then he'd go on again. Having concluded her meal, however, Tasha began looking for a way to graciously end the conversation. It hadn't been a full waste of time. She had learned a good deal about the situational realities in the surrounding regions, as the man and his family had apparently traveled around in numerous directions on their bicycles before finally settling on a course of action that led them to Bloomington on their way west.

Fortunately, Steve wandered over and extracted her, but not before he was obliged to meet Pastor Parson and his entire family. But at last, Steve was pulling King's wagon towards where the rest of the group was now preparing to leave.

"A bit of a barnacle, that one," Steve muttered, throwing a look back behind him.

"Yes, friendly enough, but apparently not one content with silence," Tasha replied, studiously not looking back.

"Well, we're all set to move along, just waiting for a few more. We'll make Bloomington for sure tonight."

Steve was right. They hadn't considered one problem, however: actually getting in. They had arrived at the intersection of I-74 and route 51 by mid-evening, but found their way blocked by armed citizens of the city. Apparently, the city was not letting anyone in or through unless they could show that they were not infected with the Disease. As it was already getting late, and because there were a large number of people ahead of them, the group set up camp for the evening.

In the morning the guards of the city began processing travelers again, and it was soon their turn. Most of the group was permitted immediate access, but King caught their attention. Though there wasn't any hint that he was infected by the Disease, his comatose state unnerved them and they held Tasha and King while they waited for a superior to arrive. Tasha's friends waited nervously directly inside the primitive barriers that had been set up, and Tasha flashed uneasy smiles at them. For the first time, she noticed that about a hundred yards away was a camp, which was ringed with fencing and guarded by citizens, allowing no one out.

The superior that had been sought still hadn't arrived after several hours, and Steve and some of the other men began to plead and argue with the gate guards, pointing out that King had no blisters or red splotches or anything that might be construed as the beginning stages of the Disease. They shared with the guards that they had been traveling with Tasha and King for more than a month and that King had always been in this state, but the guards would not be persuaded. At one point, heated words were exchanged and the guards, sympathetic up to that point, sent for more guards to ensure that they were not overpowered. Still, the superior that had been sent for had not arrived. But shortly after noon, a message arrived saying that Tasha and King would have to wait until someone who was medically trained could arrive to examine him. The note did not include a time frame.

The guards continued to process travelers even as Tasha sat there by the gate next to King's wagon, with King lying still and scrawny as always. A few more hours went by, and Steve came back to talk to Tasha, offering encouragement, but also some bad news.

"We really have no intention of leaving you behind, Tasha. If anything, we'll go through the city and pick up supplies and meet you on the other side of the city. Some of us will go with you, of course. We haven't worked that out yet. We're going to head on in a little bit here tonight and see if we can scare up some doctor or something to try to make this go faster, and tomorrow go into the city and the next day send someone back to escort you around the city."

"But ..." Tasha was alarmed, "I don't have enough supplies to last me two days."

Steve smiled at her apologetically, "I know, I really don't want to leave you. Nobody does, in fact. But we're running low on supplies ourselves. We don't want to fight these men, either. But we went around, and we each contributed from what we have left—here—this, I think, is about a week's worth of food and water for you."

Tasha felt miserable about the situation, but realized it wasn't right for her to hold up everyone on her account. She reminded herself that they had taken her on out of the goodness of their hearts and didn't have any obligation to her. She was half-tempted at that moment to reveal to him that she was their Angel of the Night and argue that they were very indebted to her, but fought off the urge and put it to death within her as a rotten thing to consider. Finally, she smiled and replied, "I understand. If they do let us through in the next day, I will not go too far into the city and will remain by the main road here so you can find us."

Steve looked relieved. "Alright, Tasha. We will see each other again very soon."

Tasha nodded but did not say anything. She met eyes with members of the group who were still some distance away from the main gate and some of them smiled, others frowned, but all waved and bid her farewell with their gazes.

After a couple of hours, the group had completely melted into the thronging traffic of travelers entering Bloomington.

That night, Tasha huddled close to King to keep him warm. She used the wagon to prop up a blanket as a shelter against the chilly wind. In the morning, she made her way back to the gate where the guards politely and sympathetically told her that no doctor had yet arrived. One offered her a warm cup of coffee, which she gratefully received. The next morning, the same ritual was repeated. The men denied her access, but gave her a cup of coffee.

Tasha peered up the road all that day to see if any of her friends were returning yet. However, no one came. The next morning and the morning after that, she was denied access to the city, and she did not see anyone coming back to escort her. She began to seriously wonder if she had misunderstood. Perhaps she was expected to walk around the city by herself. She fought back tears as she struggled against accusatory thoughts reflecting her growing sense of abandonment. Her resolve returned, however, when she forced herself to acknowledge that, if it was in their power to do so, the group would certainly return for her. Something must have come up, and they can't be blamed for that.

A few more days went by. She maintained her resolve, though there were moments when she had to fight to keep it. She was seriously considering abandoning the agreed upon plan altogether and making her way around the city when she received help unexpectedly.

"I'm sorry, Tasha. My superiors insist that a doctor will have to make the determination and they're all busy at the Chicago gate, which is a day's travel besides. We cannot let you in." The gate guard speaking was named Jeffrey, and after almost a week of waiting, they had come to learn each other's names. Jeffrey and his unit would soon be replaced by another unit, and he would not be back for two weeks. Jeffrey had been kind to her and apparently feared for her fate if the other unit was manning the gate.

"What is this about?" bellowed a familiar voice.

Jeffrey leapt back.

"I said, why aren't you letting this woman and her son enter?" Pastor Parson demanded to know. He looked at Tasha as if to say, Don't worry, but turned his attention back to the guards. "What is this about?" he repeated.

Jeffrey was at a loss for words for a moment but finally retorted, "There is concern that her son has the Disease or some other deadly virus, and we cannot allow sick people entrance to the city."

Pastor Parson was roused to anger, "The Disease? You think this boy has the Disease? Have you seen the people over in the camp?

They're bleeding out of their eyes, their ears, and their nostrils. For God's sake man, isn't it obvious he hasn't got the Disease?"

This is a line of argument that Steve and her other friends had tried, and she knew Jeffrey's answer before he said it. "Well, he has got something, hasn't he?" Jeffrey retorted. "He's just lying there, stony faced. I am very sympathetic to their plight, but I have the lives of tens of thousands of people to think about, and if I let them in and it turns out to be something horrid, besides being put to death myself, I won't be able to live with myself!"

"See here, young man," Pastor Parson snapped. Jeffrey couldn't help but smirk, as he was at least as old as the pastor. Pastor Parson continued, "This delightful and fine-looking woman has been here for how long exactly?"

Jeffrey was embarrassed to admit it had been almost a week. "A week?" Pastor Parson shrieked. "Don't we all know that the Disease starts and finishes in under a week? Who do you need to tell you that he hasn't the Disease when you can see it with your own eyes?"

"But he could have something else—"

But Pastor Parson cut him off, "You let this woman and her son in or you're really going to hear it. I will call down the wrath of God upon you, so help me God," and here he began pounding his hand on his Bible, which he had produced at some point, "And if you're not careful I'll drive God's word down your throat myself. Can't you see that I'm a pastor? Surely the judgment of a minister of God counts for something still in this day and age?" Pastor Parson was really working himself into a froth now, swinging the heavy book back and forth, and finally leaning in and slamming it against the chests of Jeffrey and the other guards who had come over.

Tasha stole a glance back at Elise and the pastor's daughters. They were standing there with their bags and bundles balanced on their bicycles, and Elise was holding the pastor's bike, too. Unsure what she had expected to see, Tasha was surprised to see that all four women were glancing nervously at the scene with expressions that she might have thought were filled with terror had she seen them under other circumstances. Tasha's attention was turned back to the gate scene, however.

"Alright, alright!" Jeffrey was shouting back at the pastor. He waved irritably at Tasha who couldn't believe the turn of events. Tasha grabbed her bag and the handle of the wagon and began pulling King through the gate and down the road, anxious to get through before anyone changed his mind. She glanced at the pastor to thank him, but the man's face was still red with fury, and he was still laying into the guards. She didn't think that was appropriate, especially given how kind they had been, but she used the extra time to get a ways down the road.

About an hour later, the Parson and his wife and children came riding up on their bikes. They stopped, but didn't get off. The pastor was considerably calmer, now. He beamed at her.

"You owe me one, dear Tasha," he smiled widely at her, winking. "Until next time!" And with that, the man and his family rode on past her, disappearing into the mass of travelers, and leaving Tasha to pull the dead weight who was King.

Tasha made it well into town that night before needing to stop and rest, deciding at that point to sleep for the night. The following morning, she noticed for the first time that there were signs pointing the way to a family registry. She remembered learning about this at some point in her journeys and decided to look into it. She put that on the agenda for the following morning, and found yet another place to sleep for the night.

She could not have picked a better place to rest in terms of information gathering. There were more people moving about here than she had noticed, and she soon learned why. She was right outside a building with a large sign painted above the door that read: HAM RADIO. Underneath that was pinned in smaller letters:

ONE OF FIVE LEFT IN THE COUNTRY,
ONE OF FIFTY IN WORLD.

She couldn't resist; she had to enter. Inside she found what seemed at first to be a farce. She entered the lobby and immediately saw that the building had been a bank. Immediately inside the lobby there were rows of chairs. Each of the chairs held a person. Still others crowded around, but as it was getting close to evening, some were beginning to filter out. She saw on a sign that the hours of operation showed an hour in the morning, two hours during the afternoon, and then two hours in the evening. She was entering at the end of the evening hours.

Behind the counter where bank tellers used to do their business, there were four sturdy-looking men with aluminum baseball bats. About fifteen feet away from them was a large table with a man operating a ham radio. The transmissions were being amplified by some speakers, so everyone in the room could hear both sides of the conversation. Tasha continued to scan the large hall for information and found a big board with an explanation. It explained that after the nuclear strikes, few electronic devices worked at all. Only machines that didn't rely on sophisticated electronics, like cars from a couple of hundred years ago, would work after enduring the EMP reaction a nuclear strike generates. The board explained that electronics could be protected, however, and that this particular ham radio station was operated by a man who had taken the time and effort to construct a

"Faraday Cage" for his radio, thus allowing him to remain in contact with surviving radios throughout the country, and throughout the world.

She listened to the conversation between the local ham operator and the person on the other side of the radio.

"Bloomer, do I understand you correctly that your city is going to begin erecting a wall? Our officials strongly encourage it."

"10-4 Omaha Ranger. Message has been conveyed and communicated. I trust that our suggestion that you begin screening travelers is being followed. It is only a matter of time before the Disease gets to you."

"Roger that, Bloomer, but so far here in Nebraska there hasn't been even a single case reported. Neither Omaha or Lincoln has seen anything yet. But we're trusting you."

"Have you heard from Jersey Joe lately?"

"That's a negative. Not for two days. Hope all is well. Spent couple of hours yesterday scanning all channels and turned up a new faint transmission. Definitely a foreigner speaking English. Couldn't connect, so I don't know where he is. He sounded terrified, though."

"Copy that, Bloomer. I picked up a signal from a gent in Japan last night around two in the morning. Didn't get a call sign out of him, but apparently they know something about the Disease, too. Then I lost him. We were already screening travelers, but when I reported that to the guards here in Omaha, they were greatly relieved to know we're not overreacting."

"Trust me, Omaha Ranger, we're not blowing smoke on this."

"I hear ya. Well, I'm about done for the evening. Anyone out there still have any questions for us out here?"

"Negative. It was good to hear that Omaha is welcoming travelers. We'll pass the word that Omaha is a safe city, because we're definitely overcrowded here. But if you can find out about other cities and get back to me, that would be great. I'm thinking especially of Des Moines."

"10-4, Bloomer. I asked around today and we did have some people last week come in who said they were from Des Moines, but the dummies didn't ask if Des Moines could sustain travelers. They're on the lookout for more from that city now and they promise to report back to me. And your cities?"

"Same as before. Clear to Rockford, but after that unknown. The extent of the fallout from Chicago is still being determined. With winter coming, I expect we'll see lots fleeing Wisconsin on account of the cold."

"It gets pretty cold in Iowa and Nebraska, I'll remind you."

"Copy that. Alright, Omaha Ranger. Sounds good. Have a good night. Over and out."

"Over and Out."

The one apparently going by the name of Bloomer sank back into his chair, apparently exhausted from being at the radio for so long. Without looking at the crowd of people, many of whom had been leaving for a few minutes already, the man packed the radio back into a box, and stowed it into a safe. Tasha left as the man was paying off his guards, and it was almost completely dark before three of them left for the night. As she drifted off to sleep, she realized that two of the guards probably remained inside to sleep and protect what was clearly a valuable piece of remaining technology.

The next morning she immediately sought out the place where the registry was located. It was in the city's downtown area, and there were people bustling about all over the place. The conversation she overheard last night was replaying in her head as she found and entered it.

The Registry looked like it was constantly under construction. There were piles of plywood and heavy wooden beams lying all over the place. Some of these were being used to erect walls for people to post information about missing family members or information about their own whereabouts, but others were used to make less than sturdy shelters for the wall postings. It was like a series of outdoor hallways with sheets of plywood erected several feet above the walls so that light could get in, and the breeze, but it was presumably protected from the elements.

Tasha had the sudden realization that it was very possible that King still had family out there somewhere. All she knew was the boy's first name, however. Where would she post it so that family members could find it? She pulled King up and down the hallways trying to figure out the system, and at last she figured out that it was all alphabetized. There were about four hallways total, and each was about a hundred feet long; large tabs jutted out indicating about where one letter of the alphabet ended and the other began. She had been confused because she had entered the Registry by an entrance marked "Success Stories." In that section, people had attached the scraps of paper that had led them to find their loved ones, or in many cases, grouped together numerous scraps that represented whole families reuniting. But in the Registry proper, there were nothing but forlorn scraps of paper fixed by hammer and nail, detailing information like names, places, directions, and other means of contact.

Was it organized by first name or by last name? It didn't seem to matter. But she found her answer when she stopped to linger by a group of men who were apparently trying to figure out the same thing.

"Should we post this by the letter F or by the letter R?" one man was asking another.

"I don't know, Lonny. How should I know? And no one seems to be in charge here to ask, do they?" the other returned grumpily.

A third man suggested that they put the note in both places.

"I'm telling you, Frank, I don't know," the second man replied curtly.

"You know, Ed, we miss him too. You don't have to be a jerk about the whole thing," the one called Lonny snapped.

"I'm just saying what's the point?" the grumpy one, apparently named Ed, retorted.

"What do you mean, what's the point?" Frank demanded to know.

"You know what I mean. We're going back home right now and we'll be able to tell Melody what happened for ourselves. We don't have to leave a stupid note—as if she's going to come all the way out here to find it even if we didn't find her—which I don't believe for a minute. This is just a waste of time!" Ed snarled.

"But we already went over that," Lonny explained patiently. "That's why we're here at all."

Frank nodded, "Right. It is possible that Indianapolis was hit, and if it was who knows where anyone is? Melody and the kids may have fled in this direction. That's just a rumor right now." Tasha's ears perked up at hearing that the men were heading in the direction she had come from.

"But it might not be a rumor, and if it isn't who among us wants to make this trip back to post this note when we can do it right now?" Lonny asked.

"I tell you, Fides has that house built like a fortress. Melody ain't going anywhere. That house is well fortified and stocked with all sorts of food and goods. They could live there for six months before they had to step out the door. She'll be there." Ed asserted, but with a little less hostility in his voice. Tasha thought Ed's voice wavered when he said that the man's wife would be there, and she couldn't help but be touched by the affection she was witnessing. Ed sniffed, and ordered quietly, "Ok, put the note under both F and R. Then let's get going. The rest of the guys won't be able to guard our trucks by themselves for much longer."

Tasha made her way to the K section as those men went about posting their notes. She made up her mind to track down the notes that they posted, deeply curious about this man's separation from his family, especially since the man appeared to live in the same general area where she had found King.

Scraps of paper and various kinds of writing instruments had been distributed throughout the registry. She sat down near a blank spot on the K wall and with pen and paper in hand, considered what to write. Finally she wrote out the following message:

> Have a young boy named King, last name unkn. Found him near Indpolis. Mother and at least one other sibling decesd. Am traveling to Om. Neb, will winter betwn. Bloom+Om. Will return him to Indpolis in future. Signed, Tasha.

That was about all she could fit on the sheet of paper. She didn't dare try to use more than one sheet, because she could see that there was no order at all to the postings and more than one sheet might get separated. Seeing that many of the postings were already blurred from the rain or morning dew, she fished through the supplies that Steve had left her for a clear plastic baggie she remembered seeing there. She inserted the posting into the baggie and sealed it as well as she could and then nailed it to the wall. Recalling that she wanted to look into the wall postings the men had left, she first went to the F section in search of a posting directed at "Fides."

It didn't take too long to find it, as it was one of the few that was unstained with water marks. She read it and then went to the one in the R section, and found that both messages were identical. They both read:

> Fides Ranthem left work crew safely by plane to the southwest night of the nuclear attack. Fate unknown after that. Waited for his return, but had to leave as job was complete. Fam in T.H., IN. Signed Ed, Frank, and Lonny.

Tasha looked at the posting with curiosity. The phrase "by plane" was really interesting, as even before the nuclear attacks there were not that many planes in the air. The country's infrastructure, economy, and dignity had collapsed after the United States lost in its war against the United Nations and its International Force—defeated in especially humiliating fashion when the Mexicans joined in, backed up by an unimaginably large Chinese army. Guns had been confiscated, factories had been sacked, roads had fallen into disrepair, and the only planes that flew were the ones flown by high officials of the United Nations. And yet Fides had flown to the southwest on a plane? There was a remarkable story behind this posting, Tasha was sure of it.

She made her way outside to ponder the new plan that had formed in her mind. Previously, she had intended to travel with Steve and her other friends into Wisconsin, but they had completely lost touch, and she didn't know where in Wisconsin they were going. With the uncertainty involved in traveling near Chicago, which she knew was a nuclear wasteland, coupled with the fact that it would soon be winter in Wisconsin, she had decided that Omaha, Nebraska was the place to go. The Omaha Ranger was right that it would still be quite cold in Iowa and Nebraska during the winter, but she was not going to try to make it all the way there. She had gleaned that the road to Peoria was sound and Peoria itself was still intact, so she thought that would be a fine place to winter. She could be there by the middle of September, and if she learned there that Rock Island or Davenport was still accessible, she could go on from there.

The more she thought about it, the more she decided it was the best plan. After all, no one was making her do anything. She could do what she wanted. She agreed with others who felt that Bloomington was too crowded and that it was only a matter of time before there was an outbreak of the Disease in the city. It was decided: Peoria. She stood up, gathered up her things, and pulled King's wagon towards Bloomington's western gate.

## == Chapter 4 ==

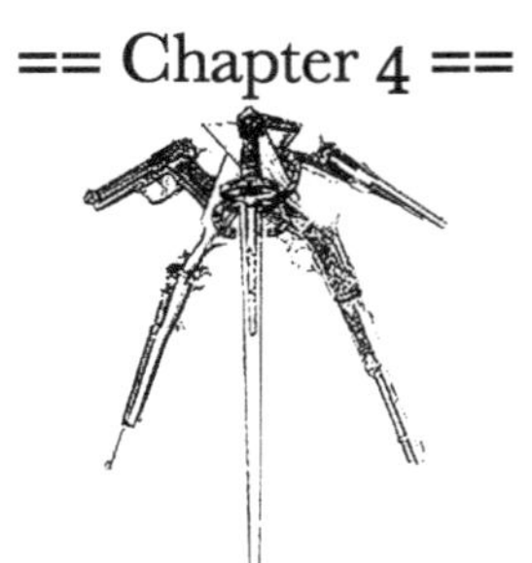

It took many weeks to get to Peoria, and she had the curious sense that she was being watched throughout her journey, but when she arrived she was generally welcomed by the community. She was able to find someone who provided lodging for her and the boy in exchange for helping to take care of the person's property. The first winter storm came early in the season, and Tasha was glad that she had decided to go no farther that year. Though King rarely made a noise and generally remained in bed, surviving only on the broth that Tasha managed to get into him, Tasha's time in Peoria was generally relaxing.

With the warming of the weather after winter, she indicated to the married couple she had served that she was ready to move west, with Nebraska as the ultimate destination. The couple thanked her, but urged her to consider staying with them for a few more months and traveling with them to their Wisconsin property to help out there for awhile, as Tasha was very competent at everything she did. Tasha would have declined this offer had the couple not promised to provide motorized transportation for the trip, and they gave the offer greater appeal by pledging to then transport them back to Davenport after she was finished. They pointed out to her that she would have taken a month or more to get to Davenport from Peoria anyway, so she'd be arriving only a little later, but by vehicle.

Tasha was unpersuaded until the couple produced an old 20th century pickup truck. They were borrowing it from a friend because they certainly had no interest in spending months walking back and forth to Wisconsin. Seeing the vehicle and contemplating the alternative—pulling King's wagon for a hundred miles—Tasha acquiesced.

So, in early spring, the four of them drove to Wisconsin to a little town called Cuba City, and from there found the large plot that the couple owned. They worked a month; their goal was to make the property suitable for renting, as it was doing no one any good sitting empty. This meant some heavy labor, but the husband did most of that, and Tasha and the wife cleaned up and repaired the farm house.

The couple's growing eagerness to return home to Peoria coincided with Tasha's own eagerness to continue on to Davenport. She wanted to have plenty of time to get across Iowa before the next winter came.

Though there was some discussion where the couple tried to persuade Tasha to stay with them, Tasha was convinced in her heart that she and King had to go west. However, another opportunity materialized when some Wisconsin relatives of the couple persuaded her to travel with them to Minnesota to work on some property there in exchange for again procuring a vehicle to make the trip, with the added incentive that they would also drive them down to Waterloo, Iowa. This would put Tasha well on her way to Omaha. Tasha was shown a map and couldn't turn down the offer. She bid farewell to the couple from Peoria, who assured her that she would always be welcome, and then waited for their relatives to obtain a vehicle and the necessary fuel, which took about a week.

They left Cuba City as March was turning into April, driving a minivan that looked like it was on its last legs. They drove up through La Crosse, Wisconsin, crossing into Minnesota on a bridge that linked the city proper to Minnesota. The downtown area of La Crosse was nearly abandoned, and there weren't many travelers to be seen. Once entering Minnesota, they hugged the ragged remains of I-90 until veering off to find the property in question, which was located near a town called Lewiston.

It only took three weeks to finish their task there, and Tasha was constantly expressing thanks for the blessings she was receiving. She was shaving hundreds of miles off her trip where she would have had to pull King in the wagon and deal with the other issues that arise when traveling by foot over so many miles. So it was that in late May, when spring was in full flower, Tasha said goodbye to the relatives. The relatives were driving back by a way where they knew they could get more fuel and also visit more family members near Dubuque, before returning home to Cuba City.

While it would have been a straight shot from Davenport to Omaha by taking I-80 straight on through, picking up her travels in Waterloo was not bad either, because route 20 was basically an Interstate in that area, anyway, and could take her to I-35, which in turn would take her down to I-80. Tasha felt confident in her hope that she could make the trip in the last few weeks of spring that remained for her and then the full summer that was available. Waterloo had more travelers than La Crosse had, but it was still nothing compared to the cramped hustle and bustle that was Bloomington.

Unfortunately, the Disease had arrived in Waterloo, and the residents were not keen on being overly hospitable to those passing through. It took some effort and some intercession by her friends before they left, to obtain the supplies she needed before leaving the town. There was also a disconcerting incident as Tasha was leaving the town—an earthquake. It didn't do much damage, but for a city dealing with so many crises, it brought them near their breaking point. Tasha left as soon as she was able.

Her travels slowed down extensively at that point, but she continued to be thankful. In a matter of weeks she found I-35, and turned south on it. The bumpy highways were still much easier on her wagon and her charge, and in the grand scheme of things, her travels were going well.

She was camping well off the road one evening in early June on account of the increased amount of travelers that were on I-35 when she was surprised to feel the earth moving powerfully beneath her. She looked around and saw that other travelers were looking around as well. Apparently, they were not imagining it. The movement turned into a rumble, and Tasha joined everyone else as they stood up. It was yet another earthquake, and unlike the one she had experienced in Waterloo, this one had real punch. The earth continued to move for a full minute—at one point so erratically that Tasha was almost thrown off her feet. When the tremors ceased, Tasha sat down and shook her head, wishing she had somebody to talk to about the event.

King was looking at her.

Tasha couldn't help gasping in surprise. She waited for him to talk, and when he didn't, she whispered, "King?"

Then his mouth opened. "I see a man surrounded by black. He gasps for breath and claws the air. He escapes an unseen danger, but others around him do not," he uttered in a voice that was much like the last time he had spoken to her. Tasha said nothing, sensing that he might continue. She was right. "The way is shut," he added.

"Way? Which way, King?" Tasha prodded him. Even as she spoke she could see that his eyes were softening. There was no longer the dull look on his face, but rather a growing sense of recognition and consciousness. The look turned from recognition to terror, and Tasha was abruptly certain that there was a boy trying to get out.

"He is trapped!" King blurted out. "The way is shut! He can't escape! None of them can! And they know it! Despair!" he cried out, and then she even saw that there were tears, too. She moved to console him.

"What is it, King? Who is trapped? Where is he? Where are the others? We shall help them!" Tasha told him, soothingly.

"I see them ...I *see* them," King continued.

"Who do you see, King? Do you see where they are?" Tasha replied. But King didn't actually seem to be speaking to her. He was staring out into the distance. He suddenly clapped his hands over his eyes.

"I see the Lizard devouring his prey ..." he moaned, trying to roll away from Tasha. She held him close and did not let him. "I don't want to see it. I don't want to hear it. It is horrible! Make it go away! Oh the Lizard-Man, he's terrible!" King wept.

Tasha was at a loss. She didn't know what to do, but she surmised that King was reflecting the earthquake somehow and also recalling the earlier incident the previous year outside Bloomington. She simply held him. After a time, his sobbing diminished, and he finally went to sleep in her arms. Looking at him in the fading light of day, she saw that this was not the same stony face she'd been tending to these many months. Some sort of peace had washed over it. A certainty grew within her that King would at last be joining her on the morn. She fell asleep with him pulled close to her, thanking God that at last the boy had awoken.

In the morning, King felt the sun warming his eyelids and forehead. He opened his eyes slowly and gazed around. He saw the dew glistening on the grass around him and felt Tasha's arms around him. She was still asleep. He slipped out from underneath her arms and gingerly stood up. His legs wobbled. He sat down. He vividly remembered the sights he had seen the night before. Nothing around him compared to what he had seen, so he strongly felt that what he had seen had occurred in his mind. This was quite perplexing as he had seen the images with his eyes open, as though directly witnessing them. He had seen them with his waking eyes. He tried to stand again.

His legs still wobbled, but he couldn't stand the idea that he couldn't walk, so he forced himself to take a few steps. A few steps were all that he could manage. He found a tree. He used the tree to have a moment of privacy and to steady his legs, and then stepped back to where Tasha was. She was sitting up, looking at him.

"Good morning, King," she said tenderly, with a glowing smile. King looked at her. She had long, brown hair with numerous silver strands. She seemed old, but not aged. A bit like a grandma, but in her full strength. She was wearing multiple layers of loose fitting clothing, topped with a heavy brown cloak that she took off now that the night was over.

"Good morning," King replied automatically. He sat down again, glad to give his legs a little rest.

"You will have to take some time, because your muscles have atrophied. I can pull you still, but if you walk a little each day, you'll soon be able to walk again on your own," she explained to him. She handed him a piece of dried, crusty bread.

"Where have I been?" he asked her.

"I'm not sure I know what you mean," she furrowed her brow.

"Don't I have a family? I know your name, but I don't know why," he realized he couldn't remember much.

Tasha wished that she didn't have to get into such matters so soon, but with the question put to her, she knew she had to tell the truth. "Well, I'm sad to say that your mother and one of your siblings are dead. You were there when it happened, don't you remember?" she gently plied him.

King strained to remember anything about the incident. He couldn't keep the tears from welling up as he realized he not only didn't recall their deaths but couldn't recall even what they looked like.

Tasha misunderstood, thinking he was remembering the horrific event she said, "I know that sometimes we see things that we wish we could forget …"

King interrupted her and blurted out in exasperation, "No, I can't remember at all! What is wrong with me?" And then, before Tasha could say anything, he added, "And things that I don't want to remember, those I see clearly. What happened to me?"

Tasha thought she knew, but she was not going to tell him anything about her theories until she'd had more time to think about it and watch him. King brushed a last lingering tear off his cheek and wondered if she was going to venture an answer. Instead, she changed the subject.

"Last night you went into a panic, King," she said. "Do you remember? Someone was in danger …"

"Yes. Well, sort of. I mean, I saw a cave or something that was already dark, but then it went completely black …" he began to explain, but Tasha interrupted him.

"Ming? What do you mean 'ming?'" she probed.

"Not ming, *mean*," he shook his head to express his confusion. Tasha had a look of recognition.

"Oh, I see. We're going to have to work on the pronunciation of some of your words," she said as gently as possible. She prompted him to continue.

"When it became black, I could still see, but it was like being blind but knowing my eyes worked and there were rumbling sounds as if rocks were falling around me," he told her, and then stopped talking, realizing that he couldn't put the rest into words. Tasha, for her part, made mental notes that for King, "wheng" was "when," "beein" was "being," and so forth. She patted his shoulder.

"You sit here, King. I'm going to check around and fill up our water jugs," she said, gathering up the jugs and walking away.

King was happy to be alone. He didn't want to think about the things he didn't remember—or the things he could, for that matter.

He used the opportunity to try walking again, but only managed a few more steps. He gazed out at the other travelers camped all around and at last spotted a big interstate road about fifty yards off. Finally, he let his eyes wander back to the camp and spotted the wagon. He realized that Tasha had probably been pulling him in the wagon the whole time, and though he had felt an instinctive affection for her when first he recognized her, it now deepened.

When she returned, there was a little bit of small talk, but finally Tasha told him that it would be time for them to get going. She explained that having begun their journey outside Indianapolis, they were going to try to get to Omaha, Nebraska, and there perhaps settle in for a few years. She made King sit in the wagon. He was embarrassed to do so, so he laid down in it instead. Tasha threw him a curious look but said nothing.

The next few weeks went slower than before, because even though King could now walk and talk, he was weak. King would take Tasha's arm and, in the morning and evenings, walk around their campsite for slowly increasing periods of time. After a mere week, he was also walking for a little ways during the day. He was driven by the humiliation of appearing to be a perfectly healthy, if skinny, boy being pulled by an old woman. Realizing that King's legs were not the only thing that had atrophied, Tasha also started him on doing push-ups and when possible, pull-ups, too. By the time the signs on I-35 were telling them that Des Moines, Iowa, was only fifteen miles away, King was walking, albeit very slowly, for more than half the day.

Tasha thrived on the new turn of events. She now had someone to talk to. Though she could not share everything with King, in part because of his own personal history and in part because he still was only a boy, there was much that she could. She told him what it had been like in Bloomington. She told him funny stories about the people in the group of old friends that she had accompanied. She told him about her time in Peoria. When King would ask about finding him, she gave him the barest details, and when he asked her about her life before that, she would describe it as foul and leave it at that.

When Des Moines seemed to be only a few miles off, Tasha turned them off the Interstate into a city that was nearby. She was looking for something but did not tell King what it was even as he peppered her with questions. She merely smiled at him somewhat mischievously. The city street was active with travelers and residents alike and many of the buildings were in good shape, but Tasha did not take him to any of those. Instead she found a more run down place and told him that this was their first destination.

"P … A … W … N. Pain? You're taking me to a pain shop?" King asked, wincing.

"I told you that English can be curious. No, it's a pawn shop, with the *a* soft and short."

"What is a pawn shop?" King asked her.

"It is a place that sells and buys and trades. It will be a good place to find you a weapon," she replied, glancing at him to catch his reaction.

"A weapon!" he declared. "Yea, let's go in!"

Tasha parked the wagon outside the door in such a way that she could see it through the barred glass door if she wanted to check on it. They entered the shop. It was dirty and dusty and someone was smoking a cigar. There were a lot of people in the shop. There was a handful arguing with the owner about the price he was offering for some item, but other than that the rest of the place was quiet as people browsed.

There was a section clearly marked "WEAPONS," and Tasha led King to it. As she did so, she explained why they were there.

"We're going into a big city, King, and there will be a lot of people. In these days, without the constraints of civilization to hold people back, you'll find that a lot of them use their liberty in terrible ways. There have always been people with no regard for decency or the law, but many of them feared punishment, so they behaved. Naturally, not all of them behaved, but you get the idea. I want you to have something just in case, a little something so you're not completely unarmed," she told him, but hastily added a stern command, "but it will be your job to wield the weapon with responsibility and only in proper circumstances."

"How will I know how to do that?" King asked her, not allowing her firm tone of voice to take away the excitement of owning some kind of weapon.

Tasha sighed. "That would be the sort of thing that your father would have been best equipped to teach you. Unfortunately, we don't know where he is, nor even if he's alive, do we? I shall teach you the best I can. But do not fear, I can speak to the matter effectively as well," she assured him.

King was only barely interested in his own question. He was waiting for Tasha to show him the weapons he would be permitted to choose from. His eyes had fallen on the glass cases that surrounded him in a U shape. The cases served as the counter as well, and a worker was behind the counter casting looks at them periodically but otherwise ignoring them. Inside the cases were knives, daggers, and even a couple of swords. There were large empty areas throughout the cases, and Tasha whispered to him that few people were trading in their weapons these days so the supply was going to get smaller and smaller. In another case, King saw items that he knew were guns. There weren't very many of them, and most of them looked like they'd seen better days.

Tasha saw him looking at the guns. "We'll be looking for a knife, today, young man," she remarked slyly, dashing his hopes.

King surveyed the knives, then, at a loss on how to decide between them. Like the guns, many of the knives looked old and barely functional, but there were many decent knives to choose from. His eyes fell on the sword.

"You're looking for personal defense?" the man behind the counter asked Tasha.

"Yes, that's right," she replied.

"You won't want those swords. They are sharp and all, but they weren't made for real use. I wouldn't trust them in a scrape," he informed her, looking at King's crestfallen face.

"No, I quite agree. For him we need something much smaller, anyway. Something that he can use around the campsite. Preferably something that is all one piece of metal. I don't want something that's going to break five miles down the road," she told the man.

He nodded in agreement and motioned her down to a case a little farther away. He pointed to a set of knives of the same sort, by the same manufacturer, but of different lengths. The metal blade was blackened, and the handle was apparently one piece with the blade, but the handle rod was wrapped in leather strands that looked to be securely bound to the weapon.

Tasha nodded her head with approval, "Yes, these look nice. We won't want the ten-incher or anything bigger than that. And not too small, either. Let's see the six-incher."

The worker pulled the blade out and set it on the counter. King knew not to reach for it and instead let Tasha handle it. She held it in different ways, examined its balance, tested its weight, and looked it over for craftsmanship. She seemed to approve. "I like that it is not double-edged. The handle I'm worried about. Looks a little like the maker wanted to rush something out before they were closed down. But I think it will do," she thought out loud. She handed the knife to King, who took it lovingly.

While King examined the blade, Tasha and the worker entered into negotiation. When it was done, Tasha pulled out a little bag with some kind of coin in it—gold, King realized—and pushed two of them across to the man. He, in turn, handed over the sheath, a knife cleaning and sharpening kit, a one piece metal hatchet, a leather belt, a belt clip, and a sturdy canteen. Both Tasha and the man looked like they'd just gotten away with murder. Tasha ushered King out of the store.

"I dare say that even gold won't be of value in the future," Tasha sighed when the door was shut behind them. She looked at King fondling the knife. "Do you like it?" she probed.

"It is fantastic!" he exclaimed.

"I'm glad you like it," Tasha smiled.

"Why don't you have a knife?" King challenged her suddenly.

"What makes you think I don't?" she countered calmly.

"I have never seen it," King explained.

"You have only been awake for a couple of weeks. Give it time," she smiled at him. He seemed satisfied with that, so she used their walk back to I-35 to lay out the ground rules for the use of the blade. He was not to flaunt it, he was not to abuse it, he was not to play with it as though it were a toy, he would have to learn how to take care of it, and then, more importantly, he was to remember to do so. By the time they reached the freeway again, she had made him quite reluctantly stow the knife on his new belt.

King was eager to enter the city now that he had something on his hip. He hadn't been afraid before. He hadn't really thought about the types of dangers that he might face. Hearing of those dangers hadn't terrified him, either. Instead, it had filled him with a sense of adventure, and it had only deepened by the acquisition of the blade. He didn't say anything to Tasha, but he secretly hoped he'd have occasion to use it. At the very least, he hoped he'd have the opportunity to wave it about without being reprimanded. He fantasized about standing up to hooligans bent on robbing them and even about rescuing Tasha from an abusive store clerk.

As Tasha had promised, there were a lot of people in Des Moines. Since King refused at this point to be pulled in the wagon when he was tired, he used the time when they were resting to look at all the people walking about. Occasionally, Tasha would comment on what they were seeing. She pointed out the numerous specially clothed citizens circulating among the travelers trying to eyeball anybody who might be infected by the Disease. She told him what individuals would cause her to be wary and what ones would set her mind at ease, and gave him some ideas on how she would make that determination.

"See that man there? He looks pleasant and well dressed. The person with him is carrying everything, though. That makes me wonder if he is a cruel bully. Let's find a different example. Sure, why not, this will do … that man is carrying the baby while his wife has the backpack. I would suspect that this couple has equal concern for each other," Tasha ruminated. She added a parting thought, "But in these days, though you have to try to draw a quick judgment, you must be aware that people can fool you. You must keep your guard up for a little ways. We may find out that there is a good reason why the man I think is a bullying taskmaster is having his friend carry everything. We may find out that the man loves his child more than his wife. Use your intuition, yes, but keep your mind open to the possibilities, both good and bad."

King listened to her, but only half-heartedly. There were quite a number of other interesting things to look at. He'd already realized by now that Tasha was clearly pleased to talk after so many months with only her own self to communicate with.

Tasha didn't allow them to sit still for too long. She was very uncomfortable remaining in the city, as it seemed quite unorganized. Omaha had sounded much more organized, and it had the benefit of having a ham radio operator. This very much appealed to her, as it allowed her the unlikely possibility to try to reconnect with King's family through the ham radio operator in Bloomington. She hoped that it was still as organized as it had sounded.

They pushed through the city in about three days. Tasha kept her eyes peeled for opportunities to replenish their supplies; she did her best to glean as much information as she could as well. During her information gathering, she learned that there was a grim threat surfacing. Apparently, groups of American Indians had latched onto the fact that there were no longer any central authorities and were arguing amongst one another about the prospect of taking the country back to be their own again. Worse, some had already acted on this principle. They were ambushing travelers, raiding cities, and generally harassing anyone who was not an Indian. Because not every tribe felt this way, there was not yet anything systemic. In fact, some of the tribes had set themselves against one another so strongly that they had already come to internecine violence. Many citizens of Des Moines expressed the hope that maybe they'd battle it out between themselves and that would settle it. Tasha believed that hope to be misplaced.

Sitting on the western edge of Des Moines, Tasha and King joined a group of travelers preparing to head west to Omaha. Merchants circulated among them, and Tasha had to politely decline their wares a dozen times. There were perhaps a thousand people sitting around waiting. Many of them were talking with other travelers, hoping to find someone to accompany them. Every now and then, a group that had formed would make off towards their destination. In the meantime, other groups were arriving and entering the city.

King asked Tasha about the many men in the area who had guns, hunting rifles mainly. She guessed that the men were escorting travelers. Tasha didn't seem to be as impressed by the guns as King was. She explained that the vast majority of such weapons had been confiscated and destroyed by the United Nations, and that many of the ones that were about these days were poorly manufactured and unreliable. Also, every day that went by when one was used was a day when there was less ammunition on hand. There would come a time, she said, when men would be reduced to sticks and farm instruments or makeshift clubs. She waved off the rest of his questions so she could speak to a party that was coming by. She wanted information and hopefully travel companions. Tasha had barely begun talking with the party when she heard her name being shouted.

"Tasha! There you are!" Tasha whipped her head around and saw Pastor Parson pedaling hard in their direction. King's face went white.

"Tasha, there is a lizard riding over here," King said under his breath, unsure even as he said it that Tasha would believe him or understand him. But Tasha did.

"I thought as much," she told him. "Don't worry, I understand."

Pastor Parson was followed at a short distance by four women. King guessed that one of them was … the lizard's wife … and the other three he guessed were his daughters. He patted his knife where it was on his belt.

"Pastor Parson, how nice to see you!" Tasha greeted him. Pastor Parson was off his bike in an instant. He took her hand before she could say anything, and bent low and kissed it.

"Dear lady, how very nice to see you. I see you have chosen also to head west as I did!" the pastor boomed. The man's wife and daughters had arrived, and King had to blink his eyes. The daughters were all very attractive, and the youngest was his own age. While all four women looked a little ragged, burdened by rucksacks, they seemed happy to be able to get off the bikes. They walked around a little bit while the Pastor and Tasha talked and then came over to join the conversation. More accurately, they stood nearby silently and watched the pastor and Tasha talk.

Tasha was cordial throughout the conversation, and that was easy enough as the pastor carried most of it. At last, he expended himself and patted her on the shoulder. He winked, "I didn't forget that you owe me one!" Then he got on his bike and pedaled west. His wife and children, catching the hint, got on their bikes and followed him. King was sure that the youngest one had looked at him.

When the family was well out of earshot, Tasha gazed at King, "So, a lizard, eh?"

"I know its weird, but that's what I see. A lizard … lizardly man. Do you believe me?" King fidgeted.

"I do. I can almost see it myself. Let's not worry about it now. Come, let's follow this group heading out," Tasha answered him, hoping he wouldn't think she was changing the subject.

It took them about a week to make the next thirty miles, but after that King no longer needed rests anymore. Tasha was pleased to see him growing in strength. While he had never looked emaciated, he had grown undeniably scrawny. In the course of their travels, she taught him how to cook some breakfast meals out of oats, corn, and wheat, and for a little while he delighted in waking early to try out some new idea for breakfast.

Pastor Parson appeared about a week after that. Tasha couldn't help remarking to King that for a man on a bike, he didn't seem to be making good time. This time, instead of jetting off right away, the pastor hung back to stay with Tasha's group. He talked with them a couple of times, but socialized with the whole group. Tasha kept an eye on him. King knew that she didn't trust him one bit, and he suspected that the pastor's reminder about her "owing" him had not been meant in play.

One morning the pastor and his family were walking their bikes near where Tasha and King were, and they were able to hear the conversation.

"The only book worth reading is the Good Book," the pastor was asserting. He had his Bible out and was pounding it on his chest.

"But Parson, the Good Book is in English, and I have to think that reading other books would help you develop your skills at literary interpretation. Surely being sure your interpretation is solid is important to Christians?" the man the pastor was discoursing with replied.

"I could just as easily say that the more you read the Good Book, the better you're able to interpret the others. But if you've already mastered the Bible, why do you need the others at all?" Pastor Parson asserted loudly.

"But can't you say that the Bible basically has only one purpose, to connect God to man? I mean, is it so wrong to have a history book covering World War II? You can't blame the Bible for not covering events thousands of years later, and such a book would be serving a different purpose anyway, wouldn't it?" the man replied, unfazed.

"Perhaps so, but what purpose could possibly compare to communicating the divine drama?" the pastor retorted.

"Well, at any rate, I can't believe you supported the UN's book burning program. Surely you knew that it would include Bibles?" the man cried out, exasperated.

"Well, as I'm a pastor and you're not, perhaps you should just leave such issues to me," Pastor Parson rebutted him, again pounding the Bible on his chest.

"Good Lord," the man sighed.

Tasha understood where the man was coming from. She angled King away from the area that the pastor was in. It didn't matter. The pastor rode off to debate someone else. King glanced at Tasha, but she didn't seem to be in the mood to talk about the exchange. To her chagrin, that night the pastor and his family camped very near where Tasha and King built their fire. They could hear his booming voice late into the night. Finally, though, there was no way the racket could keep him awake, and King fell asleep.

King sat up with a start.

Tasha sat up, too. The night had passed and it was now early morning.

"Shhhhhhh," Tasha was saying, consoling him. King realized that he had been shouting or making noise or otherwise disturbing the peace. He looked frantically around. Tasha, seeing that King was quiet, gently prodded him, "What did you see?"

King stammered. People were looking in their direction. King was embarrassed about the attention, but what he had seen was enough to frighten him, too. Tasha was waiting patiently. King spoke.

"I saw the morning star fall like lightning," King whimpered.

"What do you mean, 'saw?'" Tasha prodded him.

"I saw it! With my own eyes! It was wounded ..." King shuddered.

A number of people had come close to hear what King was going to say. One of them was the pastor.

On hearing King, Pastor Parson gave a loud cough and declared, "Ha! Stars don't fall! Stars are made up of gases of various kinds that are constantly undergoing nuclear and chemical reactions!"

Tasha angrily silenced him, "That is what stars are made of, but that is not what a star *is*." Then King made a small noise and Tasha, like the rest, turned to look at him.

King, looking even more frightened than before, but very confident in what he had seen, whispered firmly, "It did not fall far from here."

The pastor and some other men began laughing uproariously, but Tasha's face went white. Knowing that it would be no help, she could not resist finding her blade in her garments and patting it. She glared fiercely at the scoffing men.

A few nearby were not mocking King. One of the men seemed to be thinking carefully and tapped Tasha on the shoulder, possibly saving the lives of those who were making fun of King. Initially startled, she saw that this man was not being a brute, so Tasha gave him her attention.

"That thing you said about stars ... is that true of anything else, too?" the man wondered.

"It is true of most things," Tasha stated matter-of-factly.

"Is it true of people?" he continued.

"It is especially true of people. What they are made of is not what they are," she explained, softening her tone somewhat.

"That is a very interesting idea. I've never thought of that before. What makes something what it is? Is it only the sum of its parts? What about the label we give the thing? Is that part of the thing's essence?" he asked aloud, but thinking to himself. Tasha let the question hang and then responded.

"How you answer that question will determine how you set your course in this world. Thank you for your kindness to King. It will encourage him to know that not all find him senseless," she told him.

It was true. King half thought he must be crazy even though he couldn't deny what he had seen with his own eyes. That Tasha would have been nice to him was expected. That a stranger would ponder seriously what King said meant quite a bit. The sounds of the boisterous laughing still rang through the campsites, however. Apparently, what King had said had become a running joke to be applied in various contexts. Frustrated, Tasha packed up their things into their wagon and pulled it away, not even looking to make sure that King was following. After awhile, she remembered him and turned to see if he was there. He was, though struggling to keep up. Tasha had been storming along.

"We'll get to the bottom of your visions, King. I have my suspicions, but you feel free to keep sharing them with me. I know who has touched you," she comforted him. King nodded without understanding, and they journeyed on.

# == Chapter 5 ==

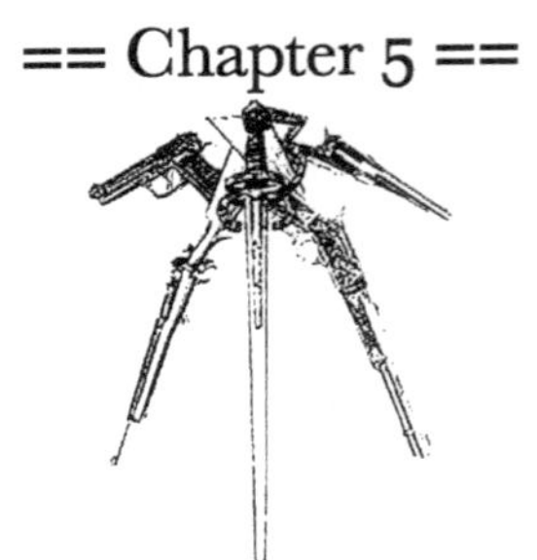

Tasha and King pressed on towards Nebraska. The signs continued to report fewer and fewer miles. Tasha patiently helped King with some of his vocalizations because he didn't say all of his words right. This made him self-conscious, but she assured him that she could help, and because of the last incident, Tasha took to having them camp as far away from people as she could, anyway. In the mornings and the evenings, since they were usually all alone, she also taught him how to take care of his knife and how to use it. King was impressed that she knew so much about fighting. The more he learned, the more his confidence grew, and the more he actually wanted to get into a fight.

One afternoon, that all changed in an instant.

Tasha and King were the only people on the road, as they often were these days. There was suddenly a dull thudding sound, and Tasha put her hand on King's shoulder. She looked around the hills and up along the freeway. There was no place for them to hide. There were trees visible on both sides of the freeway, but the forest lines were all much too far for them to hope to get to before the noises were upon them. The danger soon materialized as three men on horses cresting a hill to the north, emerging, it seemed, from some hiding spot in the woods. They bore down on Tasha and King at full speed.

"Take out your knife, King," Tasha ordered him. Her own blade was produced. This was the first time King had seen it, and he was in awe. It was longer by many inches than his own, and it sparkled no matter which way it was held. Despite the obvious superiority of her blade, King was more than happy to wave his own around. The closer the men came, however, the more nervous he became. Soon, they were on them.

The men barreled up to them shouting curses and profanity. They raged their horses back and forth past the two and did loud boisterous circles, too. The effort to intimidate them was failing. Tasha had pulled King close to her and glared at the men, her long knife plainly in view. After a few minutes of hollering at them and kicking up dust, the men, remaining on their horses, approached them head on.

"We want anything of value that you've got, young lady," the man on the left ordered her. He had a scraggly beard. All three had long tangled hair.

"You're just common bandits," Tasha replied. "What we have we need in order to survive. You know that. Anything of value we have we need to keep or we'll likely die. This, I'm sure, you know."

The man in the middle scowled at her, "That isn't our problem. You'll have no chance of surviving at all if you make us take your goods by force. Maybe someone will have pity on you, and you'll live. But you will surely die if you don't hand over your valuables right now."

Finally, the man on the right spoke. He had a long scar visible across his cheek. "Don't you see we have to worry about our survival, too? Stop trying to reason with us and give us what we want."

"I won't," Tasha emphatically declared. "Try to take it if you like. You see I am not unarmed, and neither is the boy."

The men laughed, but the one with the beard warned her, "This isn't a negotiation. You're seriously going to die if you don't give up your goods ... *including* that fine looking knife." Tasha remained silent, staring fiercely at each man in turn. Though not persuaded by her look to leave them alone, they became convinced in turn that this woman intended to defend herself.

The scarred man swore and got off his horse, quickly followed by the other two. "Why do you have to make us work for it? We're tired and hungry," he muttered. If he hoped to intimidate her in this moment before battle, he was badly mistaken. The fight was over in a flash. King barely had time to blink a few times before the men were lying down in a heap before him. They were horribly disfigured, bloody, and dead.

King stared at the sliced flesh, at Tasha, at his own knife, and back at the bodies. He put the knife away. He hadn't anticipated what a knife wound would look like.

"Come on, King. I need to find some water somewhere to clean up," Tasha commanded him gently.

King couldn't explain why he was so repulsed by what he had seen. The next couple of days he moved about in a slight daze. The incident seemed to stir up memories and warnings from before the calamities. Though he realized that this probably went back to the time when he was with his family, he couldn't remember any specifics. Tasha was careful not to push him on the topic. After a week had gone by, King was back to normal, but he handled his knife with much more respect and seriously doubted that he could ever use it as a weapon.

This was put to test much sooner than he expected. Now a mere thirty miles from Omaha, it was more difficult to avoid camping in sight of people. Tasha still made every effort she could to remain isolated, but sometimes it wasn't possible. Stopping for the day, Tasha instructed King to go into the woods to gather firewood while she prepared the evening supper.

King whistled as he pushed branches away from his face, his eyes searching the cool earth for pieces of dead wood. Little hills with little valleys were all around him. The ground was soft and springy, and sunlight shot through the woods like spears descending to the earth. He liked how the earth pushed him back up as he walked and used the little valleys as a way to gather speed as he bounced along. All of a sudden, though, he heard a rustling noise and then murmurs. He knew that the murmurs were human voices. They were too indistinct to make out. He thought to himself that Tasha would not think him wise for doing so, but he didn't see the harm in taking a few hills in the direction of the murmurs.

He crested the second hill and started down it before comprehending that he had passed several bikes leaning up against a tree. Before him were the pastor and one of his daughters. The pastor was on top, and the daughter seemed to be weakly resisting. He was saying something to her in a low voice, and though he couldn't make out what she was saying, it sounded to him like she was pleading in response. His knife was out in an instant, and the minute it was in his hand he heard a yelp.

Startled, for the first time he noticed that the other bikes were here as well. The pastor's wife and other daughters were sitting in the opposite side of the little hill. They had watched him quietly and wouldn't have said anything except King had produced the knife. The pastor heard the exclamation as well, and turned his head to look over his shoulder. He saw King and grinned. When he saw the knife, he started laughing.

The pastor rolled off his daughter and for the first time King was able to see her. It was the oldest daughter. She looked at King with fear and resignation in her eyes. She moved to try to cover herself, but she was only barely successful. King felt a pang of self-loathing as he noticed his own sense of curiosity awakened. He was distracted from considering such things by the approaching pastor. King's knife wavered in his hand. He felt certain that he would have to use it to defend himself, or he would die.

"Tell me what you see, *now*!" Pastor Parson sneered at him. King lowered his blade. He knew he couldn't use it. He knew it.

"I see a boy who has been away from camp too long," was the reply, only it wasn't King, but Tasha.

Tasha's eyes darted around the little valley. When she saw the scantily clad girl lying on the ground, Tasha's eyes narrowed in rage.

"You just move along, Tasha. Nothing here is any business to you," the pastor snapped at her.

"If you won't protect your family, and I won't protect your family, who is left to protect your family?" Tasha snapped back at him. But Tasha glanced fiercely at the man's wife, too.

"Maybe I'll just collect on that favor you owe me," Pastor Parson scowled defiantly. But Tasha's blade was revealed in answer, and the pastor took a step backwards.

"No. I think it is time for you to face the Judge," Tasha said quietly but firmly. She took a step forward, and the pastor fell back another step. The wife shrieked.

"You ... you would kill a man of the cloth?" the pastor pleaded. His bravado had dissipated in an instant in the face of Tasha's tangible resolve.

"What makes you think you are a true shepherd? It is not merely successfully completing school that makes one a genuine shepherd. Flashing a Bible around convinces no one. You do not deserve that cross that hangs around your neck. Temptation crouched at your door, and it mastered you. Very little of you remains. You should have crucified this vile passion long ago, but now it consumes you. I think I can help," Tasha asserted, her voice raised.

"He ... lp?" he whimpered, increasingly frightened by her presence.

"Yes, let me kill it. Perhaps there is a little left of you in there, perhaps not. Only one way to find out. Let me kill it," Tasha practically ordered him.

"Nooo ..." the pastor cried.

Tasha leapt forward, "I can kill it—I see it! Let me kill it!" At that, the pastor's wife shrieked again.

"Don't kill him!" the wife was begging.

Tasha looked at her, disgust mingling with compassion. "Let me do this and you will maybe have a man back," she said.

"What's going on here?" a new voice shouted. King looked in the direction of the speaker. There were several men. It was clear they had heard the shrieking and came to investigate.

Tasha stepped in and grabbed Pastor Parson by his shirt with her left hand and raised her right hand, holding her blade, high above her head. "This moment contains all moments! This is the Day of your Decision. Let me kill it! Quickly!"

"Nooooooo ..." Parson slunk back, slipping out of Tasha's hands like water through fingers.

"See here!" shouted one of the men. "You'll stop that this instant!" Tasha whipped her head around to face the men, and what they saw must have startled them for they each stepped back slightly. Tasha, on the other hand, relented. King guessed that it was not worth slaying Parson if it meant slaying the innocent newcomers who ignorantly were going to try to stop her.

Softening her gaze, Tasha nodded towards the girl on the ground, "This is that man's daughter. This is that man's family. He was raping her, or about to. No doubt this is a regular occurrence."

"Is this true?" another man demanded. The pastor was silent, but his wife nodded, tears streaming down her face.

A third man uttered an expletive. A fourth man suggested killing the pastor on the spot, and the wife began shrieking again.

Tasha sighed. "I know there are no courts worth speaking of left in the world today, but these women can't be left with this man. This man deserves punishment. Also, he refuses to repent."

"What do you suggest?" the first man asked her. Tasha had been thinking about it.

"Are you going to Omaha?" she asked him.

"Yes, we all are," he answered.

"Are you just men? If I put him into your care will you take him to Omaha and attempt to arrange for some sort of trial for him and protection for his wife and daughters? He won't end up hanged without some kind of trial?" Tasha inquired of them. There was something in the tone of her voice that communicated to them that they couldn't have extracted the pastor from her possession if they had wanted to try doing so without agreeing to her terms.

"I like to think we're good and just men," the first replied. "Jacob over there lets his mouth run sometimes, but I swear no harm will come to them. You think we should take charge of them all?"

"I do. He won't let me help him. There is nothing else that I can do for him. But he can't be allowed to roam free, either," Tasha explained. One of the men whispered to the other, and King detected some hesitation. Apparently, Tasha did as well. She fished into her pockets and produced a small leather bag. She tossed it to the first man, "That is a small bag of gold for your troubles. I think you'll find it more than enough for your troubles as we are less than a week away."

That seemed to do it. Parson's oldest daughter dressed herself, and the men bound him up. He cowered as Tasha ripped a necklace with a cross on it from Parson's neck. He winced in pain as she did so; there would likely be a raw red stripe on the back of his neck to remind him of his defrocking for some time. Then she rifled through his bag and retrieved the Bible.

She glared at Parson and declared, "I shall find some who are worthy to have these, who really are shepherds." At that, the men foisted Parson onto his feet, and they all walked back in the direction of the freeway. The daughters walked the bikes through the woods. As they were camping in different areas, Tasha and King turned away from them. The youngest daughter rushed over to King, though. She grabbed his arm and kissed him on the cheek before he knew what was happening. She ran off to join the rest of the group as they made their way to where the men had their own camp.

King had done nothing but draw his knife, knowing almost immediately that he wouldn't use it, and had still somehow won the affection of the girl. He couldn't help but smile, remembering the gentle peck on his cheek, and at the same time recall his fear and also the sick curiosity that leapt up in him even as he knew in his heart he had interrupted something sinister and disgusting.

King replayed the previous day's events in his head constantly. He combined that incident in his mind with the gruesome deaths of the bandits about a week earlier. He wondered to himself if he could actually fight if it came to it. A faint memory recalled to his mind lectures on being careful around knives mixed with depictions of the horrors of war. King surmised that he was remembering a conversation between his father and grandfather. The details weren't clear but he recalled his grandfather urging that the knives be put away and a walking stick be used instead.

He decided at some point that his problem was not simply fear. Instead, he knew that he simply couldn't bring himself to cut someone. Hitting someone over the head with a stick seemed doable, but not slicing through flesh. After awhile, Tasha extracted this from him; she solved the problem by digging out of an old barn the intact handle of a shovel. She had him use his knife to scrape off the splinters and smooth the ends. The end result was a fighting staff. This made him much more comfortable, though she reminded him that he had yet to see what kind of damage a blow from his staff would do to a person's face. He kept that in mind as he practiced the moves she showed him.

King was excited at the prospect of finally entering Omaha. There was a certain thrill to traveling through the countryside. There were plenty of adventures to be had. On the other hand, Tasha promised him that they would find a place to call home for a time, and he couldn't deny that it would be nice to settle in somewhere. A big city like Omaha seemed like a nice place to establish residence.

His excitement was cut short, however. Tasha had just told him that they were no more than a day away from Omaha when they first heard the news from people coming from the opposite direction—people fleeing—that Omaha was no longer a free city. It had been attacked and occupied by a small army of American Indians. The details were sketchy, but it was certainly clear that they could not continue on to Omaha. Given the panic that many of the travelers were in, Tasha was not content to remain on the Interstate. Unsure which direction would be safest, Tasha randomly chose to turn south.

They skirted along the eastern edge of Council Bluffs and soon found that they were confronted with I-39. In Tasha's mind, this was no better than remaining on I-80, so she backtracked a little ways. They crossed a few major roads, all of which were filled with panicking travelers and refugees, and it was beginning to seem as though there would be nothing else to do except fall back in the direction of Des Moines.

As evening fell, they were camped without a fire roughly southeast of Omaha, hidden in a grove of trees. In the morning, Tasha still hadn't made a decision about what to do when they suddenly found themselves surrounded by Indian warriors. Tasha threw herself as a shield on top of King and pointed her blade at the band of men. King blinked up at the Indians, many of whom were armed with guns, though some had bows and arrows. They were dressed in normal garb, including one wearing a suit coat, and out of step with such clothing, they were wearing war paint on their faces. The men had them encircled, and King counted ten of them.

"You will not touch him," Tasha shouted at the men. The men stared at her and said nothing. Tasha repeated her warning, "Leave us! We are nothing to you! I may die protecting the boy, but I assure you it will come at great price to you!"

King's heart beat madly inside of him. He doubted that Tasha could do anything to the men before they were cut down by bullets. And still the men did nothing!

"What tribe are you from, woman?" one of the men asked at last.

"I am not a native of your land," Tasha returned boldly.

"She speaks with courage. I think she does not tell the truth," one brave told another. There was a murmured conversation about this contention.

"Do we think only Indians have courage?" voiced one challenger.

"Look at her hair. She wears it like an Indian."

"I tell you, I'm not an Indian," Tasha insisted. "Do not continue to harass us for nothing, or if you intend to do us evil get on with it already," she dared them.

The men whispered to one another again. One of the men was elbowed by another, and this one now took over the conversation.

"What is your business? What is your destination?" the man pressed her.

"We were on our way to Omaha. Our interest was simply to find a place to live," Tasha replied, her short sword still pointing up at the Indians defiantly. "Now that Omaha is closed to us, I do not know where we'll go."

"It is a dangerous time to be wandering the hills around here," the man said to her. He continued plying her with question, "Are you sure you're not Sioux? Perhaps separated from the rest? Lost, perhaps? Maybe a scout?"

"I am none of those things," Tasha retorted shortly. "Shall we be fighting or not?"

Some of the men began laughing, and those that didn't cracked smiles. There was another murmured conversation, and the spokesmen said, "We are not the ones who have attacked Omaha. We do not think, like those, that we have a right to the land and its cities. It so happens that we are Sioux and they are Sioux, but we do not agree on this thing they have done. We are inclined to believe you but cannot risk leaving you here. We were supposed to be moving stealthily. Someone was supposed to ensure that this area was clear ..." here the man glanced at a man to his left who winced ..."So, I have to send you back so that our brothers do not know we are here. As I said, I am inclined to believe you. Yes, I must insist that you allow us to escort you and the boy away from the area, but I want to invite you to take our protection and head south. We can help you get to Kansas. We welcome courageous women like you. But you're not safe from here to Wichita right now. Will you go peacefully with my men? After that you may accept my offer, or not, but will you at least go peacefully right now?" the leader asked her.

"Yes. That is better than any other plan I was entertaining," Tasha smiled.

"Carl and Fenton will escort you back. My name is Fox Marion. Use it if you decide to accept my offer. You will find that my name is welcomed so long as you head south into Kansas, among the Indian tribes that are opposed to reclamation, anyway."

Two men stepped out of the circle and helped Tasha to her feet. Fox Marion and the other men were gone before King was on his feet. The two men introduced themselves to Tasha and King and then gently, but firmly, guided them south. It didn't take too long before they arrived at a small base camp. This was still not far enough away, apparently, for Carl and Fenton here acquired horses for them all, and they were soon riding. Again, the direction was south. They didn't stop until they'd rejoined I-35 and arrived at an old rest area.

Here they found a sizeable camp of Sioux Indians. Many of these were armed with hunting and assault rifles, but as in the first group of Sioux soldiers, some had bows and arrows or crossbows. If King thought that here, at last, they would be set free, he was soon convinced otherwise. Carl and Fenton handed them over to another group of men and then left them, presumably to return north.

The new group was strictly ordered to treat them with respect. This group of men appeared to be part of the supply and communication lines. Tasha and King were soon invited to sit in the back of a pickup truck. This was the closest King had come to traveling in a vehicle, and he was thrilled to feel the wind whipping through his hair as the truck, accompanied by an escort vehicle, bounced down the southbound lanes of I-35.

Fox Marion's idea of shuttling Tasha and King away from Omaha appeared to mean being taken all the way into Kansas itself. Initially put off by how long they were being kept in custody, Tasha decided it wasn't really a bad deal. They were getting motorized transport, and that was much better than continued travel on foot. One of the reasons why she had wanted Omaha was because it sounded cleaner and less crowded than Bloomington. Perhaps, she explained to King, another city, like Wichita, would be fine as well. Though she didn't explain why she thought this way, Tasha indicated that she hoped wherever they ended up there would be a ham radio station.

The next day they crossed into Nebraska but did not stay there long. They arrived at an intersection just inside of rural Kansas and were politely informed that they were free to go from that point on. Far from being left out in the boondocks, the intersection revealed a steady flow of traffic in all directions. Their "escorts" informed them of how to take advantage of Fox Marion's offer to go farther, which Tasha thoughtfully considered. They soon learned why the intersection saw so much traffic: Kansas City had been one of the cities destroyed in the nuclear strike a couple of years earlier, so now travelers had to go around the city if they wanted to go east or west. This meant using the roads whose intersection Tasha and King now stood upon.

"Well, King. What do you think? Wichita?" Tasha asked him. King shrugged his shoulders. Tasha thought out loud, "Mr. Marion has been trustworthy to this point. We can't stay here, and Omaha is out of the question. So why not Wichita?" It was decided. Tasha and King met a relay party on the Sioux's supply lines, informed them of their connection to Fox Marion, and were told the party was already aware of the arrangements. They were henceforth guests in the supply vehicles and could go all the way to Wichita if they desired, or do something else if they so chose.

It was not a hard decision. Arrangements were made to take them to Wichita. Unfortunately, when they arrived there two days later they found that the city was not welcoming new arrivals. The gates to the city were closed and crude signs were erected that said: Quarantine—CITY CLOSED.

"What are we going to do?" King asked Tasha nervously.

The scene was pitiable. Apparently the quarantine had only gone into effect that morning, and there were many people who had been arriving after traveling from afar, like Tasha and King, only to find their way barred. People were shouting and arguing with the gate guards. Some women were weeping and there were kids crying. It was hard to fight against the cause of the city closure, as a huge pile of dead bodies was in sight. The bodies had been set on fire, and the smoke curled high into the sky. Even the Sioux drivers that had brought them there were disoriented by the situation. They gathered with some of their fellows some distance from the city to calculate their own next moves. Having no other ideas, Tasha led King to them.

"Please sirs," Tasha implored, "Please take us to some city, somewhere. We don't have enough of the summer left to make it very far now."

"Tasha, we will not abandon you," one of them comforted her.

"We have to find out about our families. Worst case scenario for you, though, is that you come with us to one of our reservations," said another.

Greatly relieved, Tasha sat down on the grass with King to wait and see what would come of the affair. From what King could gather, many of the Sioux had been trapped inside the city when the gates were sealed, and the discussion was on how to get them out apart from storming the city. It seemed after awhile that Tasha and King's plight had been forgotten again. More Sioux drivers appeared throughout the day. As evening fell, there was a large crowd of people on the outskirts of the city. Large bonfires went up. As King went to sleep that night there was still no resolution.

By morning, the city walls had collected more than incoming travelers. Curiosity-seekers were arriving, too. Few of these stuck around, however. They didn't want to linger by a city that had apparently just been ravaged by the Disease. They only wanted to see for themselves the closed gates and the smoking corpses. By mid-afternoon an entirely different group showed up. A party of a hundred men and women on horseback appeared from the south and immediately made their way to the Sioux camp. King took these to be Sioux Indians as well.

"Look, it is our Cherokee brothers," one man called out, immediately correcting King's assumption.

As the group drew closer, it was easy to see that, while most of the group consisted of grown men, both genders and all generations were represented, too. The Sioux camp warmly welcomed the group, most of whom dismounted nearby and began setting up their own camp, but a few of whom strode over to speak with the Sioux.

"What has happened to Wichita?" a very old Cherokee began, skipping pleasantries.

"Chief Thunderfist, as you can see, the Disease has arrived here. The city is closed," a Sioux returned.

"The Disease is everywhere, but how many places have shut their walls upon such short notice? When we left Oklahoma City barely a week ago there was no word that Wichita was any worse than any other city." The Chief was indignant.

Another Sioux swept his hand out towards the smoking heap of burnt and burning bodies, "If all of the cities are as bad as this, it will be only a matter of time before every city has closed up."

The Chief sniffed at that and thought quietly for a moment before issuing his next question, "Is Fox here? And what of the Lakota chief?"

"No, we have not yet found our chief," the Sioux man returned.

Chief Thunderfist seemed sullen at this news and was not happy that only half of his question had been answered, "And Fox. What about Fox?"

"Omaha has been conquered by reclaimers, and Fox is with a large contingent of our people up in that area," the man replied.

"Doing what? Is it war already?" the Chief barked.

"No, Chief Thunderfist. We are only watching, but we have set it in our mind to make sure that the occupiers come no farther west than Omaha," the Sioux soldier stammered, trying to satisfy the fiery Cherokee chief.

The Chief pushed on his questioning of the man unrelentingly, "Which tribe was it that took Omaha?"

"Apache for sure, some Sioux. We know that Lighter's Sioux was involved. Winnebago, and we assume Omaha. These are things we seek to discover."

"You let Fox know that we will help as much as we can. He knows we have our own problems, though," the Chief growled.

"Yes sir, and speaking of Fox ..." here the man pointed to Tasha and King, "Fox sent these two down here to Wichita with his blessings and under our protection. However, as you can see, Wichita is closed. We would happily continue to protect them or take them to one of our places, but we won't be returning there for some time until this Omaha situation is resolved. Can you find a place for them with you?"

Chief Thunderfist scanned Tasha and King with eyes younger than the wrinkled face would have suggested. He gave no hint of what he thought of them but thought much, apparently, of Fox. At last, he agreed, "Yes, we will take them. I see you have no horses, or we'd ask for some for them. They will have to ride with someone." Here he looked at Tasha as though his statement was actually a question. She quickly took the hint.

"That would be fine, sir. I have experience riding a horse, but the boy does not," Tasha said to him as gratefully as she could. Thunderfist softened slightly and waved behind him.

"Son!" Chief Thunderfist called out behind him. After a moment, a boy about the same age as King emerged from the small group of

Cherokee that had been hovering behind the Chief throughout the exchange with the Sioux travelers. He was an inch or two taller than King. He wore loose fitting jeans and a long sleeved shirt. The only thing that could have suggested that he was an Indian at all was that the knife on his belt was held in a beaded sheath. King wondered how this boy could be the son of a man as old as Chief Thunderfist.

"I am Luke," the boy introduced himself to King, offering his hand.

King tried to sound casual even though he was nervous. "I am King," he said, shaking Luke's hand.

"What is that?" Luke inquired, pointing at King's side.

"That is my staff," King explained.

"A staff? For walking?" Luke squinted his eyes at the thought of a boy his age needing a walking stick.

"For fighting," King retorted indignantly. He didn't really want to go into the matter and was put off by the line of questioning. But Luke only made a noise in acknowledgment of King's answer and eyed the staff skeptically. The awkward moment dissipated when the Chief declared it was time to move. King reflected, too, that he felt more confident arguing with people now that Tasha had taken the time to correct his speech.

Chief Thunderfist wasted no time in organizing their departure. Messages were given to Fox's Sioux comrades to take back to him, and messages were left for friends and relatives currently locked in the city as well. Before long, King was sitting behind Luke on Luke's horse, and Tasha was on a horse with a Cherokee woman. The troop began heading south but only rode for a couple of hours because it was already late.

That evening Tasha tried to comfort King. There had been so much change and so many new circumstances that he was beginning to feel ill. As the camp fell to sleep, Tasha let King rest his head in her lap so that he could fall asleep. In his sleep, he dreamed.

Ratta-tat-tat-tat. Boom-Boom-Boom Ratta-tat-ratta-tat-ratta-TAT. Boom-ratta-Boom-ratta-BOOM. Ratta-Ratta-TAT-Ratta-tat-tat-tat.

King heard the drums coming from a long way off. He hesitated to open his eyes. He really didn't want to endure yet another drama. It was odd, though. It seemed to be light outside. Boom Ratta-tat Boom Ratta-tat-tat-TAT. The rhythm compelled him to look and see. When he opened his eyes, he was on a wide, grassy plain. And he was alone. He could see for miles in all directions, and all he saw were brown and green hues of the prairie. Though King had not been able to see very well where they camped on account of the evening shades, he recalled that there had been trees. There were no trees here, only the sounds of drums. Many drums. Of many types. If he knew anything of drums, he'd have known he was hearing every drum of every sort that had ever been played on the earth. The whole world seemed to tremble to the beats.

Ratta-tat-tat-tat BOOM BOOM BOOM
Ratta-tat-ratta-tat-ratta-TAT TAT TAT.

King stood up and walked in circles. There was a breeze, but it was gentle, and it made no noise. With a start, he noticed that his garments had been replaced with a long, white gown with crimson braids hanging from the shoulders and waist. The drumming grew even more pronounced. It seemed as though even the clouds were rumbling. Then there came a rolling thunder from the east:

Bum BOOM BOOM Bum Bum BOOM Bum BOOM BOOM Bum Bum BOOM the low notes made his bones quiver; the sensation was so overwhelming that he wanted to join with the drummers' BOOM BOOM BOOM—and then an answer from the west! Ratta-tat-tat-TAT Tat Ratta-tat Tat Ratta TAT! It was a dare! BOOM Bum bu-Bum-bu-Bum BAM BAM! And now the two sides were at war with each other, and King swirled around in the grass feeling the beats of a thousand—no a million—no a billion—drums of all sizes and pitches—feeling them in his bones—and in his blood—he danced because he could do nothing else.

The pounding reached a fevered pitch! From the north, from the south, from the grass, wind, sky! From the east, from the west, to the dirt, bone, star! King felt within him that if only he had the eyes to see it he would see all about him, as far as the horizon and certainly beyond, drummers, drummers like stars in the sky.

Tum Bum-Bum-Badil Tum Badil Bum Bum

B
O
O
M

And then, there was silence. Or at least, the drums ceased, and then after a moment or so the echoing reverberations ended, too. King collapsed in awe, lay flat on his back and looked up, and he jumped up! There seemed to be a trillion faces looking down on him from on high, but then he looked again and they were gone!

"What was this?" King asked aloud to himself.

He nearly fell over when came the whispered reply, carried forth on a bold wind, "Behold, the great cloud of witnesses …" and for some reason, at this point King thought he saw … which is ridiculous, of course, since he saw no one, only heard the voice, but somehow he knew that the speaker was smiling … not the smile of a jovial old fellow, but more like the cunning smile of a man whose adversary thought he had the victory, not knowing that the man held in his hand the death blow … he knew this … and the breathy voice smirked, "And they each have their sword!"

At that, King woke up with a shout, and the whole camp of Indians stared at him. It was morning and the camp had already been astir, whether it was because it was time to get up or because of King making noises, he did not know. Tasha was trying to calm him.

"What did you see?" Tasha was asking him gently, but firmly.

"Drums!" King wailed, "Terrible, terrible drums! The drums of war!"

"Shhhhhhhhhh," Tasha whispered again. The Cherokee men and women were staring at King with faces mixed with fear and curiosity. King seemed to be out of his mind and noticed none of these, but he was *not* out of his mind. He reached out and grabbed Tasha by the shoulder.

"It was wonderful, and they have their swords!" King declared to Tasha. King could see that he was making no sense, and it slowly dawned on him that he was making quite a scene.

Chief Thunderfist arrived at his side. King expected to be rebuked or ridiculed and looked away from the old man's face. But the chief knelt down beside King and asked ever so gently, "What did you see, boy?"

"Drums … in the universe … the witnesses bear arms at last … I …" King wasn't able to put it into words. It had been a dream, after all. "Right?" he asked himself silently, "Just a dream, right?" he pleaded further with his senses.

The Chief took him by his shoulders, then, and leaned in close so that only King could hear him. King was afraid of what the chief was going to say, but King saw a slight smile play on the man's face before he felt the elder's breath by his ear. "I heard them too, son," the Chief whispered. "I heard them, *too.* Did you think they would remain spectators to the end? And Iurwain Ben-atar rides with them …"

Knowing that he was not alone in his visions King could have leapt for joy, but the chief put a finger to King's lips and motioned for him to say nothing.

"Have no fear, my friends," Chief Thunderfist announced to the party. "Let's not dismiss his dreams hastily and rule him out as a child acting up. I believe he is One Who Sees, but we shall see.

Please, continue to show him our welcome."

The faces all around were visibly relieved to hear the Chief give his approval to King. Luke, in particular, sighed deeply. Initially he thought all of the worst things, but hadn't considered any of the best things. Now, Luke was in awe. The other Cherokee, too, treated him with new respect. When they broke camp and mounted their horses, Luke made an extra effort to compliment King on the fierce appearance of his staff. King smiled, though Luke could not see it, of course, since King was sitting behind him with his arms around Luke's waist. But Tasha saw it, and Tasha was pleased.

# == Chapter 6 ==

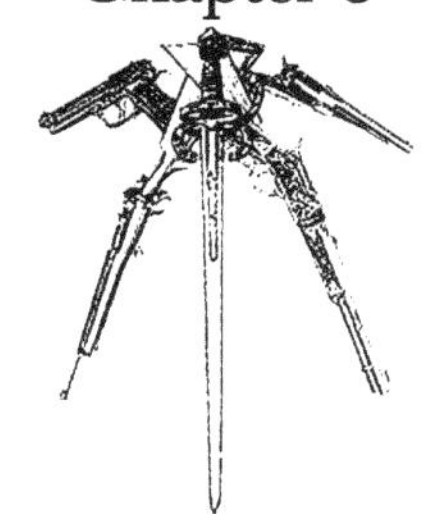

It took a month of tedious travel to finally arrive at the Cherokee reservation. To get there, they wound generally southeast from Wichita. They had a several-day layover in Tulsa but did not linger unnecessarily. King thought Tulsa was marvelous, though. The reservation was even better, although it wasn't really proper to think of it as a reservation any more—there was no more United States government to enforce whatever treaty would have confined them to that region. The Cherokee were spread throughout the region, and there was no enmity between them and the other local inhabitants since it was the Indians who gave the area strength and organization.

In the course of the journey, King had several more visions. He had another encounter with the universe's percussion and was almost prepared to welcome the incidents, when he had a series of visions that were dark and frightening. His eyes would be open, but it would be pitch black. His skin would grow cool and clammy, and his breaths would echo as though he were in a deep cavern. All sorts of terrible thoughts would assail him, such as one that urged him to take his own life. Then, as in the other cases, he would awake to Tasha's soothing voice and touch.

The region in which the Cherokee lived was called Tahlequah, and King instantly liked it. He and Luke became friends, and Tasha and King were often invited to Chief Thunderfist's residence. Here, Luke would lead King off on some wild adventure, and Tasha and the Chief would have long conversations. When Luke and King came back from their escapades, frequently accompanied by still other young men and women, they would find many other elders at the house. These too, would be deep in conversation. In this way, King met Ramaen, one of the Chief's most trusted advisors and almost as old as the Chief. A married couple from Tulsa named Philip and Mary were also frequently in attendance.

All in all, these days were wonderful. The Cherokee carefully patrolled their territory, and even after the Disease forced them, too, to shut their borders, King was still able to range across the region with Luke and his new friends. With some continued training from

Tasha, King was also able to convince Luke that his staff was not to be dismissed lightly.

Fall came and passed, and then winter was upon them. His visions still came, especially the ones where he felt like he was trapped in a cave. He had grown used to these, even if they were unpleasant. A very troubling scene began to appear in the early days of spring. He would open his eyes and see the lifeless eyes of a woman looking back at him. This scene troubled him because it did not seem so much like a vision as a memory ... but he had never seen the woman before. Now spring had arrived, and Luke took King on many new explorations.

With warmer weather, though, there were many people about, and the Cherokee patrols were working extra hard to ensure the safety of the reserve. Chief Thunderfist and Ramaen were often about at the borders negotiating with packs of travelers. It seemed that many people had barely made it through the winter on account of being shut out of one city after another, and now with warmer weather they intended to finally force their way in somewhere. The tension mounted all the way through April, and then things turned to violence.

In one instance, King found himself involved. He, Luke, and a pair of other boys were wandering along some trails well within the borders the reservation when ten travelers stumbled across their path. They were a mix of men and women and one or two children their own age, and they were as shocked to see the four as Luke and King were to see them. The surprise wore off quickly, though. The men began their menacing approach, but the four young men produced their weapons and brandished them as bravely as they could.

Not to be so easily dissuaded, the men continued to press towards them; the women also moved to join the fray. But King took his staff in hand like he was swinging a baseball bat and swung it with all his might, connecting with the chin of the man closest to him. King's friends all had shorter weapons and would have been hard put to use them once the men got within arm's length, but the staff bridged that distance easily. The man that King had struck fell to the ground like a rock, and King got another swing off, clipping a second man's hand and sending him off howling. Now reduced from five men to three, the insurgent travelers decided to try their luck a different day. The three remaining men scooped up their fallen friend, and the band of travelers followed the howls of their wounded companion back into the woods.

Patrols were immediately dispatched when King and Luke reported the event. They were fortunate: there had been a much larger group of wanderers in the trees. They had all been gathering together in little groups in order to make a grab at some of the

Cherokee's lands. King and Luke were told that they had been lucky and that they should have simply turned and run, but there was no hiding the proud look Chief Thunderfist bestowed upon the two.

Though King had no more incidents of this sort, his hosts would be busy into early summer before, at last, the rumor was well established among those wandering in the countryside that the Cherokees were not going to allow their quarantine to be violated or thwarted. But it was in early May that he had his most frightening experience in a long while. He had another vision, and it shook him to his core.

"What did you see?" Tasha gently probed. But King did not want to say.

There were no prying eyes of campers to gaze upon him with confused concern. Tasha and King had been given a small house of their own shortly after arriving on the Cherokee's land, so he was in his own bedroom with only Tasha to hear him. Even though it was only her, he simply couldn't bring himself to say.

"Come now, King. You've always told me, and I've always believed you," she cajoled him.

"No, Tasha, it was too terrible. I don't want to ... I wish I hadn't seen it!" King blurted out.

"It is up to you, King. I can help bear your burden," Tasha tried to comfort him. King began weeping, though, and she couldn't get another word out of him. He had seen a woman being brutally raped. It was more than that, though. He didn't see the scene so much as he saw her fear and panic and her utter terror. How does one see such intangibles? Never mind, King did see them. He also glimpsed the black cruelty of the perpetrator and saw in the man's heart that he was capable of far worse. Indeed, he could feel that this brutal assault was no more than sport for the man. King felt that the woman had been a token expression of the man's scornful approach to the whole world. As the vision faded, he saw the tattered shreds of the woman's dignity and smelled the cocky rage of the attacker ... and as the image popped out of existence he thought he heard, or felt, or saw, an onlooker weeping in despair at the pain inflicted on the woman and at his helplessness in stopping the attack. And King knew that this onlooker was the woman's father in some sense. King felt the anguish of both father and daughter and the dark bitterness that emanated out of the rapist. It felt as though something heavy had been placed onto his chest. He did not want to share any of this with Tasha, and he refused to do so.

What he did want to do, now, was to never experience the visions again. This one had been dreadful, filling him with an awful fear. Besides the event itself, which on its own had been horrendous, it had filled him with despair to see the father figure watching nearby, not intervening. King had the distinct impression that the father could not intervene even if he had wanted, almost as though the father was being forced to watch yet one more terrible event that had followed from one of his own poor decisions. Equally awful—and here King thought he was using the word in its proper sense—King felt that the father was seeing it from a different *time* altogether, something that even King saw could not be done apart from the power of the omnipotent and transcendent.

"Please, let me carry your burden," Tasha said again. "I can help, but you must let me."

"I don't see how you can help," King muttered, "It is in my head, not yours. In what way could you help me cease to be troubled by what I See?"

"I will be troubled for you, King. When such visions come, resolve yourself to know that no matter what terror they invoke I am the one terrified, not you," she said. Noticing King's confused expression, she continued, "Peter Stanhope would say that this is simply a law of the universe. If I am to bear one's burdens—and that is what I among others have been ordered to do—then it means that if you're still carrying it I must not be, but if I am, then you aren't. Hand your fear over to me as though it were a parcel for me to carry, and then face your visions with fearlessness, for I am certain that they come to you for a good and noble reason, as dreadful as they are."

"But how can you carry my fear? How can I stop myself from feeling a certain way?" King protested.

"I don't believe we are so enslaved by our emotions, but even if it is true to an extent, and even if you can't help it, I am suggesting that others can help you not to be afraid," she said.

"I don't see how you can take and experience my fear," King said.

"Have you not wondered about what it is you're seeing already? Is it past, present, or future? I don't think you're seeing dreams and if they are not dreams then it is happening, or did or will happen, yet you yourself are not physically present in order to witness it. If you can share in someone else's seeing, why cannot I share in someone else's fearing? If you are not so busy fearing, perhaps you in turn can bear the burdens of another," Tasha argued.

"You think I am seeing someone else's sight? Whose? How?" King demanded to know, passing over her suggestion that he might actually be able to help those in his visions. Tasha's eyes pierced his own as if to say he already knew the answer to his own question. King thought he probably did but was too stubborn to be anything but coy. He continued, "How can I be part of something so much bigger than me? It doesn't seem possible."

"You mean *finitum non capax infiniti*? If that were the case, *in morte ipsius baptizati sumus* would not be possible," then she added, noticing King's dazed look, "There once was a rescue that happened in that exact way. The rebellious were hidden inside the hero and the just wrath was poured out on the hero, who absorbed it in full. Hidden there inside him during the retribution, the promise is that they were present in his victory. Such a thing is not beyond the omnipotent, and it is the same sort of thing I am calling on you to realize, now. If I carry your burdens—really, not symbolically—it is only because another allows it and indeed, carries us both. It carries us both, and our fears, and would carry all of our fears if we did not insist on carrying them ourselves. Will you let me carry your burdens? Such an offer is rarely made and few are able to fulfill that offer," she replied.

But King had his mind made up. He announced to Tasha that he no longer wanted to receive any visions. Tasha received the announcement with a sigh of resignation.

"It is a difficult gift," she said tenderly. "I don't know if you can repress it even if you want to. I think, first, you should speak with Chief Thunderfist. Would you?"

King thought carefully, remembering vividly the look of tortured horror on the face of the young woman, "I will talk to him, but that will not change my mind."

After breakfast, the two made their way into the city center where they found Chief Thunderfist eating bean bread at an outdoor café. Ramaen was the only other person present. The two greeted them and invited them to join them. Tasha and King sat down, first wiping the morning dew off the chairs.

King inhaled the crisp spring air and wondered how to start. He hadn't needed to say anything: Thunderfist and Ramaen both knew he was there for a purpose. They were both very old men and over the years had learned how to read people well. Not only that, Thunderfist did not seem surprised to see them. At last, King decided he may as well just spit it out.

"I had another vision, Chief Thunderfist, and it was terrible. I don't want them anymore. How can I make it stop?" King blurted.

Chief Thunderfist closed his eyes in thought. Ramaen stared at King for a brief moment and then began eating his breakfast again. After a time, Chief Thunderfist spoke.

"This gift. It only comes by the laying on of hands, and the scope of the visions is proportional to the strength of the one whose hands have been laid down. Not many who have received the gift desire to set it aside, but I see in your eyes that for you it is a different matter. The ability to See, I think, was not the purpose of the gift. I think you were given the ability to See in order that you might not see," the Chief discoursed, almost to himself. King knew better than to interrupt. After a few more moments where he gazed up into the sky, clicking his fingers as though he were making calculations in his mind, the Chief again spoke.

"If I am right, then if you choose not to See you will again begin to see. I would expect that if what you See today is terrible, then what you at last see will be even more so. I cannot say, but I think that is the case. But if I am right," the Chief hastened to add, "Then you will never be able to fully set aside what you have received. The strength of the one giving the gift also determines to a degree how much or little one can set it aside. That said, if you choose not to see visions, to a large degree your choice will be respected. It is for you to choose."

Chief Thunderfist and King looked at each other for a time. The Chief was trying to decide whether or not he should inquire into the nature of the latest vision. King was pondering what memory could be worse than the latest vision. The Chief took a different tact.

"Besides the vision of the drums, what other kinds of visions have you had?" the Chief gently probed.

"By far the one that I have the most often is one where I am in a cool, damp blackness. I say 'I' but in most of the visions I am an onlooker. In this one, there is nothing to see. I sometimes think I hear breathing, or sighs and grunts. I get that one a lot. Sometimes when I see people in the same sight I see a flicker of something else at the same time. I have guessed that it is something of their character that I see," King explained.

"Ah, interesting," the Chief murmured. "I wonder if you have been given direct sight for what some people sense only as intuition …"

"Would you like to know what I see when I see you?" King offered.

The Chief laughed, "No, no, my son. Such a truth I might not be able to bear. What other kinds of visions have you experienced?"

King thought carefully and remembered the Lizard/pastor. "Not as often as the other visions, I sometimes see a person, but there is no flickering at all. Once I saw what I was told was a man, but all I ever saw was a lizard looking back at me."

Ramaen couldn't help but interject, "That's curious."

"And what about your latest vision?" Chief Thunderfist asked with raised eyebrows. "What was so terrible about it that you would reject a gift of Sight such as you have?"

King's mind was forced by the question to recall the details of the vision. The others knew this for King winced while he pondered his answer, which he delivered slowly. He had not wanted to describe the vision but he could not refuse.

"There was a woman … a beautiful woman. She was being raped by a man. That was bad enough, but another man, possibly her father—certainly a father in some sense—watched and did nothing, only he wept," King said.

"Hmmmm." The Chief murmured.

"What does it mean?" King inquired.

"Perhaps it *means* nothing. Perhaps you witnessed an event as it happened, and while meaning nothing now, it will come to mean something else later," the Chief explained.

"I had a debate with Tasha about whether or not I saw the past, present, or future," King said. "But I am struck that the 'father' did nothing."

"I have a guess as to who that man is. If I am right, he witnessed the event much as you did, except you witnessed it in the present, while he witnessed it at a future present, at the end of all things. Such things we will witness too, I imagine, before every tear is wiped away: the consequences of all our actions laid out in a long, interconnected, causal chain from the moment of the initial cause to its final effects. He did nothing because the deed was already done, but you saw it as it was being done. That is my belief," the Chief said.

At that moment, several Cherokee guards approached the table.

"Chief, there is a delegation of Sioux warriors here to talk to you. They say it is urgent," one of them said.

"We shall receive them here," the Chief replied.

"Here?" the guard asked, glancing back and forth between King and Tasha.

"Yes, here. King and Tasha will be joining us for the meeting," the Chief informed him. The guard shrugged and turned away with his companion to bring in the Sioux delegation.

"We can leave," King suggested nervously.

"After hearing what you said, why would I want that?" the Chief chuckled, winking at King.

"Alright, we'll stay," King smiled. He returned to the reason he had come, "So, where do these visions come from?"

"Your question has two answers. On the one hand, they come from the fact that you received a gift, and this I suspect you already possess some knowledge about. But the giver merely passed on what was first given to him, for on the other hand, access to information such as you see in your visions can only come from one place, and that is the Author. It can be no other way, provided they are genuine visions," the Chief explained.

"They might not be genuine?" King shuddered.

"This is perhaps not the time to speak of that. I am convinced that yours are. If your gift becomes known in the future or you yourself begin to take pride in them you may find yourself deceived. Or, you may even deceive yourself. Some messengers of light are imposters. It takes experience, time, skill, and discernment to be sure. You are not at a point where we need be deeply concerned. It would be better if instead you dedicated yourself to learning the ways of the Author. If you know his mind and understand his thoughts and agree with him on what is good, you will be able to recognize the counterfeit. Counterfeits are numerous, if not infinite, but the genuine item is only one. Know the genuine item very well, and you'll always be able to spot the counterfeit," Chief Thunderfist mused behind his wrinkled face.

"Do I see the past or the present or the future?" King pressed, returning to the question he had passed over earlier in the conversation.

"You see it as the Author sees it: as the present. All moments are present to the Author. Whether or not it is past or future relative to your own experience of time, that I cannot say. Have you ever thought to ask the Author about it?" Chief Thunderfist prodded.

"This is the first I have heard of such things," King told him.

"Tasha can tell you more, I think. As one who also sometimes sees, I think I can with confidence say that you will have more opportunity to explore such matters. However, if you decide not to see the visions, naturally there will be nothing to explore," Chief Thunderfist said, drawing attention again to King's choice. King said nothing, but thought again of the latest vision. The Sioux warriors drew into sight. The Chief patted King on the arm, "It is for you to decide. We need not speak more about it for now."

The Sioux delegation consisted of five tall and sturdy men. They wore camouflage pants but leather coats. They were accompanied by ten Cherokee guards. King noticed that the Sioux warriors had empty holsters at their side while half of the guards had side arms. When the delegation arrived, two of them stepped forward; Ramaen nodded towards some more chairs at the café, which were pulled over for their purpose. The rest of the delegation and all but three of the Cherokee guards withdrew a short distance.

"Chief Thunderfist, I am Lawrence Hantaywee. I am a spokesperson for Talutah Lighter of the Sioux, and this is my friend and associate, Nidawi. Nidawi speaks for the Omaha tribes out of Nebraska. Talutah has sent me to see where you stand in regards to reclaiming this land for its original natives, and if you disagree with our views, to attempt to persuade you to them," Lawrence began in stately fashion. He continued, "The Cherokee nation is known throughout the land as a noble race and one that is keen on good reasoning. Chief Thunderfist is known for his fairness in disputes and for his firmness in carrying out his decisions. The Lighter Sioux, the Omaha families, and a number of others believe that Chief Thunderfist will see more than many that it is just and right for the sons of the Great Spirit to reclaim for their own what was robbed from them by greed and deceit and blood so many centuries ago."

Chief Thunderfist's eyes closed, and he made a motion with his hand that Lawrence interpreted as a cue to continue speaking. Ramaen watched the pair carefully, but not as carefully as King, and King not as carefully as Tasha.

Lawrence went on. "When the white man came with his religion and his weapons and his lust for more than he needed, we were a divided people; before we knew what we were up against it was too late to unite. Today, the white man has suffered calamities of his own making. The Great Father is dead, and his office is gone. When once disease and sickness was used to purge our peoples from their places they'd possessed beyond memory, disease has come now at last to purge the land of the white man. They planted destruction and now they reap it and now we remain to start anew. We of the western tribes have not forgotten Osceola's betrayal, when he was summoned to a meeting which he approached under the white flag, only to be arrested on the spot ..." Here, Chief Thunderfist snorted contemptuously, remembering the details of the story.

Heartened, Lawrence continued, "So too do we remember in our tales how the great Cherokee nation, after abiding in so many ways the whims of the white man, was sold out and displaced in such tragic fashion that even though there were dozens of trails wet with the tears of dislocated tribes, the Cherokee's alone has become known as the 'Trail of Tears.' When our courage grows faint, we remind ourselves of the story of that valiant Cherokee, Tsali, who did not stand by as his wife was bayoneted on the journey, but rather sought to avenge her. Having done so, he fled with his family. But the white man, who had inflicted so much injustice on your people, could not abide this one thing. They tracked him down and those he was hidden with, and at the price of his life they spared those who hid in the mountains. Yes, the Cherokee Chief knows what a price in blood was paid for showing kindness to the white man and his ways. Does not Chief Thunderfist hear the cries of his fallen and betrayed ancestors in his ears, beckoning him to avenge them of their murders? Does not the mighty Chief agree with the tribes of the west that now is the time to unite and take back what was taken from us?"

Chief Thunderfist opened his eyes now and let them peer into Lawrence's and Nidawi's. For a long time the Chief stared at them and remained speechless. The delegates wisely remained silent. Finally, the Chief spoke.

"You speak of the land as belonging to us, but it never did. If we hear in the songs of one tribe of how they occupied a region beyond time and memory, we can listen to the songs of another tribe who can remember when the first tribe drove them out. The Lakota wished at one time to assert their claim against the white man, forgetting that in some cases, the land they pointed to as their own was land that they themselves had taken from the Cheyenne, which they had themselves taken from the Kiowa. Nor can I forget how old Junaluska threw his lot in with the Great Father Jackson to fight against the Creeks, and how Chief Ross sent Junaluska to plead directly with the Great Father but was utterly rebuffed. Yes, the betrayal was great, but did not the Cherokee begin the betrayal by fighting against the Creek in the first place? We did not fight for just reasons, but to win favor with the white man. How many an Indian warrior came to regret not burying a hatchet in the skull of the Great Father when they had the chance? Yes, but how many an Indian chief thought to use the white man against the white man, even at the expense of other sons of the Great Spirit?" Chief Thunderfist replied with steady oration.

"Yes, noble Chief. We all tried to play the white man's game and did not realize that a hundred or so years was not long enough to learn how to play it well. We should have driven them into the sea each time they placed down a foot. Let us not play the game anymore and push them into the sea at last!" Lawrence declared with enthusiasm.

"But would not driving the white man out of the lands they now live and forcing them to march to the Atlantic and their deaths be exactly the same as what was done to us?" the Chief retorted.

"The mighty Chief Thunderfist knows that it is different. We are only taking back what was ours to begin with," Lawrence quickly replied.

"No, that is not the case. The white men who did these evil deeds so many centuries ago certainly did evil, but they are dead and gone. The generations of men, both white and red, that we speak of in our tales are all gone now. Today, men stand alone with no government above them to tell them what to do and not to do. They are planting corn and building houses and living free, or many of them are, any way. These men had no part in the treachery of three or four or five hundred years ago. What right do we have to make them pay for it? We in the Cherokee Nation do not plan to make another wrong to avenge the wrong that was done to us. When would such a cycle end? We say it ends with forgiveness and new beginnings. You invoke Tsali, but Tsali's wife was poked, not run through. She was not killed! She lived! He redeemed himself later, but it is open to debate as to whether or not he acted wisely and justly," the Chief countered.

Now Nidawi spoke: "Permit me, Chief. You speak of forgiveness and new beginnings, and that is a testimony to how tolerant the fair-minded Cherokee have been, even giving assent to the white man's religion. Do you not see that the white man brought only lies and whiskey? Surely a learned man such as you will remember how Black Hawk described the religion of the Chemokemon? When the Sacs and Foxes were ejected from their places, we Omaha heard what he said. He said, 'If I have been correctly informed, the whites may do bad all their lives and then, if they are sorry for it when about to die, all is well! But with us it is different; we must continue throughout our lives to do what we conceive to be good.'"

Ramaen interjected, "We know the story, but Black Hawk was wise enough to point out he might be misinformed and this he was. The Cherokee received the religion of the white man because of its affinities to what we knew of the Great Spirit. The Cherokee had stories and legends and tales sight out of mind, but the religion of the white man had times, places, dates. The Great Spirit stepped into history across the seas, and we Cherokee did not think we knew the mind of the Great Spirit so well as to think he would never do such a thing. Most importantly, we saw at the time as we see today that the truth of their religion or anyone else's for that matter is not changed on account of bad men, even those men who make use of religion for their own purposes."

Chief Thunderfist nodded in agreement, "Yes, Black Hawk was wrong. For in what he called the religion of the Chemokemon it is commanded that we must continue throughout our lives to do what is good, even the good that we do not conceive rightly, but there is the acknowledgement that no man succeeds and that the Great Spirit has graciously found a way to remedy that. We too choose the way of grace. So long as I am the Chief of the Cherokee, we will not exact upon white man or red violence justified from past cruelties. We will not take the way of Lighter's Sioux or the western tribes. We hear already of the massacres in Omaha, Nebraska, and we turn our face against those who conducted them." Nidawi flushed red. "So too did we hear from Fox Marion that the quick and sudden plague that struck Wichita was hastened by a delivery of disease infested blankets. Such irony … such disgusting, treacherous, wicked irony." And Chief Thunderfist's eyes became narrow and hard as he said this last thing.

Lawrence and Nidawi stewed in silence for a time. Though almost certainly angry and frustrated, they worked hard to wear pleasant countenances. Lawrence asked if he and Nidawi could step away for a moment, and Chief Thunderfist and Ramaen nodded their assent. As the two men talked to the rest of their delegation, Chief Thunderfist leaned over towards King and whispered, "What do you see?"

King had long become accustomed to not showing a reaction when he saw something out of the ordinary, and his expressions on this occasion had also concealed any hint that he'd had a vision. King guessed that the Chief didn't actually know that he'd seen something, but hoped that he had. It was true. King had seen something.

"I see in Lawrence a wounded mountain lion and in Nidawi the glimmer of a serpent," King whispered back.

This didn't seem to surprise the Chief, but to King's surprise even Tasha and Ramaen nodded in agreement. By this time, however, the two men had returned.

"Chief, it pains us to have to lay this ultimatum at your door, but we must," Nidawi weighed his words carefully. "You have no doubt determined like we have that there are other groups forming in the region, and you must know that these would be our mutual enemies. If you are not our ally in the matter of reclamation, how can we be allies against power hungry white men?"

"I am not so certain that even if I joined you, in the end you wouldn't make the Cherokee your slaves," the Chief returned coolly. "Between a tyrant and a despot I shall not but choose to resist both."

"We are your brothers. We would not enslave our brothers if they stand by our side!" Lawrence exclaimed.

"So we aren't your brothers if we don't stand by your side, is that it?" the Chief countered.

Nidawi's demeanor had turned to stone. Very deliberately, he said, "That is the ultimatum. Stand with us or be consigned to be treated like the ones we drive before us."

The Chief did not show any recognition of the stressful turn in the conversation. Casually he replied, "You know that the Cherokee know their history and cherish it. We study it and learn from it in as many ways as we are able. Two years before our people were forced out of our homes in Georgia, a law was passed by the Federal government that required us to turn in our rifles and weapons of any kind. They said it was unsafe for us to have such weapons. We learned it was unsafe *not* to have such weapons. You may reason that this is a lesson among many other lessons that we have learned and not forgotten."

Lawrence and Nidawi didn't seem to know what to say to that.

Finding his tongue, Lawrence declared, "If the old Lakota Chief was alive, we might be able to believe that the white man and red man can live together, but he is dead."

"But is he?" Chief Thunderfist replied pointedly, not looking at Lawrence but rather glancing at King.

"Of course he's dead. He would be the first to rise to face today's challenges, but he has been silent since the calamities began," Nidawi argued.

"That is all, brothers," Ramaen informed them. "We do hope that you will change your course. All things are new. We can move forward today in a way that builds up all people who live everywhere, if we so desire. We need not repeat the mistakes of the past, including the mistake of avenging the past. We will strive for Sparrow's vision, whether he is alive or dead. If you change your minds, you will find the Cherokee are your brothers again."

Sullenly, Lawrence and Nidawi got up, nodded in respect, and left their sight under escort.

"King, I do hope you'll reconsider your decision, but believe me it will be respected. If you choose not to have them, you won't. Now, I hope you'll excuse me," said the Chief. With that, the conversation ended, and King and Tasha went home in contemplative silence.

May turned into June, and King spent it frolicking with the sons and daughters of the Cherokee nation. King and Luke roamed the hills far and wide. The borders were well patrolled, which meant that there was little threat of coming across anything truly dangerous, but each day they set out looking for as much trouble as they could find. They barely noticed that the Cherokee guards they encountered were much more on edge than they had been in previous months. The quarantine was still in effect, not only in Tahlequah, but also in numerous other cities in the region, leaving many people stranded in the wastelands and struggling to survive. More often than not, this meant desperate incursions into quarantined areas. The constant presence of refugees was only one stress on the Cherokee guards. There were also bandits and continual hints of larger foes. King and Luke were, for the most part, oblivious to such affairs.

Between wrestling matches and mock fights with Luke and other friends, King noticed that his fighting skills were improving dramatically. More than that, one day when he looked at his arms in the mirror, he saw muscles. He noted this with quiet pride but didn't mention it to anyone because, after all, everyone else was already well muscled. That included those younger than he and even most of the young girls and women.

Every now and then, Tasha would take him aside and spar with him. She discretely helped him refine his skills with his staff and even prompted him to work with his knife, though he was afraid of what it could do. He had seen Tasha in action with his own eyes, but he still felt awed when this silver haired, slightly aged, woman was able to move so quickly and so powerfully. He never thought to ask her about it.

In July, Luke announced that his father was going to allow him to go with a delegation that was going to Tulsa. He invited King to go with him, and King, remembering how much he had enjoyed Tulsa when he had first come through, quickly agreed. Chief Thunderfist wasn't so sure.

"You're good and strong, King, but Luke is several years older than you and has been involved in various skirmishes over the years, so I know that if something were to happen, he would know what to do." Seeing King's crestfallen face, the Chief added, "You may not know this, but there have been many reports that the Lighter Sioux has sent groups of their warriors to serve as bandits to destabilize the area. Also, some of our own Cherokee have disagreed with me about whether we should reclaim the land and drive the white men from it. Besides these, there are your ordinary wild men."

"Chief, you will remember that it was King who handled those gentlemen a few months back. I think he ought to be permitted to go," Ramaen interceded. "Also, Charlie is going as well."

"I would feel better about it if I knew that Tasha was going to go, too," Chief Thunderfist hedged.

King brightened considerably. He didn't know who Charlie was, but he knew that Tasha would agree to go. A few days later, King set out with Luke and a large contingent of Cherokee men and women. Tasha also rode with them, but she left King and Luke to spend their time with some of the other young men traveling with them. King, had he been alert enough to notice, would have been thankful.

Tulsa was more or less due west from the Cherokee nation. After a half day of traveling along old state highways that were well on their way to crumbling, they found a highway that led right into Tulsa. King and his friends roamed around the flanks of the group pretending to be scouts for the larger party.

On the second night, fires were started and King and Luke held court around their fire while the adults set up their dwellings nearby. Some twenty temporary tents dotted the hill they were on, and a dozen small fires were burning until nearly midnight. When the last fire went out, King and Luke were still talking with each other inside their tent.

"Did you hear that?" King suddenly whispered to Luke. Luke nodded. What they heard was the sounds of hushed whispers in the nearby bushes. They sounded like commands from one man to another and a coarse reply. King didn't hesitate, "Men! There are men in the camp! Help!"

A mere second after King yelled, the enemy flooded into the camp with loud yelling. The one second warning that King managed to provide was all that was needed to cause sentries to begin running back and warriors to grab their weapons. By the time the bandits got close enough to any tent to do damage, Cherokee braves were emerging from them, sleepy and dazed, but armed.

King and Luke and their friends also came out of their tents. The sound of fighting was all around, but very little light remained, as most of the fires were now only embers. It didn't take long to discover that these weren't merely bandits, but Indians. The Cherokee men and women joined the noise with their own, shouting that they were fighting the Lighter Sioux.

Gun shots began cracking the mirrored night. King and Luke exchanged a glance. King had his staff and Luke had a long knife, but neither weapon was a match for guns. They grinned and shrugged. It was a real adventure, after all. Accompanied now by some of their friends, they went looking for the enemy.

They didn't have to look far. There were five or six men in hand-to-hand combat at the first tent they came to, and it was easy to make out friend from foe. The five young men jumped onto the backs of the Sioux bandits and drug them to the ground. The adult Cherokee swung their hatchets with skill. King decided that battle wasn't so terrifying, after all. Picking himself up off the ground, he rushed to the next skirmish that they could find.

Between the next two tents were men firing pistols at one another, ducking around from one side of a tent to the other, and getting shots off into the darkness when a silhouette appeared. Luke flung himself to the ground and King followed suit.

"We have to find out which side is ours!" Luke shouted in the midst of the din. After a few moments, Luke had apparently figured it out, because he leapt up and ran off in one direction with King again close behind. Luke circled around the tent, going about thirty feet out of the way. The two kept low because gunshots were whistling through the dark, fired by the men that Luke had determined were Cherokee. Finally, they saw that the raider sat down with the tent at his back to reload, and the pair exploded from the dark to attack him. King's staff arrived first, delivering a blow to the man's head. King shouted out that they'd dispatched the gunman so that their Cherokee companion would stop shooting.

That companion came over at once. It was the one called Charlie.

"What on earth are you doing?" he chastised them. "Don't you know I was shooting that way?"

"Yeah," Luke muttered, somewhat apologetically.

"Well, good job I guess," Charlie said with a hint of a smile. With that, Charlie was off with his pistol, and Luke and King met up with their friends again to decide on what to do next.

That moment, Tasha arrived. She had blood on her clothes, but she herself appeared to be quite unhurt.

"I don't know if that was a good move, King," she scolded him.

"I thought it was good, I got him right across the jaw!" he protested.

"You know what I mean!" she rejoined. "You crept right into the line of fire."

"What should we have done?" Luke interjected, trying to take some of the heat off his friend.

"Found a different fight," she asserted. "Oh well, not now. Let's see what else is going on."

As it happened, the fight was actually winding down. Though the Lighter Sioux had swept in with decent numbers, they hadn't expected the Cherokee party to be as large as it was—and thanks to

King's warning shout, a good dozen Sioux were dead while the Cherokee only had a handful of men and women who were injured. None of these were harmed too seriously. The remaining Sioux, seeing that they had met determined resistance, fled into the night.

Charlie came over to King and congratulated him for giving the warning. Fires were lit up again, and men sat around them while others went into the woods to provide a guard. King and Luke and friends went back to their tents. After an hour, the pure excitement could not to keep them awake any longer; they slept contentedly with the proud knowledge of their conduct in the battle.

# == Chapter 7 ==

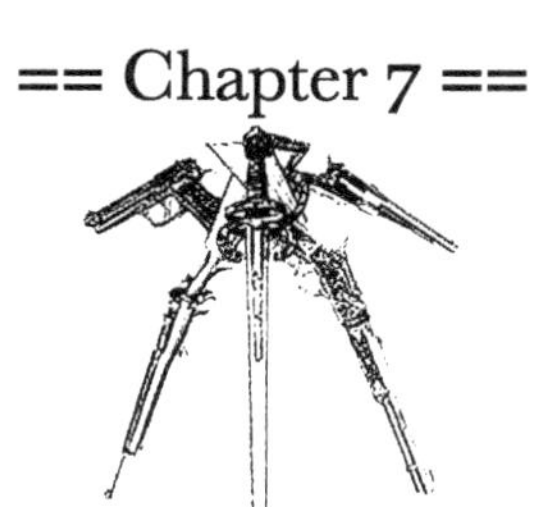

A day later, they arrived in Tulsa to what felt to King and Luke like a hero's welcome. King's warning combined with their role in taking out six or so Lighter Sioux raiders was enough to outweigh their somewhat foolish decision to put themselves in the line of friendly fire. Philip and Mary hosted a party for the young warriors, and some of the young Tulsa Cherokees attended.

In Tulsa, King discovered girls. More accurately, of course, he discovered that he liked girls in a new and peculiar way. This coincided happily with the discovery that girls liked him in a peculiar way right back. The party helped King meet a handful of young ladies, and he couldn't help but notice that the resident Cherokee boys weren't entirely pleased to have the competition.

A glorious month was spent in Tulsa. After a week, King and Luke parted company slightly as each found a few new friends in Tulsa to spend time with. To his surprise, King found that the time he enjoyed the most was with a scrawny, scrappy girl named Joan. She had dark hair and piercing eyes and, on the whole, she looked a mess. Despite the fact that King didn't find himself attracted to her like some of the other girls, she made up for it in his eyes because she liked to go out and shoot squirrels and search caves and other things that King liked to do. He was shocked to find that most of the other girls didn't really enjoy such activities.

In an odd way, one of the most appealing things about Joan was that she wasn't nearly as impressed with King's endeavors as the other girls had been. In fact, she never mentioned it. In humiliating fashion he learned why one day.

The two had been out exploring some woods with some of their other friends. The friends went off looking for some mushrooms, and King and Joan sat down beneath a tall tree that overlooked a grassy field to rest. King was using his knife to whittle a pattern into his staff.

"Why do you carry that?" Joan put to him in the direct manner King had grown accustomed to.

"I like it. When I'm in a fight, I can hit somebody and not worry about getting his blood on me," he replied, hoping he wouldn't be asked to recount for her the event that led to his carrying a staff.

"But it is so hard to use, especially in close combat," she pressed him.

"What do you know of it?" King smirked. "Aren't you only twelve? What fights have you been in?"

"I take you to be about my age or a little older is all. I don't think my age has anything to do with it," she smirked right back at him.

"Well ok, what would you use, then?" he retaliated, slightly annoyed.

"Against a staff? Nothing!" she cried out triumphantly. "My bare hands!"

"I'd clobber you!" King retorted, now really annoyed.

"You don't think I could take you?" Joan dared him.

"No, and especially if I have the staff and you have nothing," King argued, not entirely comfortable with the direction the conversation was going. Before he could say anything else, though, she was on her feet and had assumed a fighting stance. King sighed, "Come on, it isn't really fair."

"You come on," Joan snapped impatiently. "Come on before the others get here, and you find yourself embarrassed in front of them when a girl beats you."

That sort of argument was hard to resist, so King jumped up. He set the staff aside, but she mocked him for it and insisted that he use it. Standing about ten feet from her, King looked at her and saw that past her scraggly hair were brave and daring eyes.

"Don't go easy on me," she said haughtily. "I don't want to hear anything about how you went easy on me, or I'll really make you pay."

King couldn't help but laugh. Brushing aside his own long bangs he took a step towards her and swung the staff about half as hard as he might have. She stepped into the swing and punched him in the stomach. He recoiled, gasping.

"That was a nice shot," he admitted to her.

"Are you telling me that is the hardest you can swing that thing? I told you not to go easy on me!" she snapped at him. He really didn't like where this was going. How would he be able to explain to their friends why she had a broken jaw and that he gave it to her? She motioned for him to try again. He resigned himself to the fact that he'd have to really try to hit her. He opted for a thrust followed by a spinning crack to her leg. He thought he might avoid any really permanent damage to her that way and still hit her pretty good.

She easily avoided the thrust and jumped over the swing to her leg; before he knew it she was inside the swing again, and this time she got in a punch to his belly and a shove to his chest. He tumbled over backwards onto his butt in a very undignified fashion. Joan stood over him with a look of victory on her face.

"Alright, that's it," King cried out. He leapt to his feet and advanced on her without even letting her get set and ready. She still managed to duck his hardest blow, but he at least got in one glancing shot to her arm. Glad that he'd finally made contact he lost focus. Before he knew it, she had grabbed the staff with her other hand and pulled it—and him—towards her. When he hit her, she bent over and threw him over her shoulder, and he rolled quite a ways before coming to a stop. Now furious, he charged her and tackled her with every ounce of force he had. She fell backwards and together they tumbled head over heels, kicking and biting, until he was on his back and she had him straddled with her forearm across his neck.

"Now that was much better! Now you aren't going easy!" she proclaimed. King started laughing. He couldn't help it. She had beaten him fair and square. She rolled off of him and laughed too.

"Wow, am I glad we got that out of the way before the guys come back," King said, still laughing hard.

Joan stopped laughing and gazed at him inquisitively, "You don't hate me now, do you?"

"Nah," he answered. "Maybe I should, but I was stupid to think you wouldn't know how to fight. And I know women can fight because I've seen Tasha do it. How did you do it?"

"I'm probably a lot shorter than most of your opponents, so you didn't know how to fight me with the staff, but I've been wrestling around for a long time. Unlike the fathers of many of the other girls, my father believes that in this day and age even girls must know how to fight, and fight even to the death," she explained.

"Well, you kicked my butt," King said, chuckling.

Joan's no-nonsense attitude and willingness to get down and dirty made up for the fact that she wasn't as cute as some of the other girls. When King was socializing with them, Joan would mysteriously disappear. When he was ready to go off on an adventure with some of his new found Cherokee male friends, Joan always appeared just in time.

The day came when it was time for the delegation to return to the Cherokee Nation. A great party was thrown with singing, dancing, chanting and eating. For the Cherokee, they were in a good place in their history. Though most of them had no intent on a purification campaign to drive out the non-Indian, the absence of the International Force was cause for celebration. As there were no tyrants waiting in the wings, they celebrated all the more. Many of the elder Cherokee had fought against the Chinese-Mexican armies decades earlier. The sense that there might now be peace for the Cherokee was tangible, so they celebrated in earnest.

After the feast, Luke and King quickly reestablished their

friendship. For a brief moment, they thought they were going to receive a treat and be driven back to the Nation in vans and trucks that were owned and managed by a businessman in the area named Chummy. Chummy apparently raised his prices at the last minute, however, and they had to settle for traveling on horseback once again. This time, there were some wagons being pulled along with them. King paid no attention to the wagons. He saw some long, narrow crates being loaded into them, but thought nothing of it. Nor did he or Luke think anything about the extra security given to the group as it traveled back.

While perhaps misunderstanding the full purpose of the additional security, when King returned to Tahlequah he saw that security had increased there as well. The explanation given was that there was a new foe in the region. It was called the Pledge. Apparently, it consisted of packs of bandits and white men who aimed to do what the Lighter Sioux wanted to do. Chief Thunderfist was irritable for a month or so. At a council, the Chief had muttered the incoherent phrase, *"Faciunt solitudinem et pacem vocant,"* and King heard it repeated in numerous places. The feeling in Tulsa that they were coming into a time of peace was gone completely both there and in Tahlequah, but King paid little attention to such affairs as he felt perfectly safe in the Cherokee Nation.

The months flew together as King thrived underneath the watchful and protective eyes of Tasha, Chief Thunderfist, and Ramaen. Still others protected him as well, though he didn't realize it. Charlie was a captain in the Cherokee ranks and a scout. Many an incursion was thwarted by the bravery of such men, though King barely realized it.

A year went by, and then another, and King had grown a foot and put on a good fifty pounds of muscle. At some point King realized that he hadn't had a vision again like the ones he'd used to have. Instead he had what seemed more like a memory, only it was dull and dim: only the lifeless eyes of an unknown woman looking at him. He found it easier to put those images out of his mind than the visions he had received, since with the visions it was always as though he were experiencing it. It was easier to put the dead woman's eyes out of his mind … and that is what he did. But she always came back.

In about the third year, King sought and received permission to join the other young Cherokee men on patrols and defensive duty. Luke had been going out on patrols for a whole year and King couldn't understand why he hadn't been allowed to do so, but Chief Thunderfist always refused. However, Charlie and Ramaen interceded for King at last. Charlie delivered the surprising message.

"King!" Charlie said, greeting King as he sat alone in one of Tahlequah's parks.

"Hi Charlie," King said.

"I come bearing a message from Chief Thunderfist. He has decided that the time has come where you can formally help defend your friends, the Cherokee. He has insisted, though, that before you do so you experience something like what the other Cherokee experience. You have already proven yourself in many respects. You are brave in battle. You are loyal. Yet you lack something ... something that if your father was here he would have ensured you received. If you would like to fight with the Cherokee, King, you must go on a vision quest," Charlie explained.

King had heard about the Cherokee vision quest. Not all of the Cherokee still did them, but the majority did. Charlie explained further that for King, it was an invitation into manhood. If he did not accept, he could not participate in the dangerous duties of Man.

"What does Tasha think?" King asked.

"Tasha agrees but has decided to stay out of the matter, leaving it to the men to resolve," Charlie said.

"Tell me what to do," King agreed.

Charlie gave him the instructions. King was to take three days to reflect on what he was about to do and then, if he was ready, report to Chief Thunderfist. Then, he would head into the wilderness, alone, until such time as he knew it was appropriate to return. King thanked Charlie, who left to allow King's period of reflection to begin.

Three days later, King found Chief Thunderfist. Tasha was there, too. She had deliberately stayed out of sight, but she was here, now, to offer her encouragement. Charlie and Ramaen were there as well. They said nothing, though, leaving all words to the Chief.

The Chief laid his hands on King's shoulders, "Take only your knife, my son. Go, and return only when you are ready. Walk for a day in any direction before you stop to rest. When you return, we shall receive you with gladness. Be strong and courageous and open minded. Go."

King bowed his head slightly, and then nodding in gratitude at the others looking sternly at him, he turned and departed from them.

He strode towards the border of the city, heading past Cherokees who paid him no mind, having no inkling that he was on his way to find ... something ... perhaps himself. The cool shadows of the trees greeted him, and the city disappeared behind him. He trudged on and on, occasionally passing over streams, and sometimes needing to scale rocky hills. Finally, evening was upon him. He stopped in a small clearing. Unable to start a fire, he sat in the cold and dark as night came.

The noises of the woods kept him awake for a time, but he did eventually fall asleep. In the morning, he shook off the dew that had collected on his clothes. He searched around for something to eat but didn't find much. Now that he was here, he didn't know what to do.

He didn't know what was supposed to happen. The day came and went, as well as yet another night, and then another afternoon.

It was late evening and the sun was completely gone. His aloneness sunk in at last, and he wondered how long it would take before he had one of these famed visions that he'd heard about on occasion while living with the Cherokee. As the night wore on, he became frustrated. He spoke into the cool of the night.

"Where is my vision?" he called out.

To his great surprise, there was an answer immediately. It was simple: "You asked not to receive them."

He swallowed hard, staggered by the answer. Immediately the trees and the stars and the sounds of nature around him disappeared and he saw, as it were, a mushroom shaped cloud rising in the distance. Heat and smoke and the shuddering of the earth were perceived all in an instant. He felt pushed, then crushed. He panicked as he realized that he was pinned beneath debris. He fought against a sense of suffocation before realizing that though he was trapped, the crushing weight had relented, even though he could not move his legs and torso. He was, however, able to turn his head. He did so now. Looking to one side he saw the mangled, bloody, deformed face of a woman whose eyes alone he had seen up to this point. The lamps of the body were extinguished. She was dead.

He felt within himself a plunging sickness in his stomach and he swooned, feeling as the awful, gruesome sight sank in, that his lamps were going out, too.

"Is it ...? Is it ...?" he murmured in what he supposed was his sleep.

In answer the voice from before declared sternly, but sympathetically, "The Wound is Open."

When he opened his eyes next, the sunlight was beaming down on him. He felt a dull ache in his stomach as though he had been grieving, but to his own surprise he also felt refreshed. He knew, somehow, that this affair was not over, but at least for now his vision quest was complete. He sat up, collected his thoughts, and made for Tahlequah.

He had been spotted on his way in. When he arrived before Chief Thunderfist, Ramaen, Charlie, Tasha, and some of the other elders were present. Again, the Chief put his hands on his shoulders.

"You need not speak about what you have seen—or not seen. You have risked an encounter with the Divine, and that is more than many, the many who would scoff at the prospect or worse, dictate the terms of the encounter, and so not be Met," the Chief said in a measured tone. "Now," he continued, "I invite you to join us in our community with our full blessings; so too may you join us as we carry out our full duties."

King bowed his head as before. He lifted his head and saw the assembly beaming at him. A great meal was then held in his honor. Some men and women from Tulsa were invited as well, and even his friend Luke dropped in.

A few days later, Charlie arrived to give King the details concerning his duties. He was informed that he would join the border patrol. Charlie also gave him his own horse. Tasha taught him how to ride it and how to use his staff like a lance.

A week later, King was out doing patrols with the other Cherokee men. On occasion, he would see Luke and they would greet each other warmly. This was growing increasingly rare, however, as it was soon becoming clear to everyone that the peace each once thought was within grasp remained a distant dream. The Lighter Sioux and other western tribes still made incursions into the area, but now they weren't the only ones. The group called the Pledge was also sending out raiding parties, and there were roaming groups of bandits as well.

These threats arose about the same time as ammunition was growing scarce for everyone, Cherokee and their foe alike. In many towns, blacksmiths were retooling to try to learn how to make bullets, but that knowledge had been lost. The International Force had disarmed as much of the country as they could, and as part of that process factories were robbed of their intellectual property and deprived of educated engineers. People were forced to hammer out rudimentary swords and knives. They sharpened pitchforks and modified shovels. With the fading out of the firearm, bandits weren't as concerned about pushing the limits.

It wasn't long after King was allowed onto the border patrol that a small scale war broke out between the Cherokee that sided with Chief Thunderfist and the Cherokee who sided with a certain Domasi, a Cherokee elder who had abandoned the Nation years earlier in disgust. Domasi took with him several thousand Cherokee men and women who wanted to follow the path of the Lighter Sioux. However, Domasi couldn't stand to leave the Cherokee Nation in peace to focus on the white men he insisted must leave. There were numerous attacks on Cherokee farms and businesses and plenty of outright murders, and it became clear to Chief Thunderfist that something had to be done.

The war came swiftly and suddenly to Tahlequah. Banking on surprise, Domasi and his renegade Cherokee swept across the old borders demarcating the reservation and plunged into the city district, destroying buildings and plundering businesses. To their surprise, Domasi encountered no living souls. They hadn't counted on the scouting abilities of Charlie. Chief Thunderfist's Cherokees were ready for Domasi. His men and women charged out of the neighborhood to the north catching Domasi and his men by surprise.

Right there in the heart of downtown thousands of men and women battled in the streets. For a time, the battle's outcome seemed uncertain.

Several hours after it began, however, the tide turned definitively in favor of Chief Thunderfist. Charlie, accompanied by a large majority of his scouting forces and almost all of the border patrol—including King and Tasha—rushed in from behind Domasi's men. Charlie had led his band of men in a wide circle behind Domasi. It was so wide, in fact, that Domasi's own defensive flank was encircled. Reminiscent of the great cavalry charges of old, several hundred warriors descended upon the renegade Indians.

Trapped between Chief Thunderfist's fighters from the north and the slashing charge of Charlie's horsemen's from the southwest, Domasi realized that the game was up. He fled to the southeast with the remainder of his men. Charlie pursued him as far as Arkansas. Domasi's Cherokees were not heard from again.

Many heroes emerged from The Domasi War, and though King was not described as one of them, he had shown great bravery and skill. Chief Thunderfist would never attempt to give King special protection again. One of the heroes was Tasha. The story of her charge through the Domasi lines with a shining blade that they had never seen before was told and retold. She plunged through the line and through defenses all the way to where Chief Thunderfist and Ramaen themselves were fighting. No other horsemen had been able to drive in so far. Indeed, Tasha had almost immediately left behind her fellow riders.

Though the Cherokee were surprised to see such courage and skill in a woman who seemed to be getting on in years, King wasn't. He was happy for her and glad that others now had a glimpse of her that was like his own knowledge of her. Up to this point, King and Tasha had already been seeing less of each other, but now even the time of these encounters tailed off. Tasha had always been a welcome advisor to the Chief and his council, but now she was asked to be a permanent member of the council. So, while King and Tasha still had the same house that they had been given years before, with Tasha constantly at meetings and King often on patrols it was only on occasion that they spent time together.

A year or two of relative peace followed, though the Cherokee were constantly on alert on account of the growing threat that the Pledge presented from the southeast. King had quite a few trips to Tulsa during this time, sometimes accompanied by Tasha or Luke, but sometimes just with Charlie and Charlie's second-in-command, Marty. To King's astonishment, though he still found the Tulsa Cherokee girls to be attractive (and them to be attracted to him), Joan was starting to look quite pretty, herself. Each trip to Tulsa inspired more awkwardness when he was around her.

On one trip in late spring, King was a forward scout protecting a delegation from the Cherokee Nation en route to Tulsa. King was riding ahead with some other scouts, but a bit absentmindedly. Charlie, on his way to check on his patrols, surprised King, who hadn't seen him coming. King tried to apologize for his lack of attention, but Charlie only laughed.

"What's on your mind, King?" Charlie asked him.

"What do you mean?" King replied innocently.

"What do you mean what do I mean? You've only been in another world on this whole trip. This is your fifth trip to Tulsa in two months, is it not? Isn't it obvious that you have something to see in Tulsa?" Charlie smiled and King blushed.

"Yes, it's a girl. I think I like her and I think she likes me, but that is not the problem. She is a Cherokee and I am not. I wonder about my place here among the Cherokee. I would like to stay and maybe Chief Thunderfist would welcome it, but what about the girl's parents in Tulsa? Would they allow her to ..." King trailed off.

"Marry you? You're better known in Tulsa than perhaps you suspect," Charlie advised him. "You're several years from such considerations, though. You have plenty of time to show her parents that you will respect the Cherokee ways."

"I do respect the Cherokee ways, Charlie. I am deeply grateful for what the Cherokee have done for me ..." King paused, reflecting on the long list of Cherokee kindnesses, not least of which was their acceptance of him after his vision quest. He feared that Charlie would misconstrue he had to say, but it was something that had been growing on his mind ever since his time in the woods. King sighed, and said, "But I don't think I can stay here. Tasha brought me from the east, and I think sometime I should go that way to see if I have family of my own, there. I would like to take this girl with me—not now, of course!" King quickly added, seeing Charlie's expression. "What if my family is affiliated with an enemy of the Cherokee? What if they are dead? I have many questions."

"You're thinking too much about things that you can't control. Why worry about what you can't influence? You are not yet of age to receive the blessing of any parent for marrying their daughter, no matter how noble you are. You may have an opportunity to search out your family before that time. We cannot know what future circumstances will bring. Let us instead tend to this moment and our conduct within it," Charlie counseled him.

They rode on for a bit in silence while King reflected on what Charlie had said. Soon, King had another question.

"Charlie, I don't know how to act around the ones I like. I don't know what to do. Since I am so far off from being of age, as you say, how should I behave now?" King asked him, embarrassed slightly by his own question.

Charlie studied him for a moment and struggled to think of the right thing to say.

"It is a time like this when a young man needs his father and the absence of his father makes itself known," Charlie began. "Such a question lives best between fathers and sons, and I have anguish in my heart that you have no father to put the question to. I will answer it this way: Imagine that you were a father and you had a daughter. How would you like young men to speak and behave around her? Consider the question and temper your actions according to what you decide. Remember, every woman is some father's daughter. Out of respect for your own daughter—if you ever have one, of course—treat every man's daughter as you would have your own daughter treated. That is my answer to that question."

"That is a good answer and leaves me much to think about," King replied.

Charlie grinned and sighed in relief, "Good! I was totally winging it! My son is yet too young to ask such questions! Well, I must be off. Do pay more attention now and do your thinking when you're not on duty!" With that, Charlie rode off.

Charlie's advice was good advice, but King found it difficult to put all his own conclusions into action. Each time he went to Tulsa he wanted to share more of his heart with Joan but refrained, knowing that the time was not right.

Circumstances changed so that his trips to Tulsa diminished, rescuing him from the blissful discomfort he suffered when spending time there. He was needed more than ever as a scout along the Oklahoma-Arkansas border. The Pledge had officially become known as a menace. Based as it was out of Little Rock, Arkansas, King was dispatched to patrol the region southeast of the Cherokee nation. He was joined again with Luke and some of his old friends for the assignment. About forty Cherokee men on horseback patrolled the Oklahoma-Arkansas border, in particular watching the highway called I-540, which had its source to the south in an abandoned city called Ft. Smith and terminated just shy of the Arkansas-Missouri border.

There was much to see, including corresponding Pledge patrols. The Pledge was clearly not happy that the Cherokee felt comfortable coming at will into what used to be called Arkansas, but they never confronted the Cherokee patrols. Meanwhile, vehicles originating from Chummy's travel company in Tulsa en route to Little Rock drew careful observation by both sides. In the midst of all of this, King found the scenery to be absolutely beautiful. It often reminded him of the macabre sight he had seen on his vision quest. In fact, on occasion he'd wake up in a sweat, seeing it all before him anew, filling him with despair. The continued occurrence of the vision inspired new thoughts in his mind. These compelled him to realize he had to make some decisions.

One of his first conclusions was that he needed to seek out his family to the east before starting one in Oklahoma. Whatever this new vision was about, he knew it had something to do with a history he had left behind him; he felt he must uncover that history and resolve his questions about it before moving on with his life. While determined to make the trip, he didn't know when would be the best time. He felt it ought to be soon. Besides the fact that he himself was getting older and would, in a relatively short time, be in a position to seek out Joan's hand in marriage, there was a real chance that war would break out between the Cherokee and the Pledge.

He had learned a little about the Pledge. They were a group espousing an old political system called communism, though when the Pledge described it they always said it was merely an economic system. King had personally seen Chief Thunderfist sneeze milk out of his nose laughing so hard when told of this. The Pledge wanted to conquer the entire region and then redistribute it in an equal and fair fashion. King didn't bother to form his own opinion about what the Pledge wanted to do. He was loyal to the Cherokee Nation and the Cherokee Nation hadn't won that loyalty simply by being good to him, but by living in peace with one another and with the majority of the region's inhabitants. There were exceptions, such as the Domasi Cherokee and the Lighter Sioux and the constant encounters with bandits, but King thought the Chief's conduct in these instances was justified.

After a tour in the regions to the southeast, King was astonished to find himself summoned by name to a council with Chief Thunderfist. While King had often visited Chief Thunderfist and even popped into a meeting of the council when visiting Luke, he had never been specifically invited. It was the fall, and many of the Cherokee were involved in harvesting their crops. Thus, many of the scouts and fighters were on their homesteads working as quickly as they could to get the harvest in so that they could return to the defense of the Cherokee Nation. However, that meant that there were many wise men and women in the area who normally weren't there, so for the last several years the harvest had been a time when a major council was held, to which many more Cherokee were invited than usual. It was to such a council that King was invited.

It was evening, and when King arrived he saw that Tasha was already there. She was sitting at the front table with the Chief, Ramaen, and some of the other main advisors. Luke was also present and was sitting at a table near the front with Philip and Mary from

Tulsa. King was familiar with the room. It was in an old barn that had been transformed into a banquet hall. There was the pleasant aroma of various kinds of wood, and the lighting came from oil lanterns. There were about fifty men and women in attendance, with another twenty or so arriving after King.

Charlie walked over to greet him, "King! Come over here. Sit near the front. Chief Thunderfist wants you to be near the action as an observer. He has asked me to deliver a message to you to consider during the meeting." Charlie leaned over and whispered, "The Chief's message is: Will you choose to See again?"

King looked startled and Charlie added apologetically, "He said you'd understand, or you'd start to during the meeting. I don't know anything." Charlie wandered off to talk to some other men, and King found his spot near the front. He was close to the head table and could see the whole room clearly if he turned far enough to his left. Luke was on the other side of the room right across from him, and they nodded greetings to each other as the Chief called the meeting to order.

"Ladies, gentlemen, friends, family, welcome," the Chief called out, summoning the assembly to silence. "We come together for a grand council at a time of grave significance. What we decide today will impact the Cherokee people, but also on people far and wide. I do not say potentially. I say will. Let us then proceed deliberately with wit and wisdom."

In the darkened hall, the lantern light flickered, reflecting on and off the bright eyes staring back at the Chief. He paused for effect, and continued. "As you all know (and as some have constantly reminded me the last two or three decades), I am getting quite old. I suspect that this will be the last grand council that I will attend as chief of the Cherokee nation ..." here there was a collective gasp, "... and as it is also well known that my likely successor, our dear friend Ramaen, is also getting up in years, in all likelihood he will not preside over the next grand council either ..."

Shouts of protest emerged from the hall and not a few men and women stood up insisting that the Chief was mistaken. Chief Thunderfist waved them down, "Please, please. I am so old I don't know how old I am, and neither Ramaen nor myself knows who is older. The next chief should have more life in his legs. I would like to appoint my own successor, then, if you all will permit. Surely none of you will disagree with me when I say that my son, Charlie Tallstalk is a fitting leader of the free people, the Tsalagi ..."

Applause and shouts of agreement filled the hall.

"You know that when I call him my son, I do not mean my son of my own flesh and blood. That dear child of mine died in the Chinese-Mexican war, as you well know. But I do have several grandsons. I do not appoint them, and it is not because I do not believe that they are competent, but to help set a pattern and a precedent. Charlie Tallstalk is the best person for the job, and it should always be the case that the chief of this noble people is the best person for the job. In the future, I hope that democracy comes to this whole land. At that time, I hope that my example will be raised. It is so easy to keep power in the hands of a few, a single family for example, like a monarchy. When the children and grandchildren are as competent as my kin would have been, that would be no problem. But who can predict what the men and women three generations hence will be like? No, competent or not it is best if the leaders arise based only on merit," the Chief argued to the dim silhouettes.

He continued, "Yes, that is a lesson from history and not any special wisdom of my own. Is it not the case, however, that ours is now a land without a past? Can you say that it has a past if no one can remember it? So many don't. We Cherokee have not forgotten. Our stories and our lore and songs continue to be told and sung; likewise, many other tribes also continue to do so. The white men, who took to writing down their memories in books rather than minds, have no recollection of the past now that the books have been burned. For a century or more they scoffed at our story telling and could not believe stories could be accurate when told over and over and passed from generation to generation. They measured us by their own inabilities and their own lack of discipline and it is only they who were guilty of the charge they laid at our feet. It will fall to us to teach them about the past. For this reason and others, remember our history and remember it well."

Chief Thunderfist cleared his throat. He heard the echo of it because the room had become so still. The front of the hall was lit up much more than the middle and back. The lines of age etched into the Chief's face were deep and indisputable. King noticed for the first time how tired the Chief looked. Others had noticed for years. The Chief began talking again.

"There are several matters of significance to discuss tonight. I do not mean Charlie becoming the new chief. He and I have already talked. I will remain chief so long as I have the presence of mind and am alive. As of now, then, nothing in that regards changes. However, another matter I would like to raise right now concerns the Pledge. The Pledge has become mighty. Only the Cherokee Nation has stood in its way so far. But the Pledge grows restless. Its emissaries have spread far and wide seeking to accomplish by negotiation what it is willing to accomplish by force if necessary. Yes, the Pledge has even sent diplomats here. We have found that with some the words negotiation and ultimatum mean the same thing, and this is especially true with the Pledge."

"Even as we speak," the old man's voice carried across the assembly, "the Pledge has arranged an audience with the President of Oklahoma City, which many of us know as one of the only free cities within our region. The Pledge desires to come to an agreement with Oklahoma City's residents without taking into consideration what the Cherokee Nation might say. If Oklahoma City were to fall to the Pledge or the Pledge's bidding, the Cherokee Nation would be hemmed in from the east and the west. More importantly, perhaps, Wichita is a free town that is a gateway to the north, the northeast, and the northwest. The Western Tribes control Omaha and Lincoln in Nebraska, but we know that Des Moines is their next target. That is all to say that if the Pledge secures a hold on Oklahoma City, they will find the way north clear to them, and the Western Tribes, though our face is set against them, will be out of position to stop the Pledge's northern advance."

Heads nodded as the Chief spoke. Chief Thunderfist's proud yet frail body thrust his oration into their hearts. He took a breath and continued, "President Neff, the president of Oklahoma City, is not particularly inclined to negotiate with the Pledge without bringing the Cherokee Nation to the table, and so the Pledge does not know that he has sent word to us inviting a Cherokee delegation to attend the conference. Neff understands that our presence secures Oklahoma City from threats from the east and southeast, and we have always been good to the citizens of that city, as so many of them are our own kin and friends. So, we are sending that delegation, and it will leave forthwith. That requires no decision from you. What needs deciding is simply this: Will we go to war against the Pledge? It is not a matter of wondering what will happen if the Pledge is rebuffed. They will lash out, and it is nearly certain that Tahlequah or Tulsa or both will be the target. This decision will need to be made, but not tonight. Within the month I will set another date for another grand council which will convene within a couple of months from now. We will know by then the Pledge's answer."

There was a murmuring in the assembly as people shot remarks to their neighbor about some aspect of what the Chief was saying. The Chief raised his hands and the rumbling subsided.

"I urge no rash decisions, but I accept that we ought to offer some discussion on the matter. So, please follow Ramaen's directions, and he will give an opportunity for some of you to speak," the Chief informed them.

At this, the Chief sat down and Ramaen stood up. There followed a feisty debate and discussion as individuals spoke their piece. Many were for open war at the slightest provocation. Some urged patience. None advocated making an agreement of any kind with the Pledge. For the first time, King realized that there was something in this

Pledge that required his consideration. A thought percolated into his mind that the reason why the Chief was encouraging him to See again was because the Chief intended to send him to Oklahoma City as part of the Cherokee delegation. He had never been to Oklahoma City, so the prospect of visiting there in official capacity excited him greatly. He realized that he would add nothing to the delegation, however, if he were not seeing his visions. But hadn't he in fact been seeing a vision? He began thinking hard about the matter, but was distracted by the next turn of events.

The Chief stood up to address the group again. He waved his arms, cleared his throat, and again allowed his mellow yet commanding voice to permeate the atmosphere of the hall, "Friends. The counsel to prepare for the worst while negotiations are in session is good counsel, and in fact we have already anticipated that. Yes, we will be increasing our preparedness for war immediately. As soon as the harvest is in we will not simply increase our preparations, we will *prepare for war*. It pleases my ears to hear that no one is taken in by the sweet promises of the Pledge. They advocate equal distribution and argue that it was capitalism that brought the woes that came down upon the country. We know, don't we friends, that the net result in such systems is always that some people end up construed as more equal than others. Someone must decide, right? *Faciunt solitudinem et pacem vocant!* I have appointed a non-relative to be the next chief of the Cherokee Nation in order to ward off the very danger that the Pledge is flirting with. Today the people, deciding what is equal and fair, may be acting sincerely, but the next generation may not, and then it is too late."

"No, capitalism had its problems, and it wasn't the fault of democracy that the Calamities fell upon this country. It was, in fact, the abandonment of democracy. People turned over to the government the rights and responsibilities that rightly belonged to individuals, and then one day the government abused the powers that they had ... and it was too late. Nothing could be done about it. Why did the people abandon their own rights and responsibilities? There were many reasons. By far, the most pervasive reason was that the citizens of this country forgot their history and the history of all mankind. They said to themselves that it was the government's job to help people, not realizing that the more power that is given to help people, the more power there is to hurt them. By far the greatest hurt was the one that they foolishly did not expect: the utter corruption of the government. *And it was too late.*"

The Chief sighed.

"The reason I share these things with you is not because I think you need to be convinced. If the American citizens have forgotten their history, we Cherokee never have. What happened to us was a forerunner of what would happen to the country as a whole. The reason why I share this with you is because there is actually a delegation here tonight that would like to speak to us. They want to say some words. They say they are words of peace. You remember *my* words as you hear *their* words, and you decide if they are the words of peace. They have come only to present, they say, and not to discuss anything of substance at this time. Hospitality demanded that I grant their wish. Perhaps there won't be a discussion or debate, but perhaps they will allow questions? We shall see," the Chief concluded.

He beckoned to Charlie who was at the back of the hall. Charlie lifted up a lantern and waved it in the doorway. Measured discussions broke out throughout the hall while they waited for this mysterious delegation to enter the barn. King craned his neck to try to look past Charlie. When he turned back, his eyes caught Tasha's eyes, and then the Chief's. The Chief seemed to be posing his question directly to him at that moment, and King realized that he was being called to See immediately, not in a week or more in Oklahoma City. He panicked. He hadn't decided if he should choose to receive the visions! Had they even ever gone away? There was always that dead woman looking at him! The moment seemed to hang forever. The moment of free choice was upon him, and he was not equipped to make it.

More lanterns were being lit when the door opened and Charlie walked through, holding the door open for the guests. Heads turned and eyes goggled: it was a group of Texans! Their cowboy boots clacked on the hardwood floor, and their wide brimmed hats were quickly removed in a polite gesture. The delegation consisted of five men. They were smiling broadly as they made their way to the front. King noticed that each man had a sidearm.

What else did King see? Nothing else. Only the men. The Chief and King locked eyes for a moment but King looked down, ashamed that he could not help take the measure of the men who stood before them. The men were shaking hands with the people at the front table, and other pleasantries were exchanged as well. Finally, Chief Thunderfist silenced the assembly yet again and introduced the gentlemen.

"Cherokee brethren, please extend a warm welcome to a delegation from the *New* Republic of Texas," the Chief declared. King thought he detected a wry smile on the Chief's face.

"Friends of Texas!" bellowed one of the men, "My name is Jerrod Hansley; I am the newly appointed ambassador at large for the New Republic of Texas. Our president was elected just two years ago. His name is Sam Guthrie and he is a great first president for our new republic. To my right is Reverend Nolan White. To my left are my associates Chris Stevens, Harold Felts, and Jeremy Buchwald. President Guthrie sent me to the Cherokee Nation as my first assignment. We have every intention of working together with the Cherokee to secure a peaceful coexistence, and I am here to begin the process of facilitating that!"

Jerrod had white hair and was slightly balding. His face looked like it had been sun burnt more often than it wasn't. His big bellow was surely connected to his big belly, "The loss of the cities of Dallas and Fort Worth and Houston are tragic and severe blows to the morale of the people of Texas. Our spirits were lifted by the generosity shown to us by Cherokee travelers sent to aid us. We know that many other cities were lost in this country, but I doubt that the regions they were in had a friend like we had in the Cherokee! We will be in town for a week. I wanted to invite you all to come and speak with us while we're here. We're staying at the Maple Hill Inn, and we'd love to talk!"

A round of muted applause floated up to the Texans where they, beaming, accepted it. The Chief motioned for silence and, when he had obtained it, dismissed the grand council. The people began dispersing, though many stayed to socialize and discuss what they had heard. King wandered over to Luke and said hello. Philip and Mary greeted him as well. The four of them gradually made their way to the head table where the Texans were in animated conversation with the head table and anyone else who wandered too close.

"You see," the Reverend White was saying, "What we need to do is set up a government based on sound Christian principles!"

"The Reverend isn't speaking for the Republic of Texas on that point," Hansley nervously interjected. "President Guthrie is a religious man, but he has no intention of allowing a theocracy to get started."

The Reverend dismissed the interruption, "Well now, I'm not talking about a theocracy. You know, the word used to have a different meaning before slanderers got a hold of it. Yes, in their mind if you set up your government with religious principles in mind that is a theocracy. But the word comes from the Greek and means, well, 'God Rule' and there was only one instance in recorded history when there was an actual theocracy. You can have a republic and a democracy and still be based on religious principles!"

"Be that as it may, that sort of abstract conversation is of little interest, I'm sure, to the good people of the Cherokee," Hansley retorted with a strained smile on his face.

The one named Harold Felts helped change the direction of the conversation, "I think we have a mutual enemy in the Pledge. What do you think?" The question was posed loudly and to anyone who might be inclined to answer.

The Chief graciously took the question, "If the New Republic of Texas is opposed to tyranny masquerading as freedom then yes, they are mutual enemies. I don't think the Pledge has any eyes looking south though."

Hansley looked as though he would have preferred to continue talking about the definition of theocracy, but felt compelled to speak to the latent question in the Chief's statement, "We are currently evaluating our options in regards to aiding in Oklahoma's struggle against the Pledge. We haven't settled on anything, but of course that is partly why we are here."

Ramaen broke in, "We are glad you're here and hope you will enjoy your stay. If you don't mind, we're going to retire for the evening. We'll look for you in two days, as we have already arranged."

"Yes, absolutely!" Hansley replied enthusiastically, "We're looking forward to it!"

The Texans dismissed themselves and Ramaen and the Chief pretended to be leaving as well, successfully fooling most of the remaining Cherokee in the process. It was a ruse, however. When the room was cleared, Chief Thunderfist, Ramaen, Charlie, Tasha, Philip and Mary, King, and a handful of other elders remained.

"Did you see anything, King?" the Chief asked King straight away.

"No, I'm sorry, Chief. I only started thinking about it when Charlie gave me the message," King replied dejectedly.

"Well, I could have given you more warning, perhaps. Perhaps all of us could have been more available for you over the last year, and among other issues, the question of your visions could have been addressed," the Chief comforted him.

"Chief Thunderfist is sending you on the Oklahoma City trip, King. Are you comfortable with that?" Ramaen asked him.

King thought he had to share his concern that in fact he *had* been receiving visions. He didn't know how to put it, so he simply came out with it, "Well, the thing is that I haven't had any visions like I used to, but I have been having one where I see the eyes of a dead woman look at me. Actually, that's how it started. Now I see her ... broken face and body ... this vision is the only one I've seen in a long while, and it just gets worse and worse. If you send me because of my visions, I think I have to say that my visions haven't been very helpful lately."

"Well, see, that's probably the beginning of a memory, King," Chief Thunderfist corrected him. "I told you that your decision would be respected, and I think it has been. What you have to decide here as you go on, *I* think anyway, is not simply whether or not you will see the visions or have the memories, but whether or not you're prepared to have both. I am perfectly comfortable sending you to Oklahoma City before you've settled it in your mind."

King noticed an exchange of glances between Chief Thunderfist and Tasha. He remembered that Ramaen had asked him a question and said, "Yes, I'll go to Oklahoma City. I will be of service to the Cherokee the best I can."

The Chief smiled, "Very well. That pleases me greatly. Now, about that delegation, Ramaen, what have we decided?"

"You and your son Luke will tend to the preparations for war, and I will go to Oklahoma City with Charlie, Marty, King, Tasha, Leslie, Larry, Manfred and Jenny, Adsila, Tooant, and others. Philip and Mary will return to Tulsa to take inventory and stand ready. The Pledge delegation is expected in Oklahoma City in a month or so, so if we are to get there in time ourselves we will need to leave as soon after the harvest as possible, if not even during the harvest."

"We'll say the last days of the harvest," the Chief advised him, "just in case the Pledge comes early."

"Very well, perhaps during the apple harvest," Ramaen replied.

With that, the group did finally disperse. Tasha and King walked back to their house. The fall evening was cool and crisp, and the stars lit their way.

"Have you thought that perhaps it is nearly time for us to seek out your family?" Tasha broke the silence.

"I have been thinking about it for awhile now. I didn't know how to decide what would be the best time to go. You think I should go soon?" he asked her.

"Yes, I do. I would go with you, if you like. I would probably be needed to help retrace our steps. Ideally, we could find a city that had a ham radio, and we could try to contact Bloomington, Illinois. Perhaps someone there knows something," Tasha reasoned.

"Do we know of any such cities?" King wondered.

Tasha frowned in the dark, "Not any more. Omaha had one years back, but that city fell to the Western Tribes. If they still have a radio, I doubt they'd be willing to share it with us. Although, honestly, if we're going to travel to Omaha in hopes of using their radio we may as well travel back to Illinois."

"Well, I'm not sure I feel really comfortable leaving right now on a trip like that," King told her.

"I wasn't exactly suggesting that, although there could be worse times. By the time we got there it would be spring, which would give us lots of time to track down leads before we needed to shelter for the winter," Tasha thought out loud.

"I wasn't thinking of the weather," King said softly.

"Ah, yes. The girl in Tulsa," Tasha said, shooting a look in King's direction. King blushed, though Tasha couldn't see it in the dark.

"How did you know about her?" King probed.

"Oh come on, I'm Tasha. I don't have to have the gift of sight in order to see what is plain in front of my nose!" Tasha chuckled.

"I didn't think it was that obvious," King protested, still embarrassed.

"It wasn't obvious, I'm *Tasha*, see?" she laughed.

King laughed with her, "Ok, yes. It does concern the girl, at least a little. The fact is that it seems like things are going to be happening here, and I wonder if I should be here to try to protect her."

"She has a father and a mother, does she not?" Tasha replied.

"Yes, of course," King responded, not quite getting the point.

"Well, let them protect her. You tend to your own affairs. Set them in order. Then, when you're whole and intact, you add to your identity. Not before. You only invite harm on her and yourself if you proceed before fixing what needs to be fixed," Tasha advised him.

"What needs to be fixed?" King insisted to know.

"Have you not yet guessed who the dead woman is?" Tasha returned softly. She delivered the question gently, but it slammed him so hard that he stopped walking for a moment. She put her hand on his shoulder. He sank to the ground. He had known it, of course. He knew that he had. His heart was rent anew as wave after wave of grievous thought washed over him. The worst of all was the thought that he did not remember what she looked like before her features had been crushed under the weight of iron beams. He got ahold of himself and stood up. After taking a few moments to fully regain his composure, they continued on.

"It is my mother," King sighed.

"Yes, I think it is. I was there. I think I know the memory you see, because I have the same memory," Tasha consoled him.

"Do you know her name?" King sniffed, choking back a tear.

"No, I don't. That is one thing that needs to be fixed. A boy should know his mother's name and something substantial about his mother, even if she has died. He should know something of his mother's character, especially before seeking out the mother of his own children," she explained.

"Why would God do this to me?" King asked bitterly.

"It is not like that. The world is full of terrible things, but this is not because God wants to target people with calamities. If you think such things you will be consumed by despair, and you shall fail to live: the life you live in despair is no life at all," Tasha urged gently.

King relented. It had been instinctive to rebuke God, but he instantly knew that he was speaking about matters he knew nothing about.

Tasha continued, "Your mother is dead, but your father might yet be alive. I think you need your father, and I think you know that. If he is still alive, and he is a good man, then you will want him in your life before you move forward into new areas of your life."

"I don't know enough to know if your counsel is wise or not," King admitted, "but you have never let me down, and you have always looked out for my interests. You have settled it, then. The next clear opportunity to head east, let's take it."

"Perfect," Tasha declared. And that was the end of the night's conversation.

# == Chapter 8 ==

About a month later, the Cherokee delegation left on horseback for Oklahoma City. Several wagons were brought with them as well as more than a handful of extra horses. All told, there were probably one hundred members of the party, not including twenty Cherokee warriors with compound bows and reasonably nice-looking handmade swords. To King's dismay, the party didn't head through Tulsa, but rather took the most direct route which was many miles south of Tulsa and the girl he wanted to see there. His frustration went away the moment he saw the walls of Oklahoma City, however.

The city walls were, in fact, overturned semi-trailers. They had been arranged so as to encircle the entire city. The region lying in front of the trailers was formerly the neighboring suburbs, but over time it had been scavenged so completely that, except for the grid of decrepit roads that marked where city blocks had been, nothing remained to show that it had once been a thriving community.

There were numerous travelers about. Many were entering the city as they were, but many others were leaving. These were not like the refugees that King remembered from the days of the Disease. These were travelers going about their regular business. Most of the quarantines in the region, if not all, had been lifted.

Guards dressed in beige clothes and red sashes escorted the Cherokee party into the heart of the city where a park had been set aside for the delegation to camp in. They had made the trip in about six days, and they were ready to settle in. President Neff came out to welcome them and informed them that the Pledge delegation was only one day out. Word would be sent with the appointed time for the first meeting.

The Cherokee party set to work with their tents and makeshift stables; by dinnertime, they were well ready to relax. This was easier said than done, however, as quite a few onlookers had gathered to stare at them. In fact, it was so uncomfortable that a message was sent to Neff, who in turn dispatched a guard detachment to push the citizens back out of sight. After that, the Cherokee camp was kept private.

Over the next two days, the Cherokee familiarized themselves with the city. It was a busy city with lots of travelers coming in and out of it, and there were many thriving markets. There had been a decent harvest in Oklahoma City, and even though it was getting pretty cold at night and in the morning, vendors were still out with food items every day. There were also booths with other things for sale. Everything from wire fencing to makeshift weaponry could be found.

The reception wasn't exactly warm all over. Many people threw suspicious looks at the Cherokee men and women. Ramaen, upon inquiring, learned that the Pledge had sent men into the city spreading tales about the Cherokee's intentions. Ramaen responded by doubling up the guard and insisting that no one travel in groups less than three in number. Despite this unsettling development, the sights and sounds of Oklahoma City were able to make the experience generally entertaining.

At last, it was time for the meeting with the Pledge. Though the Pledge hadn't been told that the Cherokee had been invited, they had soon discovered that the Cherokee were present and the word on the street was that they weren't very pleased about it. In fact, there were now Pledge spokespersons out in the markets openly trying to persuade the people to side with the Pledge. The meeting couldn't come any sooner, but King was nervous. He still hadn't been able to come to terms with whether or not he wanted to see the visions.

Worse than that, that morning he had had a disconcerting conversation with one of the native sons of Oklahoma City. Somehow, it had come up that King had been known to have visions and the young man had simply replied, "Well, it's all in your head, isn't it? What's in your head ain't real." The comment had come as a shock to King, who had never considered it in those terms before. He had thought about sharing the matter with Tasha, but time was up. When he returned to the camp a few hours after the conversation, they were just a few minutes from leaving for the meeting.

The meeting was at the president's manor, and King couldn't help but marvel at the building. Protected by an iron fence that encircled it completely, there were several gates manned by three sharply dressed men with sharpened metal instruments. The building itself was glistening white and rose up several stories. It appeared to be a mansion connected to an office building. King had never seen anything like it.

When they entered the building, they were led through a spacious office area where there were people busily at work. King was surprised to see electric light. He had heard about electricity and had seen it at work on the rare occasion when he'd come across a working battery, but this was the first time he had seen whole rooms lit up by such small bulbs.

After some twists and turns, they were led into a large foyer, where they were met by a short bald man.

"You'll need to turn in your weapons," the man directed them. Ramaen looked down on the man, but said nothing. "Your weapons, please," the man said again. Very reluctantly, Ramaen motioned to the twenty or so that were with him, and they began taking their weapons out from their belts. Tasha was closest, so the man began there. He gasped, "Wow! This is a fine weapon!"

King looked over at Tasha and saw that she had in hand a truly beautiful looking blade. It was about a foot long, clearly sturdy and well-balanced, and it threw sparkling light in all directions. At that moment, President Neff burst into the room.

"What's going on here?" President Neff demanded to know. Then he caught sight of Tasha's blade. King found himself looking at it more closely, too. He had seen it before, of course, though he was much younger then. Tasha had made the blade famous in the battle of Domasi, but had never produced it for anyone to examine it. King realized that this was the first time he himself had really ever looked at the blade, and he had been with Tasha for something close to five years.

"That is a marvelous weapon!" Neff declared. "Can I hold it?" Tasha smiled and handed it to the president. He continued to goggle over it. "I could shave with this knife!" he whistled. He handed the knife back to Tasha and looked at the bald man, "So what's going on, Mackay?"

"Confiscating weapons, sir, as according to protocol," Mackay explained.

"Good grief, man. You don't confiscate the weapons of our guest delegates. Just the ordinary riff raff that wants to chat with me or a staff member. I'm sorry about this," Neff nodded to Ramaen, who smiled slightly in appreciation.

"What about the Pledge, sir?" Mackay implored.

"What about them? They are guests, too, aren't they?" Neff retorted.

"But are they trustworthy?" Mackay remarked a little too gruffly.

"Don't we have our own guards and don't they have weapons? Gracious. Please, Mackay, be on your way. Shoo! Now, Chief Ramaen if you could all follow me?" Neff motioned to the door of a large conference room. There was a raised platform at the front with a number of tables on it. A row of tables ran parallel to each of the walls and there was an empty area between them. It looked like this was where the city council met. The Cherokee made their way into the room and settled in on the left side, near the front.

Neff continued to apologize for his subordinate's behavior, but

Ramaen graciously argued on the man's behalf that he had only been trying to do his job. Neff finally gave up on the matter and informed them that the Pledge delegation would be along presently. Some food and drink were brought in, and Neff departed. King sat down by Tasha and began to nibble away at the crackers, meat, and cheese.

There were only about twenty of the Cherokee who were involved in the meetings. King didn't recognize all of them, but some of the older ones he knew were senior advisors. Charlie was also present and stood near Ramaen. They talked quietly between themselves for a bit before finally having some snacks with the rest of the group. Finally, the conference room door opened and a half dozen or so armed guards came in. Behind them was what was clearly the Pledge delegation. President Neff was with them, and the apparent leader of the delegation was arguing with Neff.

"Such a betrayal!" the man was snapping at Neff. "This was to be a private meeting between the Pledge and the people of Oklahoma City covering topics of interest only to our two parties. This is a bad beginning! This is bad faith if ever there was bad faith!"

"Well, now, you can see it like that if you like, but as the President of this city I decide what is in the interest of the city for purposes of our discussion, and I determined that having the Cherokee in on the conversation was certainly of interest to us. If you don't like it, Trots, you don't have to stay," Neff rejoined haughtily.

"We're here now," Trots said curtly.

"Yes, indeed," Neff snapped back.

"We can at least get it over with," Trots demanded.

Ramaen leaned over to King and whispered, "What do you see?" King could only shake his head. Prior to the conversation with the young man that morning, King had just about decided that he had wanted the visions to begin again. Now he doubted, and therefore he didn't see anything.

Tasha leaned over from the other side and told Ramaen in a soft voice, "He looks slimy to me."

Ramaen smiled at that and turned his attention back to the argument that was unfolding before them. Neff and Trots were exchanging a variety of barbs and insults practically ignoring the Cherokee who were present. Finally, Ramaen decided that they should be involved.

"I am Ramaen, a chief of the Cherokee tribes of Oklahoma. I am here to speak in the name of Chief Thunderfist," Ramaen introduced himself. King was distracted, however. The Pledge delegation was composed of about ten shifty looking fellows and five of the strangest looking men that King had ever seen. These five were short and stumpy and had distant looks in their eyes. The rest of the Pledge delegation shoved these other men around and gave them orders.

Soon, the dumpy looking men were bringing some of the food and drink that had been given to the Cherokee over to those who could only be described as their masters. The Cherokee were so enthralled by the odd sight that they overlooked the insult of having their snacks shuffled away from them. The Oklahoma City guards noticed, though, and soon after more food was brought in for the Cherokee.

The debate was well under way, now.

"It is a new day and era," the one called Trots was trying to be as eloquent as possible. "Capitalism and democracy drowned this country in despair. Yes, of course, both can work on small scales. A democracy can work at the level of a city, for example. But this is a great nation. We will have to work in close cooperation in order for everyone to thrive."

Ramaen scoffed at that, "Yes, of course. The October Revolution worked out well in the large scale, didn't it? Cooperation required organization and organization required leaders and leaders required cooperation, which of course they received, voluntary and otherwise."

"You cannot measure the whole system by the failures of a handful of corrupt individuals," Trots retorted.

"What if the system created those corrupt individuals in the first place, or at least gave them their place of influence?" Ramaen fought back.

"What would you know? You Cherokee have only your small numbers to govern. We look to the interests of the world," Trots snapped condescendingly.

Charlie laughed, "You've got to be kidding."

Ramaen, however, was offended. "If you govern well in the small areas you are permitted to govern the larger ones. How has the Pledge managed Little Rock to this point?"

"That is none of your business," Trots protested.

"It seems relevant," Ramaen folded his arms. The tension in the room had become truly palpable. Hands twitched on both sides of the room, and the guards watched everyone very carefully.

"The Pledge is different," Trots attempted to correct Ramaen. "We have more important things to tend to than the administration of solitary cities. That is why the citizens of Oklahoma City have nothing to fear from the Pledge. We will protect the city from the corrupting elements that surround it. No doubt, Neff knows the New Republic of Texas might have an interest in annexing his city and his region. Who will stand up to them? The Cherokee? No, the Pledge."

"If the honorable President Neff didn't think we would come to the aid of his city, he would not have requested our presence here," Ramaen countered.

Trots seemed to perceive that the conversation was shifting against him in a more substantial way. He changed his tact: "Very well, then. Let me put this in terms that no one can misunderstand. The day is coming when the Pledge will administer justice in this land. We are called the Pledge because we keep our word. I am telling you, it is only a matter of time. If you do not both—yes, the Cherokee too—cooperate freely with the New Order, we will have to resort to coercion."

"Is that a threat?" Ramaen growled.

"It is a promise!" Trots proclaimed. "We keep our word: If not by choice, than by force!" While Trots was speaking, the conference room door opened.

"My apologies, sir, but there are two men here who need a right to lethality permit," Mackay interrupted.

"Now?" Neff sighed.

"Well, sir, they have swords. Very fine looking swords at that. We can't set them at loose in town with these weapons without a permit," Mackay explained. King believed that Mackay was still stewing over how Neff had talked to him earlier and was really looking for a way to harass Neff.

"Swords?" Neff said. "Yes, let's see some sword." He looked relieved to have a break. Mackay left the room and returned in short order.

Two men walked in behind Mackay. They both wore long, black cloaks. The one on the right had long, silver hair. The one on the left was slightly taller and looked a little sickly. The effect on King was immediate. He felt like he had been punched in the stomach as hard as one could punch. He nearly fell over backwards, but Tasha caught him and steadied him. Ramaen and Charlie both glanced at him.

The two men walked up the center area, glancing back and forth at the scene they had interrupted. King was simply stunned. Ramaen discretely moved closer to King and finally was in whispering distance.

"What do you see, King?" Ramaen asked him.

"I have never seen such a sight," King whispered hoarsely back. "The man on the right ... he ... I see a man, a beautiful man, but he is large, so large I cannot even say ... he has ... you won't believe it!"

"Yes I will, just tell me," Ramaen insisted.

"Go ahead," Tasha prodded him.

"He has one foot on one mountain range and the other foot on another mountain range. In his hands he holds *the light of Ilivatir* and he brings death, destruction, and life. He is so terrible to behold and yet ... wonderful ..." King stammered.

"Wonderful? What is wonderful?" Ramaen continued to press him.

"It is as though I can see right into his soul, like it was made out of glass or liquid silver ... here is a *man*," King stuttered.

Ramaen smiled, said nothing, and returned to his place.

"Alright, let's see what the fuss is all about," President Neff ordered the men. They withdrew their swords and held them out to him, handles out. The president selected one sword and then the other, holding them each and weighing them carefully. "A fine specimen. I've only seen one like it, myself. And that was today," the president said whimsically.

Trots interrupted him, "No offense President Neff, but there are things of more importance than swords, and all in all, there are more fearsome weapons in the world, as you well know."

Ramaen was ready, "Yes, we all know the rumors that the Pledge has firearms. I'm sure you are also aware of the rumors that the Indians have firearms."

"Actually," Trots sneered, "We have it on good authority that this is no rumor. It is truth."

"You say it is so. It does not seem wise for this city to form their decision based on the rumors about your capabilities against the facts of our capabilities, then, don't you think?" Ramaen countered. "Why not be plain about your threats rather than rely on insinuations?"

Trots glared at Ramaen but said nothing. The tension in the room was tangible. Even the dumpy little Pledge assistants looked on guard. These men—if we can call them that—had seemed utterly oblivious to the conversation until the two men walked in. As King was recoiling in the face of his vision, the stunted men were glancing about somewhat frantically. By the time King next looked at them, they were back to their old selves, although closer observation would have shown that they were casting glances at the two men.

Seeking to ease the tension, President Neff returned his attention to the two men. "What is your purpose in Oklahoma City, gentlemen?" President Neff asked them.

"We are only passing through, sir," the man on the left replied. "We are going to Bloomington, Illinois, to try to find my family."

"Oh yes, they have some sort of a project there, don't they?" Neff smiled in recognition. "The Disease and the nuclear incidents were devastating. People were trapped all over the place. This project is supposed to be a central location to try to reconnect families and friends. I do hope you find your family, and that they are well."

"Thank you," the man responded graciously.

A sudden thought burst into King's mind: he should go with them. This was the opportunity that he had been waiting for. A significant catalyst was knowing something about the silver, valiant looking man. He had never seen either of the men before, but he knew that here were no ordinary men.

"I am concerned that people will be nervous with you in the city, however," President Neff was saying to them. "It's true that there are more potent weapons in the world, but not in this city—at least not legally. How long were you thinking of staying here?"

King exchanged a glance with Tasha. She seemed to know what he was thinking. She gave him a nod of agreement and whispered, "Do it now."

Mountain-Straddler answered, "We are ready to leave at once. Just give us a day or two to collect additional supplies, and we'll be off."

King felt that he had to interject. "Pardon me," he said, "Who is permitted to go to this project in Illinois?"

"As far as I know, it's open to anyone in the country that is trying to reconnect with loved ones. I've heard that other places may start up projects like this in the future, too," President Neff explained.

King turned to address the man who represented the people that his loyalty currently was given to, "Ramaen, you know that I came to you from that area. Tasha brought me to your people, and I have been very thankful for that. She saved my life. But I don't know what happened to my family, either. I would like to go to Bloomington, Illinois, too."

Ramaen didn't seem surprised by the request. He smiled tenderly and offered his blessing, "King, you have done well as an adopted member of our Nation. Your fighting spirit will be missed, even when we saw it as mischief. You know I cannot keep you here."

"I would like to go with these men, Ramaen. And if Tasha would like to return with me, I would appreciate her company, as she has been a mother to me," King continued.

"That is not for me to say, but you can leave with or without them whenever you like. I give you leave. And Tasha, you are released from any obligations you may feel, as well," Ramaen said.

"A new adventure seems appropriate," Tasha replied.

It hadn't occurred to King that he had imposed himself on the two men by his request. He suddenly realized the rudeness of his presumption as Mountain-Straddler began speaking, relieving King of his concern, "King and Tasha are more than welcome to journey with us. We hear there are evil things afoot in that direction," there was snickering out of some members of the Pledge, "and the more people we have, the better off we will be."

"Splendid," President Neff said jovially. "Now we can return to some other matters that perhaps may be more critical for us today," he sighed. "We need to find a way to appease the nationalistic Indian groups and keep them from slaughtering our travelers, and we need to decidedly reject so-called offers to join the Pledge. You are dismissed," the president said, handing the two men papers authorizing them to retain their swords. The Pledge spokesman snarled at the president's words, but the president ignored him, "Take up to three days, but I would suggest you leave as soon as you can. The people are nervous, and we must not make things worse."

King's spirit swelled with excitement as he left the room to join the two men, Tasha at his side. They were quickly escorted out by guards who took them all the way to the gate. Mountain-Straddler had a conversation with the gate guards about a motorcycle that was there. Finally, they were free of the guards.

King reached out to shake the hands of the two men, "You gathered that my name is King and that this is Tasha. What are your names?"

"My name is Fermion," Mountain-Straddler replied warmly.

"And my name is Fides," the other man added.

"It is very nice to meet you both," Tasha said. "Very distinctive names. I like them."

"What shall we do first?" King put to them. "Do you have lodging here? Tasha and I should go to the Cherokee camp to retrieve our belongings, but after that I suppose we can do whatever we agree to do."

"We have only just arrived in town," Fermion explained. "When they saw our weapons at the gate, they were very disturbed and ushered us to the president's manor straight-away. We have no lodging. If we're welcome, perhaps a night or two at the Cherokee camp would be a good idea."

"That sounds fine," Tasha replied, nodding in the direction of the camp. "Follow us!"

As they went, they talked. King learned a little more about the men's journey. Fides had met Fermion in Albuquerque, and Fermion had agreed to escort Fides east. Their trip across the wilderness had not been without incident. Somehow, they had even managed to acquire the motorcycle that had been discussed at the gate. King liked the two men greatly. The vision of Fermion astride two mountain ranges was now lodged into his memory, rather than his direct sight, but he felt the man's strength keenly, anyway. Fides did not yield such impressions, but King took him to be earnest and loyal.

Arriving at the camp, they agreed to rest and relax awhile as Fermion and Fides had only recently arrived and were still exhausted. In fact, as soon as bedrolls were managed for each, the two fell into deep sleep and never stirred no matter how much noise was raised in the camp. Rested, they woke up shortly before dinner, and Tasha was ready for them with a meal.

"This is a fine stew, Tasha," Fermion effused.

"Mmmmmph," Fides agreed, chewing so heartily he couldn't be bothered to open his mouth to form actual words. Tasha beamed.

"You two are not Cherokee, then?" Fermion inquired.

"No, but we have been with them for five years or more," King explained.

"King is now a trusted friend of the Cherokee, having proved himself on numerous occasions," Tasha shared while King blushed.

"Proved himself?" Fermion pressed.

"Yes, in battle," Tasha clarified.

"In battle?" Fides interjected. "You seem strong enough, but still so young."

"Sometimes battle comes uninvited and does not ask how old you are," Tasha defended King. "His battles have been many, and they have not all been against men."

"I didn't mean to offend," Fides hastily said.

"No, not offended. I am young. I don't know how old I am, exactly. Fifteen, sixteen, maybe. I have grown strong on Cherokee food, Tasha's wisdom, and plenty of opportunities to stand my ground," King alleviated Fides' concern.

The first members of the Cherokee delegation who had been at the meeting arrived back in camp. They seemed extraordinarily weary. The four of them watched the rest of the delegation wander into camp wordlessly. Many of them went to their tents to sleep. Some found a place to sit by a fire and sat in silence. At last, Ramaen arrived.

"It did not go well," was all Ramaen said.

Concluding their dinner, King and Tasha set about packing up their belongings and organizing their bags. Fides and Fermion sat and watched and chatted with them as they worked. By the time darkness fell, it was agreed that in the morning they would venture into the markets to lay their hands on additional supplies.

The following morning they discussed precisely what provisions they would need and where to obtain them. As Tasha and King had been in the city for several days already, they had had an opportunity to explore some of the market places; it quickly became a matter of deciding what would be brought with them and who would carry it.

The Indian delegates had left in the morning for the next conference before the rest of them had gotten up, but there were plenty of others who remained in the camp. To King's surprise, Charlie did not go on with Ramaen to the meeting, but rather stayed behind to converse with them. Marty, Charlie's second-in-command, had been staying behind anyway on account of being in charge of camp security. Charlie and Marty now hit it off with Fides and Fermion, and Fides in particular.

While Fides, Charlie, and Marty were getting better acquainted, Fermion fleshed out his understanding of how King and Tasha came to be together. Tasha told him about saving King's life years ago during one of the nuclear strikes.

"Where was that at?" Fermion directed to her.

"Somewhere west of Indianapolis. Honestly, I don't remember anymore," Tasha answered apologetically.

"That may make it difficult to track down King's family," Fermion observed.

"Yes, but I will know it by sight. Don't you worry about that," she grinned.

"What happened then?" Fermion smiled back.

"Well, we made it to Bloomington eventually. We wintered in Peoria ..." here, Fermion's ears perked up, "Then we zipped through the upper Midwest before finally heading south into Iowa. We were on our way to Nebraska, actually, but some western tribes were attacking Omaha right about when we got there. Some other Indians stumbled across us and escorted us south, where we were finally handed over to the Cherokee," Tasha explained.

"I rode to the Cherokee Nation with the Chief's son, and he became my friend," King contributed to the story. "He and I would roam the countryside, and one time we even helped drive off some bandits."

Fermion asked, "How did you come to be in battles?"

King was pleased to talk about such things. He replied proudly, "Well, the first time was an accident. It was while traveling to Tulsa, and the camp was attacked by a rival Indian tribe. There was a more significant battle a few years after that, though. Some renegade Cherokee actually attacked the Cherokee Nation. That was quite a battle, but my role in that battle is not nearly as famous as Tasha's."

"You, Tasha?" Fermion glanced appraisingly at her. She merely smiled.

At around noon, the delegation returned to the camp and enjoyed a massive lunch that had been prepared for them by the other members of the party. Ramaen instructed that the best food be made in honor of Tasha and King's departure and announced that that evening they'd have a real party. But there was only a short time for conversation with the delegation, as they once again adorned their faces with scowls and returned to the talks with the president and the Pledge.

Before he left, Ramaen took the four of them aside and gave them small bars of gold and silver and slabs or iron and other good bartering items.

"Accept these gifts as a token of our warm regards for you. Use them to buy what you'll need," he said. King and Tasha thanked him profusely, and Fermion and Fides also expressed their appreciation.

Finally, it was time to go to the markets. Charlie and Marty decided to accompany them. In fact, they were the ones left to carry the weight of the valuable gift, which they did without complaining.

"I wouldn't be surprised if we catch the attention of the citizens," Fermion warned.

"Yes," Charlie agreed. "We have found the reception here to be good, generally, but still mixed. The city has been attacked repeatedly by various Indians. The citizens cannot tell the difference between tribes. Those that remember that there are Cherokee here with the purpose of discussing their own safety treat us warmly enough."

They picked their way through the market looking for salted meats, water purification tablets, new boots, and other essentials.

As Fermion predicted, they did catch the eye of people in the city. Wearing their long dark cloaks, Fermion and Fides together projected a certain intimidating air, but Fermion's long silver-like hair made people visibly draw back. In fact, most people assumed simply that they were Indians as well. Though people were often taken aback by the presence of this fearsome looking group, in the marketplace their gold and silver made them instantly welcomed.

After a long shopping spree, it was time to return to the camp. As they passed through a marketplace near the camp, they heard a loud voice calling out over the crowd. Though weary from the shopping and burdened with their purchases, Fermion expressed interest in hearing what the man was saying, so they followed him over to where the man was speaking.

"Look at what government has done!" he was saying. "Democracy brought us the nuclear bomb. It brought us a terrible disease. Look at our fractured world! Today, the citizens of Oklahoma City live in a place that is protected by a wall of overturned semi-truck trailers. Is that a good thing? That is what our Republic has come to—grown men and women hiding behind ugly, tipped-over trailers! We have seen the fruit of history, and we are the ones tasting it and dealing with its poison. Why would we do the same thing over again? Why would we repeat the same mistakes of the past? We have a chance now to do right, right from the start, and so save ourselves and—more importantly—our children from having to live in a world like this for generations. We can build a nation where the individual is the most important unit, not the government, not society, but the person. Only when individuals band together and recognize that they are brothers—"

"And sisters!" a woman shouted from the crowd.

"And sisters!" the man laughed, "Only when we realize this can we understand that each person is their own law, and there is no need for any authorities above or beyond any person. It's time to live like free men and women. We can be free to be, and that means we don't have to strive for status the way people had to in the past. Why have ten chickens when you only need three? Is that not just status? Show that you are not bound by greed and avarice, and give your brother a chicken, for God's sake. Why have a million gold coins when you only need ten? What kind of free man withholds that kind of wealth—which they don't even need—from their needy neighbor's family? Why have twenty acres of land when you only need five? We should not be slaves any more to our wants. We should acknowledge our needs and, in freedom, take what we need and no more. And if everyone does this, we will finally live in a free country."

"The Pledge," the man paused dramatically, "The Pledge recognizes that not everyone thinks this way. These people are slaves—slaves to their own passions. Animals, really, muzzled with their own muzzles, doing as they are told without thinking on their own. The Pledge is assembling free thinkers from wherever they can, and already we have many that are willing to lay down their lives for freedom, if it comes to that. We are here in this city of yours right now, offering to your president the same vision for our country that we have offered to other men in other cities. We are ready, if it comes to it, to bring freedom to the land by force if necessary. That is our pledge. And those who survive—my brothers—they will receive their equal reward. They won't have to worry about government conspiracies or corrupt senators or power hungry presidents. We'll just divide it all up equally, and it's as easy as that. You need to tell your President that Oklahoma City and its surrounding areas want to be free! If your city stands against freedom and clear thought, there will some day be a battle. You need to be on the side of your human brothers, not on the side of the enslaved beasts."

"What about the Indians?" called out a man, who clearly didn't notice the Indians standing nearby.

"The Indians have no unified view. We invite them to join our march for freedom. Some will join us and some will fight us, even as some are fighting with one another. But if they insist on taking more than what they need—which retaking the country, as some Indians are calling for, obviously is—then the Pledge will match them, stone for stone, knife for knife, arms for arms," the man replied boldly.

"Does the Pledge have guns?" yelled out another voice. King decided Fermion had been right. This was turning out to be a very interesting speech.

"Guns were confiscated by the International Force. How would we have guns? We have power, might, and we are right. We will prevail because our cause is just ..."

Visibly disgusted, Fermion decided he had heard enough. He led them away from the man as Charlie explained that the Pledge had inserted a number of men like that throughout the city. Fermion was about to reply when, suddenly, they were confronted by some men who had noticed them. Ten men stood across from them, lightly armed with pipes and shovel handles.

One man in the middle addressed them: "As far as I'm concerned," he said, looking at Fermion, "we can never trust the Indians, even if they did want to join the Pledge. We know both the Pledge and the Indians have guns. You're both liars."

Tasha sighed. Charlie leaned over and chuckled softly under his breath close enough for King to hear, "The funny thing here is that out of the six of us only two of us are Indian! I told you they couldn't tell Indians apart."

"We don't want any trouble," Fides said to the man.

"Well, you've got trouble, my friend. I don't trust you, and I need to, you understand. I only trust the dead, see?" King saw that some of the men had now produced sharpened metal instruments. He set down the goods he had bought and was reaching for his knife when Charlie put his hand on his shoulder and pushed past him.

Charlie addressed the man, laughing, "You've got to be kidding me. Are you planning on fighting us in the middle of a busy market? You think Neff is going to allow our slaughter to go unpunished?"

Marty chimed in as well, "Not that you're going to slaughter us, mind you. We're just trying to make the point that you've got nothing to gain by standing in our way. Now step aside, or someone is going to get hurt."

The men did not seem to be frightened. Maybe they couldn't tell Indians from non-Indians but they could count, and by their calculations they outnumbered the shopping party. Other consumers were backing away from the argument, while still staring at it in curiosity. King and his friends stood still as the aggressors approached. Fides' group held its ground, though their aggressors were only a few feet away.

The leader opened his mouth to give the order, "Alright boys, get ..."

"Oh, what's this?" Charlie asked as though surprised at what was suddenly in his hand.

"Why Charlie, that looks like a gun to me," Marty explained nonchalantly. "I guess the man was right."

Charlie had deftly pulled his firearm out from hiding, and the barrel was now pointed directly between leader's eyes. The rest of the thugs fell back a few steps, but the leader stood paralyzed.

"You don't suppose anybody else in our group has guns, do ya, buddy? Does it really seem wise to attack a group you've just accused of possessing weapons? Did you not believe your own accusation, or was it perhaps just pretext?" Charlie asked the man, whose eyes had become wide with fear. The man trembled, and Charlie continued, "Look, I have an idea. How about you tell your henchmen to get out of our way, and to do it quickly? Then, we are going to be on our way, thankful that we live where civilization is still real and honors lives, rather than locked inside a city with scoundrels like you. What do you say?"

The man nodded obediently, and the band of scoundrels disappeared into the crowd. Charlie returned the gun to its hiding place on his person. King was still staring at Charlie in surprise. King hadn't seen a gun among the Cherokees for at least a year.

"Do you think it was wise to show your weapon?" Fermion asked Charlie as they once again made their way towards the camp.

"Actually, it's part of our strategy," Charlie explained. This is the first that King had heard anything about this, but it was Fides who asked the obvious question.

"Part of your strategy?" Fides asked.

"Yes, we want there to be strong rumor mixed with fact that the Indians really do have guns. There are plenty of people in this city who think they ought to raise an army to go out and bring down the Cherokee, and it's only because the population has a pretty good idea that we are better armed than they are that they haven't done it yet. But you've got to keep in mind, too, that it's for their own good. Chief Thunderfist would likely not choose to use the weapons. But other tribal members, and other tribes, would have no hesitation."

"So, it is true? The Indians retained their weapons despite the efforts of the International Force?" Fermion asked them.

Marty winked, "I'd answer that, but then I'd have to kill ya. You understand."

Fermion smiled knowingly but let the matter drop. When they arrived at camp, Charlie and Marty briefed Ramaen on the event, and Ramaen in turn sent a messenger to President Neff to keep him informed of the event as well as the display of the gun.

The following morning was set as their departure date, so that night Ramaen had arranged a rousing festival to celebrate the life and times of Tasha and King while they had been with the Cherokee. A roaring fire was kept ablaze late into the evening. Fermion and Fides allowed their exquisite blades to be passed around. King had never felt so cherished. He did begin to have pangs of doubt, however, though he was too young to know that it was simply the birthing signs of homesickness.

Charlie stood up and shared a long telling of the story of the Domasi War and King and Tasha's place in it. King beamed and Tasha blushed as each was given credit for their achievements. King's scouting abilities and skilled fighting with his staff were highlighted, but Charlie struggled to give King equal time as Tasha's story in this matter was much more profound. Fermion and Tasha exchanged glances, and Fermion was clearly impressed by the fighting ability of this woman who looked old (or older, at least) but didn't act it.

At last, it was too late for more reverie. Ramaen caught everyone's attention with a loud clap, interrupting Charlie who had now begun to tell the story of King and Luke taking on a gunman while taking fire from fellow Cherokee.

"Alright, Tsahli, that is enough storytelling for tonight. Our friends must leave early tomorrow, and they will need their rest," he announced. "I want to use this as a chance to say that we gained more than Tasha and King did in our friendship with them. As a token of our thanks, we have decided to let you all ride on horses as far as Tulsa. Tasha knows who to take them to, once there. Then, in order to hasten you in your journey—which we hope will be fruitful—we will pay out of Cherokee wealth the cost for Chummy's Transport as far as he is willing to take you. Now, off to sleep for everyone!"

King was delighted by this turn of events, and deeply flattered. He had hoped that the Cherokee would provide horses for Fermion and Fides, but Illinois was a long trip on horseback and they were on the edge of winter weather just as they would be heading north into it. Once he'd arrived in Tulsa, they could be in Bloomington in under a week, and then—Ah, Tulsa again!

King's heart quickened as he remembered that there was more in Tulsa than fast transportation; Ramaen had offered a gift that could only be claimed by a trip to the same city where there was a certain girl that King had grown quite fond of. Things were shaping up, he decided. He would be seeing Joan in the near future, and then he could arrive quickly in Bloomington, find his family, and be back in short order as well. He might even have matters settled at home in time to return to Tulsa in just two or three months!

The Cherokee did provide Fides and Fermion with horses for the trip to Tulsa, as King had hoped. The next morning, then, they packed the horses with as much gear as they could hold. Fides had trouble getting his leg over, but only King cracked a hint of a smile. Even Marty didn't make any smart comments as he helped shove Fides up.

"I can ride a horse, honest," Fides laughed.

They left the stable area and their friends behind as they proceeded towards the eastern gates of Oklahoma City. The city was starting to wake up. Some people poked their heads out to see who was riding this early. Those who did were rewarded with a sight right out of medieval times. After an hour of quiet travel, they saw the ramp up to the old highway, which meant that they could see the east gate out of town.

As they rounded the corner, they were confronted yet again with the same group that had accosted them in the market place. They were about fifty feet away, blocking the entrance to the ramp. They appeared to be reinforced, but no better armed. Fermion gave a grunt and set his horse at a faster trot with his sword out, held forward like a javelin.

"What are you doing?" exclaimed Fides.

Tasha silenced him, "Don't worry about him, Fides."

King glanced at Tasha, wondering what she knew of Fermion. He also caught a good look at Fermion's sword as it flashed in the flares of the morning sun. A noble blade for a noble man, King reasoned.

Fermion was off at a gallop. He let his horse drive into the group, sending them scattering in all directions. Fermion wheeled the horse around expertly so the front legs of the horse were clawing the air above the instigator's head. Fermion showed mercy, however, and moved aside, so that it was his blade that the man had to be concerned about, now. It hovered a few feet above the man's throat.

"Clarence," King heard Fermion say, "if I have to deal with you and your cohorts again, it will be with utmost finality. Do you understand?"

Clarence appeared to understand perfectly. He and the rest crawled away and finally scampered out of sight. King found himself deeply impressed by Fermion's skill and conduct. He didn't dwell on the strange fact that Fermion had known the name of the ringleader. For himself, King was just glad to get on the road. Next stop, Tulsa. And Tulsa meant Joan.

# == Chapter 9 ==

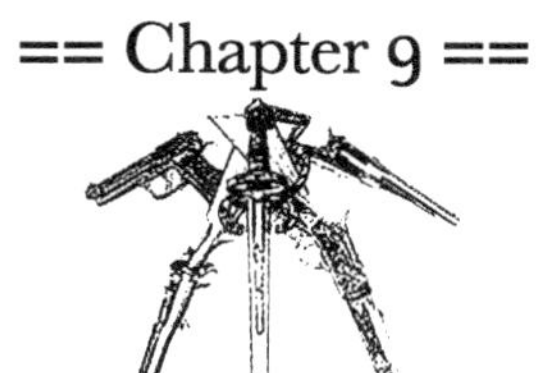

About a day into their journey along Interstate 44 towards Tulsa, the crew was beginning to settle in together nicely. The smell of Tasha's cooking woke King up. He rolled out of bed about the same time Fides did and, at his first opportunity, sat down to devour the fried potatoes and hot soup.

"Enough for a second helping, Tasha?" King begged.

"Not yet, pal. Fermion hasn't had even a first helping yet!" Tasha rebuked him. When he thought she wasn't looking though, King speared a chunk on his way back to his sleeping bag to begin packing up.

Together, the four of them put out the fire, finished packing their belongings, and continued the journey at a pace slightly above a walk. At this pace, Tasha told them, they could be in Tulsa by late evening the next day. As they went, they talked.

"How did you come to be together?" Fides inquired of Tasha and King.

"I was young at the time," King answered, "and I don't remember much of it now. But I remember that there was a huge flash of light in the sky far away, but not as far as I thought. It got very windy, and then there was a rumbling, and then it was like a wave of heat hit us and the building we were standing just inside of. The building collapsed, but I felt swept away. That was Tasha grabbing me and pulling me away from where the building was falling."

King left out the fact that over the last year or so he had been seeing the lifeless eyes of his mother gazing at him.

"I had been fleeing the Disease," Tasha continued the tale, eager to respect King's reluctance to share the full story, and aware that even now he hadn't quite remembered it all himself. "I was passing through the town, is all. There was a flash behind me. I felt the wave coming, and I saw King standing alone under the awning of a building. I was pretty close. I yanked him away as the building was coming down. Then we fell into a ditch and waited for the wave to fully pass. King was very scared. He must have only been eight or nine. He was scared silent. I asked him where his family was, and he could only point to the building." Tasha became silent for a moment, and then continued, "There was no way anyone was alive in that building. So I took King as my own, and we've been together since."

King had never really talked about the event in this detail before with anyone other than Tasha. He suddenly realized that there was a huge hole in his memory of the event. He remembered the flash of light, the collapse of the building, and more recently, the darkened eyes and crushed form of his mother. How did he get out of the building? Tasha had described falling into a ditch and having a conversation about his family, and he didn't remember any of that. How had he known his family was in the building to tell Tasha? He closed his eyes tightly. He felt that if only he allowed it, he would suddenly remember it all. He was not ready for that, so he quickly skipped ahead. He didn't notice that the rest of the group had remained respectfully silent in the face of King's remembering.

"I didn't talk for a year," he said. "It was like I had been thrown into shock. I knew my family was gone, and it changed me somehow. But Tasha took care of me. She became my new mother. At some point, I realized I had to move on. I miss them, though."

Fermion gazed on him with fatherly tenderness, "We are born to joy but are destined for sorrow. It is wise not to let the sorrow be your master, so that you can stand again to experience joy. You were wise to move on," he added tenderly. "You will always love and miss your family, but they would not want you to cling so hard to their memories that you do not make new ones. You are wiser than your years."

King nodded deferentially, "If that is so, it is because Tasha has made me so."

Tasha blushed slightly at this compliment but said nothing. Fermion studied them both carefully as Tasha related in more detail their travels from Illinois to Oklahoma.

"What family do you hope to find if you think your immediate family is no more," Fides asked King.

"I can't say for sure, to be honest. I'm sure that I must have some other relations, though. Besides, you know, maybe they got out. We'll find out," King said.

After another thoughtful silence, Fermion began sharing their side of the story up until that point.

"I first met Fides in Illinois, actually. But we only spent a little time together then," Fermion narrated. "The next time I saw him was in a tavern in Albuquerque. I had been posing as a priest in my travels because even in this day and age, a few decades after the International Force tried to purge all religion from this country and the world, a priest still gets a measure of deference. Well, when I had Fides as a traveling partner I could afford to give up that ruse."

"But what about your swords?" King probed curiously.

Fermion laughed. "They are wonderful specimens, aren't they? Would you believe I raided them from a museum?"

"I wouldn't," Tasha smiled mischievously. Fermion only chuckled, but would say no more.

"I hope you'll let me look at them more closely, at least?" King requested greedily.

"Sure, I'll let you have a look," Fermion assured him. "We should be thinking about stopping at some point here, don't you think?"

"As long as Tasha does some more cooking each time we stop, we can stop as often as you want!" King joked.

Soon, they found an area protected from the sharp wind. Dismounting, they were about to start a fire when they noticed a pile of bones. With horror, King realized they were human bones. They were held together in vague human shape by shredded rags.

"The Disease took them while traveling," Tasha reasoned. "A terrible thing, the Disease. It would rot people from the inside out as their skin and limbs start to drop off. When a person knew that the end was coming, a lot of times they, or the ones caring for them, would wrap themselves tightly in their blankets and clothing just to hold themselves so it would be easier for friends and family to bury them. Apparently these had none to bury them."

"Such a profane thing to happen under the watch of a good God!" Fides declared, his eyes welling up with tears. "Let's bury them, now!"

King quickly agreed. He had been gazing at the skulls and fighting off the impression that they, like his dead mother, were gazing at him. It took about an hour with the four of them taking turns, but eventually the graves were deep enough to hold all of the bones. Fermion said a few words befitting a man who had posed as a priest, and they got back on their way to try to find a different location for lunch. It didn't seem right to eat near the graves of those poor souls.

Journeying about a mile farther, they found a patch of grass with a nice big tree to tie up the horses to and someone else's fire pit. Tasha cooked up some more potatoes. King found a small creek nearby and took the horses to it to drink, returning to have some water himself after tending to the horses. Fermion and Fides went on ahead on foot to scout out the area ahead of them.

When they were out of sight, King asked Tasha, "What do you think it meant when I saw Fermion astride two mountain ranges?"

"It surely means he is not one to be trifled with. Apart from that, I think it means strength and courage, and the noble awe that a mighty mountain can evoke. I trust him, if that is what you're concerned about," she replied.

"Oh, I trust him," King pondered. "I just find it to be strange.

Maybe you don't understand, but in my vision he was positively huge. They were *real* mountains he was standing on!"

"What about Fides? Do you see anything there?" Tasha probed.

"No, I don't. Here's the thing, though," King thought aloud, "I didn't choose to see a vision, but one came anyway. Fermion walked into the room, and it was like BOOM, and I had no choice. Even now this vision flickers off and on so that when I see him, I see at once the man and also the giant with the torch."

King shot his hand up, "And that's another thing! I said that he was holding the light of Iluva-something, but I had no idea what that was. I had never heard that before in my life, and yet it came out of my mouth! What do you make of it?"

"It sounds to me like Chief Thunderfist is right in that you couldn't totally suppress the gift, even if you had wanted to. Some visions come as a gift, but others come on account of the laws of creation and can't be thwarted. Fermion must be such a man that his mere presence compels you to see him as he is," she offered.

"You think I see him as he is? You mean you don't think it is a … metaphor I think is the word … or something like that? How can that be as he really is?" King groped for understanding.

"Such things only make sense when you understand that there is more to reality than what we see. It is real, even if we don't see it. But you say you saw nothing of Fides?" Tasha continued to press.

"No, nothing. Should I?" he replied, perplexed.

"Maybe you should decide to allow the gift to fully work within you," Tasha concluded, signaling the end of the conversation.

King decided to think about it while carrying off and burying some of their trash and collecting more firewood. When he returned, Fermion and Fides had already arrived declaring that the road looked clear ahead of them. After eating a hefty meal to tide them over for the day, they began their ride east.

At about three in the afternoon, they saw some westbound travelers who were also on horseback. They seemed kindly enough. The two parties waved, and passed each other. About five in the afternoon they glimpsed a much larger party ahead, which was going in the same direction as they were, but on foot. Fermion stopped to consider the situation.

"Well, we know the westbound party had no troubles when they passed this group, so I think we're probably safe to pass them, too. Does anyone have any thoughts?" Fermion asked them.

"There is nothing saying that we can't break out to one side and pass them on one of the flanks," King suggested.

"We've probably only got another two hours of good light, though. By the time we catch up to them to pass them, we may very well be running out of good travel time. Maybe it would be a good idea to set up camp here and pass them in the morning," Fides threw in.

"Does it seem as though they've noticed us?" asked Tasha. "We wouldn't want them doubling back on us tonight if they are up to no good, or have some among them that aren't."

"No, I don't think they've seen us. But look—they are going to be going up that high hill. If I were them, or even when it is our turn, I'd want to see what is over that hill before I brought the full party along. I don't think we can pass them and properly scout ahead of us in the available daylight. I think perhaps we should put all of the ideas together," Fermion suggested. "Let's head out a decent distance from the road, set up camp for the night, and tomorrow morning pass them on the flank." Fermion paused. "Agree?"

Everyone agreed. Another short conversation later, they had selected a campsite about two hundred yards off the road just inside a large grove of trees. The grove had been left standing by some farmer a hundred years earlier to fight erosion, but certainly the farmer had not been aware of the service he would provide to others a century later. It did appear that others had put it to similar use as well, but it was far enough off the road that it looked as though only a few groups over the years had ever decided to come and camp there. Someone had done them the favor of building a nice fire pit, though, even to the extent of erecting stone towers on opposite sides of the pit and laying an iron rod across them to use for roasting any small animal one might find. On seeing this, King spent a little more time evaluating when the campsite had last been used to make sure it wasn't likely that its owner might return yet that night. All appearances were that it had not been used for months, though, so they immediately set to work making it their own.

King was happy that his scouting abilities were being put to good use. All three of the adults seemed to appreciate his efforts, and Fermion quickly acknowledged it.

"How about if the scout and I see where that group stopped and make sure that they aren't coming back in our direction?" Fermion suggested.

"I'm game," King beamed happily.

"I'll start some dinner. Maybe Fides can get me some firewood this time and tend to the horses?" Tasha suggested.

"Sure," Fides shrugged.

"Alright, King. Let's go," Fermion said, giving his horse a poke with his heels. This was the first time King had been alone with Fermion, and he was tempted to share with him what he had seen when Fermion had first appeared. Riding in silence, King went back and forth in his mind. He remembered the challenge that such things merely existed in his mind so he decided not to raise the matter. He was growing to like and respect Fermion and didn't want Fermion to think he was subject to hallucinations. Still, he wanted to talk about something.

"Fermion?" King began.

"Yes?"

"You know, I really don't know if I have any family left. This could be a waste of your time. Are you comfortable with that?" King asked him.

"It isn't a waste of time at all. We are going that way, anyway," Fermion comforted him.

"You know, I'm sure my mother is dead, but I don't know about my father. What do I do if I get back and find he is dead or gone?" King continued. He had really meant to address the idea of not having any family at all, but Fermion fixed upon King's example of not having his father.

"You will have to find another one, then," Fermion replied.

"What do you mean? Don't I only have one father?" King scratched his head.

"You have only one biological father, to be sure. And if he was alive and available, he would surely be preferable. Assuming, of course, the he was a man of merit. If you haven't got your biological father, however, it is too important a matter not to make up the deficit. What is at stake is not only your own wellbeing, but also the wellbeing of your children, grandchildren, and great-grandchildren," Fermion asserted.

"What do you mean?" King asked, still perplexed.

"Consider this," Fermion patiently explained, "Imagine a man who has inherited a lot of money. He mismanages it, however, so that when he dies he has nothing to leave to his own children. His children grow up not knowing anything about money management and have no money to manage themselves. So, they cannot teach their own children properly, but they teach their children some. Meanwhile, they've had a difficult life. The man's grandchildren take the lessons they've learned and the small inheritance they've received, but they still struggle to live in security and manage their money well. This all takes place because one man, one father, did not take the time to transmit good information. Presumably, in order to have received the inheritance in the first place, his own father had done well, at least in terms of making money. But in not transmitting lessons and principles, too, the cycle was broken. It will take two, three, or even four generations—or more—to recover from the broken cycle."

"I don't quite follow," King admitted.

"Well, it's an analogy. Probably a true one, but I use it to point out that there are all sorts of lessons and principles covering the whole breadth of human experience. Without a father-figure to guide you in making sound decisions, it is reasonably likely that your own sons and grandsons will suffer in various ways. If you had remained uninformed of this, they would certainly have suffered," Fermion glanced at him firmly, "but now that I have informed you, you know that you must find a way to accelerate the repair of the cycle. For yourself, yes, but also for the sake of those to come, you must learn how to walk as a man … a father, a husband, a citizen … and soon."

King thought he understood and asking Fermion to be the father-figure for him was on the tip of his tongue. However, Fermion spoke again.

"I cannot be that father-figure for you, King," Fermion informed him solemnly. "I have other tasks that I must do that I have been charged with doing. I will help you as I can while we are together, but we won't be together overly long. Besides, you do not know that your father—or your family in general—is gone."

"How did you know I was going to ask you that?" King smiled.

"You are not the only one who can See," Fermion winked at him. "But look! A riding party is coming out to meet us!"

Sure enough, there were four men riding out from the larger group who had spotted them and were now cautiously trotting in their direction. When they were close enough, Fermion gave a friendly wave, and the four relaxed slightly and drew up so that they were within a distance for comfortable conversation.

"Alo there," one greeted them. He had a wide-brimmed cowboy hat, and he looked the part. "I'm Chester. This feller to my left is my brother Felix. To his left is Samuel, and furthest down the line is Maxwell. We're out checking security and saw you again and thought we'd say hello."

"I'm Fermion, and this young man's name is King," Fermion nodded in welcome.

"You seen anything?" Felix ventured.

"One westbound group a long time ago, which I'm sure you saw as well," Fermion replied.

"Yep, we saw them. How many do you guys got? You two don't look all that fearsome, at any rate," Chester winked.

"Always more than meets the eye, don't you know? You need not fear us, though," Fermion smiled genially adding, "Only four of us, truthfully."

"We got about a hundred, but you don't have to worry about us. We're just heading for Tulsa, and we don't want any trouble with anyone," Chester assured him.

"I suppose tomorrow we'll catch up with your group, and we'll have an opportunity to chat some more," Fermion said.

"You bet. We'll save you a bit of stew even," Chester smiled. With that, the six said farewell for the evening, and Fermion and King made their way back to where Tasha and Fides already had some food waiting for them. They informed them of the meeting with Chester and Felix. After some discussion they decided that, even though the four scouts seemed good-natured, they couldn't be sure everyone in a group that size was trustworthy. With this in mind, they opted to set a watch. King volunteered to take the first one. He had a lot to think about, and he wanted to start right away.

Soon, he was alone. He watched the fire as it slowly diminished. He wrapped his blanket around him as the air grew colder and colder. He thought about his family, his missing father, his dead mother, Joan … and the very interesting assertion by Fermion that he also could See. What did that mean? What did Fermion see? In particular, when Fermion looked at him, what did he see?

As the fire finally was reduced to embers, he decided to walk around the campsite a bit. The chill breeze battered him on the cheeks. Suddenly, he was alert to something else on the breeze. He thought it was the sound of horses thundering on the plain, but it was very faint. He fell to the ground and put his ear to it, laying his palms on the soil. Yes, he felt very confident that there were horses thundering somewhere, and they were heading away from them. He perceived which direction they were going an instant before he heard the distant sound of gunshots and yelling drifting in and out of the wind.

"Get up! The other party is being attacked!" King started shouting. Fermion was on his feet before the second syllable. Tasha had raced to the horses and was leading them back when Fides had finally assembled himself. In short order and without any discussion at all, the four were on their horses racing to come to the aid of a group of travelers they scarcely knew.

They crested a small hill and saw the camp beneath them. There were a large number of fire pits belonging to the campers, and some tents were also on fire. There was plenty of light to see what awaited them inside the camp perimeter. The travelers were fighting desperately against men on horseback. Except for the dress of the riders, it was like a scene from the old west. The attackers were clearly members of some Indian tribe. There were a number of them charging back and forth through the campsite while others circled the perimeter, beating back those trying to escape.

It appeared as though the goal was full-scale slaughter. King was disgusted by the cruelty, and when Fermion let out a blood-curdling yell and descended down the hill, King was not far behind him. He laid his staff out like a spear and dismounted a very surprised aggressor. He whacked another one across the head and began working around the outside the circle, twisting, twirling, spinning, slashing, thrusting. He noticed that Tasha was on foot near him, slashing with her relatively short blade so quickly that the firelight from the camp made it appear as though dim stars were fluttering in her arms.

Meanwhile, the assaulted travelers still alive in the camp were not out of the battle; Fermion had barreled through the circling Indians to face those attackers making mayhem inside the camp itself. With their attackers' attention distracted westward, the travelers were able to see to it that some of the Indians were rapidly disabled.

A few minutes into the affair, Fides came into the area where King and Tasha were fighting off the men who previously had been trying to hem in the travelers. King also spotted Fermion darting amongst tents. Fermion's black coat fluttered behind him, and his silvery hair flashed in the light surprising many Indian riders who had not expected to meet resistance from another rider.

The attackers had probably numbered a hundred in their own right when the attack began, but the surprise entry of a counterattack of an unknown strength had thrown them into disarray. Indian

warriors were no longer pressing the attack, but kept looking over their shoulders seeking a way to regroup, or escape altogether. Within the cacophony created by cracks of gunfire, grunts, and blows, there was a steady moaning from the wounded and the dying.

The perimeter battle was a bloody scrum. By now, even King was off his horse, and the raiders were the ones now fighting as though they were cornered animals. In a very real sense, they were. King cracked a man across the jaw and heard a shrill scream behind him. King turned around to look and saw Fides rushing to save a man squirming on the ground; the man was about to be executed by an Indian raider who was straddling him. King saw Fides tackle the Indian brave and returned to his own foes.

They were nearly out of foes to fight, however. Joined by many of the travelers, King and Tasha chased off a handful of men. Fermion ran down one or two, but before long, there was no one to left to challenge. King came to where some others were standing around watching something and saw that it was Fides, who was still in mortal combat with the Indian brave he had tackled. He made a move to step in and help Fides, but Tasha laid a hand on him.

"Let the man discover his courage and the feeling of righteous indignation," Tasha commanded him. King shrugged. He watched as Fides brought the butt of his sword crashing into the Indian's jaw. The Indian fell to the ground, but after an instant, he was back on his feet with his knife.

The Indian took a step towards Fides, but froze. While King could not see Fides the way the Indian did, King could tell why he was intimidated. The campfire light cast Fides' shadow over the man, and Fides' sword glistened in the red light. There was something about Fides' stance that made it clear that he was practically daring the Indian to attack.

There was a flurry of action, and it ended with Fides still standing still and strong, but with his blade pointed right between the Indian's eyes. If the brave had not stopped himself in time, he would have impaled himself on the sword. The Indian gingerly withdrew a few steps and then, after a moment of tense consideration, he departed altogether. He sheathed his knife and disappeared into the darkness behind him.

"We must tend to the wounded," Tasha announced immediately. All those who were still in good health turned their attention to the fallen. Many of those on the ground were dead, but they found plenty who were still alive. There was a short debate about what to do with some of the injured Indians, but Tasha settled that quickly enough by coldly daring any man to try to kill one of them. One look told them that they ought to obey, but she couldn't stop them from being a little rougher than she would have insisted on. She couldn't be everywhere and do everything, after all.

Fermion was off his horse and brought his report. "A lot of them got away on horseback. I saw them checking their wounded, too, and taking some with them. I guess at least thirty riders got away. I didn't see how many got away on foot. It's too dark to give a good estimate."

"I make them to be Sioux braves," King informed them. "If I'm right, and we may find out soon enough by asking some of these, it's probably Thomas Lighter Jones. He leads a very large group of Sioux who are for reconquering. This seems farther south for them than I expected, but they move around a lot."

"We'll find out in due time, at any rate," Fermion said. He nodded approvingly towards Fides, "Fides! You put your training to good use today." Fides could only nod back in response. Fides appeared to be in a daze, and Fermion took him to the side and shared some words with him that King couldn't hear. Meanwhile, Tasha was growing impatient.

"Enough talk," Tasha snapped. "Tend to that man," she said, pointing to a wounded man nearby. Suddenly, though, a man darted forward and wrapped his arms around Fides' legs. King watched, confused as Fermion put his hand on the man's shoulder. Fermion, however, was not confused. He stood the man up and addressed him.

"Friend, this man was only doing his duty. I'm sure he would say not to think anything of it," Fermion patiently said to the man.

The man turned around to face Fermion, revealing the source of his gratitude. He had in his hands a long knife, and he was holding it by the blade. Blood was flowing out from both of his gashed hands. The man spoke, "That Indian was driving this knife into my chest, and I used all my strength to keep it from going in. I was losing strength. I owe this man my life. I—I am bound to him by blood, my own blood and future scars will serve to make the commitment real."

Fermion grew silent and stared at the man dumbfounded. Tasha approached the man and began bandaging his hands, which were badly lacerated. The man spoke again to Fides, "I will be your servant until my debt is repaid, even if it is to a violent death, or else you die of old age."

King knelt down to catch his breath while Fides protested, "I want no such thing."

"I have said it, and I am a man of my word," the man proudly protested. Fides looked to Fermion for help, but Fermion appeared to have none to offer.

"Has honor returned to this land?" Fermion asked thoughtfully. "This man offers himself to your service freely, Fides. He comes on his own free will, not coerced. Your act of instinctive courage has inspired a courageous commitment that has been missing from this planet for hundreds of years. I do not think you could release him, even if you wanted to. He is bound by his own word and will, not by yours."

"I don't know what this means," Fides said in exasperation. Fermion only smiled wearily.

"Alright then, that's settled," Tasha said bluntly, "Now help with the wounded."

The dawn brought more clarity to the scene than the night had allowed, but with the diminishing of adrenalin since the battle, people were tired, and their exhaustion brought its own confusion. The wounded had been placed into tents for care. Sioux wounded, and they had discovered that they were in fact Lighter Sioux, were also placed into tents, but were first bound. Tasha made sure that the bindings were not cruel. Some were nervous about allowing the captives to live; Tasha told them that, if they wanted an extra level of security, they could post a guard. Again seeing in her an unbending will, this is what they decided to do.

There was intense discussion among the rescued travelers about their next steps. Finally, Fermion suggested to them that they were too tired to make rational decisions; this wasn't well received. However, by about nine in the morning, with the bickering persisting yet nothing accomplished, Tasha sternly commanded everyone to speak no more about pending decisions. Instead, they worked to bury their fallen fellow travelers and some of the Lighter Sioux bodies that had not been taken away by their tribesmen. Among the dead travelers were several married couples and one whole family. The cruelty of the attack was a stench in everyone's nostrils.

While the travelers buried their dead, Fermion, Fides, and King were joined by the scouts they had met the night before, Felix and Chester, in ensuring that they were not still in danger. The five of them crested the hill and tried to track the fleeing Indians as well as they could. They ranged far and wide, succeeding only in finding the staging ground for the attack. It had been a very well planned ambush. The staging area would have been easily overlooked unless you were specifically looking for such locations, and Felix and Chester lamented that they had only looked for signs of ambush right on their route. The staging area was a good mile from the road.

However, the fleeing Indian braves did not flee to any one spot and did not seem to be anywhere in the vicinity. This was a cause for concern, as it could very well mean that they had fled to get more warriors. This could be important information to consider in deciding what to do next. They returned to the camp as people were finishing their burial duties and Tasha was distributing lunch.

Tempers flared up, while eating stew, over whether to go forward or back or, to Fermion's deep dismay, to the Pledge. Then there was the matter about what to do with the wounded Indians. Felix and Chester calmed down their fellows by telling them that everyone should get rest and sleep. Indeed, being awakened in the dark hours of the night, fighting a violent battle, and tending the gruesome cleanup in the morning had all served to exhaust people to the point of senselessness. The camp gradually became silent as people heeded the counsel of their guides. Fermion and Fides volunteered to mount a day watch and took their steeds to the top of the hill ahead of the travelers so that they could have a good view of the surrounding topography.

King sat around a campfire listening to the travelers bicker, when suddenly someone tapped him on the arm.

"Hey, I know you!" said a young man.

King saw who it was and instantly wished it had been any other person in the world. It was the young man whom he had met in Oklahoma City who had told him that his visions were all in his head. "Uh, yeah, hi. Good to see you again," King greeted him.

"Yeah, see what I mean? This is what is real. The dirt, the blood, the flesh, the violence. This stuff is real. Seeing things? That's all inside your head. You see it now, right?" the young man pressed.

"Ok, I don't know who you are or how this came up in the first place," King sighed, "but you haven't seen it. It seems too real to simply dismiss as a figment of my imagination."

"You know what they say, though?" the young man argued, "Your senses are all you've got, but it is always more reasonable to take a naturalistic explanation than anything that smacks of the supernatural. If your senses report something that appears to be supernatural, the rational conclusion is that it must only be in your head. The naturalistic explanation is always to be preferred."

"Well, I don't know about that. I can't say I've ever really thought about it like that. I don't even know what you mean by 'naturalistic,'" King mused.

"Who are you talking to, King?" Tasha said, walking over to where he was sitting.

"Well, this guy, I haven't got his name. I met him in Oklahoma City ..." King said, turning to introduce the young man. But the young man was gone.

"Who?" Tasha asked again.

Now King really thought he was losing his mind. That boy had been there as sure as anything. King looked around the rest of the camp. The young man must have left in a hurry, but even if he had gotten far enough away not to be easily spotted ... well, there weren't that many places to go in the camp.

"He was here, I tell you!" King snapped at her.

"Hey now, I believe you," Tasha defended herself.

"I'm sorry about that," King apologized. "If I find him again, I'll be sure to introduce you."

"That would be fine," she said. King barely caught a fleeting glimpse of suspicion on her face. "Why don't you have a bite to eat and then head out and relieve Fides and Fermion?"

King agreed and wolfed down the meal. Being alone seemed to be exactly what he needed. Fides and Fermion were sitting silently when he arrived. They seemed about as grateful to be relieved as King felt to have some time to himself.

He considered freshly the problem of his visions. Prior to this point, he'd had no reason to seriously doubt that he was actually seeing things that were real. Maybe the young man had a point, though. Maybe one should only trust what is seen with his own eyes, and if you see something that no one else does, the proper conclusion is that something is going wrong inside your own head. This cast the problem of whether or not to choose to receive the visions again in a new light.

Soon, his thoughts drifted towards Joan. He was closer than ever to seeing her again. Tulsa was their next destination. Fermion's counsel about his need for a father simmered in his mind and morphed into nervous thoughts about what he'd find—or not find—in Illinois.

At last, he was relieved by some of the travelers and rejoined the camp. He'd apparently missed a pretty big squabble about the ambitions of the Pledge, and Fermion was still to be seen muttering every now and then under his breath. King got a taste of the argument when he was sitting with Fermion, and Felix and Chester came over to revisit the matter.

"Now look here," Felix said. "I hear what you're saying, but surely it could be done differently. Why must it have the same results? Democracy only created a lot of rich people who were out of touch with the working man. The Pledge says that every country should mind its own business and let the working man be. And it says that every man should be a working man, and that way every man will contribute to society. And they are going to give every man a piece of his own land, and not let people become too rich or too powerful. They say that if they can implement this plan throughout the whole world, the whole world can have peace."

"But someone has to decide how rich is too rich and how powerful is too powerful," Fermion pointed out. "Surely, it's obvious that a person who says to another that they are too powerful must have enough power to impose their judgment against the other, so that there will always be some who are powerful?"

"But if those people are acting in the best interests of everyone, we won't need to worry about that," Felix retorted.

"And how are you to know they are acting in the best interests of everyone?" parried Chester. "What Fermion is arguing is that even if everything starts out with the best intentions, eventually you get people who just want to exploit their position. If there aren't checks and balances, then it's too late!"

Felix eyed his brother, "Look, I respect you Chester; a ton. A ton I say. But if democracy was so good, how did we end up like this?"

"Because people forgot why they needed the democracy in the first place, that's why," Fermion declared.

"Alright, what about what they're doing down in Texas right now. What about that?" Felix jabbed, his own Texas drawl unmistakable.

"Well, what is that?" Fermion wanted to know. King remembered the Texans who came to speak at the Cherokee council. He wondered what Fermion would have said had he been there to hear the Texan delegation talk then.

"Well, they've established the New Republic of Texas, and there's lots of talk of setting it up under the law of God himself," Felix answered. Fermion put his head in his hands.

"What?" Chester inquired.

"I'd have to hear more, but that sounds like a recipe for disaster, too," Fermion explained.

"You seem like a man of God. What's your objection?" Chester pressed him.

"Like I said, I'd have to hear more. Just what do they mean when they say that, for example. Tell me this: Is there a person pushing for that? One person in particular?" Fermion asked him.

"I don't rightly know," Felix scratched his head.

"Sure you do. Don't you remember?" Chester poked his brother, "Reverend White. Remember?"

"Oh sure," Felix recalled, recognizing the name.

"Well, with the state of things, it's important that every man's conscience be allowed to determine the will of God to the best of his ability," Fermion stated. "That is a check against tyranny of a different sort. There is no escaping the necessity of building certain moral principles into the fabric of society. Yet these should never be adopted by dogmatic declaration of a single person or a small controlling party. If they've got a republic down there, an honest to goodness republic, hopefully they're up to the task and will use wisdom."

The discussion lapsed into a lull for a few moments with everyone pondering his own concerns. Fermion seemed struck with a thought.

"When war breaks out between the tyranny and freedom, will the New Republic of Texas come to the aid of fellow freedom-lovers, or will the Texans stay home?" Fermion asked Felix and Chester.

"A lot of folks are going around talking about not being involved in foreign wars or entangling treaties," Chester informed him.

"I suppose that means that, having fashioned their own country, the rest of the formerly united states are a foreign land to them now?" Fermion growled.

"There are the folks who say that. Others don't, though," Felix comforted him.

"What do you say? Would you come? Would you ride into the north to rescue strangers from the Pledge?" Fermion replied grimfaced.

"Now there you go again," Felix complained. "The Pledge ain't gonna be attacking no one."

"We'll see," Fermion frowned. Felix wasn't ready to leave Fermion's insinuations against the Pledge go unanswered. He stirred the fire a bit, sat down, and mounted a defense.

"The basic idea behind the Pledge is that all we've got is the brotherhood of man. There isn't anyone to help us if we aren't going to help ourselves. If something is going to be done it is we that will do it. They ain't going to wait for kings or presidents or priests or holy books to solve what ails us," Felix asserted.

"It is interesting that you have suggested that Mankind has to pull itself up by its own bootstraps and not wait for kings or priests and the like. Haven't you noticed that kings, priests, and presidents are part of Mankind?" Fermion countered.

"That's different," Felix argued.

"Oh, I see," said Fermion, "By Mankind you didn't mean Mankind but rather certain elements within Mankind."

"Sure, I suppose."

"Then we're back to the small controlling minority, aren't we? Someone has to decide what is best for the rest of humanity. Let's at least be honest about the matter. You don't actually believe in this propaganda that 'Mankind must do it or it won't be done.' What you really buy into is what the Pledge thinks must be done," Fermion said.

"Alright, maybe it is like that. Still, the fact is that all of the best things for humanity have been done because of the amazingly ambitious and talented humans that kept pursuing truth. Every time someone said something couldn't be done men went out and figured out a way to do it. Fine, it is just a portion of men doing the important work. A great many other men opposed them. My point though is that Man's only hope is Man Himself," Felix explained.

"So you don't see any room in this equation for God?" Fermion probed.

"My brother doesn't really go in for that," Chester said.

"That's right," Felix agreed, "God isn't going to help us either. Probably because he doesn't exist—or, even if he exists because he certainly wouldn't care."

"What makes you think he wouldn't care?" Fermion wondered.

"We are so small and insignificant. Specks of the universe. Why should a powerful entity like God care about us?" Felix asked.

"It seems to me like the best way you could learn a reason is if God himself told you," Fermion suggested.

"That's why I said he probably doesn't exist. As far as I know he hasn't made himself evident."

"You dismissed 'holy books' a little earlier as though you knew already that they were actually the works of men. What if within one or some of these books God actually shares this information?" Fermion asked.

"Why would he bother with a book?" Felix laughed.

"You seem to know an awful lot about how a God would act," Fermion smiled, bemused. "Exactly where did you gain such extensive knowledge about how an entity you don't think actually exists would act if he really did exist?"

King thought this was a very good question. It stumped him, at least, but Felix seemed oblivious to the significance of the point. Instead, Felix focused on one of the more incidental elements of Fermion's argument.

"Obviously there are better ways to communicate," Felix answered.

"Ah, so you know the mind of an all knowing God so well as to know what all the available options were and which were the best? And you know exactly what God wanted to achieve! For of course one chooses a medium consistent with one's aims. You know so well all of God's aims as well as all of his available choices for communication. Are you sure you don't believe in an all knowing God?" Fermion smirked.

"Of course I don't, that's what I've been saying," Felix said and did not smile back.

"No, you *do* believe in an all knowing God: his name, we can now reveal, is Felix! It is Felix that knows what an all knowing God would care about and how he would communicate!" Fermion laughed.

Felix wasn't enjoying the joke. He snapped, "No one denies that the Bible was written by men."

Fermion smiled, "No one has yet mentioned the name of any of these 'holy books.' I'm glad that we have learned what was in the back of your mind. Since you yourself have named one of these 'holy books,' then let's ask ourselves: Does this book give any evidence that God cares about humanity? I'd say even if you had never read it—and so few have these days—you already know the answer. The whole point of the book is that God did care. You say he wouldn't care. Who are you to judge such a thing? If God said he cared and took action to prove it, who are you to judge? Just because you—

being all knowing and all—would have done it differently, does this mean that the whole thing was invented by men?"

"It is possible that I overstated my case," Felix admitted, quite reluctantly. "Still, there has been no word since. I don't know what you would have us do while we wait."

"Well, you mentioned that all these great things have been done by men. I would remind you that a lot of terrible things have been done by men as well. The Pledge is not the first to remove God from the equation and put their hope in their own efforts and superior vision for humanity. If you had a more balanced recollection of human history you would know that putting one's hope in the wiles of men hasn't always been such a great idea," Fermion said, the tone of his voice indicating that they were reaching the conclusion of the discussion.

"I suppose we all must make our own decision," Felix said irritably, as though trying to score a final unassailable point.

"It is funny that you mention that. It is God, whom you lambaste for being silent, who allows you that right. The Pledge, if it is anything like its forerunners, does not trust people to make their own decisions, and if history is any guide, one of the first things they'll deprive you of is this thing you lay out as your excuse for not dealing with the relevant aspects of my argument," Fermion countered firmly.

"Maybe they'll be different, like I said," Felix replied.

But Fermion just laughed, though King detected some sadness in it. After this, the conversation drew to a close. Felix left riled up, and Chester departed with a thoughtful look on his face.

That night, Fides, Fermion, King, Tasha, and now Jonathan, the man Fides had saved, discussed together whether they would stay with the travelers or not. It was quickly decided that they certainly would not accompany them if they decided to return to Oklahoma City, and clearly, going to Henryetta as some of the travelers wanted to do was inconsistent with their own destination of Bloomington, Illinois. Henryetta was on the Pledge's announced path back to Arkansas.

This point was a little more difficult because they could be in Tulsa as early as the next day if they traveled alone, but with the group, it could take as long as a full week. It also seemed difficult to imagine how they would be able to realistically serve any practical purpose if they came under attack again. Fermion pointed out that the Indians were not likely to make the same mistake twice and would come with significant force. King, who of all of them felt the most strongly that they should escort the group, argued that it was unlikely that the Indians knew the strength of those who had come to the travelers' rescue.

"We aren't far from the Cherokee nation, either," King argued. "The Lighter Sioux would be fools to try to strike us again knowing that Cherokee scouts are likely to spot them."

Fides shook his head, "I'm with Fermion. The bandits are here to make trouble, and the only difference the next time is that they'll make certain there is no help for us."

"I just don't like leaving the group to fend for itself," King relented.

"None of us do, King," Fermion counseled him. "We'll be more help if we head to Tulsa directly and send help back. Let's hope that Chester and Felix can abide our decision."

In the end the matter was settled for them. The next morning, Chester and Felix broke the news that they too had been in deep discussion about what to do and had made their own decisions. Led by Felix, many of the travelers, sympathetic to the Pledge, thought their best course of action was to link up with the Pledge delegation that they anticipated would be passing to their south. Fermion abided this wordlessly.

Chester, on the other hand would go on to Tulsa with a smaller number of people, most of whom were violently opposed to the Pledge. After some negotiation, horses were traded for provisions. Arrangements were made for the captured Indians. King grew impatient with how long the process was taking; it annoyed him to think that each minute standing around talking was one minute keeping him from arriving in Tulsa.

Finally, joined by Chester and his handful of travelers, King and his friends departed, hoping to arrive in Tulsa sometime the next day. The two groups soon disappeared from each other's sight.

The riders made good time that day and experienced no incidents. Indeed, that night when they made camp they thought they could see the glow of Tulsa in the distance. They set a guard, but the night passed without event. Late in the afternoon of the next day, the city limits of Tulsa greeted them.

Like Oklahoma City, there was a ring of defenses set around the city. Here, however, little scrutiny was given to visitors, and they entered the town unchallenged. Chester, along with the other travelers who had joined him, bade them farewell. As for King and his companions, they set up camp with the intention of finding the Cherokee in Tulsa, who would help them make arrangements with Chummy to take vehicles east.

King didn't know what everyone else was thinking as night fell and sleep came, but his concern for the travelers they'd assisted a few nights ago was completely gone. In its place was the burning desire to see Joan again mixed together with a blend of agony and expectation from knowing that she was so, so close, while knowing he would have to wait at least one more night.

# == Chapter 10 ==

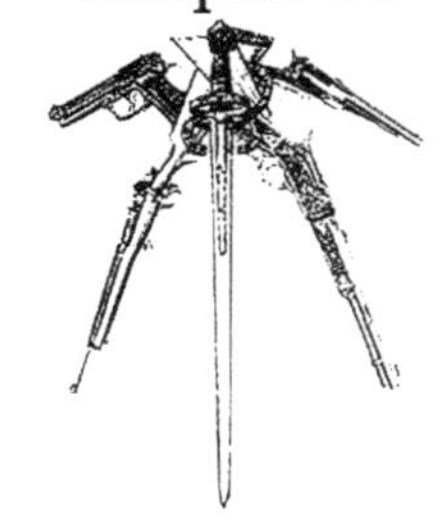

In the morning, King was out of bed before anyone else. He lit the fire, boiled the water, and began frying potatoes before even Tasha was up. He knew that the rest would insist on waiting until they had had a proper breakfast before venturing into the city, so he wanted to remove that delay early and quickly.

When they finally were packed and ready to enter the city, King had to bite his tongue: Fides requested to check out the town a little before finding the Cherokee residences. Tasha smirked, but no one else showed any realization that King was simply stewing in anticipation. As King followed his companions along already familiar streets, he clenched his teeth and said nothing.

About mid-morning, the decision was made to finally go to the Cherokee section of Tulsa. Tulsa was a clean, open city, but the Cherokees had erected two fences around their neighborhood. Both fences were tall and despite the general tranquility of the city, there were still guards patrolling the fences, both inside and out, and guard shacks were interspersed along the fence line. All this was more notable to Fermion and Fides than it was to King and Tasha, who were familiar with the security measures.

King and Tasha were welcomed immediately at the gate by a large number of people. They had met some friends in one of the markets, and the friends had returned to spread the word of their arrival. King only had eyes for one person, however. At last, he spotted her.

Joan was surrounded by a gaggle of other girls, some younger and some older, who rushed over to meet them. Many of the girls took to the horses, leaving Joan alone, if only for a moment.

"What took you so long?" Joan said softly and coyly, with a slight smile turning her lips. She brushed her long, black hair away from her eyes. King couldn't help remembering the time when Joan hadn't cared about her hair at all. Today, she cared, and the effect was noticeable.

"Been busy and all," King blushed red, "On official delegations and such, you see."

"Very important, are ya?" Joan winked.

"Getting there!" King joked. Now, though, other girls had surrounded them, some of them openly vying for King's attention. Joan slipped away, giving a fleeting glance behind her, which King of course was waiting for.

"Friends!" declared an old, familiar voice. It was Philip. "Please, come in, come in, come in. Girls, please. *Please*," he implored them to give them room to breathe.

"This is the head of the Cherokee council," Tasha explained. "His name is Philip. Philip, these are our friends and companions, Fermion, Fides, Jonathan, and King of course you know."

"Very fine. Please, come in. Follow me and we'll arrange for a nice lunch," Philip beckoned them. He led them past a shed and into Philip's house where they were offered water. Some other members of the Cherokee council were sitting with them, too.

Settled in at last, Tasha produced a piece of paper, and pushed it over to Philip, who appeared to be expecting it.

"Chief Ramaen has asked that you provide the funds to allow myself, King, Fermion, and Fides to travel using Chummy's transportation services," Tasha explained. "Jonathan is new to our party, but we trust him, and hope that you can allow for him as well." Philip examined the document that Tasha had provided him, nodding approvingly.

"Absolutely. No question. This document authorizes funding for as far as Chummy is willing to take you. I am not quite sure what that means," Philip replied quizzically.

"We have heard that in Bloomington, Illinois, a registry is being created allowing divided families to attempt to find one another and reunite," Tasha explained. "I myself have no family in that region, but King might, as well as our new friend, Fides. What Chief Ramaen is authorizing is a payment to Chummy sufficient even to pay for motor travel as far as Bloomington, if Chummy is willing to go that far."

"That is very far. If Chummy were willing to provide such transport, it would certainly cost a great deal," Philip replied. There was nothing in his tone of voice to indicate that he was displeased with the idea, but it was clear that he was skeptical that Chummy would be willing to do such a thing.

"Right now," Mary explained, "Chummy runs Tulsa as a hub, serving Wichita, Kansas City, Springfield, and Little Rock. There is no doubt he would take you to Springfield, of course."

Bill, one of the members of the Tulsa Cherokee council, spoke up: "I have traveled to Illinois before. And I mean long before. It was well before the Disease and before the nuclear attacks. I know where Bloomington is, and I know that the most direct route would be through St. Louis. As that is not possible, they would have to go to

Cairo, first, and then many miles north."

"Why is it not possible to go through St. Louis?" Fides wondered.

"It was one of the cities destroyed by nuclear attack," Philip grumbled sadly.

"So," concluded Mary, "Chummy would have to go to Springfield as normal, then to Cairo, and then to Bloomington. As I understand it, that is altogether three times longer than his normal run to Springfield, and he will of course want to be compensated for his trip back."

"We can only know if he's willing to do it by asking. The question is whether or not we have anything to offer him that'd he'd take as payment," Bill mused.

Philip explained some of the considerations that were involved. As they lived in Tulsa, they had many opportunities to deal with Chummy. Much of this was old news to King, but he listened as Philip described Chummy. He was a tall, pudgy man. Apparently, he had been an engineer at one time, but before that he had grown up on the farm. Adjoining that farm, owned by him and his father (now deceased) was an old junk yard filled with all sorts of ancient vehicles. Chummy's skill as a mechanic proved to be very profitable for him, which was good, because by all appearances, Chummy enjoyed profit.

He had brought a number of vehicles into working order and had somehow managed to procure enough fuel to keep his fleet in action. The source of his fuel was unknown. In exchange for motor transportation, people were willing to give over many of their valuable items. People got tired of walking from place to place, and as times were getting more and more dangerous, the sooner they were at their destination, the better. Chummy was not likely to give them transport to Bloomington out of the goodness of his heart. A trip of that distance would require far more than just room for passengers and their gear. It would require additional vehicles and therefore more drivers to bring the fuel with them sufficient for the round trip. Chummy would also want to send along some of his security forces to protect his assets. All in all, they'd have to provide a great deal of incentive to persuade Chummy to make such a trip.

For a time they sat in silence, and King noted that Fides was fidgeting somewhat uncomfortably. He wondered if he had the same question, so King asked, "It seems that there is something being left out. Isn't it easy enough to ask him what it would take, and then see if it is available?"

Philip nodded towards Fides and Fermion, "I apologize for our discomfort in this matter. It is not meant to be rude. The problem is that we already know what Chummy will want, and we are not so sure ..."

Tasha seemed to grasp the concern immediately, "I assure you that

Fides and Fermion are completely trustworthy. In fact," she continued, "I give you my word that you can speak of anything in front of them that you could say in front of me and King."

Tasha told them all about the mighty battle they had had with members of the Lighter Sioux and, in particular, Fermion's and Fides' conduct in the battle. Convincing them that Jonathan was likewise trustworthy was much more of a challenge, but when the circumstances were explained and Fermion vouched for him, Philip finally acquiesced. At that point, naturally, the men in the room wanted to see their weapons.

As they marveled at the fine swords, Philip suddenly gasped in recognition of some fact. He smiled slyly, "I do believe that we received word of your battle, actually."

"Oh?" Tasha cocked her head.

"Well, things begin to make sense!" Philip declared, glancing back and forth between Bill and Mary and other council members present.

"What though?" Tasha persisted.

"Never mind that. Let us simply consider the matter settled that you can be trusted. In fact, now it seems plain that we have something to show you," Philip explained as the council members nodded in agreement. "We need to take a trip to the shed."

Philip led the way to the shed. A young man sitting outside the shed smiled at them, and King realized that this particular shed always seemed to have a young man sitting outside it. In they went. For all intents and purposes, the shed appeared to be nothing more than a normal machine shed. There were all sorts of shelves filled with supplies or assorted machine parts. In the corner, there was what appeared to be a little office. A large metal contraption was in the middle of the shed. They paused around it and talked about it very briefly, almost as though it were part of an act.

After pointing out several features of the machine, Philip led the way to the office. He opened the door to the office, moved a cabinet that was on tiny coasters, and revealed a staircase descending into blackness. He gave a nod, and they all followed him down into the dark. There was the sound of fumbling, and then the sound of a switch being thrown. They were suddenly immersed in electric light.

Before their eyes was revealed rack upon rack of military issue weaponry. There had to be hundreds of guns and boxes and boxes of ammunition. Besides this, there appeared to be all sorts of military supplies stacked around as well.

"This," Philip explained, "is what Chummy will want in compensation."

"But does he know you have such weapons?" King asked, in awe of the sight.

"Chummy and his family grew up in this area," Bill said. "His family and our families all know one another very well. These weapons came here on his trucks a decade or more ago. Though we made a great effort to make sure that they were not seen, that very effort fueled his suspicions. On occasion, he has subtly suggested payment in arms for transport when we have asked for it, and naturally, we laughed as though he were joking. He has been satisfied with normal payments of goods prior to this. But there is no doubt that if we seek transport as far as Bloomington, he will want weapons as payment."

"In all the times we visited here, we never knew of such things," Tasha said. "What are they all for?"

"I can tell you a couple of reasons. Obviously, with attempts by foreign authorities to fully disarm the citizens of this country, we realized we had to retain arms. They were to be used only when it would seem as though it would make a difference. Now they remain here in Tulsa for several important strategic reasons. For one thing, in event of a need to muster an army, we know that we can, at last resort, use these weapons to purchase Chummy's entire fleet—or even commandeer it, if necessary. For another, we can make use of Chummy's vehicles to rally quickly and deploy quickly, too. In the event of any kind of invading force trying to commandeer Chummy's fleet—something that is a real threat—we also will want to be able to repel that force. If an army gained Chummy's fleet, they would have a real strategic advantage," Philip said, laying the situation out for them.

He continued, "We know that many of Chummy's drivers at least have handguns. Now, the Pledge is based out of Little Rock, and Chummy provides transportation to Little Rock. So, we know that the Pledge is aware of this strategic asset not too far away from them. The Pledge is not likely to be deterred by a few armed drivers. Chummy, we think, is well aware of the threat. We think, too, that the Pledge knows that we have so many Cherokee here in Tulsa for the specific purpose of protecting Chummy and his fleet. However, if the Pledge knew that there were military weapons floating around Tulsa, rather than be deterred, it'd find the temptation overwhelming. Naturally, we have enough guns to repel it, but we would not by any means have enough men to hold those guns."

"What strength do you make the Pledge out to be?" Fermion inquired.

"It has at least five thousand warriors, according to our spies," Philip replied gravely. "Come, let us go. We don't like to talk about these weapons in our houses, even with the security we have. Now you know. We have put great confidence in you and your ability to preserve our secret." Philip led the way up the stairs. Once they were all out, he moved the cabinet back into place. Once again, they congregated around the machine in the middle of the shed, and Philip said, "If anyone asks you what you did in this shed, you tell them about this nifty machine that I am so proud of!"

Once back at the house, they found themselves again in the dining room, where Mary served them a fine breakfast. King ate quickly. He wasn't very hungry. He kept getting up to go to the window. Finally, he saw what he was looking for. Joan was making her way across the yard!

"Uh, I'll see you all later," King announced to the group. They were all in deep discussion and hardly noticed his leaving. He slipped out of the house, and he and Joan quickly escaped the compound. In short order, they were walking hand in hand through the streets of Tulsa.

All that day, the two roamed the city talking quietly and keeping to themselves. In King's mind, Joan had matured much more into a woman than she had been even a few months ago. King thought, possibly, she perceived that he was more of a man today than she had remembered, too. Such perceptions were not the subject of their conversation, of course. They talked about useless things, but King pondered the deeper matters he thought might be true that were right below the surface.

Finally, late in the evening, they walked back to the compound. Joan slipped a kiss on his burning cheek in the shadows of one of the houses, and they departed.

When King woke up in the morning, he learned that a very big decision had been made in his absence. A significant offer was going to be made to Chummy to try to persuade him to take them all the way to Bloomington. It was decided that the meeting would be the next day, and King was quick to see the opening. As quickly as he could, he slipped away to Joan's house. She saw him from a distance, and before long, they rejoined the streets of Tulsa.

They wandered to and fro; as evening took hold, they found a secluded clearing in a park. They sat down and gazed at each other wordlessly.

"Do you want to marry me?" Joan asked him at last.

"You know I do," King confessed.

"So why don't you ask me?" she wanted to know.

"I—I need to settle some things. I need to make this trip and get whatever I find squared away. Then I'll be back, and I'll ask you. I promise," King explained, half-heartedly wondering if he wanted to go through with the journey.

"Great! I'm looking forward to it," she smiled. She put her arms around his neck and kissed him with a single, passionate kiss. He instinctively pulled her close, and then in a panic over the new situation and the potential it harbored, he leapt up. Joan watched with mirth as he danced around the little clearing.

"Wow, ok. That's something I'm going to have to think about!" he declared.

"You can think about it all the way to Bloomington and keep it as a reminder for why you want to come back," she laughed.

"That's a memory that will endure, no doubt about that! You didn't have to worry, but this cinches it for sure!" King babbled.

With darkness on its way, they decided they needed to return to the safety of the Cherokee compound. When they arrived, they sat in the swinging chair that was on her parent's porch until, finally, he couldn't keep his eyes open. She gave him a peck on the cheek, and he went back to Philip and Mary's house and fell fast asleep.

It wasn't until late in the morning that King rolled out of bed. As usual, he had missed a lot. They were expecting him to join them in the conversation with Chummy, and he had clean forgotten about it. Chummy was the last thing on his mind. Around lunchtime, the five of them, accompanied by Philip, made their way to the eastern edge of Tulsa.

Though the rest of Tulsa hardly compared with the tranquility of the Cherokee complex, those outside the complex appeared to have a very good life. Philip explained to Fermion, Fides, and Jonathan that, ultimately, everyone benefited from Chummy's success. Chummy had so much wealth—and wealth was not merely measured in pieces of paper and coin anymore—that problems of proper storage arose. He couldn't help but share liberally with the rest of Tulsa's inhabitants.

The negotiation with Chummy went on for a time, and King found it impossible to concentrate. He paid attention well enough to notice Chummy calling the Cherokee bluff about not having guns. For the most part, King stared dumbly throughout the conversation, his mind on Joan and nothing but Joan. The meeting ended without a clear resolution. Chummy would consider the offer and send word on his decision.

They would not have to wait long.

The six had barely arrived back at Philip's house when a young man from the complex's guard shack informed them that a messenger had come on behalf of Chummy. Chummy was on his way, personally, and asked if they would please remain at Philip's residence. Philip accepted the message and told the guard to send Bill to him immediately. They were settling in when Bill arrived, and he and Phillip had a private conversation.

"I suspect that they are going to have a few more guards on hand and send out some spies to make sure Chummy is not coming in force," Fermion remarked. He was probably close to the truth; Bill hastily left the residence, and Philip returned to them looking slightly perplexed.

But Chummy came alone. He was escorted to Philip's residence and came into the living room, where everyone, including Mary and Bill, was relaxing with some hot coffee.

"Look," he began, "Philip, you and I go ways back. Our families have known each other for at least a hundred years, and our fathers went together to the war in the south and shared the same fate. Through thick and thin, that's us. Right?" Philip nodded to Chummy, who continued, "Alright, I know that you have ..."

"We don't say the words, even here," Philip interrupted.

"Alright, well you know what I'm talking about," Chummy continued. "But we can bet that the Pledge has got its hands on some, too, and besides, if you've got them, we can be sure other Indian tribes have them, too—there certainly have been enough murders out in the wild to prove that—and you know that all of my vehicles would be very tempting for any of them. My workers report more and more problems. It's only a matter of time, I think, before they come here to take over my operations. I understand that they would be here sooner than later if they also knew ... Well, you know ... so you won't let me have any. Fine, I get that. Here is the deal I will offer you."

He stopped for a minute to enjoy a drink from a tall glass of water that Tasha brought him. He wiped his mouth on his oversized coat sleeve, and continued. "I'll agree to have some of my men take these five as far as Bloomington. I would say that I'd decline Bill's land altogether, but I think those men who take you will need something like that for compensation. So, it'd be for them, really. I hope you understand."

"Well, I was already prepared to let it go, Chummy, so it's all the same to me," Bill replied.

"You know, Chummy, I should at least ask you whether or not you might be willing to sell the vehicles and fuel," Philip joined in.

"Oh no, that's out of the question unless, you know, we really had the type of transaction that I desire in mind. I need all my vehicles. I've assembled all the intact vehicles I can. I've only got enough extra to serve Oklahoma City, if I could ever secure the route," Chummy countered.

"Well, it was worth asking," Philip said.

"No problem," Chummy said, brushing aside any notion he was offended. "So, here is what I'm going to ask. I'll send the men and vehicles out with you in exchange for that parcel, but also for your assurance that if there is an attempt on me and my fleet, you will help defend us, even if it means bringing out your treasure." Now that it was out on the table, Chummy was quiet. He had nothing more to add.

There was quite a pause after that, which King hardly noticed lost in his own thoughts as he was.

"Of course we will have to consider this offer of yours. It is a very modest proposal compared to what it could have been, but as you are asking us and the rest of the tribe to possibly die for you and your business operations—and of course, the people who help you—I cannot make such a decision without first clearing it with the Cherokee Council. But I will not hesitate in calling a meeting of the council. In fact, I will call a meeting as soon as you leave, and I will send word to you no later than supper time tonight about our decision," Philip countered.

"I understand. Incidentally, when would you like to depart?" Chummy asked. King's interest was suddenly roused.

"Fermion?" Philip redirected the question to him.

"We want to go as soon as possible, but recognizing the preparations that might be involved on your end, I would say we could allow at least two days," Fermion pondered aloud.

"I think we can probably do it in one day. Would that work?" Chummy replied. King was disappointed. Two days? Only two more days with Joan, and then they'd have to part again? However, Fermion nodded his assent, and Chummy left to make the preparations.

After he was well out of sight, Philip smiled and said, "Well! Who would have thought we'd get something more out of our willingness to protect that man?" Everyone agreed, and general conversation followed, but finally, people dismissed themselves from the company. Wanting to make good use of every available minute, King quickly went over to Joan's house.

Again, the two of them took to the city. This time, however, King caught her father's gaze as they left, and King felt a bit of anxiety. King and Joan spent that day together, and then the next. Finally, the moment of parting was determined to be the following morning. The Cherokee community threw a huge feast in honor of their trip, and the two of them felt obliged to be there, though they wanted nothing else but to be alone. King made sure he was packed and promised her they would manage to sneak some alone time in.

The feast was a glorious affair. Fermion surprised them all by dancing some of the ritual dances. Many of the tribe decided that although, Fermion had denied being an Indian, he must surely have some good blood in him at any rate. That's the way they put it to one another. King watched Fermion dancing and cheered along with everyone else. Tasha sidled up to him.

"So, King. You decide to join us," Tasha poked him.

King blushed, "Not entirely a free decision or one without a price."

"I suppose in some respects all decisions are like that," she smiled.

Joan came over and looked questioningly at Tasha.

Tasha laughed, "Go on! I'll talk to him later!"

Joan led King away by the hand just as some other girls began walking in King's direction. King had already been forced to dance with some of them, and Joan wasn't about to let it happen again.

The feasting and the dancing went on into the night. After a time, people began telling stories around the fire, and King and Joan slipped away. They found themselves at her house. They checked carefully to see that they were alone. By all appearances, her family was at the feast. With the lights off, they sat very close on the couch.

"I'm going to miss you," she murmured after a time.

"It hurts already," King admitted. She lay down and pulled him on top of her, kissing him. This time, he was ready for the situation. He ran his fingers through her hair and caressed her cheek. All the while their lips were tightly locked. There was no Tulsa, no feast, no house: the universe existed only for them.

And then the light flicked on.

"Excuse me," Joan's father, Bardia, said sternly. King was so startled he fell off the couch with a bang. Joan sat up abruptly, and King bounced himself off the floor and discovered he was now sitting in the recliner. Nobody said another word.

Bardia was a man whom King had met off and on. He was a Cherokee warrior who was often out on patrols. He had always spoken kindly to King, but as King's affection for his daughter had increased over the last couple of years he had also withdrawn slightly. King didn't know what he was thinking, and didn't know what he should say.

"I'm sorry, I'll go ..." King began.

"No, wait," Bardia commanded. Then he pointed to Joan and said, "Go to the camp fire. King will join you there."

Obediently, Joan straightened up her clothes and hastened out the door and into the dark in the direction of the feast. King waited for the hammer to fall.

Bardia sized him up, staring steadily at him. At last, he addressed him, "This is my daughter, you realize. She is not yet eighteen and without a doubt, neither are you. I would like to know where you two think you were heading."

"I hadn't really thought about it," King admitted, his head hung low.

"A truer thing you probably have never said," Bardia told him. "That's usually the problem. In centuries past, and certainly in many places still today, it is said that emotion cannot be controlled—that we are slaves to our feelings. On that view, no matter how we acted we were justified so long as it was done in obedience to our emotions. It is not so. Bad decisions are always crouching at the door. We all must master our impulses, or we shall be mastered by them. Do you understand?"

"Yes," King said in a humble undertone, "I do, and I'm very sorry."

"Do not be dismayed, King," Bardia assured him. "I still hold you in very high esteem. I respect you. You have done great things for the Cherokee, and I know that you will do great things for Joan, if she becomes your wife." King looked up at that, and Bardia continued, "Yes, I would approve of your marriage. I don't disapprove of your desires, King, only I am concerned that you hadn't yet considered the most proper context for their manifestation. Do you understand?"

"You lost me," King acknowledged.

"A fire belongs in a fire pit. Fire is not bad. But if you play with fire, if you let it get out of control, if you let it past the stones, you risk being burned or burning someone else, or destroying property. Fire is good, but in order for it to be of best use and not hurt anyone, it must be kept in its proper context: the fire pit. Do you see?" Bardia explained patiently.

"Yes, I do now. I am very sorry," King repeated.

"As they say, it takes two to tango," Bardia smiled. "I will address these issues with Joan, too, but not until you're gone. Let me explain just one more thing."

"Ok," King acquiesced.

"There are worse things than death and there are greater things than a moment's passion," Bardia began. "The greater things always include the smaller, but still good, things. Do you know that marriage is preparation and it is training? In the family, one learns how to love others and be good to others, but it is not the case that this is meant only to be useful for the family. If you cannot be good to the ones you love, you will find it difficult to be good to the ones you don't love. Do you see?"

"I'm not sure … I think so," King replied.

"When you learn how to be good to the people you live with you also learn how to be good to the people around you, in the community or what not. So, a good marriage in a community filled with other good marriages is good for the community. I'm not saying that marriage is simply a tool for the government to create certain kinds of people—namely, whatever kind of person the government decides to create," Bardia clarified parenthetically.

"No, being married is a good thing in itself. The security it offers to the father and mother and to the children is a good thing. But a marriage out of control can hurt people: present and future. It is not only about the husband and the wife, but also about their children and grandchildren, and their children. Even as you must be careful when you make a fire, you must be careful when you make a marriage," Bardia continued. "I say these things because I know that you have never had a father to tell you. Chief Thunderfist and Ramaen and others could not provide it. We have all known this. I am sharing this with you because I am *Joan's* father. I cannot be *your* father. King: you must find your father, or find a man who will be as one for you. It is important that you design your fire pit well, and your father is the one to teach you."

"What if my father is dead?" King asked, tears welling up in his eyes.

"Then it is as I said, you must find a man who will be your father. And if you can find no man, seek the transcendental. A good man would have directed you there, anyway," Bardia said compassionately.

"What if I cannot find one?" King cried out, nearly weeping.

"You see, King, waiting for the conditions to be right to marry my daughter is living a life of hope. You live today in a certain manner, knowing that after a certain time things will be right. The control that allows you not to despair when I merely insist you wait in regards to my daughter's body is the same one which allows you to overcome your fear and doubts about the future and trust that what you need will be provided, *when the time is ripe*," Bardia explained.

Then, more thoughtfully, he added, "Yes, and realize that it is sometimes the case that the need is never satisfied. Yet, the person who lives in the sure hope that it will be provided is a different man than the one who despairs of it ever coming to pass. I want you to be a man of hope, King. So, look expectantly to the future fulfillment of your desires—all of them—but do not accept a crusty morsel today in exchange for a glorious feast tomorrow out of fear that the feast will never come, that there may be nothing beyond the morsel. Do you understand these words?"

"I gather that you think I ought not to be afraid that I won't find my father, but live hoping I will find him. Also, I think you're saying that just because I am afraid I might die on this journey I am getting ready to go on, I shouldn't grasp for a momentary pleasure with your daughter, but rather wait for better times to come," King said slowly, thinking it through.

"Yes, all that and more," Bardia said. "Do you think it is a coincidence that Ramaen gave permission to pay Chummy for a ride all the way to Indiana? Do you think it is a coincidence that Philip felt compelled to show you and your friends our arsenal? Do you not see?"

King jerked his eyes to meet Bardia's. "What do you mean?" King demanded to know.

"You know exactly what I mean," Bardia countered. "Some

things have been seen, and so, preparations have been made. Some things Chief Thunderfist would have liked to have seen, but he cannot. You, however, could, if you so desired. I am given this message to give to you, King, from Chief Thunderfist: be a man of hope, even unto death."

"Chief Thunderfist has seen that I die ...?" King stammered.

"No, you don't understand. You see, a man of hope and a man of despair will both die. But how they live their life will be utterly different: the man of despair is dead as he walks. Just be certain that you place your hope in things that are worthy of it," Bardia encouraged him.

"Mr. Ehrk ..."

"Call me Bardia."

"Bardia, I do not deny that I was improper with your daughter, but I really don't think we were going to do what you think we were going to do," King offered gingerly. King had been thinking about it, and he simply didn't see it happening.

"Oh, that is probably the case," Bardia smiled. "On the other hand, we sometimes end things differently than we thought we would when we began them. What you need to understand is that this moment was Seen. It was appointed as an opportunity to explain these things to you." At this, Bardia's smile faded, his face turned grave, and he continued, "It is the last opportunity we have to try to explain to you why you must choose to See. More hangs in the balance than you know."

"I don't understand," King shook his head.

"No, I suspect you don't. But you must trust that Chief Thunderfist would not lie to you. If you trust him, you may hope that you will come to understand. Now, enough of all this. Go to my daughter and say your farewells," Bardia said, taking King by the arm and guiding him to the door.

King walked slowly away from the house. It was one of the most perplexing conversations he'd ever experienced. He knew, without knowing how or why, that there was something much more to it. When he met Joan around the fire, she was surprised to see him. He came along side her and kissed her gently on the cheek. There was nothing to say.

Knowing that he would have to get up early to begin his journey, after only a few minutes he walked her back to her house. He didn't feel like talking, and he was feeling somewhat humiliated, too. He kissed Joan again on the cheek, went back to Philip and Mary's, and went promptly to bed.

The sounds of engines in the Cherokee complex stirred them all from their breakfast, and a great crowd of people came to watch as they loaded up their supplies. Chummy had not come to see them off—too busy, no doubt—but the men he had sent seemed very capable. There were more of them than he expected, too. The foreman, a man named Tom, informed Philip of the rumors that the Pledge was on the move northward from Little Rock, though not towards Tulsa. That, of course, was the very direction they were going, so they had decided on sending a few extra men.

Altogether, Chummy was sending along ten men to operate and accompany the vehicles. One of the vehicles was an old jeep that had been cleaned up. Closer inspection revealed it to be an old military vehicle, and where there had once been mounted a machine gun, there now was an impressive looking crossbow. The jeep carried three men whose sole purpose was to protect the rest, though the whole crew could take care of themselves and operate that crossbow if necessary.

It did not take long to get loaded, as both parties were well organized. After no more than an hour, the four vehicles rolled out of the complex. The caravan wove through the city streets and finally found the open road towards Springfield, Missouri. In front was the jeep. Winter was in full swing, though fortunately it was mild. As such, it would have been pretty cold for those in the jeep, except they had been doing this for so long that they knew how to keep the heat in and even make some more right inside the vehicle.

Next was one of the passenger vans. It carried some of their supplies and two of Chummy's men, Fides and Fermion, and of course, Jonathan, who refused to be too far from the man he had vowed to protect. Next was a small flatbed truck, loaded with some boxes of tools, parts, and other supplies, as well as quite a few barrels of what they presumed to be gasoline. Finally, in the rear was another passenger van carrying Tasha, King, and some more of Chummy's men. Though the roads were bumpy from disrepair, they were still able to speed along at forty to fifty miles an hour.

King was distracted. His eyes saw the scenery flash by, but none of it registered. He replayed the earlier night's conversation in his head. A sick feeling in his stomach reminded him of his embarrassment. Bardia had gone out of the way to say that King was still in good standing with them, but he had noted that Joan had not been present to see them off. On the whole, he felt out of joint with the world.

King had been watching the scenery, but Tasha was watching him.

"Something is the matter, King?" she probed.

"Nothing," King offered half-heartedly. He didn't want to lay bare his humiliation before Tasha.

"You understand that there was more to the conversation than just impropriety with Joan?" Tasha replied. King jerked his head to regard Tasha under new light.

"How did you know?" King demanded.

"Isn't it clear by now that it is believed you play a vital role in what is going to transpire in this country? You have a gift that you choose not to employ. It is rare that one has such an abounding overflow of sight like you do. It is felt by those who see less than you that what you're choosing not to see is …" Tasha trailed off.

"Is?" King prodded.

"Is going to result in a calamity," she explained, nervous about putting such a burden on him.

"You don't understand," King protested. "Some of the things I see are terrible nightmares. You call it a gift, but I have seen things I would never want to see. Why would I choose to open myself up for them again?"

"Because sometimes it is necessary to come to grips with terrible truths in anticipation of future joys," she retorted.

King shrugged. He didn't know what to say about that. He wasn't even sure he knew what it meant. Tasha continued.

"You must know that it is not good for you or Joan for you to be apart. If circumstances had been different, you could have stayed and even had her parent's blessing. They admire you, King. Know this: if you return a man, they will receive you warmly. Don't worry about the situation any further," she asserted.

"I don't know how I feel about you guys talking about me," King sighed.

"Who said we talked?" Tasha said, looking away.

*Just then, King blinked his eyes and opened them to see a great darkness. It was cold and clammy with not even a single source of light. He heard breathing and movement and maybe a hushed tune being sung.* As quickly as it came it was gone. King saw signs indicating they were passing through Carthage, Missouri, rather than the damp blackness.

"You saw something, didn't you?" Tasha smiled.

"Yes, I guess. But I didn't want to," King answered. "It was the old one where I am immersed in darkness and there is moisture all around."

"Interesting," was all Tasha said.

After that, conversation ceased for a time. King returned to his thoughts and Tasha to hers. Tasha moved up to the front to talk a bit with Chummy's men, and King sifted through recent events in his mind. While he still felt uneasy about the night's events, Tasha's words had been of comfort.

The caravan stopped at Chummy's garage in Springfield to get more fuel, thus conserving the fuel that they were carrying. They shared some conversation with the mechanics and drivers who were based there, specifically looking for any information of interest regarding the east. There wasn't anything more to be gleaned than what they had already learned, so after a quick hot meal, they bundled back into their vehicles and were driving again.

The road got a little rougher after Springfield. Because of the radioactive destruction of St. Louis, they would not be able to use the direct route with the nicer highway. A smaller state road would have to do. Route 60 was their path to Cairo, Illinois, and it was bumpier by far than the interstate.

Sometime in the late evening, they stopped and switched drivers. In the early morning, when darkness was fading into light, the caravan stopped again. Weary travelers crawled out of their vehicles to stretch out. It had been a long ride.

They were in an old picnic area. The sun rose fully while they walked around, stretching. Clearly, at one time this park had been well maintained. It still retained some of its former glory and beauty. After a short time, they realized that the old buildings had actually been commandeered as residences. Some of the people who lived there came out to greet them. These seemed to be somewhat simple, but nonetheless very good, people.

A little later, they were joined by travelers who were on their way on foot to Springfield from Cairo. Some of these had come from Tennessee, and informed them for the first time Memphis had been one of the cities destroyed several years back in the nuclear attack. King and Tasha knew that already, of course, but it was the first that Fides and Fermion heard it.

"So," Fermion had observed, "Cairo is really the best way through the heart of the country."

"It's basically the only way," Chummy's men answered.

That made Fermion quiet for a little while, but after a nice hot breakfast, he returned to normal. Tasha had gone on a walk on the trails after breakfast. When she returned, they all jumped back into their vehicles. They said their farewells to the good people at the old national forest's picnic area, and were off. They had hopes to be in Cairo before noon and in Bloomington by late evening, unless they decided to spend some time exploring Cairo. None of them had ever been there, but they were told it was an exciting place to visit.

That was not to be, however.

## == Chapter 11 ==

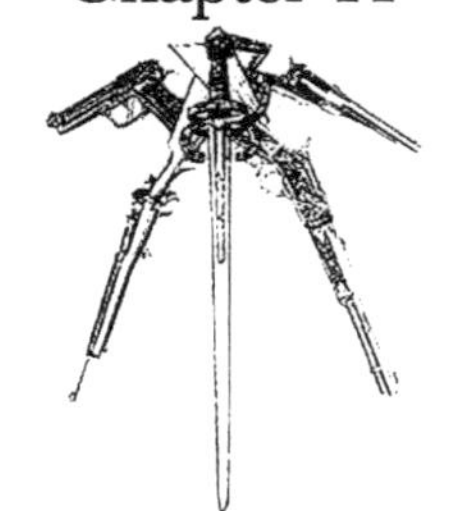

It seemed as though everything was going according to plan. Their ride since Springfield, Missouri, had been relatively swift, even if bumpy. They made it all the way through to a town named Poplar Bluff without incident. However, about an hour's ride after Poplar Bluff, they were suddenly confronted with their advance vehicle, the jeep, coming back towards them at full speed, flashing its headlights at them. The other three vehicles screeched to a halt right there in the middle of the road. The man arming the crossbow jumped out of the jeep and ran over to the window of Tom's van.

King and Tasha and the men who were in their van watched as the folks in the jeep had conversed with Tom. Clearly, something was not right. There were rapid exchanges between Tom and the other fellow. Finally, the man ran back and told their driver to follow Tom's vehicle. He pulled his van off the road and drove it towards the trees. The other vehicles soon joined them.

"What's going on?" the men demanded to know from Tom.

"Trouble ahead! A Pledge army, perhaps. Lots of men!" Tom blurted out. Sure enough, they could hear engines in the distance, though they couldn't make out if they were moving towards them or not.

"Hearing that Cairo was the primary way through the country here, I realized it had some obvious strategic advantage," Fermion said. "I bet that Cairo is not at all prepared for a Pledge war. The Pledge's time of diplomacy and verbal persuasion must be over. We must warn them."

At that, Chummy's crew, normally nice and decent men, began to swear. Tom settled them down and spoke on their behalf, "We didn't agree to get caught in a fight with the Pledge army. We'd be willing to hide for a time, if it were possible, or maybe see if there are any other bridges across the Mississippi and try them, but we're not going to tangle with something like this. I think the guys are right to protest."

King grabbed his staff and cautiously ventured to scout ahead. He kept to the trees and bushes. He listened carefully and realized that the engine noise had drifted off to the north. Seeing nothing else, he returned to the group, which was in discussion about taking another path to avoid the Pledge army that might be ahead of them.

King interjected, "I went and listened to their engines. They haven't come any closer, but I'm sure that they have moved north. Do you think we are very close to this road here, going north?" King asked, pointing to a road on the map. Sure enough, between them and the Pledge army was a northbound road connecting with the road heading east that they had discussed as an option for evading the forces.

"So, they've got some maps, too. They have anticipated what we might do, and they are putting out a blocking party. I'd wager they've done the same thing to the south," Fermion mused.

"They probably don't expect us to go all the way around. They probably are thinking we'd try to find a way to cut across the countryside, off the road, to try to get around them. They might not go all the way north. And by the time we retreat that far and go around, I bet they are all well along," Tom suggested.

"We'll need to decide soon," Tasha said urgently. For his part, King welcomed the excitement. It took his mind off the things he'd been pondering for so long. This was action. Meanwhile, the conversation was continuing.

"If I were them," Fides said hesitantly, "I would not rest until we were hunted down completely. It's obvious that we were on our way to Cairo. They'd expect that we'd want to warn them or get ahead of them. I bet we'll soon see some coming our way, and they'll follow us right around if they have to. We'd have to completely elude them, or make them think we've completely retreated, or something like that, or they'll relentlessly pursue us to keep us from spilling the beans."

"You might very well be right," Fermion said. "Quick, let's have a decision. Are you and your men willing to try going around to the north by taking this county road up from Poplar Bluff?"

Tom was getting ready to say that he was when it became too late, really, to do anything. The sounds of engines started getting louder and louder as Fermion was asking his question, and some of Tom's men were making their way to the top of the rise during that time to see what there was to see. After no more than a moment or two, three pickup trucks came into sight. In the back of each were a good half dozen men who appeared to be well armed, if only with clubs.

"Well, we're outnumbered by this lot, but not by much," King whispered. He had no reason to whisper, but it seemed like he should. "Maybe we should try to take them?" he added more eagerly.

Tom gasped, "We are not weaklings, but we are not soldiers, either."

"But if we did defeat them, that would give us time to get away," Fides replied. A couple of the other men swore at them. What they didn't realize was that they were not quite as well concealed as they thought, and the pickups suddenly veered off the road heading in their direction.

"Well, this is a beast," Tom cursed.

"Well this is the moment, really. Retreat is not an option. We can either take them on right here on foot, or we can try to take them on in our vehicles," Fermion declared, taking out his sword. Fides took out his as well. Chummy's men appeared to be emboldened by the sight of them, and even King found himself thrilled by them. He thought for a moment that he might even be willing to trade his staff for a weapon like that, but then thought better of it.

The decision had been made to confront the vehicles by charging into them, since they were faced with pickup trucks filled with the men in the back, while their group was in enclosed vehicles. They were going to leave their fuel truck behind and use the vans to play chicken with the Pledge scouts. They peeled out of hiding and were only some fifty yards away from there when the vehicles met.

Much to the surprise of the Pledge drivers, the vans did not slow down at all as the vehicles drew nearer. If anything, they sped up. Surprised, the Pledge trucks turned to get out of the way, sending some of the more eager soldiers, who had been leaning out in readiness to jump when all the vehicles came to a stop, tumbling out. They did not quickly get to their feet. Yet they were better off than those who remained in the trucks, because both vans managed to smash into the rear ends of the trucks as they turned away; it spun one of the trucks out, sending Pledge soldiers flying through the sky. Those men did not get up at all.

The other truck had only been smashed in the back corner and kept going forward a little farther. One man was badly injured at the impact and flipped up and over the roof of the van as it passed by. They might have kept driving back and forth crashing into trucks and soldiers except that it turned out that at least one of soldiers had a gun. He stumbled out of the back of third truck, which hadn't been hit at all, and got a shot off at the van Tom was driving.

King watched as Tom almost lost control of the vehicle and had to slow the van down to a near stop in order to regain it. In that time, the truck had pulled out to hem the van in. The gunman fired another shot at the van, now a still target; things were looking grim for a moment, until the jeep zipped by. One of the steel arrows loaded into the crossbow zipped through the air and struck the gunman dead. The jeep kept going, meaning to circle back around with another arrow loaded.

As their vehicle circled around, King and Tasha whipped their heads back to see that the other van had stopped and its occupants had stumbled out to fight off the men. Chummy's employees in the van with King and Tasha began shouting at one another and demanding that the driver take them back around. King checked to make sure that he still had his blade strapped to his thigh and readied his staff. Their van was now aimed at the melee.

The van pulled up and out poured Tasha, King, and the four who were with them. King waded in with a certain glee. He cracked a few heads and ducked a few blows. In one of his strikes, his staff broke into two equal pieces. Fermion and Fides were not far off, and Jonathan was tackling people and dragging them to the ground. King saw that Tasha was handling herself well, too. There was a frightening moment as one of the Pledge men found a gun and emptied it into one of Chummy's men. Infuriated, the man's friends fell upon the gunman and beat him to death. The tide was clearly turning against the Pledge scouts. When there were only four or five left, they withdrew to one of their trucks and drove off towards Poplar Bluff, the town they themselves had passed through earlier.

The battle over, the travelers took a moment to catch their breath and tend to their own wounded. The man who had been shot dead was named Luke and had been one of the men in King and Tasha's van. Tom confiscated the gun, searched the body of the gunman for ammunition, found some and pocketed it. He was all business when he called them to attention.

"Friends, we can't go on ahead and face more of this. We have brought you fairly close to Cairo, and you should have better luck sneaking by that army on foot than we would with a vehicle. But if you want, you can have the jeep," Tom told them.

"Let us put a little distance between the army and ourselves," Fermion suggested after they had loaded Luke's body into the backseat of the van. "Let's all go back to Poplar Bluff. There were lots of abandoned homes there that we can find shelter in for the night if need be. But at least we can find a warm place to talk." Tom was fine with that, so they climbed back into their respective vehicles and drove back to the fuel truck. Two men jumped into the fuel truck, and they started their short drive back to Poplar Bluff.

King and Tasha reentered the van. The men were mourning the loss of their friend and were casting cross looks at King and Tasha. King and Tasha sat quietly, saying nothing. King tried to keep his eyes forward so as not to catch a glimpse of the dead man in the seat behind him. Meanwhile, their van followed the ones ahead of them at high speed. They passed a sign indicating that Poplar Bluff's city limits had been reached. The driver suddenly gasped and cursed.

"What is it?" Tasha demanded to know.

Ahead of them were thousands and thousands of men marching in their direction. The pickup truck that had escaped them and fled in this direction was now parked near some other vehicles. King saw the astonished looks on the Pledge faces. Two of the Pledge jumped up onto a truck.

"Turn around!" Tasha shouted earnestly. But it was too late. The first rounds were already coming towards them. What Tasha had noticed before the driver was that on top of that truck was a heavy machine gun. Loud popping noises and puffs of smoke made it clear that they were being fired upon. The van ahead of them, with Tom and their fellow travelers was taking fire.

Tom's van swerved hard and their van followed suit. Everybody was thrown to one side of the van, and the driver struggled to keep control of the vehicle. Just then, machine gun rounds began streaking through their van as well. One of Chummy's men slumped over.

"Neil!" the driver exclaimed, looking over his shoulder. "Patrick! Check Neil!"

Patrick pulled Neil up but lifeless eyes were all that greeted him. Patrick leaned him forward and saw the entry wound near the spine. A bullet hole could be seen in the van seat.

"He's dead! He's dead!" Patrick wailed.

The driver cursed. Tasha had moved up to the next seat to confirm that Neil was actually dead. With heavy eyes, she returned to her spot next to King.

"Look! They're turning off!" Patrick exclaimed, pointing to the vehicles ahead of them. There was a dirt road heading into the trees. It appeared to be someone's driveway from a long time earlier. After a bumpy ride they rolled into a clearing where sat an old, decrepit house. When they stopped Patrick leapt out of the vehicle, followed by everyone else in the van.

"Neil is dead!" he wailed to the rest.

"We have no time to give him a proper burial," Fermion said firmly, but compassionately. "Listen to me. We need to park the truck and the jeep here behind this house, back in the woods. We can try to find an appropriate place to leave your friend's body while we do that. But then we need to get into this van, and we need to drive as fast as we possibly can toward Cairo. The enemy in front of us is not likely to know about what has happened to their friends yet, so we'll have the element of surprise. We'll drive through their camp at fifty miles an hour, and if they move, they move. If they don't, they're dead."

Tom scratched his head. "But aren't they likely to have guns, too?"

"They surely might, but they aren't likely to have them trained back behind them. It's risky, but we can be sure that the main army is going to be coming to look for us, and if we don't hurry, they'll get a message through to the forward guard for sure. We're trapped. We can go back in the direction where our presence is known and even expected, or we can go ahead where we are not known or expected. And there are fewer men. We must do it now—right now!" Fermion argued.

"Alright, it's settled. Patrick, get a grip. Take Steve and find a place for Luke and Neil's bodies. Chris and Manny, go park the jeep and the truck back there in the trees. We'll try to get back to it sometime. Then hurry back! Five minutes! Go!" ordered Tom.

The bodies of Luke and Neil were carried out of the van. King helped carry some of their effects, and finally, a slight gully was found where the bodies were laid. In under five minutes, they were back to the vans.

"What are we doing?" King asked Tasha.

"We're going to ram them," she replied coolly.

"Ram them?" King was confused. Chummy's men were staring ahead, stone-faced.

"Yes. You'll see," Tasha replied, apparently not entirely pleased with this strategy. However, when they pulled back onto the main road they saw that the pickup truck and the machine gun truck were driving in their direction. There was no choice, now. Tom's van had rapidly accelerated and they followed suit. They were headed right for the Pledge forces they knew to be ahead of them.

Driving sixty miles an hour on such roads was a bumpy endeavor. King clutched at the seat ahead of them to keep his head from smashing into the ceiling. They crested a slight hill, and the Pledge army was revealed to be sprawled out ahead of them. Tom's van sped up rather than slow down.

Tasha shouted at the driver, "Faster! Follow them through!"

King watched in amazement and horror as their van barreled through the Pledge camp. Surprised men leapt out of the way, and every now and then King felt the crunch of some item or box crushed beneath the van as it whizzed its way within the camp. Apparently, the element of surprise had been all theirs. As far as he could tell, none of the Pledge men were seriously injured by the vans, but in at least one case the van's mirror clipped a man who didn't get out of the way fast enough, and that couldn't have felt good.

"We made it!" Patrick howled with delight after they emerged from the other side of the camp. Even Tasha was smiling. King was pumping his fist. Earlier he had delighted in having some action, but upon learning that he was faced with thousands of men and having seen the evidence of what a machine gun could do, he hadn't been looking forward to a new conflict. They were also buoyed by the fact that the road beneath them had improved. They were flying down the Interstate now. King watched the signs inform him that Route 60 had turned into I-57.

"Holy crap!" the driver blurted out.

"What?" Tasha, King, and Patrick blurted out simultaneously.

There was no need to answer. The sight was evident to all now. Before them was yet another army, but this one did not have the dismal gray uniforms and the wearied eyes that the Pledge men had. Before them were ranks upon ranks of men and beasts stretching back as far as the eye could see. They were adorned with bright colors and magnificent crests and dazzling shields. They were ready for battle. They were formed up to the north and to the south. They hadn't seen the army as they had been driving, because it had craftily concealed itself behind the earthworks of an old, intact overpass. By the time they passed under it and saw what was on the other side, it was too late.

"What now?" Patrick shook his head wearily.

"Armies behind and now an army ahead. We have no place to go," Tasha sighed.

"They're getting out of the other van," Patrick noted. Apparently, Tom had decided there was no sense in running anymore. They appeared to be confronted with a massive army numbering close to ten thousand.

Though this was a stunning thing to encounter, having only recently escaped the clutches of another army, there was much about this one that was unique. It looked as though it were a scene from a Revolutionary War battlefield, or an old European one, perhaps. There were flags and banners waving all up and down the line, and they were waving even now, as units communicated with one another. The men were neither dressed like modern military men, nor quite like what one might expect from medieval soldiers. Many of them had a silvery-looking, but obviously thin, armor on their bodies, and even on the warhorses. Crests of different colors were overlaid over the silvery armor, clearly indicating different units.

The army had left the road clear, trusting their concealment to the earthworks; now, about forty men on stout horses took to the road to confront the travelers. The riders spread out along the road and within the space between the two sections of the army. Five of them trotted a little farther forward from the others and appeared to be waiting for the occupants of the van to come forward.

King followed Tasha as she led the way forward to where their friends were waiting for them. Tom and his crew looked pretty nervous. Once together, Tom glanced at Fermion and said, "Well, let's go. Fermion, you do the talking!"

The twelve of them walked slowly towards the center emissaries. As they drew closer, they were able to make out the details of the army facing them a little better. There were several ranks of archers, and they could see that some of the horsemen had lances, though most had long broadswords. In the third and fourth rows, there looked to be men armed only with sticks and clubs. These looked nervous and even somewhat timid.

Tasha leaned in close to King's ear so that only he could hear and whispered, "What do you see, King?"

King had been thinking the very same thing. He realized that here again was another time when his gift would have come in handy. Torn still between skepticism and a growing willingness to See now that Fermion had slyly admitted to being able to See as well, he had still not come to the point where he had openly decided to again receive the blessings—and curses—of the gift. The truth was that, by and large, he didn't see anything different from anyone else at this point. Oddly, he did think he could hear music.

Not wanting to start a conversation about whether or not he had a gift of Hearing as well as Sight, he merely answered honestly, "Nothing. I see nothing out of the ordinary."

Soon they were within thirty feet of the five emissaries riding out to meet them. After they had come within speaking distance, the emissaries dismounted and approached them. Seeing them close, King knew that if he could See them properly they'd be as magnificent as Fermion had appeared when he had first Seen him. Four of the five emissaries were men: handsome men whose stern eyes also exhibited a piercing compassion. A woman rounded out the group. She had a stunning beauty about her. King couldn't take his eyes off her.

"Your weapons, if you please," one of them demanded politely. Tom and his men flashed weak smiles, because they really didn't have all that much to show. The men threw forward their thick clubs that they were accustomed to traveling with, and Tom at last remembered he had a gun, which he threw at their feet. Jonathan gently tossed his long knife ahead of him. King produced the two parts of his staff that had broken over the head of one of the Pledge soldiers. Tasha threw her dagger into the middle of the road.

Fermion pulled his cloak aside revealing his sword and nodded towards Fides to pull his own weapon out. The two of them placed their swords next to King's broken staff and the dagger.

"My Lord," gasped one of the emissaries, addressing the tall man, "I believe those three weapons are from my own stores." The emissary was pointing at Fermion's, Fides', and Tasha's weapons.

"Interesting. We'll have to hear the story of how they have acquired them," the taller man said. "Are you with the Pledge?" he demanded to know.

"The Pledge is our sworn enemy, my Lord," Fermion said, bowing slightly. "In fact, we have only just escaped its armies. They are coming now to Cairo with a force that will at least match what you have here. We have fought with some of them and lost some friends, but we are here now and will fight alongside you, if you will grant us the honor."

The beautiful woman now spoke, "A force to match what we have here? Our scouts tell us their force is much smaller than ours."

"Indeed, my Lady. We know the force that you speak of," Fermion replied. "At first, we thought that was the extent of their army as well, but when we were trying to retreat and hopefully get around them so that we could warn the city of Cairo, we fell against a much larger force just coming into the city called Poplar Bluff. That force alone has as many soldiers as I see here. I should add, too, that they have guns as weapons—I don't know how many—and I see that you have no guns nor armor that could repel bullets. They fired a machine gun that sent a round through the side of the van over there and killed one of our comrades. The first army must only be a forward element, perhaps a probe or perhaps even something meant ultimately for diversionary purposes."

King thought he heard horse hooves thudding in the distance as the tall man's demeanor soured slightly in reaction to Fermion's news, "This requires new consultation, if it be true. But how to know if you are speaking the truth and not just a scouting party for the forward element? I believe we might be able to find out the answer to that question depending on the quality of your account of how you came to possess these weapons. They, at least, are not what we expect to see in the Pledge."

By the time the tall man had finished his statement, everyone had noticed that horsemen were inbound. Before they could arrive, the leader of the emissaries nodded to Fermion, "These are my advanced scouts finally returning to report. Tell me, truthfully, can we expect an attack by the force that you consider the 'forward element' today, as we anticipate?"

Fermion seemed ready for the question, "No. Though the forward element has a handful of vehicles, they have no horses to ride and appeared to be traveling mainly on foot. They are at least twenty miles from us, and still encamped. They might march double-time though, and try to attack you in the morning if they know you are here. But if they have no idea of your presence, I submit to you that you won't see them until the morning of the day after tomorrow."

"Alright, it is not much—after all, if you were the Pledge we'd expect you to know perhaps that much—but it is something. Let us see," the noble man replied, beckoning for his scouts who had finally arrived but had waited patiently for Fermion to finish. "Well, you heard him. What do you say?"

"Sir, he is quite right. We have heard from our forward scouts through the signal flags that the army has only now begun to pull up their tents and make their way towards us, and at no great speed. We appear to have arrived with plenty of time to spare," the man said.

"And an army behind the army?" the tall man inquired further.

"Sir?"

"You weren't here for that. Right. This one says that beyond the army that we know about is another army that is our match in size, and has guns as arms. Do you know anything about that?"

The man's face, though as profoundly otherworldly as some of the others around them, went pale white. "Sir? No, sir. We know of no such force. I will signal ahead and dispatch some of our best men to find out. How much farther behind?"

The tall man nodded towards Fermion, who replied, "Not more than five or ten miles, my Lord. It was very near Poplar Bluff when we encountered it, and that was not more than forty-five minutes ago."

King marveled at the change of language that Fermion was

employing. Referring to people as "Lords" was not normal speech. King began to wonder if perhaps Fermion was in fact Seeing something that he was not.

"Such advantages one has when they have mechanical vehicles," the tall man was continuing. "Well, you may be a Pledge spy, but if so, not a very bright one to tell us such information. I will hear your story and decide your fate." He turned to a person on his left who had not yet spoken. "Apparently, we do not fight today. Dismiss the ranks, but put out a large guard."

"Yes sir," the man replied and promptly left to give out the orders. The flash of flags giving out the signal all along the ranks was a sight to see. You have not seen such silent precision wrapped in choreographed dance. Meanwhile, the tall man motioned to the captives to come with him. He wanted to hear a story.

The soldiers slowly disassembled as they followed the tall man and his men and women to the rear of the lines. After it had become clear that they were not going to die, at least not immediately, King had more studiously examined the faces of the beautiful warriors assembled around them. He had noticed that there were not only men, but also a fair amount of women among them.

Off to the right side, behind a hill, lay a huge tent city. To the left side, farther back, was another tent city, and it was in that direction that the poorly armed men they had previously observed went, though not alone. Even as they were all returning to their tents, a good five hundred noble looking archers and swordsmen on horseback trotted out in the direction of the Pledge armies to serve as a watch and, if necessary, an obstacle, should the Pledge army try to march on them unexpectedly.

After a long walk, more or less in silence, they arrived in the center of the tent city. There, a very large meeting tent was waiting for them. Maps of the entire region, Illinois, Kentucky, Missouri, Tennessee, and Arkansas, were suspended on the inner walls of the tent. A large table in the middle of the tent had even more maps laid out on it. It was clearly a war room. They heard their vans being driven up somewhere out of their sight. It was about this time the man who had given the orders to disperse the army arrived at the tent. King and his companions waited for whatever was next. The swords and Tasha's dagger were placed on the table. The tall man gave an order, and chairs were brought in for the guests to sit in.

Fermion, however, remained standing. The tall man gave a gesture to Fermion, who said, "The story that I have to tell cannot be told in its entirety for reasons I hope my Lord will allow me to keep concealed. However, I shall tell you what I can here in public, but perhaps I could share more in private."

"We'll see if that is warranted. Please tell your 'public' story," the man answered him.

"Many years ago now, I volunteered for and was dispatched on a very important mission by my own Lord. As part of that mission, I worked with a group of people protecting a very valuable treasure, the worth of which surpasses all anyone might imagine. It is a treasure one might sell everything to obtain. It cannot be measured in any currency now in existence on this planet. Part of my mission was to help secure that treasure, and in the course of that business, my friend here—Fides—was sent as a construction worker to help. In the course of events, the man who possessed the sole key to access the treasure became nervous with rumors of the times. It was after the Disease had been unleashed, but before it had arrived in our parts. Therefore, he took Fides as a ransom and me as a mediator, and he used an airplane to carry us all the way to New Mexico. I suspect that he has now fled south into Mexico. However, those entrusted to protect the treasure had access to many weapons, even though we were few in number. I chose these two swords from what was available, knowing that they might be of use to us. When we arrived in New Mexico, it was not without any weapon."

"However, Fides was struck immediately with the Disease even as we got off the plane. Knowing nobody in the area, I found finally a good and decent man in the town, possessing a deep good, and a willingness to risk all for that good, who agreed to care for Fides until he was either well, or dead. At great personal risk to his own being and his wife's, he cared for Fides. I remained in the area, roaming to and fro, and received occasional word of Fides' health. I eventually learned that he had indeed survived the illness, so I awaited his inevitable journey home. Fate was with us as we found each other in a tavern near my home. Fides showed great courage in defending me against bent men. Since then, we have been journeying together towards Bloomington, Illinois, where we hear that there is a repository of information to help families reunite."

"Though I have no family of my own, Fides does. He left his family to work on the project I was associated with, and it was on the very same night this country was attacked by nuclear weapons that we landed in New Mexico. The only items of machinery that have worked since, as you well know, are purely mechanical devices that do not rely on electronics. Fortunately, we were not affected by the atmospheric event that caused that, since we were already on the ground. Nonetheless, we could not fly back."

"Along the way, we were escorted to see the president of Oklahoma City, also on account of these weapons, and it was there that we met King and Tasha, who also had fled the Disease at one time and had become welcome in the Cherokee community. King apparently is in a similar position, having family in the Illinois region.

They sought leave to join us in our journey, and we welcomed them. They have helped us both against rebel Indians who wish to reclaim the country they believe—with reason—was robbed from them many centuries ago, and then again against Pledge scouts. This man, Jonathan, was saved from death by Fides, and now in gratitude travels with us in order to repay his debt. I should say that these men over here are hired men who have agreed to drive us to Bloomington. Hired or not, they have shown great bravery in helping to defeat the Pledge scouts, and of all of us it is they who have endured the burden of cost, having lost two of their friends in the ordeal."

The tall man spoke again. "That is a fine tale, filled with courage and honor. These are themes we well appreciate. It explains how you came to possess these swords, but not how they came to be accessible to you in the first place. Also, as you indicate that this Tasha only more recently joined you, it does not account for her dagger."

"I cannot speak to that, my Lord," Fermion replied. The tall man nodded towards Tasha. King had never really thought about Tasha's weapon. Though in retrospect he saw that the quality of most weapons had greatly diminished over the years, the fact that Tasha had a weapon that was so much better was something he had chalked up to it being made when factories were still producing good work. Yet, her blade and Fermion and Fides' weapons were attracting an awful lot of attention. King thought maybe there was more to the story after all, and he turned attentively to hear Tasha's answer.

"My Lord, I am afraid there is no interesting story behind my acquisition of this fine weapon. I found it many years ago, in the woods. I considered it, at the time, a gift from God, and hope it may yet be returned to me," Tasha said. With a start, King felt that she had told the truth, but not the full story. He had always known Tasha to be the most honest and direct person he had encountered. She was being coy. He was sure of it.

"Found it in the woods, eh? Well, Nagro, how do these stories sound to you?" the tall man asked the one who had made a claim to them earlier.

"These blades have a curious look about them that would be more at home back in the light of my own homeland. I know of no one from our party that brought them, so I cannot say that they must belong to me. I only argue that they are not of this land. I believe there are some among our party who might know the lore behind them, though I don't, myself," Nagro replied.

King had only come to grips with the fact that Tasha had given a diplomat's answer when it sank in that the strange warriors were talking about different lands. His mind began to swim in a sea of uncertainties.

"Oh, so they are not really yours?" the tall man sought clarification from Nagro.

"Well … I think they are, but they don't seem the same, either. I am certain at least that they did come from my land," Nagro returned.

"And yet this is the public story," the tall man pondered. "There is more to tell, is there? Still, you seem sincere, and genuine. Frankly put, you are just the sort of men and women I'd expect with such weapons, and I am inclined to trust you and believe you, and even to admit you into our army with high rank. What say you?" the tall man asked his friends.

The woman replied first. "I do believe that I'd want to still hear what he has to say in private before bestowing such honors. And, I am thinking that I would want the counsel of Gongral and Dolam first. I am thinking we will want it anyway in light of the news of a coming larger army."

Nagro agreed, "I, too, would like to hear the more private words, and I also would like to submit these weapons to the examination of Falda and Leredo. Like Henryetta, I think that counsel is required at any rate in light of the changing facts on the ground." The woman's name was Henryetta, King noted.

"How small of a party is required to ensure that the privacy you desire is maintained?" the leader asked Fermion.

Fermion replied, "It is no insult to my friends who have agreed to take us to Bloomington, but I would only want Fides, Jonathan, Tasha, and King to be allowed to hear the other things I might say. Of your own party, I see that there are five of you who govern this army, and that you seek counsel only from an additional four. So, I would be comfortable speaking with my friends and you and your counselors—just the fourteen of us, then."

As the final arrangements were being made, King's heart leapt with excitement. He was being invited to the private party, and his heart warmed with the honor. His curiosity was further fueled at the thought that he would hear Fermion say what it is that he Saw. King believed without a doubt that it would be spectacular.

At last the five leaders departed. Guards were set around the tent and food was brought to them. King had that feeling again that he could hear music and shortly after they began to eat the food that had been brought to them, there was indisputably the sound of song—not only Heard, but heard by all. The strange people were singing in the tents around them. There were rich harmonies and not a single voice out of key. Every voice was superb, and the timbre of the whole was such that, despite there obviously being many, many voices, it sounded as though there was only one person singing the different parts. They were singing:

*One breath is all it takes*
*One mighty breath to come*
*and makes the stone arms move*
*and gives the shadow form*
*It lives, it lives, it lives, he lives.*

King exchanged glances with Tasha. Tasha exchanged glances with Fermion. Fermion exchanged glances with Fides. There was something remarkable going on, and King felt like he was being tantalized with sweet drops of water though he was otherwise parched. In his heart he began to plead for relief. That meant Seeing, and he knew it.

Finally, glorious looking people arrived to escort them to the private meeting, and the men of Tulsa were left behind. They were taken to a tent that they were told belonged to men named Falda and Leredo. Their weapons—the swords, the dagger, and the gun—were brought with them.

Falda and Leredo's abode was something to behold. It was brightly colored, and looked like a wigwam. From the top of it there spun out wisps of smoke. Not smoke as from a fire, but smoke as from pipes. Indeed, pipe smell was what greeted them as they entered the tent.

One man was saying to another as King took his turn stepping through the door, "Proper fourteen-twenty, indeed!" Seated around the circular tent were the five that they had already seen, and in the middle, opposite the entrance, were four very odd looking people.

The one who King was led to believe was named Falda was dressed in a long white robe. He had long, grey hair coming down both from his head and his chin. Around his neck was a thick necklace of gold. In his hands, however, were a pipe and a flint for lighting it. The other man sitting next to Falda greatly resembled Falda, except he wore a long black robe and no jewelry. He was puffing on his pipe and staring at Fides, who in return was staring at him. At that man's side was an older woman. Dressed in a dark forest green, she seemed stern, but friendly. She declined the offer of the pipe, which was handed to her. At the side of Falda was a young-looking man. He was not wearing a robe, but rather garments made from very nice looking leather. He was wearing a vest made of the same silvery material King had noticed much of the army wearing.

The five that King had already met were also seated close by. The tall man sat next to the man adorned in leather and silver. The one called Henryetta was next to him, and next to her was a very proud-looking man. He looked absolutely regal. On the other side was the one who had been ordered to dismiss the troops. Next to him was the one they had heard was named Nagro. All of them were stunningly handsome, or beautiful, if either word could fully convey the profound depth of pristine appearance they possessed. Even the three older people in the middle were wearing robes cut from marvelous cloth.

The tall man began his introductions. "Starting from where Fermion is are people you have already met. That is Peder, Henryetta, and my name is Yuri, Yuri Ryson. Next to me here is Leredo, and next to him is Falda. Helping him to cloud up our meeting with their incessant smoking is Dolam." Falda and Dolam's eyes twinkled at the rebuke. "Next to Dolam is Gongral. Leredo, Falda, Dolam, and Gongral are our most trusted advisors. Next to Gongral is Calvin, our master-at-arms. And finally, Nagro, whom I shall add is so valiant that though he deserved to rule this lot, and if truth be told, ought to do so even now, has deferred leadership to me. I am not worthy to lead them. Indeed, even when I come to those who are my own it will not be mine to lead them."

"We call ourselves the Shadowmen, and we ask that we be spoken of by that name, too," Yuri added. King didn't think the name fit. They were not shadowy at all. They were vibrant, brilliant, and shiny.

Yuri spoke now to his friends and counselors, "Next to Peder is a man named Fermion. As I understand it, this is his friend, Fides. These are the two in possession of the fine swords. Then Jonathan, the faithful friend. Then it is Tasha, who had the dagger. Finally, King."

"Nagro tells me that he thinks the weapons came from our land. May I see them?" Falda asked. Peder handed all of them over to Falda for inspection. Falda and Leredo looked at each weapon very carefully, with a hint of recognition, some gasps, and some appropriate expressions of appreciation of the quality of the craftsmanship. At last, Falda delivered his verdict, "If they are from our land, they look different than they ought. They do not seem to belong here, either, so I suspect there really is more to them than we can see. Still, I do not think we can lay claim to them in any way. We should return them, I think, to their apparent owners." Peder took the weapons and returned them.

"Now then," Yuri said, "Let us hear what you wanted to say in private."

Fermion seemed eager to speak. "I am of the Nephilim," he declared. "I have been tasked to protect a treasure that surpasses all worldly estimation. It is important that I escort my friend, Fides, to Bloomington. He must find his family, but then he must go with me so that I can accomplish my task. He possesses the only key."

Under Fermion's direction, Fides produced an odd looking necklace from under his shirt. This was definitely a new development, and King realized that Fermion was not the only person who was more than the naked eye could see. Still, the most curious thing of all was Fermion's announcement that he was "of the Nephilim." This was a completely new term to King, and he had no idea what it meant. It was clear, though, that Fermion thought it was significant. King swelled with glee. At last Fermion would reveal what these people were really like. To Fermion's surprise and King's disappointment, the council didn't seem to have any more knowledge about the Nephilim than King did.

"What is this … 'Nephilim' … you speak of?" Dolam said aloud.

"I have not heard this term before," Peder said.

"Nor I," Nagro said. Around the circle it went, with no one having heard the term before. Clearly, Fermion thought he was speaking to his own kind. King felt like he had been kicked in the gut. Just as he had been ready to set aside the lurking doubt that he had been imagining things, the discovery that Fermion had himself been misled—even though he had Sight—was devastating. King couldn't help glowering. He felt betrayed.

Fermion's own disappointment was on full display when finally someone said, "I think I have heard of the Nephilim." It was Yuri, and he had a very reflective look on his face. "But I must confess that I do not know very much about them. But I have heard of them, from my readings." Fermion's face now brightened considerably.

"Fides," Fermion said quickly, "show us your book." It should have been interesting to King that Fides not only had a mysterious necklace around his neck, but also an ancient book, but he was still stewing in his anger and angst at his perceived betrayal. Had he been conned by Fermion? Perhaps he was being conned by all those who had urged him to See, even Tasha and Chief Thunderfist! Perhaps it was all in his head after all. Fermion, who had hinted that he could See was proved a liar! The conversation continued as King gazed about darkly. He had been taken in. He was sure of it.

King's attention to the conversation was suddenly brought home when he heard Yuri suggest to Fermion, "I wonder if we do not in fact serve the same Lord."

"If so," Fermion offered carefully, "it might follow that neither are you from this world."

King glanced back and forth at the two men. Were they lunatics? From different worlds? It was odd enough to be referring to people as "Lords," but to talk as though they were from different worlds? King felt his lips tighten into a slight sneer, but even he couldn't help contemplate what other world the Shadowmen might be from.

After a long pause, Yuri answered, "You are right, of course, in some ways. We are not of the Nephilim, but I am not so sure it can be said we are not from this world. We have our own tasks given to us, but we are not permitted to speak of them with others, and I am afraid—I mean you no insult—that I do not think we are permitted to speak of them to you, even though I am certain we are in the same army."

"I certainly understand," Fermion replied.

"For my part, I believe every word he has said," Nagro said. Peder concurred and, in turn, the rest assembled there did as well. King now felt that he was surrounded by people who were plainly nuts. When people start talking about being from other worlds and other people take it seriously ... well, King felt that things had gotten out of hand. There would have to be extraordinary evidence for such an extraordinary claim. In a daze and disheartened, King noticed that the conversation moved on to a topic interesting in its own right.

King allowed himself to hear Fermion tell Yuri and the council, "My Lord, I am very concerned that you are not prepared to deal with the weapons that the Pledge has."

"You mean guns, I suppose?" Yuri asked, not overtly concerned.

"Yes. The days of lining up in ranks, as impressive and formidable as it seems, ended a long time ago. Perhaps they could return in some situations if the lethality of the guns employed were more limited. However, we encountered a machine gun that sent rounds clear through the panels of our van and killed a man. If they have enough ammunition, they will be able to kill all of you, especially with you grouped so nicely together." Fermion seemed uncomfortable to have to share this news with them. It was almost as though he was disappointed that he even needed to. King again noted Fermion's apparent inability to See, after all.

"We believe our armor is sufficient to stop a bullet from a gun," Nagro informed Fermion. At this, even King gasped.

"It is lovely to look at," Fides blurted out, "but you can't believe it can stop a bullet round?"

"Here is a gun," Yuri said, "How about a demonstration?"

At this Nagro stood up and invited Fermion to shoot him in the armor, but Fermion adamantly resisted.

"That is insane!" King blurted out, and then silenced himself out of concern that he had spoken his mind about more than guns and armor. He noticed indistinctly that Tasha had glanced at him.

Finally, they agreed to the demonstration, but only if Nagro's silvery armor was placed over a wooden beam. Everyone exited the tent together. Someone quickly procured a large wooden beam and placed Nagro's armor over it.

Fermion took the gun, which had been previously owned by a Pledge scout, but more lately handled by Tom. He carefully aimed the weapon, which was not by any means the most powerful handgun in existence, and fired. The armor, impressively, did not let the bullet pass. At first Nagro beamed at the success of the armor, but when

Fermion had to dig the armor and bullet out of the wood where it had become embedded, a look of concern came over all of the beautiful faces.

"The weapons, or at least one of them, that are coming to you are much more powerful than this one," Fermion said, showing the indentation in the wood. "I admit I am amazed that your armor kept the bullet from going through. It is a remarkable thing. Yet, I do not think you need only be concerned with keeping it from going through, if you see what I mean."

There was a cloud of dark contemplation that hung over them all as they absorbed this demonstration. At last, Yuri told them that, given this new information, they may want to speak with them some more. Fermion, of course, said he'd be available, and they were at last dismissed. They were led back to another tent, and King sulked the whole way there.

## == Chapter 12 ==

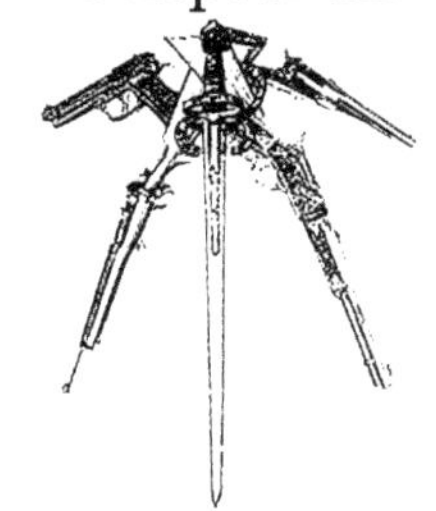

The tent they were led to had been stocked with fruits and breads. King wasted no time in grabbing some slices of dried apples and then rounding on Fermion who, to King's dismay, seemed to be ready for him.

"Now what is all this nonsense?" King demanded to know. "Here I have been trusting you and now you spin out a story like that!"

"Your anger seems misdirected, King," Fermion replied coolly.

"People from other worlds? Lords and Ladies? You thought they were the Nephilim, but you were wrong! I always thought you were holding out on us with something, Fermion," King retorted, "but to learn that it was something that no one has ever heard of, anyway, I have to say ... well, I don't really know what to say. What is the Nephilim?"

Fermion said nothing and continued eating some nuts that had been provided. When he didn't respond for a time, King turned his attention to Fides, "What about you? Did you know he was a Nephilim? And are you one as well?"

"Yes, actually I did," Fides admitted. "But I am definitely not of the Nephilim."

"Well, then, can you tell us what it means to be 'of the Nephilim?'" King continued straining to mask his impatience.

"Well, I wish I could. Other than knowing that the Nephilim are not to be trifled with, I can't say much more. Well, there are some things I could add, but it seems to me like Fermion ought to answer them, not I. To tell you the truth, I am mainly in the dark on the matter," Fides confessed.

Fermion spoke at last, "Fides, bring out your book." Fides produced the ancient book, which Fermion took from him. He waved it at King. "Do you know what a Bible is?"

"I have heard of Bibles. I know my father was interested in them at one time. Obviously, I've never seen one before," King said.

"Did your father ever teach you anything about what the main message of this book is, or anything else about it?" pressed Fermion, tossing the book back to Fides.

"No, not that I can recall. I don't recall much about my father anyway. I was much younger, then," King explained.

"Well, as I have been trying to explain to Fides for many months now, it will be very hard to understand what the Nephilim is without taking the time to at least acquaint oneself with this book's contents," Fermion said, taking the book back from Fides and tossing it into King's lap. "Can you read?"

King caught the book and tossed it back to Fides without looking at it. "Tasha taught me how to read a little, but mainly just sounding out words so we could read the old signs we saw," King replied.

Fermion turned his attention to Tasha, "So, can you read?" Tasha nodded. "Can you teach him more, so he can read this book?" Fermion asked.

Before Tasha could answer, King objected. "Now, wait just a minute. First of all, I'm sure there were some very good reasons for destroying this book. I think it likely that it must mean everything in it is all rot, for one thing. Second of all, that is a huge book. When am I going to read it, even if I could read?"

King felt nauseous. He knew he was really throwing out any objection he could find to divert attention from the real issue, which was his sense of being betrayed or suckered into thinking that his visions were not hallucinations. King felt that he had let too much out of the bag already and was backtracking and throwing out chaff to cover up his real interests. However, even as he engaged in the tactic, he was uncomfortable with it and didn't know why he couldn't be direct about his true feelings in the matter.

Fermion appeared to be oblivious to such undercurrents, however, and played along, "Perhaps you do think it rot. Assume it is, even. I assure you, unless you at least have some knowledge of the contents of that book, what I have to say will be simply unbelievable. I wish it could be otherwise, but it isn't. But, ok. Let me ask all of you a question, and perhaps we can give you a hint. What do you think will happen to you when you die?"

Here was a question that King hadn't thought about before. It is true that he was afraid of death and simultaneously thrilled at beating it back, but he had never taken the matter to its final conclusions. He had a fleeting insight that it wasn't death he was afraid of, but rather the pain of dying. Whether or not there was something on the other side of the veil hadn't crossed his mind. As he thought about it now, he remembered some of the old stories, the ancient answers, dealing with this question. For some, it was thought that after death there was punishment forever, and for others paradise. He didn't recall what conditions were laid out in the tales for who received which reward.

Jonathan broke the lingering silence, "I suppose that there are only a few basic options. The obvious one would be simply that we cease to exist, and our body returns to dirt. The other option is that one of the old superstitions is right, and we will continue to exist in some form or another. Given how many of the superstitions speak of heaven for those who do right and hell for those who do wrong, I'd say the odds are good that perhaps there is a reason for that, and that goes right along with the belief in an afterlife, too."

"Well summarized," Fermion said. "And the Bible obviously has its own views, and a more particular set of positions on the matter. Pretend for a moment that the Bible is right about what it says. Do you know enough to know what the Bible says about the afterlife?"

Fides lifted his head to attempt an answer, "Well, eternal life in heaven for those who do good and eternal life in hell for those who don't. I know that much."

"You forget faith, Fides. And grace," Fermion said. "But that's good enough for now. Keep that in your mind, and assume, if you will, that something like that is truly the reality. Have you any thoughts about what a person might do with eternity?"

Jonathan had been deep in thought. He measured his words slowly, "That is a very interesting question. I suppose I had always imagined one simply sat in a massive church on a much softer pew, and instead of listening to a preacher, one gazed upon God. That was the impression I always had growing up, and I must confess that it never seemed all that appealing to me. I never really took it seriously, because to tell you the truth, it was hard to imagine how a heaven like that was any different than hell."

At that, Tasha made a snorting noise, but said nothing. Instead, Fermion clapped his hands and smiled. Confused, Jonathan continued, "I suppose from what you are trying to get at, that you think that heaven is something different, something more than that?"

Fermion laughed heartily, "Indeed I do! Absolutely!"

King's demeanor remained sour, and his growing bitterness could be restrained no longer, "This is all well and good, but it still helps little in understanding what you mean when you think you are a Nephilim. Although it makes me wonder if you are not a little crazy."

There, it was out. King was glad he had gotten it off his chest.

"Well, now we are getting into areas where you would have to acquaint yourself with the material in that book," Fermion replied, completely side-stepping the insinuation that he was insane. Fermion cryptically added, "I am not going to throw my pearls to pigs."

"There is no reason to be insulting," Fides chastised Fermion. Fermion merely sighed.

"Alright," Jonathan mused aloud, "let me see if I understand the basic premise of your hinting."

"Go ahead," Fermion invited. King tried to make sense of Fermion's dodge as the conversation progressed.

"You claim to know what is on the other side of death, and what we do with eternity. In other words, you are saying you are some sort of eternal being," Jonathan offered.

"Sure. Although I had a beginning, I'll have no end. But you've got the gist."

"Ok, for what purpose have you come to us, then?" Jonathan inquired further.

"You heard me explain it to those people," Fermion said. "I am here to do my master's bidding. I have several objectives, and then my time is done. And no, I won't tell you more of that purpose than I've already revealed," he added, anticipating Jonathan's next question.

"Hogwash!" King exclaimed.

"I wish it was," Fides said quietly.

Like everyone else, King turned his attention to Fides.

"Go on," Tasha prodded him.

"We hadn't told you this part of our story. When I began my journey home I went first to Albuquerque. I spent some time getting to know the citizens and picking up bits of information about my journey east. Well, one evening I went to a tavern for a drink. I used the rest room there, and when I came out, there were some scoundrels harassing a man, a priest. That man was Fermion. Well, something burned inside me when I saw that. I had once considered the priesthood myself. I don't know if that was part of it or not. Anyway, I stepped in and before I knew it I got myself clobbered, and the rascals were about to kill me off when Fermion stood up with that sword of his. He didn't use it, though. Instead, he put it down and held open his hands. Inside his hands a super-bright fiery globe appeared, and as if driven by thought, it suddenly flashed towards the men who were about to kill me. They weren't killed, but they were incapacitated, and bits of the globe sparkled on the wall. Fermion pulled me up, and we left before more trouble could arrive. You know, if I hadn't seen it myself, I wouldn't have believed it. To be honest, I don't rightly know what a 'Nephilim' is, but having seen Fermion exert his power in that way, I am inclined to believe that he is whatever he says he is," Fides concluded.

"I insist on a demonstration," King argued. A demonstration which was witnessed by all would go a long way in settling his persistent doubts.

"I am afraid it is not as simple as that, my friend," Fermion cautioned him.

"So, you can't reproduce it? It was merely a miraculous event, and we will have to simply believe you and Fides?" Jonathan interjected. King welcomed another skeptical voice.

"I'll say this about it, and no more for now. A man may disbelieve another man when he claims that he can deploy a nuclear weapon, but we would not want too many demonstrations before we gave in and believed it. And the man with such a weapon might be mature enough to know he does not parade his arsenal merely because others doubt it. If others wrongly perceive it as weakness in that man, or deception, it can't be helped. If the wielder of such a weapon is mature, he will not allow another's cynicism to force him to do what he knows ought not be done," Fermion explained.

"I wish I understood a word of that," King sighed.

"I get it," Jonathan said.

"I do too," Fides added, "but you are leaving out a lot, aren't you?"

"Yes, I am. I have already shared with you more than I thought you could conceptualize, and I admit, you have gotten on admirably. To go farther would be foolhardy. The rest of you will have to simply decide whether or not I look like a lunatic to you, if I have a habit of lying, or else, failing these, perhaps it is reasonable to believe that I am telling the truth," Fermion concluded, casting a steely gaze towards King.

"So, now what?" Fides asked Fermion.

Fermion scratched his head, "Well, I admit I am perplexed. I know who you are. I know who the Nephilim are. But these people around us are neither the Nephilim, nor of your own world—I am sure of it. But for the life of me, I don't know who they are!" Fermion slapped his knee and laughed, "Boy, let me just say that He likes to throw curve balls when He gets the chance! But to not know the power of Adam's guns? To think a sheet of silver would be enough? Who are these noble, but foolish people?"

"Is it important to know the answer to that?" Tasha inquired, but King was still wondering who the "He" was in Fermion's comments.

"No, you're right, Tasha. It is none of my business," Fermion agreed. "I have my orders. They have theirs. My orders are not their business, and their orders are not mine. I know what I need to know, and what I need to know concerns getting that necklace around Fides' neck to Peoria, Illinois just as fast as I can."

At that moment, the tent flap was pulled aside, and the man who had guided them to the tent thrust his head through the opening. King had been too busy sulking before to notice, but now he noticed that the man was hideous in appearance. Fighting the urge to recoil, King looked down at his feet. The man asked Fermion, "Your services are desired, sir."

Fermion grabbed the Bible from Fides' lap again, tossed it back into King's lap, and followed Redemptus out of the tent. King glanced at it and towards Fermion, but Fermion was already through the entrance. He thumbed through the Bible gingerly. It looked to be a hundred years old, and there were numerous notations written in the margins. It had been marked up with comments and shortened words, followed by numbers. He hadn't been entirely truthful to Fermion. He could read reasonably well. Still, as he skimmed through the book he realized that he didn't know what he was looking at or where to start. He intuitively sensed that he would need more than literacy. He would need a guide.

"Well, I'll say I don't buy this whole Nephilim business, but Fermion strikes me as the most honorable man I've ever met," Jonathan exclaimed.

"I think he might say the same about you because of your pledge to me," Fides said.

"If you would have seen the way you fought the night you saved my life, you'd understand why I'd sooner think you were from a different world than I would Fermion. On the other hand, you didn't have flames burst out of your hands," Jonathan replied. "I'm not sure I believe you on that, my friend, but I have made my vow, and even if it's to a lunatic, I'll keep it," he winked.

"Go on!" Fides exclaimed, chucking a dried chunk of some fruit at Jonathan, who laughed as he evaded the toss. At that moment, they could hear singing again from somewhere in the camp:

*The old stick bears a leaf*
*The rock bigger than the biggest can move*
*Is in my pocket and the*
*Sword is in its sheath.*

King's heart and soul resonated with the song. In fact, after a moment he realized that there was music beyond and behind the music. It seemed like an additional choir was singing a harmony and this somehow gave the tune real, physical substance. King felt that if he were in the midst of the singers he would be able to reach out and grasp the melodies as they washed over him, heaping handfuls of the stuff into his pocket. Or maybe it would be more like standing in a stream as water rushed by. The music was like the water, and if he had liked to he could dangle his fingers in the hymn just as he could watch the current of water form circular waves around his fingers.

Fermion came into the tent, and the singing abruptly ended. They could hear trumpets and horns immediately followed by the sounds of the camp awakening into action.

"What's going on?" Tasha asked.

"They asked me for my counsel, and I gave it to them," Fermion replied.

"What was your counsel?" Fides wondered.

"I told them that they're going to get a lot of people killed with their camp out in the open like this, for one. Secondly, I told them that they need to consider guerilla warfare rather than their current approach. Thirdly, I implored them to respect the power of the weaponry they are facing, and fourthly, they should deploy immediately and not delay."

"From the sounds of the camp," Jonathan said, "they have certainly moved on the fourth suggestion."

King thought that for an insane person, Fermion showed remarkable good sense with his advice to the Shadowmen.

"Yes. Though they did not think guerilla warfare was a very honorable way to fight, they saw the wisdom of it. They were giving out the orders even as I was on my way back. By the way, our weapons are outside the door. King, they have given you a new staff. Jonathan, if you like, they have offered a sword from their stores. I suspect Tasha is content with her weapon." Fermion was rattling this off while pushing them out the door. "Our escorts have already been led to the vans, and we are to go to them, now, and be on our way."

"But what about the feast?" King asked, always depressed to miss a chance to eat a good meal.

"No feasting tonight. They are going to fall back towards Cairo to some positions that might give them a chance to hold the city—even against a few heavy machine guns, if they play it right." Fermion was walking quickly, and they all struggled to keep up.

They had to go past Falda and Dolam's tent to get back to their vans, and both Falda and Dolam were standing outside it, watching them intently. Fermion nodded solemnly to them but kept going. When King was near, though, Dolam attracted his attention.

"A word, son?" Dolam asked him. King was confused that Dolam would take an interest in him, and he looked ahead where the rest were still following Fermion. Tasha saw what was happening and backtracked.

"Don't worry, King. I'll make sure they wait," she told him. "Talk to the men," she said firmly, and then ran to catch up again with the rest of the party.

King lingered uncertainly, but the two old men gazed on him sympathetically with their pipes still blowing rings about the breeze. King figured he ought to wait for them to talk since they were the ones who summoned him.

At last, Falda spoke, "Something seems on your mind, son."

"I don't know what you mean," King replied, still dazed to be having the conversation.

"It's simple. Is something on your mind or not?" Falda remarked casually.

"Ok, yes, I do have things on my mind. Who doesn't?" King answered.

"Fair enough," Falda replied. "And yet, you seem to be engaged in a battle in your mind. It is as though you were settled on something, but a seed of doubt has now given rise to a ravaging vine suffocating what was ready to bear good fruit."

"In battles, a helmet is always a good idea," Dolam interjected, "And battles of the mind are no different. Where is your helmet, I wonder? Lost in despair, I think."

"I don't mean to be rude," King stated, honestly trying not to be rude, "but I don't see what any of this has to do with me or why we are having this conversation. I've got to go. They're waiting for me."

"It is true that I don't have Sight in this place like I did before, but I do see that you have something on your mind, and you'd best say what it is," Dolam asserted. "Pretend like it is possible that we will never see one another again. What harm, then, is there in sharing your burden with us? Perhaps we can carry some of it."

It was an interesting tact, and King couldn't find a retort. Also, the sudden revelation that here again was someone who apparently could See caught him by surprise. King decided he ought to tell them.

"Look," he began, "for some reason I can See things. Not just see, mind you, but See. I've been told that it is a gift, but some of the things I've Seen are horrific. So I asked not to See things anymore, and with few exceptions, I haven't. Well, I've been told that it is important and good for me to See, but the decision is mine. In the meantime, though, I began to fear that it was all just in my head. A hallucination or a delusion. That said, I had really started to come to the decision to accept the gift again, because I felt that Fermion could See. When I saw that Fermion thought you were of the Nephilim I realized that he couldn't See after all. Perhaps what he thought he Saw was all in his head, too. I'm being played for a fool."

Falda and Dolam stroked their respective beards.

King interrupted their thought and summarized, "It really comes down to this: Is it real? Or has it all been happening inside my head?"

Dolam beamed at him, "Of course it is happening inside your head, King, but why on earth should that mean it is not real?"

"What do you mean? If something is happening inside my head it is just a figment of my imagination, don't you think?" King was taken aback.

Falda corrected him, "That might be possible. Certainly if it was *only* happening inside your head, that could be a concern. But think of it. We are standing here having this conversation right now, and you're experiencing it. Everything you think you're experiencing is in fact mediated to your brain through your senses. That is to say, if we take your sight for example—not the mystical sight you're concerned about, but your regular sight—the light is allowed to pass through the lenses of your eyes, but you do not actually have a mechanical one to one correlation between that light and what you see. The truth is that what you see is reconstituted by your brain. That is to say, even what you are experiencing right now is going on inside your head. What you see, what you hear, what you touch, taste, and smell ... all interpreted within your brain and experienced within your mind, ultimately, and yet you have good reason to believe that it is not *only* happening inside your head. You take it for granted that your senses are getting you real, objectively and independently existing information about external reality. You might ask yourself, therefore, whether or not you can make any statements about reality if you're concerned that it is 'only happening inside your head.'"

"Well said," Dolam puffed on his pipe.

"Thanks," Falda puffed in return.

"That is way over my head," King grinned.

"I doubt it," Dolam smiled back at him. "I suspect the truth is that you asked a hard question but didn't have a mind to tolerate a hard answer. This is a common characteristic of the human race when you come to study it. They ask questions like 'How could God allow suffering?' and then, when the answer takes longer than a sentence, they conclude it's all smoke and mirrors."

"Sometimes they really don't understand," Falda winked at Dolam.

"Alright, truly said. Allow me to put my answer this way," Dolam reasoned, "If forever and ever you were the only person seeing mystical visions or hearing prophetic words, then perhaps you might dismiss your experience as a self-contained delusion. If, on the other hand, you continue to come across people who likewise claim to have such a Sight or to have received some prophetic word, then you have good cause for at least being open to the possibility that what you're seeing by Sight might be externally real, after all."

"Yes, yes, very good, Dolam," Falda clapped. "Let me elaborate! One thing you must not do for sure is prejudge the matter. You're just waking up to the world and discovering that there are other people about. You know that to a large degree, such mystical visions are somewhat rare, or else we wouldn't be having this conversation. But how do you know that they are impossible, just because in others it hasn't been reported as a common experience? You do not have the universe under a microscope in order to examine each part to state with certainty what is real and what is unquestionably impossible. But when you're confronted with people who have a similar experience of the world as you do, that offers a certain measure of corroboration, does it not?"

"Excellent, dear Falda," Dolam smiled. "My turn. Now, perhaps it is not wise to trust any person's account of reality just because. A person might in fact be a lunatic, and his stories the fruit of his lunacy. If they are sane and reasonable in all other matters, however, then what justification do you have for dismissing their accounts of mysticism on first blush? Don't you see that would be to prejudge the matter? Fermion has indicated that he has Sight. Does he strike you as otherwise irrational or unreasonable, or does he seem to possess extraordinary good sense?"

King knew the answer to that. "He seems to have pretty good advice and solid moral character," he admitted.

"Well then," Dolam concluded with a flair, "let us not demand more evidence than is reasonable. Do not say, 'I think this extraordinary, so I demand extraordinary evidence!' because after all, that prejudges the matter. You might be quite wrong in thinking something is extraordinary. Usually what ones decides is 'extraordinary' is deemed so relative to one's already held fundamental beliefs about reality. There is nothing inherently wrong with such an assessment, but it does pose a problem when what you're trying to do is establish in your mind those fundamental beliefs in the first place. If you're still in the business of trying to settle your beliefs about the nature of the universe, I suggest that rather than seek exceedingly high demands for evidence as though it were *proportionate*, look for evidence that is *correlative*."

"I don't know what you mean," King confessed.

"See now, Dolam, you've gone too far," Falda chided his friend. "King is going to begin to wonder if he is not the only audience you have in mind."

Dolam laughed, "Ok, let me explain. Quickly, I know. You have to go soon. Correlative. If a man says he is the map maker for the region do not prejudge the claim because you believe such a claim to be extraordinary. Instead, see if he does actually have expert knowledge for the region. Does he seem generally trustworthy? Or is he shifty? Does he seem to be out for material gain that you can tell? Similarly, if a man claims to have Sight, and seems on other grounds to be trustworthy, then he ought be able to do things in line with that claim. We have agreed that Fermion is trustworthy, have we not?"

"We have," Falda hurried Dolam along, "More quickly. The boy has to go."

"And in fact it is because it seemed like Fermion failed in this instance to have Seen that you have your doubts in the first place, correct?" Dolam asked King.

"Yes, that's right," King confessed again.

"But you know from your own experience that just because you have Sight it doesn't mean that you always See. So why hold Fermion to a standard that you yourself know to be unreasonable?" Dolam concluded.

"Has no one given you any insight at all as to what, why, and when you might see things?" Falda probed.

King remembered now that he had been advised a little, while he still lived with the Cherokee nation. Still, he wasn't quite confident that Falda and Dolam's advice summed up the matter. He was rushed for time but decided to raise another objection.

"See here, though. It seems then that a person could say just about anything, and so long as he otherwise seemed sane and was trustworthy you should just believe him," King protested, "On that view, a person could just pop in and say that he was God, and if he seemed reasonable and trustworthy we should believe him."

"No, not at all," Falda corrected him.

"Did we not say that there ought to be a correlation between the claims and the man's deeds and abilities? If a man claims to be God, but his sole talent is making poached eggs, we need not take the man's claims seriously," Dolam explained. "Likewise, if a man claimed he made a map of the area but was perpetually lost, we might reasonably conclude that the man could not be trusted on the point."

"In the case of a claim to divinity," Falda maintained, "one ought have in mind what kinds of things could only be done by a divinity, and it makes no sense assuming that accounts of those things should be dismissed on their face if, in fact, the very question you're examining is whether or not there is a God or that he is acting."

"What things did you have in mind?" King wondered.

"Oh, many things. It is a discussion for another day. The point is that you can't prejudge the matter, nor should you assume that you have a full grasp of the nature of reality so as to know that something is or is not possible, or that a certain claim is lunacy on its face. Fermion didn't claim to be God, did he?" Falda asked him.

"No, he claimed to be a Nephilim," King replied, "whatever that is."

"Well there is part of your problem, then. You don't even know what a Nephilim is, so you can't even match up his claims with his deeds. For all you know, a Nephilim experiencing Sight is a little different from you, or happens under different conditions," Dolam explained. "Your job is very simple, my dear, skeptical son. Determine what kind of events would be correlative to the claim, and then look into the evidence for whether or not the events really happened. If you don't know what kind of events to look for, then figure that out. If such events seemed to actually have happened, it is no refutation to offer that you think such things couldn't actually have happened. If the evidence is good, your job is to man up and conform your beliefs to reality."

"Yes, you think about that, young man!" Falda cried out. "We've got to get you to your friends!"

With that, several men appeared from around the tents and quickly shuttled King away from the two old men. King didn't even have a chance to respond. He got one last glance off and saw them waving and that was it. When King reached the vans, people had just gotten in, and Tasha was waving at King to hurry. He scrambled in, just in time. It seemed that only Tasha had noticed he was gone, and to King's relief they hadn't had to wait for him.

"Good conversation?" Tasha asked him.

"Interesting, to say the least," King shook his head. The vans started moving and King buckled himself in.

"I like them," Tasha stated matter-of-factly.

"Yeah, I do too. They seemed to know an awful lot about the very things I had on my mind. Coincidence that I would encounter two men well versed in my particular issues?" King glanced at Tasha.

"Coincidence? If you like," she smiled. King fell into contemplation, and Tasha let him. The ride to Cairo was under way.

When they arrived in Cairo, they were not challenged by anyone to gain entrance into the town. It was eerily desolate, in fact. Until they reached the downtown area, they were not sure that there was even anyone in the town at all; once they pulled their vans to a stop, they saw people walking the streets in the dusky light. There were older men, women, and children. Their company quickly gathered a crowd around them. Working vehicles were rare things to see in these days. However, everyone knew what was brewing to the west, so beyond the novelty of the vehicles many of the inhabitants wanted news. The local bars soon heard about their arrival, and people began peeking out the windows and even coming out to see what could be seen.

They quickly learned that it had been no more than a week earlier when the Shadowmen had come, set up camp south of the city, and sent in a delegation to meet the leaders of the city. This was the first time the people of Cairo had learned that they faced any kind of threat at all, though obviously rumors about the Pledge had been around for some time. Indeed, some of their own people had joined the Pledge. It took some convincing, but the Shadowmen were very persuasive and very earnest. Once persuaded, the men had assembled and journeyed west in order to defend the city. When King asked why they had no defense set up at the city itself, the people only shrugged and said that if the Pledge arrived at their city it meant that their men had been killed, and they saw little reason to live on if those they loved would never return. After all, they added, they were all too young, too old, or too weak to fight. King didn't know what to think about that.

Their escorts raised objections for extending the trip. Tom explained that fuel was getting low. The old vans got very poor mileage, and despite the fact that they had very large gas tanks, there was little point in denying that taking the vans all the way to Bloomington without having their fuel truck with them was simply not possible. There was some groaning and sniping about leaving that fuel truck behind, but Fermion pointed out that the presence of the fuel truck probably would have encouraged the Pledge to keep pursuing them. It was determined that there might possibly be enough gas in the tanks for the escorts to get back to their fuel truck. Obviously, though, if they wanted to do that there was a significant obstacle standing in their way, that is, the ten thousand men in the Pledge army.

The situation was not positive, then; there wasn't enough gasoline to go on, the city they were in was undefended, indefensible, and demoralized, and they couldn't get back to their fuel truck. This made Tom and his friends quite a bit annoyed, but as they couldn't do much about it at the moment, they left all decisions unmade and sought and found lodging for the night. Cairo was a peninsula, and in the old days, there were bridges coming in from all directions, but now there appeared to be only two to the south. The one they'd have preferred, the one bleeding into I-57, was out, as they had discovered earlier.

King had a lot on his mind and, as there wasn't much to do, shortly after dinner he told his friends that he was going off for a walk through the town. The sun was still up, but it was hovering not too far off the horizon and throwing off amber hues. In due time, he found himself in the city square. There were benches all around the square, and in the middle was an empty platform that King supposed used to hold a statue. He reasoned that it had probably been made of bronze or some other metal and had been carted off to be melted into something useful.

After a time, an old man, barely able to put one foot in front of another even with the help of his cane, came and sat down on a bench not too far from where King was sitting. He glanced over at the man. His wrinkled face and other features could be seen clearly, but he was far enough away that if King had wanted to have a whispered conversation he wouldn't be heard.

There he sat.

The winter air was quite crisp, though not harsh. It kept him awake, and he was glad because he felt that he really needed to make his decision about whether or not he would receive the gift. His discussion with Falda and Dolam had been confusing at times, but he did have a sense of their points. He reasoned too that denying the reality of his visions was connected to his assessment about the rest of his reality. His visions had been of such a nature that they seemed at least as real—often *more* real—than his normal experience of reality.

Not knowing what kind of consequence would come, but ready to surrender to his own experiences and to the arguments that he had heard from so many since he first left the Cherokee nation, he breathed a deep sigh and wondered if he needed to say anything to seal the deal. Somehow, it seemed he ought to.

"Ok, well then. Look, bring the gift back. I accept it," he said aloud but under his breath. In a softer voice, he said, "Please don't hurt me."

Though he did feel a burden lift, nothing else changed. He laughed at himself because, of course, he didn't have any reason to think anything would change. His smile faded away, and he put his arms up on the back of the bench and tried to relax.

Something about his scouting training always kept his ears twitching, so he didn't relax long. He started looking around because he was sure that he heard engine noise. In fact, he thought it was probably a motorcycle. That didn't necessarily warrant concern, but working vehicles were always of interest.

No sooner did he decide that the faint noise was the sound of a distant motorcycle then the sky cracked open in the city square. A gash was rent in the fabric of reality about ten feet off the ground, and out of it screeched a roaring motorcycle. King jumped up in surprise, tripped backwards over the bench, and tumbled onto his backside. He rolled over and stood up as the bike roared around the square much faster than was safe and making turns that the laws of physics would have suggested could not have been made.

King threw a glance over to the old man who had come to sit down and noticed that the man hadn't made any sign that he saw or heard the motorcycle. King feared that perhaps the old man was dead, because even if he was deaf and couldn't hear the great dragon roar of the motorcycle, it was so loud that King felt the vibrations in his bones, and the old man would have felt them too.

The bike zipped by King and screeched to a halt, leaving a long black streak of burnt rubber on the sidewalk. The rider dismounted from the motorcycle. He was wrapped in a thick cloak and was wearing goggles. He strode over to where King was still standing and sat down on the bench. He took the goggles off and motioned for King to sit down, which he did, though he sat as far away as he could. He could see the man clearly now. His hair was a mop, but was long and windswept. He seemed small in stature and had a small smile that seemed genuine enough.

"Expecting someone else on a bike?" the man put to King.

"Uh, I wasn't expecting anyone, not even a bike," King admitted.

"Alright then, well, here I am! Rich Mullings at your service," the man declared, extending his hand gregariously to King. King shook Rich's hand but pulled back as soon as he could. Rich didn't seem to notice. He continued talking as though King had reciprocated with warmth.

"Yessir, and I think you made the right decision," Rich said, looking King right in the eye, "You have a gift my friend. Perhaps we all might have had the gift if things had gone differently. But there it is, it is something that few have and you're one of the few. You don't understand that what you see is not something less or some shadow, but something more. Not shadow, not image, but a glimpse of the substance. Oh, and there is so much to see!"

"Thanks Rich, but I've got to ask, I mean, you just drove a motorcycle from out of who knows where. I assume that this is real ... you seem real ... but ok, are you an angel?" King suggested.

"Heavens no!" Rich smiled at him. "I have been dispatched for this moment as a special provision. We may or may not meet again. Our happiness will not be diminished one bit if we do not meet because we will know—or at least I hope—that we will both know the One who is the source of our joy. You have never been formally instructed in these matters, but it has been decided that it is too important to allow you to continue on in ignorance. At least, not too much," he winked.

"I don't understand …"

"Of course you don't. That's why I'm here," Rich laughed.

"Ok, explain then," King sighed.

"Look over there. See that old man?" Rich pointed at the man who had sat down a little earlier. King nodded. "Ok, now what do you see?"

King looked at the man for a moment and concluded that the man was a case study for why Cairo needed to be concerned for its safety. Here was a man who was so old and frail that if the defense of the city rested on this man's valor the city was certainly lost.

"I see a broken, old man," King told him.

"Close your eyes," Rich instructed him. King did as told. "Now open them," Rich commanded. King did. Rich pointed at the old man, and King turned his attention to him but the old man was gone. King was again startled to his feet.

The old man was now a ruddy young man who was fast asleep on the bench. To his amazement, when King looked upon the young man he could see inside the man's mind and glimpse the man's dreams. These dreams were not taking place inside the man's mind, however, but were being recreated in the city square. The city square was still there, but the dream was superimposed onto the square. The streets faded in and out of old comfortable kitchens with family members darting here and there with laughter only to be replaced with scenes of some distant farm. Then the city square was a graveyard, and the young man was sitting next to a newly dug grave with a small headstone and weeping gently. King suddenly realized that he was not seeing the man's dreams, but rather his memories.

The memories wove in and out of the city square, and at any given moment King found that he was standing in the midst of fields of corn or watching as the young man was lying in a ditch as bullets flashed over him. The young man had been in a war. King watched as other young men died, or were wounded, and this one comforted them, or wept over them. Scenes of ecstasy were replaced with scenes of agony and despair which were replaced with mundane scenes. The man's life was flashing before King's eyes, but King was standing within the sight. The man's body grew older as the visions cascaded around King, but King saw that there was something about the man that didn't change at all, something which remained perpetually youthful. It was, among other things, a sustaining sense of dignity, a sense of identity that did not change merely because the body or circumstances changed.

"These are not his memories, King," Rich corrected him. "You're seeing them as they are actually happening. Past and future are a fiction. All moments are present to the One who sees, and he sees them forever more, for each person, and his seeing imputes to them reality. You're seeing not the past, but past presents. A person's full identity is the sum of every present, and only One can hold them all in sight at a single time. This is a rare glimpse and is above and beyond even the powers of your gift."

King felt hot salty tears welling up as he revised his view of the old man. The visions had ceased and he saw again only the old man, and yet King now knew that the valor of such a hard working, loyal, passionate man could in fact serve the city. King felt embarrassed and ashamed. He had seen the man's victories, his defeats, his glories, and his losses. The man he saw now was tired, indeed, but his old body only told a small part of the tale of who he was. He was seeing only a slice of the real man.

"He looks so helpless and weak, and yet his spirit within is as strong as before," King beat back his sorrow, "His aging body cannot match his strength within. Why must it be this way?"

"Be this way? This was not the way things were meant to be, King, heavens no. But they will be made right, you can count on that. Plans are in motion, prices have been paid. Lift your head, the final redemption is near," Rich said. "But see what it is that you have Seen. What other person is able to look at a man or woman and know not only that there is a whole tapestry that is their life but to have glimpsed into it? We take for granted that what we see with our eyes is all there is worth knowing. It is not so. It is *not* so."

"Is it all for nothing?" King asked him. "Will he see his loved ones again?"

"He will see the Lover, don't you see? What follows after that is better than we imagine. We can hope that he will. I hope that I will, but that is not where I place my hope. I place my hope in the things that I do know and not the things I don't, and I know that we start with the Lover and that is contentment enough. Whatever great glory we imagine might be the reality will be better yet. No eye can see, no mind can conceive what is being prepared," Rich explained.

"Who is this lover? What is it to say that there is more to reality than what we see?" King pressed him.

"Child! Listen! There is more that rises in the morning than the sun! There is a loyalty that is deeper than mere sentiment and a music higher than the songs that I can sing! The stuff of earth competes for the allegiance we owe only to the maker of *all* good things! So do not stand on shadows and falsehoods! If you weep, weep only as a man who is longing for his home!" Rich declared.

King again heard a song on the wind. Like before, it had that strange feeling that, if he could find it, he could cup his hands and scoop it to his mouth and drink deeply of it. Rich was not done.

"Every morning the Author wakes up and dances on the plains. The birds are adorned for his joy and the sky serves as the canvas of his artistry. The ways of Men are not his ways, but he invites Men to follow him and gives them the strength to do so—if they accept the gift!" Rich was practically singing, and King knew that the song he felt he could taste on the wind was a song that Rich was feasting on in this present moment, though perhaps standing from a different vantage point.

Rich continued, "Our deliverer is coming, my friend, with power and might and glory. The old tales are true, the old stories have life still. You can put your hope in that! He has heard the whole world cry. He will ride to mend the broken hearts with mighty warriors to his left and to his right, with horses pounding through the canyons. He has made this promise ... he will return!"

Rich was crying now, big tears falling down his cheeks and drenching the wisps of long hair that flew in and out of his face in the breeze. King couldn't help but cry now, too. He heard ... or felt the song ... that Rich was singing, and the smallest morsel was enough to fire King's soul. Then, suddenly King saw Rich's life flashing before his eyes. He saw glory and shame, agony and pain, and a defiant shaking of the fist at death which seemed to have gotten off the last blow and had not yet been answered.

The vision of Rich's life faded away and together the two of them regained their composure. King suddenly wondered what his own life would look like if it flashed through the city square as a series of past presents on display. Would he want to see it? He didn't know.

The sun had dipped completely below the horizon now. There were still crimson streams streaking across the clouds, and Rich was looking at the scene with a slight smile.

"What do I do with the gift?" King asked Rich.

"It is no accident that you have it," Rich assured him. "What you do with the gift I honestly don't know, but now that you've chosen to accept it I trust some purpose will be achieved. Quite possibly, though you may find it unpleasant to consider, some purposes have already come and gone and are now lost. Nothing can be done about that. Press ahead, and make the best good use of the information you gain through the Sight. That is all there is to say. Know that it is a gift you could choose to use for evil, so proceed cautiously. Still, realize that there is nothing that you will See that was not meant for you to See. Whether the vision is given so that *you* can act upon it or so that another may gain from it is something that must be determined each time it happens."

"By another you mean the ones I relate the vision to?" King inquired.

Rich was wearing a crafty smile, "I expect not only them."

"Who else?" King asked.

"One never knows. The point is that it is a gift that has wide reaching consequences and should not be treated lightly," Rich counseled.

"It seems like a lot of responsibility," King sighed.

"It is! But it is an honor to have it," Rich answered.

After a short silence, Rich made as though he was preparing to leave. King now thought he heard something else. It was a familiar, rhythmic cadence.

Rich smiled, "The drums!"

"You hear them too?" King exclaimed. The pounding was now all around him, though he could see no drummers. The ratattats of the snare drums and the thunderous booms of the bass drums and the march as to war fully immersed them. Rich was on his feet, dancing and whirling with perfect abandon. He lacked even an ounce of self-consciousness.

"Oh ho, I hear them! Love's Unborn is with them! As is my kid brother! Their day will be a day to behold!" Rich shouted, tears again streaming down his cheeks. The drums continued all the while that Rich was getting his motorcycle and rolling it over to the bench were King was still standing.

"Where are you going?" King wanted to know. In fact, he wanted to go with Rich, wherever he was going. "I can ride with you! Don't you need a companion?"

Rich laughed long and loud. The drums faded away as his motorcycle began revving. Astride the bike, Rich put his goggles back on. "Who says I'm alone?" Rich shouted over the noise.

Rich waved his hand and, as though out of a mist, a hundred, no, a thousand motorcycles emerged. Sitting on each was a man or woman (it was sometimes hard to tell) dressed in brilliant white clothes, which seemed to shine even though the sun was no longer in the sky. The thundering roar of their motorcycles made even King's spine tremble. Strapped to each person's thigh was a shimmering sword—no sheath—and each wore goggles over their longhaired heads—no helmets. King wondered if they had been present all along.

Rich laughed again, and it was amazing that even in that din his laugh could be heard as clear as anything, as though it were the only sound in an empty church. Rich gave a signal, and the hundreds of riders peeled out of the square and disappeared in individual flashes of light into the space-time continuum in the environs of Cairo.

And then there was silence and a steady ringing in King's ears. He would be hard pressed to dismiss this experience as "happening only in his head."

The old man had disappeared from the square at some point.

King hadn't noticed when he left, but he wished that he could go and talk to him now and hear his stories and learn more about him. King started back to the inn they were staying at and kept his eyes peeled for the man, but did not see him.

Back at the inn, darkness and quiet reigned. Everyone had gone to bed. King thought it was just as well. He had a lot to think about. He found his bed and fell into it. A slight murmur of a tune from a distant land was in his ears, but he was too tired to analyze it. He welcomed it uncritically, and slept.

King was startled from his sleep by Jonathan's loud shouts. Jonathan thrust his head into King's room and shouted, "Come quick! Fermion is on the roof to see and insists that you come as soon as you can. There is fighting!" King scrambled out of his bed and grabbed the staff, which had been given to him by the Shadowmen. He made his way up the stairs to the roof and found Fermion and Tasha peering off to the south. They could see down the road leading to the bridge that they had crossed the night before. The people looked like tiny stick figures from this distance. They couldn't see the bridge itself, because the road bent away into a narrow forest. Fides was the last to emerge onto the roof, arriving as Fermion pointed and exclaimed, "Look!"

Down the road, they could see men dressed in dark brown and green clothes, appearing a little like soldiers. They were firing around the corners of buildings, and others were lying down. Their targets were men in white or grey cloaks who were posturing across from them beyond a clearing. The men in robes controlled the road to the bridge, but that was all. Both sides had guns, but from the sounds of the battle, it was clear that each side had only old hunting rifles and shotguns, not military gear.

"I don't know what those men in dark colors are all about, but I have a sneaking suspicion about the white-cloaked men!"

"Who do you think they are?" King asked.

"A long time ago there was a vicious organization devoted to establishing a so-called pure white race in America. They were dealt some hefty political blows and were pushed underground. I hadn't seen anything about them in my studies of the last century. I could be wrong, but if it is them, then by all means, we side with the men in darker colors," Fermion declared.

Tom and a few of his men had joined them on the roof. "What are we going to do?" Tom asked.

"I think we need to find out what is going on, exactly. This is a very important strategic point. Cairo is at the nexus of the north and south right now. Cities both south and north of any size apparently were destroyed in a nuclear blast. Whether or not there are other bridges to get across these rivers I don't know, but in any case, we know about this one. We would not want this city to fall into enemy hands if we could help it," Fermion explained.

"Isn't your business north?" Tom inquired nervously. He didn't want to be around any more fighting.

"Indeed it is, but also I am to do good as I have opportunity. If I can stand in the way of evil or stand up for the innocent, I should. If I fall, I am convinced my master has someone ready to carry out the rest of my orders. And my orders include doing good as I have opportunity. Who is with me?" Fermion asked.

"I am with you, absolutely," Tasha declared.

"What are your intentions?" King wanted to know. He was prepared to receive visions again, but didn't know what he thought about possibly receiving them so soon.

"Right now, only to find out the situation in more detail," Fermion explained.

"I think I can certainly go that far," King replied. Fides and Jonathan also indicated that they were ready to check it out, but Tom and his men declined to go with them. Tom told them they would try to wait for them, but gave no promises.

King now thought he heard a machine gun off in the distance. In fact, King decided there were at least two guns.

Fermion agreed, "I bet anything that Cairo's Shadowmen have arrived again, with the Pledge at its back. Quite the confluence of powers! Let's go find out what is going on!" Everyone bounded downstairs and gathered up their weapons and cloaks and trotted south at a jog, staying close to the buildings along main street. After about a ten minute run, they were well within sight of the outskirts of the town, but still not with any hope of truly seeing what was occurring. They could see some of the brown and green clothed men lying prone. Their weapons pointed south; occasionally, puffs of smoke could be seen and cracking sounds could be heard as the men acquired targets and fired.

They looked for a higher vantage point so they could see what was going on, and King was the first to notice a tower rising up from a levee. They ran to the top of the levee and climbed up the stairs to the top of the tower. They found it was already occupied, however.

"You there, stop right there!" a big burly man shouted, surprised, but not so surprised as to fail to keep his gun leveled in their direction. "Identify yourself!"

"My name is Fermion. I think we are allies!" Fermion hastily explained.

"We have few allies, so I wonder about that," another man snapped at them.

"Who are you fighting, then?" Fermion probed.

The burly man replied, "They call themselves the Copperheads."

"That is a distantly familiar name," Fermion answered. "What do they stand for?"

"They want to make a new country out of the southern states, ruled only by white people," the last man replied.

As the conversation proceeded, King prompted the visions to return if they wanted to. He felt that he might be able to use them to decide if these men could be trusted or not, or if they were noble. The visions did not come. He kept waiting for Fermion to appear once again as a mountain-straddler, but even this didn't happen. King eyed the men as Fermion continued to talk with them, fighting back the slight doubt in his mind that despite his conversation with Rich he had been fooled, after all.

"Another old power rises to fill up the void," Fermion sighed. "Yes, we are certainly opposed to such people," he told them. "We are also violent enemies of the Pledge, not merely the organization, but the ideology. Not only that, but we oppose also the Indian nations who wish to reconquer the continent. As far as I know, there are no other groups to ally with or oppose, though I confess that thirty minutes ago I did not know about these 'Copperheads.' If what you say about them is true, we certainly stand against them," Fermion patiently explained.

"Well, you've got all the right enemies, then," the burly man said. "What do you say, Emory?"

"Well, they clearly started out on this side of the skirmish, and he's saying the right things, so let's give them the benefit of the doubt," Emory said. Emory and the other man, whom they learned in short order was named Perry, lowered their weapons and began looking out one of the tower windows again.

"One Simus," the third man said, introducing himself. King couldn't help looking at Simus a little extra long. Simus was one of the first black men he'd seen up close. He was familiar with the dark red hues of his Cherokee friends, but Simus was barely a shade lighter than pitch.

"Pleased to meet you. So, what do we have here?" Fermion inquired, gesturing to the skirmish playing out below them.

"We've got about two hundred and fifty men, all armed. The Copperheads number about a thousand. We think they only have as many guns as we do, though. It's hard to say what the situation is," Perry explained.

Now King did have a flash of something. It wasn't sight so much as recognition. These men were not merely ideologically opposed to the agenda of the Copperheads, but personally and intimately opposed. Here were three men who were part of a band of brothers, joined like three strands that could not be easily broken. One of the strands was under attack, and the other two would not stand for it.

The men smelled (in the vision King felt that he could smell it) of loyalty, courage, honor, and action. It was only a flash and it was interesting as far as it went, but King smiled slightly ... happy to know that Rich hadn't been a figment of his imagination after all.

"Ok, but why are you here?" Fermion pressed him. King leaned in and whispered to Fermion that he trusted these men. Fermion's expression did not change, but King sensed his gratitude.

"We've come to Cairo to reach what they are calling the Shadowmen. The Copperheads have been racing us the whole way. We lost contact with them a day ago, and evidently, they crossed the river somehow. They came up the southern bridge, but we made it across the other bridge, which comes across there, a bit ahead of them." Perry continued, "The Copperheads basically want to do what some of the Indian tribes want to do. Too bad we can't let them fight it out between each other!"

"We have spent time with the Shadowmen," Fides offered.

"That's true. Do you wish to join them in their fight against the Pledge?" Fermion asked.

The three men glanced at one another. Emory answered, "You could say that. No offense to you all, but I have no reason yet to trust you more than to leave it at that. It is important that we find them before the Pledge finds them."

"Do you hear those horns?" Fermion asked.

"Sure do," Perry replied, gruffly. "Can't figure out what the blazes that's all about, either."

"Worse than the horns is that other sound we hear," Simus said. "We're quite confident that we can hear heavy machine gunfire in that direction."

"Those horns are the Shadowmen, and the heavy machine gunfire is the Pledge," Jonathan explained.

Fermion very hastily explained to the three that they had spent some time running from the Pledge on their way to Bloomington and, in doing so, had run into the lines of the Shadowmen. The three listened to this with interest, and not a little concern.

"We can't hold those bridges against heavy machine gunfire," Perry muttered. "We can't even hold them against the Copperheads."

"They are about to get squeezed," Fermion pointed out. "The Shadowmen have a good ten thousand people. They don't have guns, but they do have bows and arrows and a lot of brave men. They're coming for Cairo because they know they've got to hold it or the Pledge will be able to control one of the primary north-south gateways. If the Copperheads are inbetween you and them, they are in for a nasty surprise."

"That may be. We were just getting across our bridge when they started shooting at us from the ruins of Fort Defiance; we managed to both arrive here at about the same time. Down that road are a thousand men, many of them armed. I think if anyone is going to get squeezed, it's going to be the Shadowmen. It won't take many snipers to pin down that bridge long enough for the machine guns to come and finish them off," Emory said.

"For future reference, does your force have a name?" Fermion asked.

"They call us the Rangers, and we take the name gladly. We're just a large group of average Americans whose folks never gave up their guns. Now we only wish we had better than hunting rifles. We have been pestering both the Copperheads and the Pledge for a decent while now, but we can see things are coming to a head. We have been trying to rally people to us as much as possible, but except for a handful here or there, people are reluctant to take a side," Emory lamented.

"Apathy sucks," Simus growled. King could see from Simus' expression that he had been the victim of inaction before. King wondered if he would yet See it.

"They'll be roused of it soon enough if the Pledge gets its way, but it will be a long time to throw off the burden placed on them," Fermion said. "But take heart! Your immediate concern is the Copperheads, and if we can, we want to make sure it's they that get sandwiched and not the Shadowmen."

"It's the Shadowmen we are here to find anyway, so I guess you're right. I guess our only choice is to try to make the effort to push them back across the bridge," Perry said, looking eager to go after them.

"Think of it this way," Fermion pointed out, "if you're engaging their whole force, perhaps they won't even notice the army sweeping in behind them."

"That's a fat chance, but it's worth the effort. Simus," Emory instructed, "go pass the word. Let's send forty men out into that open area to the west and try to flank them. Let everyone else know that once I give the cue, we're going to do an aggressive push. Tell them that the Shadowmen need us to draw the Copperheads away from the bridge. We're going to threaten them so much that they bring to bear all they got, and then, when I give the cue, we're all going to retreat into the city to try to suck the Copperheads in even farther. Go!"

King joined his friends as they accompanied the Rangers in their attack. The plan, however, quickly fell to pieces, but not adversely. Even though the Copperheads outnumbered the Rangers, the Rangers were better armed and had better aim. It descended into a rout. The Copperheads fled before them, surprised at the bold assault. King had no opportunities to swing his staff. All the while, the sounds of trumpets and horns and machine guns grew louder in the southwest.

At last, the Copperheads mounted a defense. King observed the skill and rapidity that Simus displayed in the face of changing circumstances. Bullets whizzed over their heads, forcing King and his friends to hunker down behind trees. Simus, however, braved the bullets and darted between positions issuing orders. Though King spotted more black men among the Rangers, they were mostly white people; in stark contrast to the attitude of the Copperheads, all of the Rangers took Simus' orders without hesitation, even Emory and Perry appeared to defer to him. On matters of strategy, Emory and Perry were in charge. In matters of actual combat, Simus was in his element, and the Rangers understood that.

After thirty minutes of exchanging light gunfire, they heard trumpets again. This time, the horns rang clear and close. They thought they could hear a low rumble. The Copperheads all suddenly jumped up out of their positions and began running for the eastern bridge.

"No doubt the Shadowmen have arrived," Fermion declared. The grey-cloaked warriors were beating a hasty retreat to the east even as they spoke, and the Rangers were looking at one another in confusion.

"Well," Perry said, "let's go meet 'em."

# == Chapter 13 ==

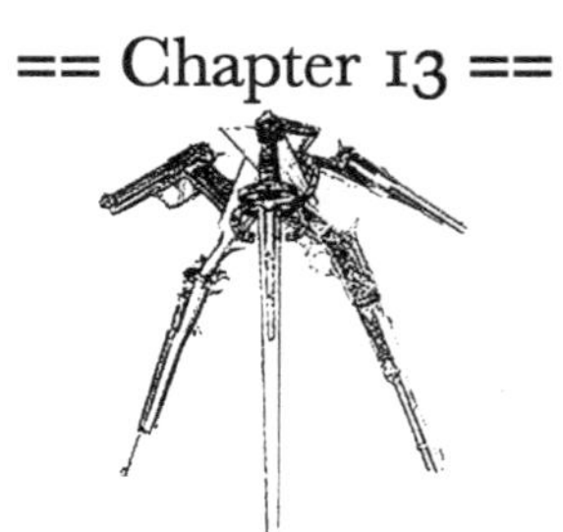

Simus led a detachment to monitor the fleeing Copperheads; the rest of the Rangers followed Emory and Perry, who cautiously approached the spearhead of the Shadowmen's force. That spearhead consisted of five hundred horsemen who had bounded across the bridge, and many of them were hauling store wagons behind them. These were dumping out dozens of men from within them, turning back around, and heading across the bridge. But two hundred very fearsome looking riders remained and were glaring ominously at the approaching Rangers. In the background, they could hear more trumpets and horns and the staccato heavy machine gunfire. The riders formed a line. Behind them, four or five hundred soldiers were getting their bearings. They had apparently had quite a ride and had been jostled thoroughly. King noted that even more wagons were coming across the bridge towards them and, alongside them were men jogging.

While this was going on, four riders formed up in the middle of the line of cavalrymen and trotted out in their direction. King felt shivers go down his spine when he saw them. Though they weren't very tall, they had the demeanor of kings. Clearly, they were of the Shadowmen. The four closed the distance in good time and greeted the Rangers walking out to meet them. King took his cue from Fermion, who followed a little behind the Rangers but remained within listening distance.

"Hail! Friend or foe?" called out one of the riders in the middle.

"Friend, and at your service, sir," Emory shouted out to them as they drew even closer. Now they were within normal speaking range. Perry and Emory stepped forward. "You must be among the Shadowmen, and we have come to bring a message to your leaders, and help you in your struggles to the best of our abilities," Emory continued.

"We will see that you at least see Nagro, and, if your message is worthy, he will decide and refer you to Yuri Ryson, our leader," the stocky prince said. "Right now, we are all in great danger. The Pledge is tied up a little ways from here with some of our archers, but we expect it to arrive with significant firepower. I trust you hear the machine gun fire."

"Yes, we do. How can we be of service?" Emory replied.

"My recommendation would be for you to get away from here as soon as you are able. We do not have the capability to resist their weaponry. Already, many men have been killed and wounded," he said solemnly. "We have killed only a few of the enemy in return. Nonetheless, we have been on the march since last night in hopes of getting here in time to properly account for that demonic gun. We have had to make up the difference by ferrying our foot soldiers in our supply wagons. It is a very dire situation," the man explained.

"I assure you that we don't consider machine guns to be weak weapons," Perry interjected, "but as you can tell, we all have guns. I bet our range is better than the range of your archers, and I bet we can teach the Pledge a lesson in respect!"

"They have guns, Dor!" one called out to their spokesman.

"Heavens," Dor exclaimed, "and you are willing to fight with us?"

"Without being asked," Perry declared.

"Dor," another of the four said, "all we need is something to keep the Pledge guns at bay long enough for us to get our people together and across the bridge."

"Agreed, Thamson. Tell me, friend, who were those men in grey cloaks we saw as we came across the bridge? I don't know who was more surprised to see each other, us or them," Dor asked.

"Those are the Copperheads," Emory answered. The four only returned dumb expressions, so Emory added, simply, "Enemies."

"That much we could tell. How many men can you spare?" the one called Dor wondered.

"We can send you one hundred men, each with his own rifle. It should be enough to send a nasty surprise to the Pledge. We need the rest to make sure the Copperheads don't try to come back across this other bridge," Emory said.

"More than generous." Dor turned to one of his fellows who hadn't spoken yet, "Greene, get us fifteen to twenty wagons over here immediately to get these marksmen across the bridge. Yuri will know what to do with them."

As Dor was issuing his order, Perry and Emory turned around and were barking orders to their own men. Simus, having rejoined them, was already selecting some of the squads that were to go forward. The hundred men or so chosen began walking towards the bridge. Greene had turned his mount around and thundered back to the line, which parted for him; a number of soldiers from the line peeled off on Greene's command, and they were now sending empty wagons back to pick up the Rangers.

Shadowmen soldiers on the Cairo side of the river now numbered one thousand. Many of these had begun moving towards Fort Defiance, which was the remains of an old fortress situated near the bridge. Those who had arrived there sat down in exhaustion to await the next move.

Dor turned his attention back to Emory and Perry, "What are you called by?"

"We are called the Rangers," Emory replied. "I'm Emory, and this is my friend Perry."

"It would seem that our meeting is timed perfectly to help each other," Dor said. "I don't think that either Nagro or Yuri will be over soon. They will want to make sure everyone else is across first. In light of that, we should make some arrangements between you and me about any preparations we think we should make."

"Can you tell us what kind of forces the Pledge is bringing?" Emory inquired.

"They have three large vehicles that are each mounted with heavy machine guns. They have four more vehicles that are loaded with men with rifles such as you have. It is embarrassing, but this force of no more than forty or fifty has managed to rout our army of ten thousand. We have good information that behind these is an army of ten to twelve thousand, mainly on foot," Dor informed them.

"I'm pretty sure we don't have twelve thousand rounds," Perry said to Emory.

"I think that is a safe assessment," Emory sadly agreed.

"If we could get their cursed machine guns silenced, we have more than enough manpower and courage to take them hand to hand!" blurted out Thamson.

"By my measure, you have about two hundred riflemen," Dor observed. "That may be what we need to do exactly that."

Fides interjected, "If the goal is to keep the bridge, shouldn't you want to deploy your guns mostly on the other side, and hold that? Otherwise, won't it end up simply with each side holding one side of the bridge?"

"Right you are," Dor said. "But even that is better than how things are looking now. I am afraid our plans have been thoroughly dashed. If it weren't for some men who shared with us the true extent of the enemy's weaponry, I suppose we would all have been cut down in the open some miles west of here."

"I believe that we were those men," Fermion said. Dor studied them.

"Yes, you do fit their description. Thank you very much. If only we'd have known sooner. Many are wounded, and some fine friends are dead." There was a deep sadness in Dor's eyes. "You were right—our armor does wonders at keeping the rounds from going through, but it's not as though the rounds bounce. We have been on the march since an hour after you left," he recounted. "Not knowing what the enemy's intentions were, we thought it wise to retreat as quickly as possible. And oh the grumbling!"

"How was I to know?" said one of the three.

"Blessed, I certainly don't mean only you," Dor back-pedaled. "The men of Cairo were especially unhappy. First to learn the rumor that they faced heavy machine guns, and then to learn that after trotting them out all that way to meet the threat we were going to triple-time it back? If I were them, I'd be upset, too."

"Plans?" Tasha reminded them. Emory and Dor began collaborating and as their plans didn't involve King and his friends, they made their way back to the inn to see if Tom had remained or fled. On the way back, they heard the Ranger's rifles cracking in the distance and a temporary silencing of the machine guns. Many of the men of Cairo who had been with the Shadowmen had crossed the bridge and were walking back to their city. Dozens of wounded were being helped back as well. On seeing the wounded, Tasha left them and began tending to people as she was able.

The rest continued to the inn and Tom, who had been watching events from the roof, came down to meet them. Fermion brought him up to date over the course of a hastily prepared meal and released Tom and his men from their obligation to drive them to Bloomington. The sense of relief emanating from Chummy's crew was palpable. King and his friends set about replenishing the crew's stores for their journey back to Tulsa; it was a small gesture, but all that could be offered under the circumstances. Their goodbyes were amicable enough.

After settling matters with Tom, they decided to make their way back up to where Tasha had been tending to the wounded and see how things were going. They found that the town had roused from its daze; the men of Cairo had returned, many of them wounded or dead. Many of their families were out looking for them, tending to them, or mourning for them. Some of the Shadowmen were also in the city, roving about on horses and sizing up the town's defensive infrastructure.

Finally, the friends arrived near the levee where the Copperheads and Rangers had first squared off, finding that the whole area had been turned into a hospital of sorts. Two hundred men were lying on the ground and being tended to. They noticed that Tasha helping and went to greet her. They found her working alongside some other women. King's jaw dropped; they were beautiful.

His instinctive assessment of their appearance was jarred, however. One of them seemed familiar to him. The more he looked at her the more he thought he recognized her, though he couldn't place her. She paid no attention to King. In fact, none of the women gave them more than a glance. Like Tasha, they were hard at work on the wounds of the men who were lying all around.

Fermion nudged King, "Let us go." Fermion then nodded towards Fides and Jonathan, who caught the hint as well. These women were all too busy for casual conversation. Down the road towards the south bridge, Fermion led them. In the plains where the bridge emptied, they found that thousands of people were milling about. The Ranger's rifles could still be heard in the distance, engaging the Pledge's heavy machine guns and riflemen.

"Look," Fermion said, pointing towards some tents that were being erected. "We might find the Shadowmen or Ranger leadership over there." They hastened in that direction but did not find anyone in charge there; those they sought were yet in combat. Having no further objectives, they remained in the vicinity.

Finally, all of the Shadowmen and men of Cairo were across the river, and the Pledge gunners had relented and withdrawn. Weary Shadowmen warriors streamed into the camp, and the men from Cairo continued on into the city. King saw that the Shadowmen didn't seem quite as awesome to look at as they once had. Waiting required patience, for the leaders of the Shadowmen were not soon in coming, but finally, they saw Yuri, Nagro, and Dor, heading their way.

Yuri was the first to speak, "Fermion! We owe you a debt of gratitude. You were right in every respect. Your counsel was right on. If we had tarried even an hour longer, the size of our army would have been measured by counting up how many rounds of ammunition the enemy had, and calculating the difference."

"My lord, it was my honor and my obligation," Fermion replied, bowing slightly. Yuri continued to heap accolades onto Fermion, but King was distracted by the sight of the two wizened men, Falda and Dolam, entering their tent. King slipped away from his friends and made his way over.

"Hello?" King called out politely near the entrance. Dolam peeked his wrinkled face through the door.

"King! Dear boy, please come in!" Dolam exclaimed. King stepped through the door and saw that Falda was grim-faced.

"We have met again," King said happily.

"Yes, yes, that is a pleasure, of course," Dolam smiled, but he nodded towards Falda, "but circumstances could be better. We have lost many a man, and even some good friends. Falda ..."

Falda glanced over at King and tried to put on a glad face, "It is a delight to see you, son. So, have you arrived at any conclusions?"

"Yes, well, yes. I had quite the experience last night, and I've decided to accept the visions," King replied.

"Excellent," Falda murmured.

King could see that the man was in emotional pain, but didn't know if he should speak to it or not. He didn't know if it was polite to call attention to the man's loss or impolite not to. He ventured to comfort Falda, "I am sorry for the losses of your friends ..."

"Thank you, King. The passing of the son of Bundo pierces me to the core, but this last adventure was his best to this point. He has his breath, and that is a very good thing, for now his adventure has really begun. I do not grieve like the rest of men. Not all tears are evil," Falda sighed.

There was an awkward silence. Falda and Dolam both were staring off into space, and King didn't know what else to say. He was relieved when someone else poked his head into the tent. It was Nagro.

"Ah, you're here," Nagro said, stepping through the entrance.

"Yes, I am here," Falda replied softly.

"He is gone, Falda," Nagro gazed at Falda tenderly.

"I felt his passing. It is time, then. A final goodbye, I hope, and all hellos after this," Falda winced, stuffing his pipe into his pocket.

"Many more of our dry bones will find their breath yet, dear friend," Dolam laid his hand on Falda's shoulder.

King slipped out the door as Nagro also moved closer to comfort Falda. He noticed that there were other Shadowmen grieving as well. Not all of them, however. Others were hastily setting up tents, watering horses, and moving supplies around. He saw Perry and Emory in conversation with Yuri. He had a sudden insight flash through his mind that Yuri was with the Shadowmen, but he was not one of them at all. King closed his eyes and opened them, and then he was back to normal.

"What is this new thing?" King wondered to himself. He was having thoughts that he knew were not his own. They were not visions, per se, but they were still from without. He kept walking.

He finally spotted where Fermion, Fides, and Jonathan were standing. They were talking with some of the Shadowmen. He recognized one of them as Calvin, their Master-at-arms. He was just leaving.

"Peace!" Fermion declared to Calvin as he walked away. At that moment, Nagro reappeared.

"Many thanks again!" Nagro said to Fermion, pumping his hand in gratitude.

Fermion wouldn't hear of it, "Truly, please, don't mention it."

"We shall mention it often and think of it even more often. What a blunder we made!" Nagro shook his head sadly. "I am afraid I cannot stay and talk," he said suddenly. "I have a solemn duty to perform."

"We understand," Fermion assured him.

Nagro gazed at them with his probing eyes, "We will be forming ranks two days from now to meet the Pledge. Yuri has invited you all to fight with us, standing side by side. Will you join us?"

"Most likely, sir," Fermion answered. "We are obviously honored by the invitation. However, we must consult with our friend, Tasha, and also take into consideration our own particular mission," he added, nodding towards Fides. King noticed the nod and wondered what he had missed while he was gone.

"That is understood," Nagro replied. "The invitation is open. I must go, now," Nagro said, shaking Fermion's hand again. King watched as Nagro strode over to where Falda was standing with some other Shadowmen. He glanced around at the flurry of activity. People were coming and going at Yuri and Calvin's command.

King recalled to his mind the latest piece of insight about Yuri, while the others talked about their next move. Fides suggested examining the bridge defenses, which they did, and then, with no other objectives for the moment, they decided to go and see how Tasha was. King, while present through all of this, remained lost in his thoughts. What did it mean to be with the Shadowmen, but not one of them? The obvious question was, What are the Shadowmen? What makes them special? Why did they have a sparkle about them before, something almost unworldly, and now not so much?

He was jerked out of his thoughts by a voice saying, "No, I think it's fair to say we didn't. Peder won't steer us wrong—or at least, we know he'll do quite his best. And Yuri is not here for no reason at all."

They had been walking behind the three for some time, and King hadn't even been paying attention. There really was a grand mystery afoot. Yuri was not here for no reason at all. He was here as the leader of the Shadowmen, but was not one of them. Did the Shadowmen know the answer to his questions?

The crowd of travelers on the road was parting.

It was Nagro again, but now he was on his way back from the direction of Cairo. Behind him were Falda and Leredo, and behind them were Dor, Greene, Thamson, and Blessed, bearing among them a stretcher. On that stretcher was a body, but it was covered in a brown blanket. There was clear sorrow etched on the faces of the stretcher-bearers. Now that they were not on their horses anymore, King noticed for the first time how short and stocky these men really were. They passed without looking to the right or to the left. Behind them trailed another pair of Shadowmen, but King hadn't seen these before.

"I would say that is Lobi," declared the young man who had mentioned Yuri's name. The girl he had been speaking with began crying, and the other man with them consoled her. Soon that threesome went in a different direction, and King saw the hospital field before them. It was cluttered with wounded and those tending to them. The beautiful women that King had noticed before were present, but now Dolam was here, too, along with the Shadowmen woman King remembered by the name of Gongral. King spotted Tasha at work and led the way over to her.

"How do things seem, Tasha?" King asked her when they drew near.

"Well, we simply do not have the supplies we need in order to save many of the worst wounded. Those we have tried to make as comfortable as possible. Many of them could still be saved if we had basic surgical instruments. It is very sad," Tasha replied.

"Is there anything you need? Any way we can help?" Fermion asked her.

"No, we are very well helped. Over there is a woman named Margory. Go and ask her, but as far as I know, we have all the blankets, water, and bandages that we need."

Margory did have a use for them. They wanted to move people from the field into the houses, old hotels, and inns that were in the city proper, so the four of them spent a good part of the morning and afternoon being stretcher-bearers. Often they broke off into pairs, so as to be more efficient. Sometimes King was sent running with some message or errand because he was still young enough to have energy.

Margory, a sweet but assertive young woman, had sent him to the Shadowmen camp, and on his way back he suddenly found that he was blind! *King toppled over into the dark and rolled over, bracing himself against the ground with the palms of his hand. What he felt wasn't the road. He was back in the cave, that old familiar cave. He smelled the damp air and heard his breath echoing off the walls. He thought he heard a noise, and yelped. Then he heard someone call out, "Who's there?"* King leapt to his feet, startled, and he was back on the road in Cairo.

"I may have gotten more than I bargained for, allowing these visions to begin again," King muttered, rubbing his eyes. He returned to the medical area but soon afterwards Margory decided she didn't need anymore help. King and Jonathan made their way back to the inn, where Fermion and Fides had already arrived.

King couldn't sleep that night. Several times he stepped out into the streets and took a brisk walk. He sat for a long time in the lobby of the inn. He had too much on his mind. Late into the night he began to drift off but was startled awake again by the sound of distant machine gunfire. He opened his eyes and saw it was still dark. Fermion was at the window scanning the road outside the inn.

"See anything?" King inquired groggily.

"Nope," Fermion replied tersely.

"Hey, has Tasha been back?" King suddenly wondered.

"No. I suppose she's still tending to the wounded," Fermion suggested.

"I can't really get comfortable anyway, so I'll go and check on her," King said, throwing his cloak over his shoulders and grabbing his staff.

"Give her our regards," Fermion said, still gazing out into the street.

"Will do," King replied, opening the door and stepping into the crisp, cold air.

It didn't take very long for King to get to the hospital area. The streets were quiet and empty, and there wasn't anyone to distract him. When he arrived there, most people were sleeping. Margory was sleeping, as were as two of the other women King had seen, but Tasha and yet another woman were still wide awake roaming through the fields and tending to men and women as they had need.

"Hi, Tasha," King greeted her.

"King. What are you doing up?" Tasha glanced up at him. King was silhouetted against the stars.

"I couldn't sleep. I thought I would come check on you," King answered.

"I'm fine. That was very sweet of you to come. But you must go back and get some sleep. You'll need it," Tasha instructed him.

King grinned, "Soon I'll be old enough that I won't have to listen to you anymore."

"Oh heavens, dear. You passed that age a long time ago. Now do as I say this one last time and go to bed," Tasha ordered him kindly.

"Yes ma'am," King obeyed. When he returned to the inn, he was able to fall right to sleep. It wasn't for long, though. It seemed as though he had just closed his eyes when he opened them to Fermion shaking him awake.

"Time to get up, King. The battle will probably start this morning rather than tomorrow as they had thought. Come," Fermion cajoled him.

It took even more effort to rouse Fides and Jonathan, but at last, the four men were walking towards the plains of Cairo. They didn't bother to wake up Tom and his men to let them know they were leaving, their goodbyes had already been given. As they neared the camp, the din of its preparations greeted them. Men and beasts were forming ranks. The four made straight for Yuri's tent. Nagro and Peder were in deep collaboration with Yuri. Calvin and Henryetta were in conversation with Perry, Emory, and the master tactician, Simus.

Seeing that Fermion had arrived, Yuri nodded to him, "Emory, why don't you run your plan by Fermion and see what he thinks?"

"Alright," Emory agreed. "We are working under the premise that we don't stand a real chance keeping those machine guns from coming across. We can unleash a hail of bullets on them, but they've got armored vehicles. It would be a lucky shot indeed. So, we save our ammunition and let them come within our range, which of course is their own range—no need to tell us that. The priority of the Rangers will be to take out the guns so that it's a fair fight for everyone. The problem is that doing this lets them get quite a lot of people over, while it would have been preferred to keep them off the bridge altogether."

Perry continued, "A good length of that bridge is fully exposed to the length of the ruins of Fort Defiance. So, we think with two hundred and forty men firing on it, and with some of Yuri's archers in the trees right where the bridge finally turns into the road, we might stand a decent chance of knocking off the guns."

Emory concluded, "We also don't know how many guns they have, ultimately. We know what we saw yesterday, which was three heavy machine guns, each mounted on an armored vehicle, and about thirty rifles. In an army of ten thousand that seems like the tip of the iceberg. But the Copperheads have a thousand men, and they could generate weapons for about a quarter of them."

"Twenty-five percent of ten thousand would be two thousand five hundred rifles coming down that bridge," Fides pointed out.

Emory shrugged. "We just don't know, really, what they have."

"And what of the rest of the army?" Fermion asked.

"Once we believe the machine guns have been disabled, we will charge," Nagro said.

"That's pretty straight forward," Fermion chuckled skeptically. There was no more time to try to come up with a new plan, however. Battle was near. In fact, they could hear the sounds of engines on the other side of the river getting louder and louder. King and his friends were invited to join the ranks of the Shadowmen, and they were quite happy to do so.

"Come, let's get you horses," Henryetta smiled at them warmly.

"Thank you, Ma'am," King smiled back. While it was true that the Shadowmen had lost their luster, Henryetta was proof that it was not all lost. Soon all four of them were mounted and assembled along with the Shadowmen. They were in the second rank. Though it was still pretty dark, King could see that the majority of the army was Shadowmen warriors. The men of Cairo had shrunk in number.

King couldn't see very far to his right, but to his immediate left were Henryetta and her contingent. Henryetta was in soft conversation with a man who had received a blow to the forehead. The scar could be seen prominently in the moonlight. King spotted a massive man, eight, nine, ten feet tall, King couldn't tell, standing alongside the horsemen and fidgeting. Behind Henryetta's friends, Dolam and Gongral roamed back and forth tending to last minute details. King spotted the grotesque face of Redemptus and averted his eyes.

Only a bit ahead of them all was Yuri, who was peering unblinkingly towards the bridge. The sun was beginning just now to send flares up over the horizon. King was able to see that the Shadowmen ranks were stacked dozens deep. There were spears, swords, and shields. There were cavalry and archers. It was a formidable display, but everyone knew that it was nothing in the face of even one heavy machine gun.

The sounds of rifle fire snapped the night air in half; the Rangers were firing from Fort Defiance, which overlooked the bridge. The sputtering sound of several machine guns erupted in answer. King could see the muzzle flashes from where he was perched. He gripped his staff tightly. He wanted to go down fighting, not picked off like a defenseless animal.

Signal men began flashing flags, and Yuri blurted out what it meant: "Get ready! There are men on the bridge now, and they are on their way!"

One could now see that the bridge was thick with men all the way back to the south side of the river. The north side was held by the Rangers, but under covering fire from their fellow soldiers, many of the Pledge were already pouring off the end of the bridge. Still others were leaping off the side of the bridge to the ground if they were far enough along to do so safely.

"Like they say," Henryetta said to her friends, "it was an honor and a privilege to fight by your sides."

"We'll make it, you watch, Henryetta!" blurted out one, stoically.

"Dearest Newt," she replied, "We hope, yes, but we have higher hope, do we not?"

"Hear hear!" two lanky men near the end shouted back to her, clanging their swords on their shields.

King tried to stare forward and pretend that he didn't hear what was being said near him. They were tender goodbyes, and they were not for him.

Henryetta leaned over and kissed the scarred man on the cheek, "Harold …" and then circled over to the man to Harold's left and kissed him, too, "Roland …"

"Cut it out now, you're going to make us blubber," Roland sniffed, wiping at his eyes. Henryetta did stop. She returned to her place and cast a sad look over to King, but then the sad look went away. It was replaced with fierce determination.

Nearby, in the direction of Peder's kindred, King heard people chanting a little tune. The tone of their voice and the words seemed to be designed to remind those around them of some story known only to them and to stir them to bravery and courage. King couldn't make any sense out of the verse but he never forgot the words:

*Cheeripeep's father gnaws on a rope*
*The Lion escapes and so catches our hope*
*Dry bones will have breath*
*Why not dry lines?*

In the meantime, the situation had deteriorated a great deal. Many Pledge soldiers were across, and the Rangers and some Shadowmen archers that had been positioned with them were in hand to hand combat in the ruins of old Fort Defiance and the surrounding trees. Worse, two trucks had gotten across the bridge and into the plains. Each truck had a machine gun mounted on the top.

The machine guns were distracted for a time on the harassing Ranger snipers, but at last, one of them turned its attention to the Shadowmen ranks. The truck began firing off rounds in their direction in five second intervals.

"It's fixing our range!" Calvin shouted. Yuri cursed and galloped his horse over to consult with Nagro. By this time, a third vehicle armed with a machine gun was across the bridge. A decision apparently made, Yuri galloped back to the middle of the line and stopped next to Fermion, only ten feet from King. Yuri raised his hands to his mouth to issue his order—presumably an order to charge—when Fermion reached out and grabbed his arm.

"Belay that order," Fermion said. It was a command.

"Can you do something as a Nephilim that can remedy this situation?" Yuri hastily asked him, unconscious of the imposition.

"I can try, and you have nothing to lose," Fermion returned, grim faced. King watched with interest as Yuri nodded his assent. Fermion drove his heels into his steed's side, sending it bolting out towards the first rank, and then through it. Fermion was now in the wide open. His sword was pointed at the Pledge, and his cloak flapped behind him in the wind. King muttered under his breath. Then he blinked. Then he opened his eyes.

Before him, the entire scene had become transformed. The ranks of the Shadowmen and the interspersed men of Cairo appeared like glittering gems in a bath of light. Fermion was the Mountain-Straddler once again, only now he was riding a comet across a black abyss. To King's surprise, where the Pledge line ought to be, there were still a fair number of diamonds twinkling back at him. He hadn't expected to see people of merit—for that is what he guessed it meant—in the Pledge lines. A cold rock formed in his stomach as he then saw what he had expected to see … gurgling up above the Pledge line were massive, dark tentacles, thrashing about at the sky. Hideous serpents leapt from spot to spot. A black ooze seemed to ebb and flow in the midst of the Pledge line. The Mountain-Straddler with his lightning lance seemed bent on piercing it.

Then King blinked and he saw things the way he was used to seeing them. He knew better than to ask himself which appearance was the real one. Most likely they both were.

The machine guns began firing in Fermion's direction and were answered by hundreds of Pledge riflemen. Fermion was halfway across the plains. With a start, King realized that the bullets were not getting through. The enemy's aim was fine. Their bullets were exploding in the air around Fermion, who seemed to be protected by a faintly visible silvery sphere. The Pledge gunners stopped firing as they realized that their bullets were having no effect.

Fermion pulled within forty yards of the advancing enemy, and dismounted. As he did so, he took his sword and thrust it into the dirt. Then, he stretched his hands into the sky, and a ball of fire appeared between them. King made himself blink. When he opened his eyes Fermion seemed to have an actual sun between his hands. It grew larger and larger against the backdrop of the Pledge's greasy shadow. In utter disbelief, King saw that the sun was being fed from shoots of flames from Fermion's body, in particular, but not exclusively, from his head. King blinked: there was Fermion again, as usual, but still with what seemed to be a blazing star in his hand!

There were gasps of disbelief and incredulity all around King. King was as startled at that as he was seeing Fermion on fire.

"We're all seeing it!" King blurted out in excitement. "Do you see that?" King laughed excitedly, poking Jonathan hard in the ribs.

"I see it, I see it!" Jonathan shouted. Fides was whooping.

All at once, there was a strange green flash, and the star between Fermion's hands disappeared. A green sphere now appeared around Fermion, but it was in fact only a wave of some kind, and it rapidly spread out in a circle from him, first encompassing the Pledge army, which was closest, but quickly enveloping the army of the Shadowmen, too. Then it was gone, zipping out into space behind them all. Fermion collapsed to the ground next to his sword. His horse turned around and trotted back to the first rank. Both armies faced each other in stunned silence, staring at the fallen figure between them.

Nobody knew what had been accomplished other than being treated to a marvelous and mysterious light show. A series of shouts came out of the Pledge ranks: they were renewed orders to press the attack. Once the Pledge soldiers began rumbling slowly forward, the Shadowmen observed that a wave of panic had overtaken their enemies. The vehicles were not moving. The weapons, as a whole, were not firing. Members of the Pledge who had rifles were checking their weapons' mechanisms. Some were able to fire, but most could not. Even some of the Ranger's guns had failed. Most importantly, the heavy machine guns were not firing. Yuri realized the significance of this fact before the Pledge commanders did.

"Chaaaaaaaaaaaarge!" Yuri shouted. The first rank, greatly encouraged, surged toward their enemy. After they had gone fifty steps, the second rank also began running to engage their foes. The third rank moved ahead as well, under the direction of Calvin, but it stopped short to await direction. Enemy commanders did finally figure out the effect of the crazy man's deed, and issued loud and urgent commands to meet the charging army, but the circumstances had changed dramatically. Now, the fine swords, shields, and armor that the Shadowmen possessed were superior to the weapons possessed by their enemy. That is to say, their enemy had no swords, had no shields, and had no armor. They had various dangerous instruments, but none as efficiently lethal as those possessed by the Shadowmen. The Pledge army didn't have time to reflect on that, because Yuri's wrath was quickly upon it.

Shortly after the first rank had begun thundering forward, and before the second rank had begun making its move, Fides had shouted to Jonathan and King, "First to Fermion!" The two sides had crashed into each other causing them to lose sight of where Fermion lay. Horses from the second rank were now in the full thick of battle. If Fermion was not pummeled to death by Pledge soldiers who came to him first, there was a chance he could be trampled to death by their own forces. The three of them tried to get into the area, but simply could not.

Even though the advantage had significantly changed, the Pledge remained a violent threat. The Shadowmen brought five thousand people crashing against three thousand, but the Pledge was effectively and efficiently getting its men across. In no time at all, they had four thousand, then five, and then six.

King found himself separated from his friends and could no longer determine even the general direction in which Fermion lay. Pledge soldiers were around him, now, so he had to pay attention to the threat they posed. Soon he was in full combat. His staff whirled around with power, and he jabbed to his left, to his right. His staff did not negotiate with those it came in contact with; it spoke decisively, and King told it what to say.

It was a romp. All around King were Shadowmen, Pledge, Rangers, and men of Cairo. It was so crowded sometimes that King didn't even have room to swing his staff. He received a small break to rest as he was jostled together with allies so tightly that he couldn't even move.

"Alo, King!" cried out a man at his shoulders.

"Hi there! I don't know you," King confessed.

"No, of course not. But I know you. You can call me Mike!" Mike introduced himself.

"Think we'll get back into the action?" King asked him with a toothy grin.

"Indeed, indeed. Temporary relief, you see. We'll get space yet," Mike laughed, wiping sweat out of his brows.

"I think I see some space coming now," King told him.

"You're right. I see it too! I'll see you later, to be sure!" Mike exclaimed. And then, like an accordion opening up, there was room again for King to battle and people for him to battle with. Mike disappeared into the scrum. King continued to crack as many heads as he could and carefully avoided hitting allies. He was on his own for several minutes, not knowing where he was or where any of his friends were. Suddenly, he saw Peder fight past his position, and because he recognized Peder as one of the leaders of the Shadowmen, he tried to fight his way in that direction.

He tripped and fell over a fallen person and saw that it was a Shadowman bleeding profusely from the chest.

"Oh, sorry! Lord, can I help you?" King stammered.

"Get Odo or Crisp, that's all!" the man offered weakly.

King stood up and gazed around to see if he could find the people the injured man was speaking of. He heard a sudden shout of pain and turned back to see a Pledge soldier with a pitchfork spear the man in the stomach.

"He was already hurt on the ground, dammit!" King snarled in rage. The Pledge soldier didn't get his weapon in the air in time to block King's heavy swing of his staff. The man's skull caved noticeably, and the man crumpled and was still. The staff itself was now cracked in two and was barely held together by a shard. King snapped the staff completely in half and looked about for the next soldier to smack with the pieces. At that moment, two Shadowmen fought their way through, and the wounded man smiled in spite of his pain and gasped, "I knew you would come, Odo. Knew it, Crisp. Give Luva my love ..."

"Thank you kindly for saving him," one of them said to King. He didn't know whether it was Odo or Crisp.

"I don't know if he'll make it," King apologized.

"Make it or not, he'll *make* it, don't you see?" was the reply.

King shrugged. Such comments were coming to be expected out of the mouths of the Shadowmen, and King didn't think he had time now to sort it out. Furthermore, he was distracted from the conversation on account of spotting Peder at war next to the giant of a man he had spotted cavorting with Henryetta's detachment. He made his way for the giant. After some effort and a few swipes of his sticks, King had joined Fides and Jonathan. The giant had Fermion securely around his neck. Dor and Thamson were there with Peder and a fair contingent of men from Cairo. They were all intent on getting Fermion out of the melee and to safety.

Fides noticed that King had joined them and saw that King's staff was broken. He laughed and called out to King, "Broke another one, did you son?"

King laughed in reply, "You can't believe how hard some of these people's heads are!"

They emerged on their side of the battle with no Pledge soldiers in the vicinity to trouble them. Horses were brought to them, and the giant laid Fermion's body gently over one of them.

"Here is his sword," a man said. It was a fighter from Cairo.

Yuri had found his way back to his reserve lines and ordered Fides to take Fermion to Cairo for care, and to retire from battle. Then Yuri turned his attention back to the battle at hand. Both armies were now in full force. Sporadic rifle fire could be heard from behind them as they began making for the road.

"Take good care of'im," the giant growled at Fides.

"Tally ho!" Dor shouted out, following the giant back into the fray.

Fides and Jonathan led the horse carrying Fermion up the road towards Cairo. They passed dozens and dozens of wounded men, and occasionally wounded women. Some were on stretchers, but many were being carried, or even dragged, by their comrades. King walked ahead, trying to clear a path. At last, they reached the hospital clearing. Men and women were working quickly but calmly to address the wounded that were laid at their feet.

Initially, they laid Fermion down there, but quickly realized he didn't have any normal wounds. They grew uncomfortable waiting. Several attendants didn't even give them a second look, so they decided to scoop him up again and head back to the inn, hoping Fermion would come to with some rest. They laid him on the floor in the main lobby, and then Jonathan and King went to the roof to see how the battle was going. After a time, they came down to report that the battle was still raging fiercely on the plain. Naturally, they couldn't see much of it from where they were, but they could get a general sense at any rate.

It was about then that Fermion whispered. They didn't recognize it as a whisper at first. They thought it was merely a deeper breath, or maybe a sigh. Then he did it again, and there were clearly two syllables to it. "He's talking!" Jonathan had declared. Fides put his ear right up close to Fermion's mouth.

"Taaaaa-sha ..." Fermion whispered, ever so faintly.

"He's trying to talk to Tasha," King said.

"Tasha isn't here, Fermion," Jonathan told him, kneeling next to him.

Fermion's eyes had been closed throughout this, but with Jonathan's words, Fermion's grey eyes flashed open. He reached up and grabbed Fides by his cloak, and with what must have been every ounce of energy he had left, quite audibly said, "Get Tasha!" And then he collapsed, and was very still.

"King, quickly! Go get her!" Fides commanded. There was fear and concern in Fides' voice, and King felt it too. He rushed out the door even before the command was complete. He turned to the right to make his dash towards the hospital area. He screeched to a stop, a long black sword pricking his belly. King was confronted with one of the short, dumpy looking fellows that he recalled served the Pledge delegation back in Oklahoma City.

"Back it up, boy," the stumpy man sneered.

King didn't even need to blink. He saw the man in all of his slime and grease, and then he did blink. The whole scene turned into inverted colors, as though reality had a contrast switch. The slime and grease went away, and he saw the usual stunted slave, but thought for sure there were serpents dancing inside the man's eyes.

"What do you want?" King blurted, backing slowly towards the inn. "What is your name?"

"Our name has changed, but we are still many," the man growled. "Now, open that door and in you go!"

King pushed through the door with the man's blade still at his belly. Jonathan and Fides whipped their heads in surprise that he had returned so soon, and then seeing what was happening they leapt up.

"What is your business?" demanded Fides, flashing his sword.

"This is one of the Pledge slaves," Jonathan blurted out, pulling his sword. The dumpy man flashed an evil smile, but didn't move. Fermion's body seemed to shake in the slave's presence.

"Get out of here!" came a woman's voice from somewhere behind the man. It was Tasha, but a Tasha enraged. King saw a flash of light that was only his own to see and then it was Tasha, just Tasha, for the Pledge slave was flung from the doorway. Tasha grasped both sides of the doorframe, and it seemed as though the whole building quivered. She threw a golden glance in King's direction: "King! Jonathan! Be sure he keeps running!" Then she stepped through the door and it seemed as though she filled it to the top. King didn't waste any time. With one of the lengths of his staff in hand, he rushed out the door, Jonathan following closely, in pursuit of the stunted man.

The man could be seen running ahead of them, not too far off and with a discernable limp. He threw frightened glances over his shoulders. King had outpaced Jonathan and was gaining on the little man.

"King! Watch out!" Jonathan shouted out to him.

King took his eyes off his prey long enough to notice that there was a band of Pledge soldiers loose in the city alleys. Indeed, King now noticed that there was one on one combat here and there. The dumpy man disappeared into the growing crowd of combatants.

"Let's get back!" Jonathan counseled.

"You bet!" King agreed. Pledge warriors were beginning to flood into the area. The two made double-time back to the inn. King burst rushed through the door, which was still open.

"The tide of the battle has changed! The Pledge is in the city!" King shouted. He noticed with shock that Fermion was up and alert.

"We need to get out of here!" Fides exclaimed.

"I think you're right," Fermion admitted. "I feel much better, but I still lack the strength. If it seems as though we can have no more good effect here, I confess we ought to get you and that key out of the grasp of the Pledge. If the Shadowmen have collapsed, we five will not be able to resist." Tasha helped Fermion to his feet. "We need to head north, immediately," he continued. "We shall hope that the tide changes here, but anticipate that it won't."

They quickly gathered their things, such as they were. It didn't take King long to finish, and he was sent outside to scout out the situation. About ten minutes later the other four came out of the inn, and Fermion led them to the north. King glanced at their faces; Fides seemed to have acquired a scowl in the last few minutes, Fermion a look of weariness, and Tasha, sadness.

They set up camp about five miles away as the sun began to go down. Fides was sullen, and the atmosphere was tense. King found out what had happened. Fermion had insisted that Fides leave his magnificent sword back in the inn, along with Fermion, who actually had left his sword. There was no conversation about it. Fides sulked. Ironically, Fides dropped his sword in a nearby river while trying to get firewood, and he lost the blade for good. With the object of the tension gone, the camaraderie returned.

That night, King slept deeply, but he had troubled dreams. In the dream, he was in a fight, a battle to the death. He needed a weapon or he was going to die. He reached out in panic but could find nothing. He felt the plunge of a knife into his chest and was left to die. He ran his hands over the wound, and the blood streamed out over his dark hands. King's body twitched in his sleep as he forced himself to dream a different dream. When he woke up in the morning, he had forgotten all about what was in his head that night as he slept.

# == Chapter 14 ==

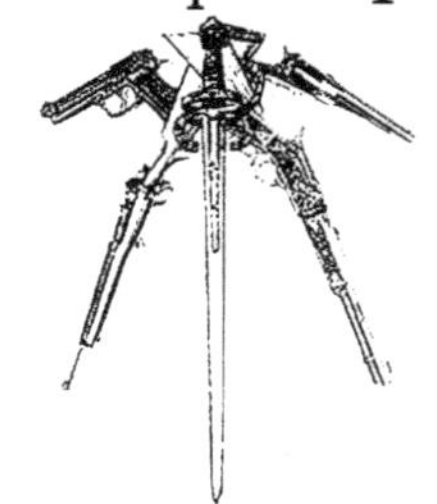

The smell of earthy forest was the first thing to greet King when he woke up. This was followed by the awareness that his muscles were tight and stiff, and was soon accompanied by the realization that he had various cuts, scratches, and bruises. In the adrenalin of the battle he hadn't noticed receiving the wounds or exerting himself, but now the toll on his body was indisputable.

Fermion took King aside at breakfast.

"You have decided to See, then?" Fermion gazed at him.

"Yes, more or less," King conceded.

"Are you committed to that decision?" Fermion asked, confused by King's answer.

"Actually, I am. How can I not be after I saw you flare up like a burning globe?" King laughed.

Fermion smiled, "Yes, I suppose you make a good point."

"I had made the decision beforehand, but ... whatever it is that you did encouraged me. I wasn't the only one who saw it, you understand? All this time I sort of wondered if it was all in my head. When I see you ... I haven't told you this before ..." King stammered.

"No, I don't want to know what you see when you See me," Fermion stopped him.

"Alright, my point really is that now others can see that there is more to you, too," King said.

"Comfort in numbers?" Fermion glanced at him.

"I guess you could say that," King admitted.

"That is not entirely unreasonable. On the other hand denying your own experience of reality is never a good step, no matter how many are arrayed against you. But I do understand. I hope that you will stay strong to your decision," Fermion advised him.

"I think I will," King said.

"Good. But look, the others are returning." Fermion said, changing the subject as the rest arrived after their morning rituals.

The decision was made to move closer to the road so they could glean from passersby what had happened in Cairo. Though they could see people on the road, none was close enough to talk to. They observed, though, that everyone was heading north out of the city, as though fleeing.

Around lunchtime, they stopped to have a rest and a snack. One of the benefits from their time in Cairo was that they'd had time to restock their stores. They had salted meats and tasty loaves of thick bread. They had been able to clean out their canteens properly, too. While they were resting, they heard the familiar sound of horses trotting on pavement. Looking to the south, they saw the Rangers coming in their direction.

"I don't think they have two hundred and fifty men, anymore," Jonathan said while they were still out of earshot.

"It's safe to say they've had better days," Tasha remarked.

The Rangers, having caught sight of them, rode over and dismounted. Emory and Perry approached them wearily and clearly burdened with sadness. He received no dramatic visions of them, but he did have a clear sense that the men embodied bravery derived from principle.

"Greetings," Emory called out.

"Emory. Perry. It is good to see you," Fermion replied. There were handshakes exchanged. Other Rangers whom they had become familiar with also gathered around while pleasantries were exchanged. Finally, Fermion gently asked, "What news do you have?"

"Well," Perry began, "I guess you could call it a victory. Cairo has not fallen."

"It seemed as though it had before we left," Fides exclaimed in pleased surprise.

"Well, it wasn't Cairo that they really wanted," Perry replied.

"Oh?" Fermion intoned.

"Yes, we are certain that they only wanted passage to the north. No doubt, actually taking Cairo and holding it would have been critical for them, but if they could have gotten by us altogether, I shouldn't think they wouldn't have tried," Emory explained.

"What is it to the north that they want?" Fermion wondered.

"Don't you know?" Emory threw a piercing gaze at Fermion.

"I do not understand," Fermion returned, confused.

"When we first encountered you and the Shadowmen, you will remember that we had a message for the Shadowmen. After we delivered that message, we learned that you had developed quite the reputation in their eyes. They instantly wanted your counsel. Clearly, they didn't have an opportunity to get it, which is one reason why I am going to share it with you now. It also seems that they think it might be relevant to you. They have instructed me to share the message with you. Here it is. We learned some time back that the Pledge leaders had recently changed their minds about their goals and the speed with which they wanted to achieve them. That is because they learned of something in Illinois that they thought could help achieve the final goal—world conquest, really—with more ease," Emory explained.

"So, they were actually on their way to obtain this thing, and not simply to gain a strategic hold, is that right?" King asked.

"That's right. We knew that the Shadowmen were moving to stop the Pledge, but we feared that they would go about things in the wrong way if they misunderstood the Pledge's intentions. I suppose we are lucky, all in all, with how things turned out," Emory continued.

"But what is it they want?" Jonathan pressed them.

"Come on, man. Fermion knows!" Perry blurted out.

"I only have a dim awareness of what you mean, I confess," Fermion said. "I know my own mission, and I know how important it is, but I cannot imagine how what I am sworn to protect would specifically help the Pledge."

"Alright, I'll come right to it," Emory decided. "The Pledge believes that the Ark of the Covenant is buried somewhere in the north."

"The Ark of the Covenant!" exclaimed Fermion.

"The Ark of the Covenant?" asked Fides. King was with Fides in not knowing what Emory was talking about.

"Ok, I'm going to harass you every night from here on to read some of Corrie's Bible, Fides. Believe none of it if you will, but at least you'll be informed," Fermion growled at Fides.

"The Ark of the Covenant was a chest carried by the ancient Israelites thousands of years ago," Emory patiently explained. "It was specially blessed by God, and God's presence went with it. Wherever the Ark was, there was success. The Pledge leaders calculate that with the Ark, they have a win-win situation. If it is not a magical mechanism to gain success, they will be able to exploit the superstition of the masses, at least. It would be a propaganda field day for them. They could show, too, that they were not opposed to religious expression. If it does have magic, then all the better."

"That is amazing," Fermion said, still dumbfounded. "How did they come to this information?"

"That, I cannot say. I do not know," Emory replied. "Is it true? Is it true that the Ark of the Covenant is in North America, of all places?"

"About one hundred years ago it was claimed that the Ark had been discovered. Of course, it had been missing for thousands of years, smuggled off and protected when it became evident that the nation of Israel was going to be defeated. There was all sorts of publicity. I would not be surprised if it was the real Ark. However, after a year it disappeared again. It was stolen from a museum in Jerusalem, and no one ever learned how or why. In fact, they were still in the process of deciding if it was the real thing or not when it was taken." Fermion paused. He thought for a moment, and then continued. "However, I know much of what is to the north, and as far as I know, it is not the Ark of the Covenant. I did not see it or hear of it, and I think I would have. I could be wrong, but I do not believe the Ark of the Covenant is there. But I would not want the Pledge to lay hands on what is there, either."

"What is there?" Perry asked.

"I am not permitted to tell you that," Fermion reluctantly admitted.

"This is all very interesting," King interrupted them impatiently. "I still would like to know how the battle fared!"

Then Emory told the story. He told it slowly and methodically, with Perry throwing in excited interjections, as he was known to do. The battle had not actually ever turned bad for them. What had happened, though, was that since the Pledge commanders had, in reality, only wanted to get past the Shadowmen army, they had collected their wits and focused on taking the bridge that the Copperheads had escaped over, and which the Rangers had used to enter Cairo. By sheer numerical superiority, the Pledge managed to erect a wall of soldiers to serve as a barrier. Behind the barrier, the majority of the Pledge found their way to the bridge across to Kentucky. Attempts to head them off failed, even though, thanks to the Ranger's message, they knew the attempt was possible and even likely. In the course of this escape, the Pledge mounted a surprise attack on the opposite flank. The Pledge soldiers, along with their strange, stunted slaves, forced their way into the city, as though looking for something. Emory paused in his story.

"Slippery folks. We didn't understand what was going on. We lost some good men, there," Emory said softly. "But afterwards we learned that there was a key to whatever was protecting the Ark, and that key was with you, Fermion. Maybe they do not know about the key, but after the display you put on, my friend, it's possible they simply wanted to take hold of you. At any rate, we think they were looking for you. We chased them from house to house, but in the end, the sneaky fellahs were able to escape and get back to their own lines and across the bridge to Kentucky."

King and Jonathan exchanged glances. Each guessed that Emory was probably right.

Emory told them that the Pledge army was now in Kentucky, though a thousand or more dead had been left on the flood plains south of Cairo. The Shadowmen had lost men, too, so the break from fighting was welcome. Some of the neighborhood blocks in Cairo had been torched, unfortunately, so the city itself had taken a wound. Emory explained that, as far as they knew, there was no good way to get across to Illinois from Kentucky anywhere close by, but there was a lock and dam to their northeast that, with some ingenuity, might be reformed well enough for the Pledge to get its army across.

With a better grasp of the full situation, the Shadowmen Army was, at that very moment, making plans to pursue the Pledge. However, the Shadowmen had decided the "key" needed more protection, and for that reason they dispatched the Rangers, who readily obeyed, to escort Fermion and his friends northward.

"So, tell us about this key you have, Fermion," Perry jumped in.

"I'm not the key. He's the key," Fermion replied, nodding toward Fides. Fides pulled the awkward necklace from beneath his shirt. "That cannot come off of his neck without the right code being entered. Any attempt to take it off without that code will kill him and destroy the key. Any attempt to open up the structure that key was designed for, without the key, will result in that structure being destroyed."

"So, we actually need to keep Fides away from the structure?" Emory inquired.

"No. Actually, as I said, opening the structure without the key will cause the structure to explode, destroying its contents. I have no doubt that the Pledge would make the attempt. This cannot be allowed to happen," Fermion explained.

"It is your mission. Ours is to accompany you for as long as it is necessary, and regardless of our own preferences. The Rangers are at your disposal, Fermion," Perry stated.

"I take your services gladly, and consider you as free men whom I would never dispose of. Serve me while seeking to serve also the men who follow you," Fermion corrected him.

"It is well said," Perry rejoined.

"How many men do you still have?" Fermion asked.

"We only have one hundred and fifty Rangers. We count the women accompanying us in that number," Emory replied. "Only one is a Ranger. The others are friends who have come with us a long way and wish to continue with us, but can leave whenever they please."

"I am sorry for your losses," Tasha offered gently.

"That is much appreciated," Emory returned.

"The map, Emory," Perry reminded him.

"Oh, yes. Here," Emory said, producing a map of the region. He spread it out between them and pointed at it. "As you can see, that lock and dam I mentioned is not all that far from here, and in some ways, as much on the way to Bloomington as our own way. We risk being cut off if we don't hustle. We should use our time advantage as much as possible to get past this point," he was jabbing his finger at lock and dam number 53, "and head for Bloomington with as much space between them and us as possible."

"The Shadowmen are going to try to stop or delay them. It is agreed that we must keep them from obtaining the Ark of the Covenant, but even more so it is our goal to put down the Pledge army altogether. So, we don't want to let it get away," Perry interjected again.

"Very well," Fermion said. "Let's finish our meals and then be on our way again. What are the chances that you have horses for us?"

"Very good!" Emory laughed. They all rose to go and get the horses that had been set aside for them. Perry led the way to the horses, but Emory turned aside to give out orders to the Ranger remnant. They found the horses lashed to three other horses, which were guided by three women.

"This is Misaluva. This is Charis. And this is Melody," Perry said, introducing them. All three women were stunningly beautiful. King didn't think he was the only person to notice, either. Jonathan, for example was opening and closing his mouth with a smirk playing at his lips, too nervous to say anything.

They all climbed onto their horses and situated themselves.

"It is a pleasure to meet you," Charis initiated with Fides.

"Delighted," Fides was saying. But Jonathan had found some courage and introduced himself to Melody, and King watched in mirth.

"Melody, my name is Jonathan," Jonathan said.

"How nice to meet you, Jonathan," Melody replied cordially. When Jonathan looked as though he was stumped for something else to say, Melody nodded towards King, "And who is your friend?"

"Friend? What friend?" Jonathan answered absent-mindedly. King poked him with one of the halves of his staff. Everyone laughed as Jonathan blushed.

"My name is King," King answered for Jonathan. That was about all King could get out, either, because he too felt his tongue was tied. Melody was extraordinarily lovely, and though she was older than King, this didn't stop him from considering the possibilities. To his disgust, hours later he realized that his beloved Joan never crossed his mind.

"Are you a Ranger?" Jonathan said, delighted to have found a coherent thing to say.

"No, I'm not. I am a companion to Charis," Melody replied, nodding towards Charis who was in conversation with Fides.

"How did you come to be with the Rangers, then?" King joined the conversation.

"In search of adventure and fellowship, danger and loyalty. In a word, a life worth living with people worth living with," she stated seriously.

"And you found what you were looking for with the Rangers?" Jonathan asked.

"Eventually, yes," Melody smiled, "But not at first. It is a long story and it begins with sorrow. However, that part of the story is not mine to tell, but Charis's, and it will be up to her if it is told."

And so the conversation went on, though Melody did most of the talking. That day they kept the horses on a fast walk, eager to get past the point where they were afraid the Pledge might be able to get ahead of them or even intercept them. The three women took turns finding out all there was to know about the traveling party that King was with. The men even had occasional opportunities to answer their questions! At some point, he didn't know when, he realized that he had seen all three women before. They had been working alongside Tasha to help the wounded in Cairo. Charis seemed even more familiar, but he couldn't put his finger on it.

All in all, it was a pleasant day for everyone. The conversation was light and even jovial. One wouldn't have guessed that the previous day there had been a great battle and they had lost many friends. That evening, they made camp on the shores of the Cache River. Again, there was good conversation. A dozen or more campfires were made, and everyone roamed from fire to fire, socializing. It wasn't much later than 10 p.m. when they began to drift off to their beds. By midnight, all were asleep, save Fermion, who had agreed to take the first watch.

In the morning they moved hastily to break camp. They wanted to be ahead of the Pledge army. Forgoing breakfast, they quietly and quickly packed up their belongings and started to the north at a steady pace. There was a lingering unease. It was entirely possible that they might stumble across the Pledge, in which case there would certainly be fighting.

After about three hours Emory directed the riders to take a break at a rest area they had come across. They were only about ten or fifteen miles from the place they most expected to meet the Pledge if it was going to be met at all, so Emory decided to send ahead some scouts. King eagerly volunteered to join that group. He welcomed the opportunity to assist his friends, and scouting was something that he had some experience with. Emory had no objections.

King was gathering his belongings and situating his horse when he felt a tap on the arm. He turned and saw a man who looked vaguely familiar. The man was grinning at him as though he was a long lost friend. King smiled and then noted that the man had a staff in his hand.

"King, it's me! Don't you remember? It is me, Mike. We fought alongside each other briefly in Cairo," the man said. King slowly remembered bumping up against the man in the midst of the melee. Neither had been able to move because so many people were in the battle.

"Yes, of course, now I remember!" King replied.

"I thought I would ride out with you guys today," Mike told him.

"I don't think I'm in charge of giving permission!" King joked.

"No," Mike laughed loudly, "But I wanted to give you something first. Here, a staff!" Mike was still wearing a big droopy grin, and when King didn't reach for the staff, Mike realized that King thought he was joking. A more serious look came in his eyes. "This staff was given to me by one of the Shadowmen to give to you, King," Mike explained.

"I don't want to break another one of their staffs!" King smiled.

"I think this one is special. He says that it is oak, but a special oak that won't break. At least, he doesn't think it will. Anyway, it was seen that you broke your previous staff, and the Shadowmen insisted you have this one as proof that their workmanship is better than you may have thought after your first one from them," Mike explained, the toothy grin again creeping across his face. King surmised that he was simply a happy person and couldn't resist being joyful.

"I don't know if I had thought to hold it against them. I swung the staff pretty hard," King tried to be gracious.

"There is no sense in trying to make me feel better about the matter. I have nothing invested here. I'm merely delivering a staff and the message. Do as you will, but if it were me, I'd accept the gift," Mike winked.

"I suppose I don't have a reason not to, do I?" King said, taking the staff in his hands. It was perfectly balanced, and the wood gleamed as though it were a royal scepter.

"Nope. I'll see you in a bit, now. Hurry up! They won't wait for sluggards!" cried Mike, jogging away to join the scouting group that was forming.

"There was a unique fellow," King muttered under his breath.

King finally had his affairs in order and had time to tie a rope to the staff that he used so he could sling it behind his back. He rode up to the group and saw Perry and Mike in merry conversation. He listened in and learned that it was also plan-making, but on account of Mike's perpetual gleefulness and Perry's general good nature it had sounded like light banter.

"We're off!" Perry declared at last. With that, King followed the fifteen or so other men ranging ahead to scout.

They double-timed it for a couple miles before finally slowing down. Perry divided the men into three groups of five or six. One group he sent to scout one side of the road and another to scout the other side. King was in the last group, which kept to the road. Except for Perry, he didn't know the men in the group. Perry kept looking at his map, but the rest of them fanned out on both sides of the old Interstate highway and kept a keen eye on their surroundings. King couldn't remember exactly what they were looking for. He knew that they wanted to evade the Pledge army if it made a dash to the north, but didn't know how they might pull that off. His question was answered an hour later when he saw the signs for Interstate 24. They were on I-57, but the concern was that the Pledge would connect with I-24, which merged with I-57.

The scouting parties on the flanks rejoined Perry on the road, and Perry had new orders for them.

"Ok, these Interstates come together at an angle about two or three miles ahead. We're going to stay in three groups. My group is going to continue ahead on I-57 and take a position where we can monitor the intersection of the two highways. I want Mike's group—here, Mike, look at the map—I want Mike's group to take this little road here that cuts the corner all the way across to I-24. I want Clayton's group to take that same little road, but then turn left on 37 here and follow that up to I-24. Be sure to keep an eye on your rear, though, Clayton. The straightest shot for the Pledge is 37, so even if that road is clear when you get there, it might not be for long. Hold your positions for about an hour or so, and then send messengers up to the merge. An hour after that everyone else can ride on up, though clearly we'll end up needing a rear guard," Perry patiently explained.

"No problem," Clayton replied.

"Just one thing. I want King to go with Mike's group and Kim and Mark to go with Clayton's group," Perry added.

"That's going to leave only you and Jeff," Clayton pointed out.

"Yes, but I don't expect to have trouble whereas you two groups are heading directly into danger. You'll need every man we can spare, and three is the most I can spare!" Perry ordered.

That signaled the end of the conversation. As Mike's and Clayton's groups were taking the same road for a time, King fell in with the ten men taking the old exit ramp that led to the road Perry wanted them to take.

Knowing that they were now heading directly into the area where they might expect a Pledge encounter, conversation came to an end. Mike and Clayton agreed to take either side of the road where trees would give them some cover, and the two groups wormed their way along carefully in sight of each other along their respective tree lines.

There were a number of smaller roads that emptied into their own that they approached cautiously, but only once they reached the town nestled between the two Interstates did they really go on alert. The name of the town was Goreville and it was eerily quiet. The road coming from the south that they were so worried about, 37, pierced Goreville right down the middle. They carefully wove their way through the abandoned streets. When 37 was visible, the two groups broke off from each other and they led their horses at a slow walk, so as to be able to hear the sounds of many men marching.

When at last they reached 37, they found that Goreville did have a citizenry. Perhaps there were even more in the surrounding buildings, but there were a goodly number of them gathered outside a general store, and the Rangers quickly convened on them for information. The Pledge may have come up I-24, but it had not come through Goreville.

This made matters simple enough. Mike's group would proceed to I-24, and Clayton's group would leave a few men behind on 37 to make sure their rear was covered. These lucky men were treated to beer and coffee and cheese, but the manager of the general store sent the rest of the group off with rolls, and they gladly took them with many thanks.

With Clayton's group behind and considerable relief in not stumbling across the Pledge in Goreville, Mike led his men south where they found a road that would take them to I-24. King knew that Mike was a jovial man, and that made the seriousness of his warning all the more obvious when he told them all to be quiet and pay attention.

A couple of hours later they had struck I-24, and Mike's caution appeared to be unnecessary. There was no sign of the Pledge.

"Marcus, you and King ride north. Let Clayton know that it's clear to this point, and then go on ahead and meet up with Perry and let him know," Mike ordered, his wide grin fixed on his face again. "We'll be along in due time as a rear guard."

Marcus was the opposite of Mike. He was grim and grumpy and hadn't said a word the entire trip. He nodded to King to follow him, and then he set off without a word. King didn't mind too much. It was nice to be back on an Interstate. Marcus moved them along at a quick pace, and it wasn't very long before they found Clayton and reported their news.

Clayton sent them along with a few other men to ride north to Perry. When they finally arrived at the merge, Perry wasn't there. It took a few minutes to realize it, but the main body had already passed that point. They could barely see them on the horizon heading north. Marcus said nothing and started out to meet them.

Soon they came upon the rear elements of the Rangers and Marcus stayed behind with them, letting King go forward with the news they had gathered. King saw Fides and greeted him, "We went south a little bit while we were waiting for you guys to catch up. We didn't see anything. I think we're safe." King reported. King surmised that Perry had already communicated something of the sort, but he thought he should ride up to where Emory was and make sure he knew the full story.

Emory graciously received the intelligence that King had to offer. Orders went out to keep pressing forward, even though it was already very late in the day and everyone had been on their horses for a long time. When at last they reached the city limits of a town named Marion, Perry convinced Emory that they had probably put more than enough room between them and the Pledge, at least for the evening.

Despite the fact that they knew they'd have to get up early in the morning, once again people stayed up late into the night talking. Perry and Emory provided great conversation. Emory would tell stories in his straightforward way, and Perry would interject with more colorful commentary as the tale would go on. It was their way, but without the imminent threat of battle surrounding them, they both gave into it whole-heartedly. Between the two of them, they managed to summarize how the Rangers had come to exist and how they had come to be opposed to groups like the Copperheads.

King didn't hear all of that account. He found himself joking around with Jonathan. Through the course of the evening, it became clear to King that Jonathan had given up his eyes for Melody and had taken a shine to the woman named Misaluva, instead. Though most couldn't tell this because it had grown dark, King was next to Jonathan at the fire and could see him throwing glances her way. If that weren't enough, he'd lean over and whisper declarations in King's ear meant to make him laugh, comments like "Wowsers!" and "Mama!" King really liked Jonathan.

As the night went on, residents from Marion came to visit them. Loud arguments sprung up between the Rangers and some of the men when it was learned that the Rangers opposed the Pledge. Not all of the men of Marion were of that mind. Before long, Marionites were arguing with one another and with the Rangers that were willing to take up the fight. King could hear the quarreling from afar, but was content to hover around his own fire and enjoy the company of Jonathan and others who happened by.

Finally, it became too late. They spread out their blankets even as the last men of Marion left the camp for their own beds. King saw Tasha lie down nearby as his heavy eyes finally closed with a thud. He fell into a dreamless sleep.

He awoke to the sound of Jonathan shouting. "Hey there! Help! Foes in the camp!" he was shouting. It took a moment for King to register that something was going on, but at last he yanked the blanket off, grabbed his staff, and tried to find out what the source of the problem was. He heard the sounds of tussling in the dark near the edge of the woods, where Fides and Fermion and a handful of others had gone to sleep. King squinted into the dark. If he didn't know better, there were dozens of men in mortal combat! He rushed ahead as someone produced a bit of light. It was hard to tell friend from foe, so he was reluctant to begin swinging.

"Step aside, King," Perry said, arriving on the scene. Behind him were Emory and a handful of other Rangers carrying rifles and torches. The increased light helped a great deal. Rangers rushed into the melee, and King could see that Tasha, Jonathan, and Misaluva were already engaged in the fight. King made a move to join them, but Perry stopped him again. He quickly realized why. A number of Rangers with rifles had come up to them and had taken a knee.

The command to fire was not given immediately out of fear of hitting their own, but as the numbers thinned and the Rangers could pick out their friends, Emory gave the command to commence firing. The Rangers fired carefully and selectively, only when they were sure of their shots. It didn't take long for the assailants to figure out what was going on, though it was much too late for them to do anything about it. When there were just a few of them left, some of them decided a mad charge was their best bet. The Ranger snipers let them get within ten feet to make certain that the shot was sure and dropped them one by one.

For a moment there was calm, but then came a burst of orders.

"Clear up!" Emory ordered.

"Check those men!" Perry demanded.

"Sentries, check in!" Emory snapped angrily.

"Seal the perimeter!" Perry shouted.

King rushed in now to see what had happened and saw Jonathan on the ground and Fides clawing his way over to him. Fides began shouting, "Hey, Tasha! Someone help Jonathan!" Tasha arrived and so did Charis, who began barking orders.

"Put pressure on that wound there, and there. Hold the arm up. Quick, put pressure there," Charis was saying. King backed away in order to give them room to work on Jonathan as well as some of the others who were injured. He watched helplessly and nervously from a campfire that had been stoked to a full blaze nearby.

Fermion was in conversation with Perry and Emory over two of the bandits who were unharmed and their prisoner. King wandered over to listen in on the conversation. Emory had agreed that the two would be allowed to live and would be handed over to the men of Marion to handle. Finally, Emory turned to Fermion, "Who's Jack?"

Fermion explained the story of the encounter with Jack and his men back in Albuquerque. King recalled that this is when Fermion and Fides had first met.

"Well," Fides said, "we'd forgotten all about them, hadn't we?"

"We sure did," Fermion concurred. "But we'll be able to safely forget about them from now on," he added.

King joined Fides and Fermion as they went to check on Jonathan. Tasha and Charis were working together to stitch the many wounds in Jonathan's left arm. Jonathan was still out cold. They joked that this was probably a good thing. When it seemed that there was nothing else to be done, everyone crawled off to bed. This time it was with the knowledge that Emory had set a substantial guard.

The next morning, Jonathan was one of the first to wake up. He began complaining immediately and cursing and swearing, but the only response was that people laughed and applauded him. Tasha hushed him and tended to his wounds. King wished him well and then wandered up to the leadership to see if he was needed. It was clear that he would be welcomed again as a scout.

After a time, Fides and Fermion joined them. Apparently, Jonathan was too weak to ride but insisted on coming along anyway. After some men from Marion arrived, it was arranged to obtain a wagon with which to haul Jonathan in. Misaluva agreed to pull that wagon. King couldn't help grinning at the thought of how happy that would make Jonathan.

"King, would you be willing to join the rear guard?" Emory put to him.

"Absolutely. Glad to be of service," King agreed.

"Let me introduce you to Aiken. A bunch of men from Marion have agreed to join the Rangers and help us in our cause. He's one of the town leaders, and I've asked him to lead the rear guard," Emory explained.

"Good to meet you, Aiken," King said, shaking his hand.

"A pleasure," Aiken replied. Aiken looked to be in his mid-forties, perhaps about the same age as Fides. His weathered face had a pleasant look about it, and he displayed a gentle smile.

"Shall we go?" King asked.

"Yep," said Aiken.

Each went to his horse and rallied with the men whom Emory had already dispatched to be the rear guard. On his way back, King wished Tasha a pleasant morning and inspected the cart that had been acquired for Jonathan. Jonathan was in for a bumpy ride, but men were still tinkering about in an effort to improve it.

The party moved off to the north in due time, and King and his company watched from their position about a half-mile south as it departed. There were merely twenty men in the rear guard, though Emory had dispatched scouts even farther behind. Most of the twenty were riflemen. Their task was to stall and delay any Pledge units that tried to approach, so that the main body might have time to react intelligently.

King quickly took to Aiken. Aiken was well respected by the men and women of Marion. He didn't seem to ever raise his voice, but when he issued an order he issued it firmly; even the Rangers that were with them obeyed. Aiken knew the area well. As they continued north they passed through various small towns, and Aiken would ride with King into them and spread the word about the Rangers and the coming Pledge.

Rumors of the Pledge had long been heard in the region, but the Rangers were the only ones to bring firsthand knowledge of them. Many of the men and women in the towns immediately began arranging for a defense, though in some places the old debate about whether or not the Pledge had the wrong idea broke out. Some citizens reported that relatives had already headed south to join the Pledge. Of those who had remained in the towns, there were many who expressed disgust for the Pledge. A great number of these chose to join the Rangers outright, quickly gathering their belongings and horses, leaving their towns behind, and rushing to catch up with the main body of Rangers as it passed through. So many men joined the Rangers on account of the persuasive words of the Marion Men that Perry began calling them the Mighty Men of Marion. The name stuck.

"So what was life like with the Cherokee, King?" Aiken asked him. Several days had passed, and Aiken and King were now in the advance guard. They were scouting ahead of the main body and even ahead of the advance guard itself. Though they kept a sharp eye out for signs of trouble, the deafening quiet of the woods around them persuaded them to believe that there was no immediate concern. Small talk was acceptable.

Aiken also knew his local history. The Trail of Tears which the Cherokee had followed to Oklahoma led through the southern part of Illinois. That was centuries before, but there were still monuments. He had been surprised to hear that Cherokee Indians still lived when King had first told him about his time with them.

"Very noble and very honest people, I would say," King ventured thoughtfully. "The ones I stayed with were, anyway. We actually had to fight a battle against other rival Cherokee once, so I guess you can't speak too generally."

"That is the thing, I suppose. Though for communication's sake we have to put people into groups, there are always many exceptions, and we can't be too quick to judge," Aiken agreed.

"That's right, though with the Cherokee there weren't many exceptions," King said.

"Now, are Fermion and Tasha Cherokee?" Aiken inquired.

"No, it is as I said, Tasha rescued me from somewhere in this area and took me West. As for Fermion, we met him in Oklahoma City with Fides. There is much I could say about Fermion, though I doubt you'd believe me," King replied.

"You wouldn't know until you tried. You know, we've heard stories from the Rangers about Fermion," Aiken offered cryptically.

"Stories?"

"About the battle of Cairo," Aiken prompted. It seemed inevitable that King would have to speak about the event. He hoped he could avoid talking about his visions, though.

"Well, I saw it with my own eyes. Fermion charged the Pledge lines, and a small sun blew out of him and disabled the Pledge's heavy guns. Call me crazy if you like, but I saw it with my own eyes," King affirmed.

"You've been traveling with him. Surely you have an explanation?" Aiken wondered.

"I can give you the one that he has given, take it as you like," King said. Aiken nodded, so King continued, "He says he is a Nephilim. Don't ask me what a Nephilim is. I take it that he is some sort of being from heaven—if you believe him."

"An angel?" Aiken asked.

"No, a human, but sent with a mission. Something about there being a life after death that is really living and not the singing of syrupy hymns forever, and for him that meant coming here on an adventure," King tried to explain, knowing full well he didn't know very much.

"We'd actually heard about the Cairo thing as you may have guessed. And I also heard that he had called himself a Nephilim, but none of us knew what to make of that. So I guess the question is do you believe him?" asked Aiken.

King realized he did. "Yes. There was a time when I didn't, but I have always known there was more to Fermion than the eye can see. Now thousands of people know it. They saw it with their own eyes, even as I did."

"There is more to everyone than just what we see, I think," Aiken stated.

"I think that is true. Not just metaphorically true, either, but actually true," King replied.

"Yes, that is what I meant."

King studied Aiken for a moment wondering if he too had seen visions. King changed the subject.

"What about you? What is your story?" King asked.

"Well. I've always lived in Marion. This whole area has seen hard times. We sent a lot of men to fight in the war with China and Mexico, and when the International Forces came trotting through to set up a power center in St. Louis, a goodly number of us put up a fight. I didn't fight in the war or against the IF. My wife and children were deathly sick. I had a girl and a boy, and without good medicine they ended up dying. My boy was eight and my girl was ten. My wife had the same illness." Aiken answered somberly.

"Was it the Disease?" King interjected.

"Nope. Just some run of the mill disease that they probably could have cured a hundred years ago, before all the calamities. Well, my wife ended up dying a year or so later, but not so much from the illness, I think—rather from a broken heart," Aiken sighed. His eyes were watery.

"I am very sorry, Aiken," King intoned softly.

"Well, thanks for that. Nothing to do about it. I can't say that my heart wasn't broken, either. I guess you basically have to make a decision eventually to let yourself heal and go on, but some don't. But my heart aches even now. If God is sending men from heaven that's a comfort, I say," Aiken said.

"Do you believe in God?" King put to him.

"Oh sure. In the fullest sense of the question. I believe he exists and I trust him, knowing he knows what he's doing, too. I know that death and disease weren't his idea, and I know that his idea was not to start over but to meet it all head on. He defeated death, don't you know, and some day he'll be along to set it all right," Aiken replied.

"What makes you think all of that?" King wondered.

"That's what Christianity is all about. Christians believe that God came down and endured our suffering before kicking some tail," Aiken stated matter-of-factly.

"Are you a Christian?" King pressed him.

"Certainly. I'm a pastor. Well, more or less. We've one Bible in Marion, and I was one of the few who knew where it was kept hidden. The Bible is a collection of documents that Christians believe give us the historical knowledge we need to know what God did so many years back," Aiken explained.

"Your Bible is hidden?" King asked him, trying to piece together what he could recall of accounts of the time before he was born.

"That's right. The IF came through and confiscated guns and religious books. All kinds of books, really, but especially religious books. A lot of people did what they could to hide guns. My father was the pastor in town, and he made sure to hide a copy of the Bible," Aiken told him.

"Fascinating," was all King could say. Talking about God was not something that King was used to doing. He wondered now if all this time the visions he was experiencing were from God. If they weren't simply his brain misfiring and they actually corresponded to reality somehow, then God might be a good explanation. The thought was startling: Why would God care about *him*? Even more perplexing: How could he learn more so he could test this explanation? King realized it might not be a coincidence that he had fallen in with and grown to like a man of sorrows who claimed to know something about God. Felix's objections several weeks earlier suddenly seemed to have more weight and he recalled the conversation between Felix and Fermion with a little more sympathy for Felix.

"A pretty tough time. And what with the Disease," Aiken continued while King fell into contemplative silence, "Things became even rougher for a time. But the Disease has run its course. The IF has withdrawn. The Chinese and Mexicans have withdrawn. There are no government controls at all, though many groups trying to set up some. Everyone has been put back to square one. In a sense, the world is fresh and clean, and we can start over. That's why I'm against the Pledge. Anyone who knows their history knows that whenever the Pledge's ideas have been tried, they've always failed."

"People seem to have strong feelings about the Pledge," King admitted.

"As right they should! I don't know what we're going to do, but going their way is a recipe for disaster. I like the Ranger's approach, though I don't know where it's going to take us. Escorting Fermion and Fides with more than two hundred men and women … if it ain't the Ark of the Covenant waiting for us up north, I don't quite get it. But the Rangers are good folk, and as you may have gathered I don't have anything holding me in Marion anymore," Aiken said.

"You heard about that Ark of the Covenant business? Do you think it's up north?" King asked him.

"The Rangers talk and talk, so of course I heard about it!" Aiken smiled. "As for whether it's up north or not, I reckon that depends on whether or not you trust Fermion."

"So you heard about what he said, too!"

"Like I said, the Rangers like to talk. That's ok, so do I, and so do my friends who have joined the Rangers," Aiken laughed. They noticed that men were coming to relieve them, and so the talk turned to other things.

# == Chapter 15 ==

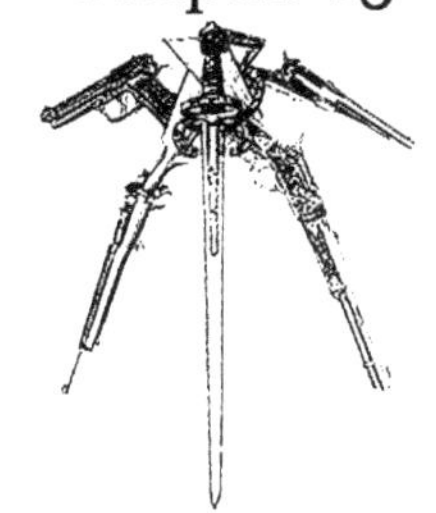

The weather became erratic as they traveled. While it had been a mild winter there were still moments of discomfort. The region began the transition from winter to early spring. The mornings were still cold and wet, but there were several days in a row where the sun's warmth paid for it all. After about a week of the welcome warmth, flowers began blooming, but it was too soon: there was a hard frost and they had to hide a little longer.

King and Aiken were together constantly. King's previous companions received Aiken as one of their own, while Aiken was seen less and less in command of the Mighty Men of Marion. Nonetheless, the Marionites deferred to Aiken for important questions, but these were few and far between because of Emory's skill in planning ahead and Perry's skill in executing orders and carrying out Emory's plans.

One day, several men from Marion came and pulled Aiken away from the campfire where King was sitting with his friends and fellow travelers. King watched them take Aiken out of earshot and then take up some pressing matter with him. The men gesticulated wildly, and Aiken glared at them resolutely in reply. Finally, it seemed that the men had achieved their purpose as Aiken threw up his hands in surrender. The men left and Aiken began walking back towards them.

"I think we've put poor Aiken in a spot, Fermion," Jonathan said to Fermion. They, like King, had watched the exchange.

"It will be fine," Tasha said.

"So you know what this is about?" King wondered.

"We do," Fermion replied. "The men of Marion asked me about the incident in Cairo and have heard that I am a Nephilim. As time has gone on, they have begun to wonder if attaching themselves to the Rangers is akin to joining a cult or fringe group," Fermion surmised. Aiken had returned.

For a few minutes Aiken poked at the fire pit. His friends from Marion had succeeded in persuading him to broach the subject, but he clearly didn't like it.

"Come, Aiken," Fermion counseled, "tell me your concerns."

Aiken glanced up at Fermion and couldn't help smiling at Fermion's perceptive abilities, "I somehow think you know what they are already."

"The Rangers saw it with their own eyes, but the men of Marion only heard about it from the Rangers. They asked me about it, and I shared with them what the Rangers had learned—that I am of the Nephilim. Some others were near when I explained what that meant. I can guess at their reactions," Fermion said.

"That is about the way of it. I had heard some bits about your deeds in Cairo and even something of your Nephilim claim. This is the first I had heard anyone was concerned about it. Now, some are concerned that we are in the errand of a fraud, or worse, a sorcerer. I could not tell them what you meant by the Nephilim so as to assure them. It is something I don't know," Aiken confessed.

"You might know more than you think, but you'd have to know Hebrew," Fermion comforted him. "But I will tell you about the Nephilim, and then you can decide for yourself and take back whatever counsel that you like."

"Very well, let me hear it," Aiken agreed. King leaned forward so as to hear better. He had wanted to hear more on the topic himself, and he had heard that Fermion had, albeit reluctantly, talked about the matter with some of the men and women traveling with them. King had been patrolling and had missed it.

"It is very simple, really. I think you will find it easy to grasp though it remains to be seen if you will find it easy enough to believe," Fermion began, gazing at Aiken while using a long stick to stir the embers of the fire. "This universe is one of innumerable creations, for the Creator delights in creating and even more in the created responding in love and affection for him, of their own free will. This particular creation that you live in is a fallen one, but not all creations are fallen. Can you tolerate the notion that other universes exist by a word, even as this one does?"

"It is an interesting thought. Not one that I've thought about before to be honest, but not one that seems objectionable provided you already believe there is a Creator," Aiken replied.

"And you do believe that, unless I misjudge my man," Fermion threw a glance at him.

"Yes, I do believe that."

"Very well. Now, as I said, not all creations are fallen, though some are. The Creator hopes that they will remain unfallen, but on account of his desire for reciprocated affection from free-willed creatures, he is careful in how he appears to them. This is all the more the case when the first decision to reject Him is made. The Creator sends out men and women from his other creations into his new creations in order to offer guidance and counsel. This guidance is intended to instruct the new creatures in Wisdom. Such Wisdom might allow an unfallen creation to continue to live in full fellowship with Him, but for a fallen creation the hope is to ward off the more horrific evils and so preserve the lives of men for the Mending that is in store for them. For the Creator is not content to let his creatures alone in their brokenness, but strives to make a restoration of all things in light of his perfect need for justice and his perfect desire for mercy."

"My dear man," Aiken laughed nervously, "if you are the Nephilim, you're quite a bit too late! Grievous horrors have befallen this creation while you were needed!" King couldn't help agreeing, though he said nothing. Jonathan glanced back and forth between the two men. Tasha sat on a log with her eyes closed.

"I wasn't finished!" Fermion smiled. "The Nephilim come early, yes, but they come again later. They are like bookends. They come in the beginning so that the story of that creation might proceed in Wisdom, but when there is a fallen creation they come also in the end, so that the story of that creation might end as well as possible."

Fermion paused, and then added grimly, "I am one who comes near the end."

"You don't seem like the sort of man to tell lies or fairy tales, Fermion. Nor do the Rangers seem like the kind of folk to exaggerate and spin legends. If it were not for their account of your deeds in Cairo, I should wonder how I might know if you speak the truth about such a mission. You would not give me a demonstration, though, would you?" Aiken asked. He knew the answer but tendered his question hopefully. Who would not want to see such a thing?

Fermion grinned at Aiken, "I would not, because I am not a toy, or a plaything of men. I will tell you, though, that if your race had not fallen into disobedience, you too would be able to do as I do and See as I See. What they thought in Cairo was a ball of fire was no such thing—it was a spiritual weapon that appeared as fire to our material eyes."

"A spiritual weapon?" King interjected.

"That is, it was thought," Fermion replied.

"Thought is spirit?" King scratched his head.

"No, but the mind represents spirit. We are not mere physical beings. We are amphibians, experiencing the physical world but breathing the spiritual air. And if you were unfallen, you would be able to see that which you live and breathe within. But it is not so, at least not yet," Fermion said. "Not until all things are birthed anew."

"Fascinating," Aiken chuckled.

"You believe me?" Fermion glanced at him.

"I will have to test this against what I already know to be true. It is the first I have heard of such things," Aiken replied.

"I would not have it any other way," Fermion answered.

"So I must know: were you from a fallen or an unfallen creation?" Aiken wondered.

"Unfallen."

"So how did you come to be a Nephilim? How does one 'get' from one creation to another?"

"By Thought. By Word. But it is only appointed to those who have died and passed on. Those living in an unfallen world live on to this day, filling ever and ever with more Wisdom and delighting in life and adventure," Fermion explained.

"How does one die in an unfallen world?" Aiken asked, confused.

"It isn't easy! I died in battle."

"Battle! In an unfallen world!" Aiken exclaimed.

"A battle not against men, but against another kind of enemy, something like the *hnakra* if that helps, but something we need not discuss here," Fermion said.

"But what about your wife and children?" Aiken demanded to know. King thought that was an excellent question. Jonathan was now leaning so far forward out of curiosity he might have fallen into the fire if he wasn't careful. Tasha made a small, sniffing noise, which King might have mistaken for a suppressed sob. When he glanced at her, though, she was still sitting with her eyes closed.

"Most Nephilim come from fallen worlds. Death is a bitter thing, but all the more so in a world where it has not been invited. But in my world, we all spend an allotted time as trained Warriors before we are permitted to raise a family. Once the time is up, you're free to marry and raise children, and you will not be called to battle again. If battle calls upon you, however, you will be able to stand strong in defense of those you love," Fermion answered.

"Fascinating," Aiken said again. Fermion smiled. King had seen enough by now not to heed the whispers of doubt and derision that mounted in his mind. He set aside such thoughts and commanded them to be silent. They obeyed.

"You still believe?" Fermion asked again.

"You can't make this stuff up! There is the testimony of the Rangers to take into account as well," Aiken replied.

"Perhaps it can be made up, but the truth is always more than we can imagine, not less. No eye can see, no mind can conceive of what is prepared for those He loves," Fermion acknowledged.

"Well, I will do my best to appease my friends. They are brave and noble, but they don't want to be taken in, either."

"The fear of appearing the fool in the eyes of others, or being had by a fraud, is enough to keep many a man from tasting and seeing," Fermion counseled, casting a glance at King and then at Fides.

"You speak a true word," Aiken said solemnly.

"Is it settled for now?" Fermion inquired.

"It is." And it was. Aiken went back to his friends and gave them his judgment. He reported to them later that there was still a measure of skepticism but they were willing to stand or fall by the judgment of Aiken, who in forty years had not let them down.

Their travels were without further incident until they drew closer to Effingham. They had begun discussing whether or not they ought to proceed to Bloomington where the family contact center was or if maybe Fides should go home first to see if his family was there. This led to contemplating whether everyone should go on to Terre Haute if Fides went, or if it might be better to divide the party with some escorting Fides and the rest going to Bloomington. The ultimate destination was Peoria. It was in Peoria that Fides would be able to rid himself of the treacherous key around his neck.

However, the closer they came to Effingham, the more anxious Fides was to go home, first. They were, relatively, much closer to Terre Haute than they were to Bloomington, and Fides remarked often that any trip to Bloomington without finding out what could be found out at home would only make for a longer trip later. After all, if there were no sign of his family in Bloomington, he'd have to go all the way back to Terre Haute, anyway. The counter argument was that, in such a case, Fides could go on to Peoria first from Bloomington and rid himself of the key, finally being unburdened from the tie to that city. Fides was definitely leaning towards a trip to Indiana first. The matter was left unsettled until Effingham itself.

As for King, he didn't have a strong opinion. When he reached Bloomington and the family registry was not as important as simply making sure he did at last arrive there. The farther north in Illinois he traveled, the more he found himself thinking about his own family. Tasha's memory began in Bloomington. She could tell King that they had arrived in Bloomington from the south and east, but that is all she could say. Still, there were times when King glanced at her and wondered if it was truer, rather, to say that it was all that she *would* say. King didn't know Tasha to be a dishonest person, however, so he thought little about such doubts.

Yet it was a fact that they were now approaching from the south and a little east, so King became progressively more contemplative. Perhaps this town was where his family had lived, and he was now passing by it! Or perhaps in this town Tasha had made her rescue! Might there be some old witness who could lead him home? He would have become immersed in such fantasies if it weren't for his ever growing relationship with Aiken.

Due in part to their growing affection for each other and also for King's ability to scout and Aiken's knowledge of the area, Emory had given them charge of the advance guard. About twenty of them rotated back and forth between the main group and the forward elements, and more often than not, Aiken and King would probe even farther ahead than the advanced guard itself. They would wake up early, and Aiken would give orders (or receive them, as necessary) and leave a half-hour before the rest of the group. They would be a mile or more ahead before the fires were out in camp.

These days, the road signs were reporting that the town of Effingham was drawing closer and closer. They had been traveling on I-57 but the signs also reported that another major Interstate was drawing nigh as well, I-70. Effingham was a fairly large city with many occupants, and there was still some debate amongst the leadership as to whether or not they would go through it or around it. Aiken urged that, for the sake of the Key, they should go around.

Finally, the day came when Effingham was less than a day's march away. A certain tension began to build up, and Emory asked all the scouts to be on a heightened sense of awareness. Few had to be told and certainly King and Aiken didn't. There were many more travelers on the road around them. This was in part because of the warming weather, but it was also due to the fact that Effingham was a more populous city. So it was that Aiken and King found themselves perched upon their horses scanning the wilderness a mile or two shy of the I-57 interchange with I-70.

"To be honest, King, I wouldn't think we're a very good advance guard if we don't take a peek at our flanks. I-70 is a big road. It is in the same shape as any other road these days, but still many men could travel on it if they wanted. An army, even," Aiken confided in King.

"There aren't supposed to be any armies in this direction. We ought to be ahead of the Pledge army as it is," King countered.

"Too true, but I'd like to know where they are rather than suppose. And do you suppose they might have gone around us?" Aiken replied.

"Then Ranger scouts are not worth their salt and neither are we!" King laughed.

"True again, but perhaps we can redeem ourselves by checking on the eastern and western approaches on I-70," Aiken smiled.

It was decided. They trotted back towards the main advance guard, which they knew would be making its way in their direction. When they reached it, they informed it of their plans and Aiken singled out from the guard two men he knew from Marion to come with them. These men would scout out to the east, while Aiken and King would check out the west. The remaining men would keep communication lines open with the main body.

They turned around, and together with the other two men from Marion, they traveled alongside one another until there was a wide open patch that would allow Aiken and King to cut across the open fields to the northwest. They said goodbye to the other men, and soon they were galloping across old corn fields that had become overrun with corn and weeds. The fields were still somewhat soggy from snow that had only recently melted and an earthy smell of rotting vegetation filled their nostrils.

"Look! A river!" Aiken declared after a time.

"I could do for a drink," King said, getting off his horse and leading it to the banks of the river.

"This is the Little Wabash river. This is the only part of it I'm really familiar with. I know it stretches out to the southeast from here, but I have only once or twice followed it. From this point, we have only to pass through a mile or two of forest and field and we'll be able to see I-70," Aiken informed him.

"Terrific," King answered between gulps.

At last the water break was over, and with only a little difficulty they found a place to ford the river. They were in the woods now. King liked being in the woods. One of the things he liked about scouting was that it often allowed him to roam through rough terrain and yet say he was just doing his duty.

They had not gone far, however, before they spotted trouble.

"That sounds like a large group of men, don't you agree?" Aiken whispered. They both leapt off their horses. They hooked the reins over branches to secure their mounts and crept forward. It didn't take long to find the men. They were making enough noise for a hundred though when they finally spotted them there were only fifty. The woods and trees grew thinner as they approached the men and it became clear that they were on the skirts of I-70 itself. That gray river could be seen just inside the horizon. Finally, the available cover was spent and they could go no farther. They turned their attention to scrutinizing the large group of men they had stumbled upon. The men were a mere fifty yards away and were not keeping a low profile.

"Fifty or so men. All on horses. I can pick out some rifles among them and more may have them," Aiken whispered.

"Does it seem as though there are leaders? I think so," said King. "See, that man there going back and forth between the small groups. I think he is giving orders."

"Hmmmm," Aiken murmured. While they continued to watch an order was apparently carried out. One of the small groups mounted up and rode at speed to the west.

"That is a curious thing to do. You don't suppose they are runners much like we have runners?" King suggested.

"If so, they must have someone they are running to. Perhaps they are an advance guard? We can hope not, but should act otherwise," Aiken replied. They backed through the underbrush back into the woods to their horses.

"So?" King asked.

"I say we ought to think the worst. You need to ride back and meet up with one of our own runners. Word must be sent to the main group that they should proceed no farther until we've sorted out these men. Give the message and return. I'll monitor them and wait for you here, or follow them in parallel," Aiken ordered. King immediately obeyed. He threaded his horse through the woods until he found the place he crossed the river and then set his steed across the corn fields at a hard gallop. He was spotted by some of their own advanced guard who had come close to that point already, and two of them raced out to meet King, closing the distance and hastening the delivery of the message.

King explained the situation to them quickly and they, in turn, raced back to deliver the message. Soon there would be more scouts dispatched in their direction and more men to carry messages need be. This required the delivering of the message. King glanced over his shoulder as he neared the edge of the corn fields and saw his message spiriting away to the south as fast as fast could be.

King returned to where Aiken's horse was still tied. He tied his own up again and crept forward until finally he was next to Aiken again.

"Anything new?" King asked.

"These men are starting to move northeast, and the men who we saw leave before have not returned. We could probably follow them in the woods for a bit before we needed to get our horses," Aiken answered. That is what they did. The riders were themselves riding parallel to the road, but carelessly. None of them looked to their left or their right. Their confidence was owed perhaps to the fact that, upon further inspection, nearly all of them carried rifles. The riders ambled on and it was easy to follow them.

"I feel something," King whispered suddenly.

"Eh?"

But King had his ear to the ground. Aiken smiled. He hadn't seen this before. King always surprised him.

King picked his head up and gazed to the west. Finally, he offered his conclusion, "If I didn't know better there is a bit of dust kicking up in that direction. I feel a slight rumble on my ears. It is very slight, but I think it is real. This may be the advanced guard we are tracking, and it may be the main army that is coming."

It seemed to be a sweeping conclusion based on such little evidence, but Aiken knew that King had been trained with some of the best scouts the world had offered.

"I see over there a large tree that has fallen out into the plains and tall grasses around it. It is on a slight hill and extends out toward the Interstate. From there I might be able to see both the doings of the advanced guard and the upcoming main army, if that is what we are seeing," King said.

"That large tree is less than forty yards from the men as it is. Seems risky," Aiken frowned.

"That's nothing!" King smiled. King began plucking grasses and jabbing them into his coat and shirt. He found a broke branch with fifteen dried leaves still on it and inserted the branch behind his head so that the leaves formed a spanning crown behind his head.

"Nice," Aiken smirked.

"Now watch," King retorted. He jogged a bit down the line of woods until he found a good spot, and then threw himself on his belly. He threw one glance at Aiken to make sure he was still there, and then began crawling forward through the tall grasses and assorted young saplings. In this time, the men he was stalking had gone a little farther away, but had stopped. By the time King found his tree and his cover, the men were about a hundred yards away, but King could see their projected path for a good mile. He turned his attention now to the southwest.

He barely contained a loud gasp. There were a thousand men on horseback trotting in his direction, following the line of the trees. They were only about two hundred yards away and closing fast enough that King doubted he could make it back to the woods in time not to be trampled in the attempt, and to go quicker might mean being spotted. He was debating what to do when the army dismounted to the man and began walking instead. They were still coming in his direction. He turned his head to check on the advanced guard. Most of these were gone, but several others were riding back to meet their friends. King was stuck.

He took some time to improve his concealment. The tree had a thick trunk, and the bottom half of it was soft and rotted. He burrowed underneath the tree and pulled more grasses over him. He worked to give himself a vantage point and finally, with some effort, he could still see the oncoming approach of the main army while remaining quite invisible. He could not, however, see the advanced guard, and he had only just contented himself with his position when the men he saw traveling back finally passed by him. He wondered what Aiken was thinking. By now, it was certain that Aiken had seen the men and had himself withdrawn a ways.

Like their advanced crew, the main army was loud and inattentive. King could hear them from a long ways out. He realized that they were going to pass right over his position and he hoped that he had done as good of a job concealing himself as he thought he had.

Then they were upon him. He could hear various conversations, and more than one rider walked over to his log and kicked it, or jumped on it. It takes some time for more than a thousand men to pass by. He listened more closely to what they were saying.

"We'll hit Effingham tomorrow. They won't rush us, I think ..."

"No, we'll meet the Cairo Pledge up by ..."

"Bloomington has only twenty or thirty thousand men and women. We'll be at least their match, but I don't know how we'll meet up with the eastern force. Somehow we've got to get word to the southern Pledge ..."

"We'll organize into regiments and squads once we're all together ..."

"How much bigger is the eastern force? I don't want a bunch of strangers ordering us around just because they're bigger ..."

"The rest will catch up ..."

"No, Cairo sapped them but they're still effective ..."

And on it went like that for four or five minutes and then the conversation became less interesting. King heard people talking about their women and what they plan on buying in Effingham, and then the army was past him. King dug his way out of his spot and crept back to the woods. Aiken was waiting for him.

"Good grief, King. Risky, like I said," Aiken chastised him.

"But I heard some interesting comments. It was well worth it. There is another Pledge army, Aiken! Maybe more than one!" King blurted out. He explained the story in a rush and tried to remember some of the more specific details like the names of places. Because he was not aware of the geography of Illinois, however, most of the names faded quickly from his memory. Only Effingham and Bloomington did he recall.

"Well, I was watching pretty close. There were about ten men in pretty close conversation the whole way, and they looked to me to be leaders. They passed pretty close to you. I don't think they were badly misinformed," Aiken declared.

"Tens of thousands: Bloomington's match! And we're taking two hundred and fifty men right into the thick of it!" King remarked.

"We have to get back!" said Aiken. The two found their horses and made off as quickly as they could. They ran into some Rangers and told them what was seen, and these went on ahead to keep tabs on the army. King and Aiken fled to the south as the sun was shedding its last scales for the day. Finally, they spotted the camp and galloped all the more urgently in search of Emory.

"What's going on?" Fides asked them, but King marched right up to Emory.

"There is another Pledge army!" King exclaimed.

"You're sure of it?" Emory inquired. This was unwelcome news.

"Yes, absolutely. We were right when we spotted those riders in thinking that they too were an advance guard for another party. We sent the relay back with our hunch to make sure that you didn't come too close, and then sought cover to watch. After about twenty minutes, we saw what I hope was the full body. There were at least a thousand men," King explained.

"Why do you hope it was the full body?" Jonathan asked.

"I shouldn't like to think there were even more than what we observed," Aiken answered for King.

"We think it was the full body, though, because we didn't see any others and we watched the full force pass us heading north," King said.

"But that's not all," Aiken reminded him.

"No, there's more. Even though I think we saw the full force, I think there really must be many more. Tens of thousands more, *somewhere*," King shuddered.

Perry's face went pale. Emory spoke, "What makes you say that?"

Perry screwed up his eyes trying to make sense of the message, "How can you think there must be many more while insisting you saw the full body?"

"Well, after the advanced guard went past, I thought I spied another vantage point to check things out from. So, I crept to it, and hid. Soon, the main group arrived. Well, I'm pretty lucky. I didn't expect so many people. There were so many that they walked right over my position. I heard some of them talking. Most of it was normal conversation, but they clearly think they are on their way north to meet a much larger body," King said.

"Perhaps they are expecting the force that we defeated at Cairo?" Fermion suggested.

"That's what I thought, too, but they seemed to know about the defeat in Cairo, and they included them in their estimated strength. I couldn't make out everything, of course. However, I definitely gathered that they thought they had at least a force of some twenty to thirty thousand, not including the Cairo force."

"You're sure about that?" Emory pushed him.

"Definitely. They passed right over me. They were talking about divisions and regiments and squads and a southern force and an eastern force and a western force. I didn't look to see at the time, but Aiken told me later that he thought their leadership went past near where he saw me hide. I am confident of this information," King added emphatically, annoyed that he was being doubted.

"This is a ruffle in our plans," Perry thought out loud.

"It sounds like they are on their way to take Peoria right now," Tasha suggested.

"It doesn't add up very well, though," Emory said. "We have been south, and I think we have a pretty good idea what is there. Though we heard of various smaller sized units of the Pledge, the groups we heard of were, more often than not, just like some of the roving bands of renegade Indians or Copperheads. We know of no group the size of the force at Cairo. And a western force? To the west are St. Louis and the Mississippi River. St. Louis is supposed to have been annihilated and should not have any population. I confess I know nothing about what is to the east."

"I'd stake my life on this information," King declared.

"I don't doubt you," Emory said, finally alleviating King's concerns. "In fact, I very much believe you and think you have the right view of things. What it means, though, is that we are operating on some very bad assumptions. It would seem, for example, that we are walking headlong into an army that is overwhelmingly large. Even the unit you saw is bigger than we are."

"Time to go off-road?" Perry suggested.

"No doubt," Emory agreed. "Our rear guards haven't been reporting anything behind us, but with I-70 passing so close we can't be sure. Let's make that our first step. Let's re-encamp a bit north of this little town on my map," he said, pointing to a dot called Watson. "Let's break camp right now, set up camp over there, and reconsider the matter," he ordered.

The orders were immediately delivered. The Rangers had complete trust in their leaders, so there wasn't even any grumbling. The fires were put out, the ashes hid as best as could be done, and the horses were repacked. Emory sent King and Aiken off to the east into the fields and woods to find a suitable place that was within a reasonable distance. They didn't have to go far to find a good sized hill that could conceal their position from any passerby on I-57. Camp was reset, and more armed scouts than normal were posted in a perimeter around their new position.

"Ok, what to do?" Emory opened the conversation among the leadership after the camp was settled.

The conversation ranged between subjects. Fides informed them that he now felt more than ever that he ought to go to Terre Haute and investigate his homestead before making for Bloomington and Peoria. Perry did not want to give up either town without a fight and Emory reminded Fides that the key around his neck was needed in Peoria, subtly asking Fides to choose between giving up his burden first which might be of aid to the whole nation or searching for his family which would ease only his own mind.

As that conversation went on King began to have his own thoughts. The Rangers and the men they had gathered in the small towns of Illinois numbered two hundred and fifty, maybe three hundred at the most. What good would such a small number do against a combined Pledge army of thirty to forty thousand? At best, they could merely hope to arrive in time to warn the residents of the threat arrayed against them. What good is that warning when there is nothing to be done about it? But King thought he had some ideas on how the scales could be balanced.

He knew where there were brave men and women who had the interest of the whole country in mind who might ride to the salvation of Bloomington. Though he knew the numbers were still far less than twenty thousand, indeed probably less than ten thousand, he recalled that they had a critical advantage: guns. Lots of guns. As King contemplated the affair, he realized that what Fides would need in order to get safely to Peoria was a grand distraction. If the Pledge could be pitted against a determined and well-equipped foe, then perhaps the Key could slip through. And yet someone would have to summon the Guns. Someone would have to go. It might already be too late.

King knew at once that he too was facing a choice. He had come all this way in search of his family, but to return to Oklahoma City might mean never finding them. The way was precarious. He reasoned that remaining with the Rangers might give him the opportunity to unwittingly defend his living family, even as he was ignorant as to who they were and where they were. No sooner did this thought cross his mind than did another thought, that perhaps arranging for Cherokee reinforcements might in fact be exactly what his living family needed. It was a hard decision to make.

While King was making hard decisions in his own mind, the council was making their own. As King slowly regained awareness of the conversations going on around him, he realized that plans had been made. Fides, Charis, Melody, Misaluva, Jonathan, and perhaps a half dozen Rangers would go on to Terre Haute, and then seek to rejoin them in either Bloomington proper or Peoria. Tasha, King, Fermion, and the remaining Rangers under Perry and Emory would press on to Peoria. King knew he must speak his mind now or never.

"I've been thinking," King began explaining some thoughts he'd developed. "That southern force we defeated in Cairo will soon be at our backs. The Shadowmen are likely to be behind them, but as it was, the Pledge force to the south is a good match in size and capabilities for the Shadowmen. What lies ahead is a force that is two or three times bigger, than even the Shadowmen. Even if we had everyone available, we would not be able to successfully resist."

"My boy," Perry said somewhat ruefully, "we do not retreat."

"No, no, no," King corrected him. "I'm not calling for a retreat. I'm saying that we need more men. More armed men, preferably."

Perry didn't quite see the point, so he scoffed, "Well sure, but where are we going to get more armed men?"

"Actually, I can think of a place," King said hesitantly. There was a lingering pause. King glanced first to Tasha and then to Fermion. Then he locked eyes with Jonathan, and finally he and Fides shared a long gaze.

Growing impatient, Perry blurted out, "Well, ok, you can tell us where we can find them now!"

Fermion gave the explanation. "We had an opportunity to meet with some Indians back in Oklahoma who were heavily armed and extremely disgusted with the Pledge. I do not know how many their total number would be, but they would be extremely well armed. I'm not talking about hunting rifles, here. I'm talking about military hardware."

That gained Perry's attention, "Oklahoma? That seems far."

"Yes, it could take some time, and someone will have to make the trip," King pointed out.

"It could take months!" Perry objected. However, the decision had already been made with silent looks.

"It very well could take months. You will have to try to postpone a confrontation if you can," King said.

"Ok, but who will go?" Emory brought the matter to the point.

"I will go," King asserted.

"You are only a boy!" Perry objected again.

King thought he had earned more respect than that and struck out in his own defense, "I am man enough for this!"

Aiken interrupted them. He addressed King, "I do not doubt your capabilities. I do hope it is no slight if I say that you would want a fellow warrior at your side. I will be that warrior, if you would permit it."

"That would be fine!" King agreed. He was somewhat surprised. He had expected Tasha to volunteer if anyone would, but he knew Aiken would be a worthy companion.

Perry was about to say something, but Emory poked him in the ribs. Emory eyed King across the licking flames of the camp fire, "I cannot keep you, of course. It is a noble effort, besides. As for trying to postpone a confrontation, that may not end up being within my power. I support you in your quest."

"Tasha, will you come with me?" King turned his attention to the woman that had been his guide for as long as he could remember.

"We have come far together, King. You no longer need me. I know you aren't asking out of necessity; you certainly are man enough for this task. Still, I feel that I will be needed to the north. At the very least, to tend to the wounded; I think there will be many. I hope you will forgive me," Tasha spoke with some apprehension, not knowing how King would respond. King was surprised, but saw that Tasha had been distancing herself from him for many a week. He knew in that instant that she had been letting him become more independent, and allowing him to go was her judgment that he was ready. It was bittersweet, but his affection for the dear old lady swelled.

"It is settled, then," King said. "We'll leave first thing in the morning."

"We'll need some new people to serve as our advance guards," Emory said.

With King's new information not much in the plans changed. The only difference was that King would not be heading north. There would be a three way split, though. King and Aiken would make the long and difficult journey to the west, Fermion and Tasha would head north with the Rangers, and Fides and Jonathan, accompanied by Charis, Misaluva, and Melody, would first seek the family of Fides in Terre Haute. That night King went to bed and could hardly sleep for all the excitement. Fides had his quest, and who knows what it would bring. King said to himself that he too had a quest, but he knew what it would bring: men and fire sticks in abundance, the salvation of Bloomington, and the destruction of the Pledge.

The dew was upon them the next morning. The scouts had reported that the Pledge army that had been discovered had continued away from them, and as yet there was no hint of impending conflict. King and Aiken checked their packs, and Emory saw to it that they had as many supplies as could be arranged.

Perry came over to make amends for his comments the night before and offered some supplies of his own: his pistol and the ammunition that went to it.

"No, Perry. Thank you kindly for your apology and the offer," King told him, "but I am going to count on pretending to be a common citizen, and these days common citizens don't carry guns."

"Bah," cried Perry, "Fides would not take a weapon either, and for a similar reason. You seem to forget that while the Pledge might overlook a common citizen, a common bandit will not!" But King was not to be persuaded.

Emory wasn't to be persuaded either after he heard King's plan in full. He marched over with Fermion and Tasha at his side, but only Emory was perturbed.

"What is this I hear about you heading into St. Louis? Don't you know it is a nuclear wasteland?" Emory complained.

"It is also the most direct route to Oklahoma and the Cherokee nation," Aiken informed him.

King reasoned with Emory, "Look, if a Pledge army can form up somewhere in the west it had to come from somewhere. If not St. Louis, it crossed the great river somewhere, and we will be able to find that crossing, too. There isn't time to turn to Cairo."

King had expected Fermion to back Emory since he had strode over with him, but Fermion surprised him by coming to his defense, "It is his quest, Emory."

Fermion's word settled the matter.

## == Chapter 16 ==

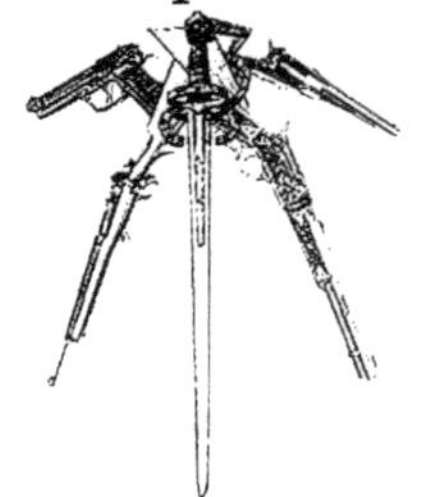

After an early breakfast, the hour of parting was at hand. King embraced them all in turn. Tasha held him close and relinquished him slowly. Jonathan shook his hand and rubbed his head and tried to look like it didn't affect him, but began to cry anyway. Then he and Fides said their farewells. He, after all, was also leaving the main body of Rangers, though he had a few more going with him.

Fermion put his hand on his shoulders, "You may not yet know your father, King, but he would be proud of your effort here. If I am ever given the opportunity, I shall tell him personally. We shall see."

Charis came over with Melody and Misaluva with her. "We haven't talked as much since we first met, King, but I really respect what you're doing and wish you well."

"Thanks, Charis," King blushed. She really did seem familiar. Then Charis hugged him, and then Melody and Misaluva were hugging him too. When Jonathan was looking, King mustered up his courage and took the hand of the closest beautiful woman he could find—it was Misaluva—and bent down and kissed it gently. "My lady, the honor was mine," he said, winking at Jonathan.

Jonathan burst into laughter, "King, you dog!" After recovering from the shock, Misaluva laughed too, and soon all those around who witnessed it or heard about it laughed long and loud.

Jonathan blushed and King blushed too, amazed at himself for what he had done, but Misaluva kissed him on the cheek and said, "Well met, my friend."

But it really was time to leave, and there were tears all around. King shook a few more hands, and Perry slapped him on the back. Fermion nodded knowingly at him, and Tasha smiled and choked back a tear as a mother might do. Aiken had respectfully stood back as King and his friends exchanged their farewells. When they appeared to be ended, though, he strode over. Yet Tasha lingered.

Tasha put her hands on Aiken's shoulders, startling him.

"Aiken, you're a good man and have been a worthy friend to King and to the rest of us. I want to thank you ..." Tasha said.

"Of course, yes, my pleasure," Aiken stammered. He instinctively tried to pull back out of social habit, but Tasha clung to him. He marveled at the strength of this old woman, for he knew he was a strong man, yet he could not move under her grip.

"I want you to have something," Tasha began.

"No, really, such things are unnecessary!" Aiken tried to be polite. But Tasha shushed him.

"Be quiet, Aiken, and receive what I have for you," she said, letting go of his shoulders at last and extending her hand towards him. Nestled in the palm of her hand there was an object. Aiken reached for it and took it into his hand. Tasha gazed at him as he lowered his eyes to see what it was.

"I said once that I would find a man who was worthy to possess it. I have known for a time that you were that man. Take it. Let it be a token of friendship between us, a symbol of a price paid so that though we part today, on account of what is symbolized, we know we might meet again," Tasha recited solemnly.

Aiken took the cross and the chain that held it and put it around his neck. He was speechless, but Tasha wouldn't let him talk anyway.

"Go now in peace," she said. "You have your charge. You know what to do. I need not dwell on it. Depart now in favor."

Aiken nodded his head in deference to the ancient respect that Tasha commanded of him. Without another word either to him or to King, she left to join the Rangers who were already beginning their trek north. Ready at last, King and Aiken struck out on their horses for the wastelands of St. Louis. King threw a glance over his shoulder, and for a moment he thought he saw a silvery river winding north and five sparkling stars trotting on their steeds away from him towards Terre Haute. The journey was on.

The idea was to make a straight shot towards St. Louis. I-70 might have been close enough for that, but they didn't want to take a route they knew had so recently been traversed by the Pledge. They cut across the country knowing that I-70 angled down in front of them. They would pick it up again near a town of Vandalia and would hopefully evade any Pledge units that way. It had the remaining benefit of still being a reasonably straight path.

At first they journeyed in silence. Something like grief came over King as he left his friends. He had been with them for many a month, and the Rangers had become close even if not as close. More than that, he felt like he was walking away from his one best chance to find out about his family. He had set out to find his father and his surviving family in order to set things right so that he could return to his dear Joan whole and intact, in order to start his own family.

Aiken had surely left behind beloved friends as well, but they had said their farewells long before. Aiken spent so much time with King out scouting that his leadership had slowly passed to other men of

Marion, though he was always well esteemed and still had led the advanced units. Now he was heading west to a region he knew was desolate. He without a son, King without a father. This was not lost on Aiken, but it was not clear if it had dawned on King.

They rode with haste as they were able, but when others were traveling nearby they slowed so as to avoid raising suspicions. They passed through little towns as quickly as possible. They reached Vandalia on their second day, and were resolutely informed by more than one person that there was very little to see to the west. Why would anyone venture into wastelands? The talk was all about the Pledge, but they dared not ask questions. The Pledge had emerged from the Wastelands, and that was the first these people had heard about them. King and Aiken exchanged thoughtful glances. Perhaps St. Louis was not as desolate as people believed.

Early on the third day they started seeing signs. The signs displayed warnings and prohibitions and detoured people away to the south or the north. By the end of the day, the signs now had even more ominous messages such as: "You Are Entering the Desolation Region" and "Beware! Radioactive Fall Out!" They spotted something else that caused them even more concern: guards.

They certainly looked like average citizens, but they eyed any westbound travelers with deep suspicion, and occasionally upbraided them and badgered them into making a detour. They had probably been spared because they were riding on horses, while the others were on foot and in reach. They had witnessed several such encounters and concluded that they needed to get off the Interstate and find roads less watched. That night they camped a stone's throw from a little town called Lebanon.

On the fourth morning, they did their best to escape the watchful eyes of the locals. They ranged north and south, occasionally coming within sight of what looked to be some sort of wall. It was not apparent that it was guarded, but there were citizens about and King and Aiken didn't trust them one bit. They ended up retracing their steps and returning to the environs of Lebanon to camp for the night.

"We're four days in, but we could be a lot farther if we really worked these horses," King sighed.

"Hard enough with snooping town folk about. Add in these guards, and we've got to be real careful," Aiken replied.

"Can I see the map?" King asked Aiken. Aiken handed it to him. The two had been given a very old, hand drawn map by the Rangers. It had been copied from a copy of a copy of a quality map, such as they had decades ago. This one was starting to fall apart. The Rangers had only let it go at all because they had recently made a new copy of it for their own use. It charted the borders of the individual states, rivers, the Interstates, and occasional important roads and cities. The detail around St. Louis was scant.

"I think there must have been bridges where each Interstate goes across the Mississippi. We needn't go through the middle of the city. I don't know what this one is called," Aiken pointed at one of the Interstates, "But it swings down to the south, outside the city, and hopefully outside its mythical desolation. It is also more on the way."

"If that one is blocked, we can hope to find another way across farther south. I agree. There is no sense in taking a more northern route," King concluded.

"Excellent. The light is fading. I'll take first watch," Aiken said. King was exhausted and more than happy to take Aiken up on his offer. The days were growing longer, though, so they shared some small talk for a while. Aiken kept the fire going, but at last King dropped off.

*"Who's there? Who's there I say?"*

*King opened his eyes.*

*"I'll find you and run you through! You'd best come clean. Declare yourself!"*

*He felt the cold and clammy dark air and knew where he was. It was the Black Cave and the Voice Within It. The voice was not far away.*

*"I'm not crazy, I say! Here and then not here! Going on and on with naught but my own breathing, and then there is you! With your heart beating! Declare yourself! I'll be upon you in half a moment!"*

*King leapt up in the dark. The voice was coming his way. He groped in the dark for anything to put his hands on. He had no sense of direction but one: the direction of the Voice. King, for one, did not feel compelled to reveal himself to a voice in the dark without more information. He retreated as quietly as possible away from the voice.*

*"Aha! I've got you!"*

*King had slammed unceremoniously into some sort of rocky wall. He had let out a grunt quite against his will. He sat down with his back against the wall and listened to the soft padding footsteps plodding towards him. There simply was nothing else he could do.*

*"I know these caverns like the back of my hand. Been in them long enough! Yes, I know exactly what nook you're in right now. Speak and you might yet save your life! That is your only hope now."*

*King dared a response: "Hope is vain, I think. You have me cornered." He felt something like hopelessness descend upon him, weighing him down, pressing on his chest.*

*"Hope! Hope is what has kept me alive, and you, the bringer of hope!"*

"King! Wake up!" It was Aiken, shaking him. King's eyes fluttered open. It was no longer pitch black. The stars might not be as bright as the sun and moon, but they are light enough when there is none at all. Remembering his fear he lashed out with his arms like one trying to save himself from drowning.

"Oh man, I've just barely been saved!" King declared.

"It was a dream, King. Have no fear!" Aiken comforted him. But King knew better. His visions were different than his dreams. His dreams felt somewhat real as he slept, yet he always knew it wasn't quite real. His visions were always at least as real as his waking world, and more often than not they were more real, more substantial than reality itself. This had been real. He had been in the cave. He knew it.

"No. No, I'm afraid it isn't a dream," King said, getting a hold of himself. He sat up and drew close to the fire. Aiken drew back wondering what King meant. King looked at him and said, "Aiken. I must tell you something I have not told you before. You may think I'm crazy, but I'm not. I think if you can accept Fermion's explanations, you may accept mine. But, well, hang on."

King told him all that he could think of about the visions he'd received. He recounted how they began and some of their recurring themes. He told him about his decision not to See and then his decision to See again and what this had sometimes meant.

"But each time I See the cave I'm there for a little longer, and the person that is there senses me more. He nearly had his hands on me this time. I don't know what will happen when at last he catches me," King trembled. "You don't think I'm crazy, do you?"

Aiken shook his head, "No. No, I don't. It is a unique account by all measures, but you're not a person who lies. If we were compelled to dismiss all accounts merely because they were unique, we'd have to dispense with virtually all we learn from other humans. You don't lie, and that settles it."

"I haven't had this vision in some time. I have sometimes had glimpses of Sight the last month or so, but not very many and not this one again. I fear for my life," King replied, comforted that Aiken believed him.

"What did the man say to you at the end again?" Aiken bent his head in thought.

"Something like hope is keeping him alive, and I am the bringer of hope," King said.

"Those are not the words of a murderer, unless my sense of judgment fails me now in my old age. If this happens again, I suggest you speak to him right away. Something of profit might emerge," Aiken counseled him.

"That is not something that occurred to me to do. I'll try it," King agreed.

"Well you have another hour or two before it is your turn for the watch. Maybe you'll have your chance yet tonight," Aiken said.

So King went back to sleep, but no more visions, nor any dreams, came to him that night. Aiken let him sleep a little longer but when, at last, he could stay awake no more, he let King take his turn. The night passed without further event.

The conversation was casual and light as they shared a quick breakfast. Haste was still the order of the day, so after tending to the horses they packed everything up and buried the fire. They followed the road through a small town called O'Fallon and quickly came across yet another ancient highway. It was I-64. They debated briefly whether or not they should take it since it was I-70 that they had spotted the Pledge on, but they recalled the sentries they had spotted and guessed that all the major roads would have them. Their map could not be trusted to tell them how far out of the way they might go if they strayed from a main road, but it couldn't be helped. They stuck to the back roads.

"Don't you think we'd start seeing signs of an actual nuclear wasteland in here sometime?" King thought out loud.

"I was thinking the same thing. I'm trying to work through some kind of scenario that would account for the universal belief that St. Louis had been wiped out, when in fact it was spared," Aiken ruminated.

"The city seems to have been a large one by all accounts. It must be some operation to keep the truth concealed," King said.

"Indeed," Aiken agreed, "Which is another good reason to stay away from the guards. What lengths would they go to in preventing the truth from being revealed?"

There were many more signs expressing dire warnings and predictions along their path even though they were far off of the main road. They continued to bear southwest, and the lush woodlands bore no indication that there was any truth to the warnings. They came to an intersection of many roads and here discovered that there was an armed outpost positioned by it, closely monitoring the travels of those nearby.

The sentries, guards, and soldiers let them pass, but it was only under a keen eye. They passed through the intersection warily and were glad to put the soldiers behind them. Several miles down the road their anxiety dissipated some, and they slowed down to give their horses a break.

"Have I told you about Joan?" King asked Aiken, making an effort to conceal the fact that his stomach had fluttered even as he asked the question.

"No, who is Joan?" Aiken smiled.

"She will be my wife. She waits for me in Tulsa," King smiled at the thought.

"You left behind a woman to make this trip? That is some hardship!"

"She was too young. Well, I am too, more likely than not. Her parents would not have let her marry yet. I left to seek my family and set things right here and return with everything in order. It seems that plan has become delayed," King sighed.

"All in good time. It sounds like her parents expressed their views on this?" Aiken tilted his head at King.

King wasn't interested in sharing the details of that exchange so he said, "They did. Yet they offered hope and confidence that the right time would come."

"Ah, it is nice to hear that there are parents who act in wisdom. That is not always the case today, and from the stories I was told from my own parents, not the case in the past, either," Aiken remarked.

"What kind of stories?" King wondered.

"All kinds of stories. Most parents tend to want to protect their children, but sometimes they let them be exposed to the dangers of life too soon, or didn't equip them to face those dangers at any rate. That is my experience. But my father told me that in the days of his father and grandfather it was even worse: children were brought into the world without parents, for example."

"Without parents?" King was confused.

"Yes," said Aiken, "They used technology so that a single man might have a thousand or more children and they would never meet. Many times this was done in the name of kindness, for couples who struggled to have children because of health issues. Yet many were born for couples who could not have children because of the nature of reality. Boys without fathers, girls without mothers. As often as not, their own flesh and blood were ever unknown to them."

"I don't see what technology could achieve this. What happened to the children? What happened?" King frowned in thought.

"They grew up lost and detached and knew that they were missing something. By the thousands they sought their blood parents, even in cases where the ones who had raised them had been loving enough. This was the tragic selfishness of that time: they insisted on having children brought into their relationship so that they could feel whole, but this at the expense of the children, who would feel empty," Aiken explained.

"What happened to these children?" King probed.

"They have left behind their mark. They strove against the world as the world collapsed around them, and had no moorings. They looked to fill up their empty places with whatever seemed would work. When you don't know what goes in a place, but you feel something should go there, you may heedlessly insert something dangerous or toxic," Aiken ruminated.

"But ought not the parents you speak of have known better?" King wanted to know.

"Them? Heaven's no! The thought didn't cross their mind. What they were doing had never been done before, but the notion that some dire consequence may come out of it for the children they insisted on having was the least of their concerns. When, decades later, the children went searching for their real mother or their real father or turned to destructive habits to provide for their lost sense of identity and namehood, the adoptive parents had the gall to look surprised. It grew even worse ... at first technology allowed a single man to sire a thousand children for a hefty profit to him with no lasting responsibilities, but then technology reached the point where they could clone a child from nothing more than bits of DNA."

"You're beginning to speak of things I don't understand. A sense of identity? Namehood? DNA?" King asked. He was fascinated by the story, but frustrated that he knew so little.

"Let's start with DNA. It was discovered that information is what drives living systems. Like a map, or a blueprint, DNA was like a language that carried out operations that resulted in virtually every step of human development and activity. From the tiniest cells to our largest organs, our DNA is what made it happen. Animals, too, have DNA. It is the language of life. Well, if you scrape some skin off your hand, there is DNA in the skin flakes. There is DNA in your hair and even a tiny drop of spit in your mouth. Amazing, don't you think?" Aiken glanced at him.

"Yes, I would say so. I cannot see this information you speak of, though," King confessed.

"No, of course not. It is very small. You would need advanced technology the likes that we will probably not have again on this planet for some time. But there was a time when they could. And from the smallest bits of DNA they could create whole humans. Do you understand?"

"You mean that they could take the DNA contained in my skin and make a whole human being out of it?" King was incredulous.

"More or less, yes. They got to be very good at what they were doing. They never stopped to consider whether or not they *should* do the things they were able to do," Aiken sighed.

"What do you mean?"

"Now we come to it. You set out for Illinois in search for your family. Your mother you believe is dead, but your father and siblings you hope are alive. But you believed that you had a father and a mother. You wanted to learn what they were like because you instinctively perceived that you would bear some of their characteristics. You would find out who you were by learning who they were. You too have a lost sense of identity. You too have lost your namehood. That is, your parents gave you a name, and to you the name represents a reality … latent in that reality is their love and respect for you. In all of this, you know at least that you were born out of a loving embrace—they had sex, King—" Aiken chuckled at King's dumb look and then continued, "and so you can make some guesses about who you are and why you're so named."

"So, I am like that generation you spoke of. In my case, it was not that my parents had sought a child at whatever expense, but rather conflict and war came upon us and we're separated. Yet still I search … I *must* search …" King murmured.

"Yes, very like that. But now let's think of our cloned children. When they are of age, their scientist father tells them proudly that they were crafted from the scraped skin of his left hand. Such an identity! Why was the child brought into the world? The child guesses: to prove that it could be done! And why stop with scraped skin? What about pieces of bone marrow? How about a nose hair? And if you could create a child from the DNA found in the hairs of nostrils, why not hair elsewhere, say a butt hair? Behold, your identity, my child! Carefully cultivated from the hair of a grown man's ass! Just to prove we could! That is your identity: Thy father is Balaam!" Aiken cried out. He clenched his fists as he thought about the subject and then continued on, "So you see, there was a whole generation, maybe two—hundreds of thousands, if not millions—of young people who grew up in doubt of their identity … or in contempt of it. Oh sure, they tried to reason with them: 'DNA is DNA. From a hair or from a skin cell or from the joining of sperm and egg into an embryo. No difference.' But there was a difference, and those who were born that way knew it and would not be counseled otherwise."

"Surely you overstate it when you say they did these things just to prove they could! Could they not prove it simply by starting the new life out and then ending it early on, and spare the children the shame of such a source?" King despaired.

"But think of what you're saying! To create life out of various mediums just because you can is bad enough. Is it better to start the life and then destroy it? Is this really an ethical escape? But you're not far off. For a time that is exactly what they did, and they were content. They created life at will, but then destroyed it to escape the charge of destroying life. You see how it worked: so long as they desired it, they pounded their chests at their successful creation of life. 'Look at us! We created life!' they called. But when the organism became a burden, whether in the womb or outside it, it was merely a mass of cells and devoid of any need for ethical considerations—and thus easily disposed of. Such clarity of thinking they possessed! Yes, they were content for awhile with creating cloned humans, and then content for awhile creating organs by themselves here and there. But Nobel prizes were not easily won. Nor did governments fail to see the value in being able to produce men and women to their own liking. As soldiers perhaps, but more often as workers—slaves, if you will. There were only the beginnings of those possibilities when hell poured out on the planet: nuclear holocausts, wars, the Disease. I confess that even in light of the horrific loss of human life that came from those events, I do not feel altogether sad. We can imagine that right now the world's governments might be breeding slaves by the millions for their own nefarious purposes. This is horrific in itself. If we must choose between horrors, I will take the one that ends with men living wild and free," Aiken declared, his eyes like burning coals.

"You have recounted amazing things. I am beginning to understand how things have come to be the way they are today. I understand more of myself and my quest to find my family before settling down to start my own. I see that I am not alone in this desire; it is part of our natures that cannot be denied," King summarized.

"Denied? Yes, but at peril," Aiken corrected him.

Such perils had evidently come to fruition. They passed the next few miles in silence. These were deep things. King's heart resonated as Aiken had spoken about things that had begun and almost begun. He made up his mind that he would not stay in the Cherokee nation, but would definitely ride back, both to help his friends whom he had sought help for and also to make another attempt at establishing his namehood.

"I remember my father," Aiken smiled, starting up the conversation out of the dead silence.

"Oh?" King prompted him.

"In my earliest memory he was so large, and I was so small. I didn't think a larger man lived on the planet. He was strong! He could lift me up and twirl me around and toss me about! I would strive against him, and he would let me win! There was often tumbling involved. He had a hearty laugh, though also a fierce temper. He would sometimes apologize for it. He rarely exerted it against me or my brothers and sister, or my mother, but … sometimes. When he was in anger he was like a rumbling maelstrom that one should journey far to avoid. He taught me to fight and he taught me to pray and he taught me how to treat a woman. He was a fine man and brave. He hid the town's only Bible at great personal risk, and even hid others of the Book as they fled from their oppressors. I am honored to be counted his son," Aiken reminisced.

"He sounds like a fine man," King remarked.

"He was! Flaws and all, he was! He was my mountain to conquer, my dragon to slay! For years he was my rugged battleground to march upon. I remember the day I first drew blood!" Aiken laughed.

"You drew his blood?" King chuckled.

"Yes! I was nine or ten, I don't know. I hit him with a closed fist right on the lip, and he started bleeding right away. His lip swelled up, and it was black for two days!" Aiken continued laughing.

"Was he mad at you?" King asked, smiling.

"That was the thing! Not at all! He said to me, 'Now you know your power, don't you? You can cause even your father to bleed!'" Aiken recounted. He added, "My mother wasn't so approving. She wanted me disciplined, but he told her that it was good for a young man to know his strength, and it was better to learn against his father than not at all, or too late. I remember her, too! Standing there with her hands on her hips glaring at my father! I didn't linger! I escaped!"

King saw that Aiken delighted at the memory and laughed throughout the story, and yet his eyes were moist. King felt it best not to speak. After at time, Aiken continued, "Yes, I miss them. Death is a terrible foe, even if defanged. And ... and I had looked forward to my son having memories of me ... But it is I who have memories of him and he has gone on! I had longed to tell a strapping young man that my daughter was too young for marriage; those years are snuffed out, not to be restored!" Aiken choked back a sob. His chest heaved as he struggled to regain his composure.

"Yes, King. We shall find your father, and we shall make sure that you are whole for Joan. I shall help. And though I weep for my lost loved ones, I do not weep as though they were forever lost," Aiken managed to work out at last.

King felt like he ought to say something. Aiken was spilling his heart out to him. King knew that that kind of honesty meant that Aiken held him in high esteem. The best that King could manage was, "Thank you, Aiken, for all your words and your friendship to this point. I thank you."

Then silence overtook them again as they trotted across the roads and fields of southwestern Illinois. When they had guessed it was about five o'clock in the afternoon they decided to set their horses off on a gallop in the cooling of the day. They relaxed their horses about an hour later. They saw a little ahead of them another important road, and the road they were on was ending. They would have to choose between north and south or to continue across the open fields. The Mississippi river was not far, now.

They saw a small town not too far to the north and decided to head into it to see if they could get a sense of direction before camping for the night. Immediately, they noticed that the buildings were well cared for. There were people about who didn't seem to be travelers, rather contented citizens. Content, yes, but not very friendly. They tried to start up casual conversation with several of the citizens, but the men and women didn't seem to want to talk to them. It was only as they were nearing the north edge of the town that anyone had anything to say to them, and it was an uneasy exchange to say the least.

"Where do you think you're off too?" the man berated them.

"It's getting dark. We're going to go camp out in the fields," Aiken replied unapologetically.

"There ain't nothing to the north, don't you know? You ain't got no business going that way. Likely to die of radiation poisoning you keep heading up that way. I'd just as soon turn around if I were you. Camp to the south of the town, and then on the morrow head south or east if you like, but for your own good go no farther north," the man snapped at them.

"We are not in your power, sir. We mean only to camp for the night and have no plan in mind for the morning. Counsel we might have taken, but orders are a different matter. Tomorrow we'll make up our own minds!" Aiken retorted.

"Suit yourself!" the man barked and walked away.

"That was a conversation to remember," Aiken said after the man was out of earshot.

"Look, Aiken! Behind us!" King whispered hoarsely. Aiken whipped his head around. A mile or so down the road the tiny figures of about nine men on horses were trotting slowly, but deliberately, towards them. They were looking right at the two of them. Their intent seemed clear.

"Sentries, I'd say!" Aiken declared. "I wonder if they've been summoned to deal with us."

King saw the horsemen, but saw something else as well; along with their distant silhouettes he saw them as though from nearby. From the nearby vantage point he saw a murky shadow proceeding before the men, like a black curtain. Through the veil, the men themselves appeared like black blotches. Fear coursed through him as he clutched at the reins of his horse and cried out, "Foes, Aiken, foes!"

He drove his heels into his horse and raced into the north with Aiken close behind. The other horsemen quickly gave chase, but had apparently been taken by surprise by Aiken and King's quick action. They had a good head start and sped off with good hope that they might elude their pursuers. However, they didn't know the area. They didn't know if they ought to stick to the road or dart off to the side to try to lose them. As they followed the road it twisted around, and they saw to their left wide open flood plains and perhaps the Great River itself! But it was all exposed. They would surely be spotted darting across the fields, and they could not be sure they'd find a bridge anyway. They sprinted ahead a little farther in a quest for woods to hide in. Though it was getting to be late in the day, there was still an hour or two of good light for a search party. They would need excellent concealment, if it could be found.

To their dismay, the road opened up and revealed itself as an Interstate! As they had feared, the Interstates were well guarded, and this one was evidence of exactly that. Immediately ahead of them and breaking off to the northeast, they saw a high wall had been erected on the inside of the freeway. There would be little hope of hiding that way. Moreover, numerous guard towers were spread along the length of the highway. They were quite trapped. Aiken spared a look at King, but King merely spurred his horse on to the north even farther. Whatever was to the south was worse than guard towers and walls, Aiken concluded, so hastened to catch up to King.

The first guard tower they raced by was empty. The next one wasn't, but the men in it hadn't been very attentive. As Aiken and King thundered past it, following the bend of the road to the northwest and towards the river, the men called out commands to halt. Another guard tower loomed ahead of them; this one was occupied, and the men in this one were paying attention. They began shouting at the two long before their horses had drawn them near. When they had come within fifty yards Aiken and King spotted rifles being pointed in their direction. King showed no sign of slowing down, but he did veer away from the tower as far to the left as he could as he passed it. The men were hollering at them, but not shooting. At least not at first. Soon, shots began coming their way, but they were poorly aimed.

The signs told them that they were on a road called I-255. Faintly visible in the distance was a cut in the land with a rising dome over it. They guessed that this was the river and a bridge over it. They were correct. Though new hope filled their hearts as they dashed to the west and the river, their horses could not sustain the speed that they were being driven at. The uneven concrete was treacherous even at a walk for both man and beast, but they were taking it by storm. Finally, they saw a large stand of trees where they could stop for a few minutes and let their horses rest. It could not do as a hiding place as all would guess that they had entered the woods when they weren't spotted on the road, but it would do for a few minutes. It might even do long enough for the sun to go down so that darkness might come to their aid.

The sound of galloping in the distance proved that this was too optimistic. The riders were not bothering to follow the road. They were cutting across the fields and coming in their direction. Aiken and King still had a good lead on them, but couldn't squander it. Their only hope was to get across the bridge and hopefully find that there was more cover in Missouri. Since it wasn't a nuclear wasteland as the rumors had insisted, this didn't seem implausible.

They exited the woods and put their horses into a fast jog. Their pursuers couldn't ride their beasts to death either, so a fast trot might preserve the buffer between them. They could see the bridge looming on the horizon. They were not more than a mile away. After about a half mile, they put their horses into full gallop again. A glance behind them revealed that the black riders had emerged from the stand of trees they had taken brief refuge in. Now they were fleeing over the bridge!

The river stretched out to their left and their right. In the fading light of the day, the waters seemed murky and uninviting. They had meant to seek cover on the other side, but it was not to be. As they reached the west side of the bridge and began sprinting down it, they found that they had ridden right into a well defended and well attended out post. They had been seen coming from a ways off, and a dozen men on horses were waiting for them. One or two of the horsemen had rifles. They hadn't noticed the guard tower in the dimming of the night, but now they could see that it too was armed with rifles. There was nothing to do but surrender. Their horses were happy to stop.

"You there! Stop!" called out one of the guards. It was unnecessary; they had already stopped.

"We are no one's enemy," Aiken returned.

"Riders who ignore sign after sign as you must have in order to have gotten this far have their credibility on that count diminished to begin with," the man retorted.

"What is your business? What is your intention?" demanded another man.

"Only to ride west to Oklahoma," King answered him.

"That is the end of that hope," the first man glowered.

The conversation was interrupted by shouts from the top of the tower, "Ho! A party of a dozen or so horsemen at the bridge!"

"Good grief. What are our guards doing on that side of the river?" complained one man in the picket line hemming Aiken and King in.

"Letting us do all the work," smirked another.

"It may be some of our sentries," called out a man from the tower, "Looked like Stan and Murdoch a bit, but they've all turned away!"

"Likely it isn't Stan and Murdoch, then," the first man said to himself. Then to King and Aiken he said, "And lucky for you. If I read this right you were running for your lives. Does that seem right?"

"I think you're an insightful man and an able leader. You're right," Aiken explained, trying to butter the man up as he went. "We were afraid of those men."

"You still may not pass. No one who comes into St. Louis, leaves. That is the rule. But now, perhaps, you will not be imprisoned. Reconcile yourself with the fact that this is now your home. Tonight you sleep in the tower, and tomorrow we take you to the judge who will decide the manner of your staying," the man told them. King opened his mouth to say something, but Aiken motioned for him to remain silent.

The guards were kindly enough to them. It probably helped that they were not raiders, but rather refugees of a sort. They put their horses in the stable with the other horses. Aiken and King were led to a small room on the first floor of the guard tower. There weren't any windows, and the door was barred behind them. For all of that, the beds, at least, were in good shape, and they were given blankets and fresh bread.

"This is a pretty pickle," King said, enjoying his bread.

"Yes, but don't give up hope. I assume that you saw something in the riders, something terribly fearsome. I count us blessed to be here rather than overcome by them," Aiken answered.

"They are dark men. A darkness covered them, I should say. I felt as though I could see a cold hand pulling a thick black blanket across them. Whether the men are dangerous on account of the hand or because of their own hearts I cannot say. But I saw murder on their minds, never mind the source," King explained.

"We shall trust your Sight," Aiken answered, taking his own bite of the bread. "I refuse to believe it is random, and if it comes we ought to pay heed to it."

"I agree, though it is hard to agree when we find ourselves in prison!" King smiled.

"Prisoners perhaps, but with fresh bread and beds!" Aiken declared. "I haven't slept in an actual bed since joining you and the Rangers a month ago!"

"And I haven't slept in a bed since ... Tulsa, I think, months and months ago!" King replied.

"You win! I'll race you to sleep tonight!" Aiken cried out in mock defeat. He lay down on the bed and pulled up a blanket. He was asleep in mere minutes. King didn't see any reason to stay up. He too curled up in a bed and murmured a word of thanks for the bread and blanket. Soon he was fast asleep as well.

The smell of frying fish woke them in the morning. The dark worries of the night before seemed beyond them. Aiken pounded on the door and, as politely as he could, informed the guards that he needed to use a rest room. The guards hollered back from the other side that someone was coming along with a key.

"I hope we get a bite of that fish," King moaned, rubbing his eyes.

"I'm not worried about fish right now. I'm worried about leaking.

I'm getting to be an old man," Aiken grimaced.

The door opened and Aiken practically pushed the guard along. Not long afterwards, Aiken was returned to the cell looking much relieved.

"Ok, now I hope we get a bit of that fish!" Aiken remarked. "Perhaps they fry it and make us smell it, but as punishment don't let us eat it!"

"Good grief!" came a muffled but clearly exasperated voice from the other side of the door. "You do complain!"

The door opened and trays were handed to each of them with some of the fried fish and more fresh bread. Mugs with hot coffee were handed to them next. After finishing their meal, the door swung open again. It was the man who had first addressed them the night before.

"It's time to come along. I'm Jasper. What are your names?" Jasper inquired.

"I'm Aiken. This is my friend, King," Aiken answered.

"Alright. The judge will see us in about an hour or so. It takes about thirty minutes to get there, so we'd best get off. You'll take your horses and we'll ride next to you. Your staff will be removed for now pending the judge's decision," Jasper explained, leading them out of the tower and to the stables.

"Since we are trapped in St. Louis forever, either as prisoners or as freemen, can you at least tell us now what accounts for the fact that all around the region men speak of St. Louis as a desolate wasteland? I look around and see buildings and trees and grasses and many people. I think an explanation is in order," Aiken asked Jasper.

Now accompanied by about ten men, Jasper smiled and said he would explain more once they got farther down the road. They followed the Interstate a little ways, and then they exited it and began traveling along a wooded lane. Then Jasper kept his promise and began his explanation.

"You will remember that five, six, maybe seven years back the Disease began ravaging the eastern regions of this country. Well, St. Louis was among the few cities to attempt to set up a quarantine. Oh sure, other cities had tried somewhat. The truth is that most people just couldn't believe the threat was real. At the time, though, St. Louis was a center for the International Forces. The leadership of St. Louis was able to get good, up to date information about the state of things both close and far. We knew it was real. So that was the first step. We began building our walls and erecting our signs long before the first nuclear bomb dropped.

"When the first bombs dropped we were just reaching the point where we could effectively keep everyone out we wanted out and keep in everyone we wanted in. That is no small feat, mind you! St. Louis is a large city! You no doubt saw our wall! It stretches for miles around the city, and people who come up to the wall are yet too far away to see the city proper. After we thanked our lucky stars for not being among the targets of the nuclear attack, we realized that we had a unique opportunity. If we could spread the word that the city had been destroyed, then we wouldn't have to bother with multitudes of diseased men and women trying to infiltrate our city, thus putting at risk hundreds of thousands of us. Indeed, as it was the Disease still did pop up here and there. We lost something on the order of fifty thousand men, women, and children to it, but it could have been much worse. Our management policies were effective.

"One other thing we learned by virtue of the presence of the International Force in our city: most of the power centers for the International Forces had been destroyed. The IF was withdrawing. They were attempting to return to their own lands across the seas in a vain hope to avoid the disease and also future nuclear attacks. The mayor saw the chance and took it. We rallied together and attacked and destroyed the International Force in St. Louis. It went radio silent in St. Louis, and the scattered remnants of IF units across the country presumed that the city had been struck by an atomic weapon. This helped fuel the rumor far and wide."

"What did this all achieve for you?" Aiken asked, perplexed.

"Well, in the first place, no one comes this way. We are perfectly isolated from the world. No one knows we're here. We don't let anyone out to tell them. The Disease has run itself out by now, of course, but in a future outbreak we need not be concerned about that, either. If enemies from overseas return, they too will avoid the area in the belief it is hopelessly contaminated. Meanwhile, we are completely self-sufficient. There are probably a million residents in this city these days, and no one knows we're here! And that is precisely the reason why you can't leave now that you're here," Jasper explained.

"But the Pledge came from this direction!" King pointed out.

Jasper's confident look faded and some of the men in the party frowned, "You've heard of the Pledge, have you?"

"We have! It is precisely because of the Pledge that we are headed to Oklahoma!" King replied.

"Wisely, I think, but you should be safe here," Jasper replied, thinking that King meant to hide from the Pledge.

"I have the distinct impression that the Pledge is aware of the truth about St. Louis," Aiken intoned. Jasper winced again.

"I don't know much about it. I know that the Pledge is a kind of army that is not the kind you'd think would be welcome in this city. Certainly most of the residents would reject and resist them. Still, the word is that a Pledge delegation came and rallied a sizable amount of

St. Louis residents to join them. They departed the city only a week ago and are now headed towards the east. It is a wonder that they were allowed to depart. It seems to go against the very philosophy that we've been operating on for these last years. My job is not to lead St. Louis, though. My job is to guard that bridge and as far as I know, the policy has not changed!" Jasper ended with conviction.

"If you don't mind me saying so, I think the time of your insulation is coming to an end," Aiken stated. "If you knew much about the Pledge, you'd know too that it is only a matter of time before they turn their attention to St. Louis."

"These things are out of my hands ... and yet I agree with you," Jasper replied. "But you're in my hands, and I must do as ordered. So, we are drawing near to the court. The judge is named Judge Martins. He is a good and fair man. If you're honest about where you have come from and where you were going and why, I expect he will grant you citizenship. But do not lie! Not even a little! If you are imprisoned, there you will stay for two years to have a good hard think about the matter; only then will you be given another chance to come clean. So be truthful!"

The court turned out to be a converted grade school. They tethered their horses to posts outside the doors, and half the men stayed outside to loiter while the other half escorted them inside. A woman greeted them and said that Judge Martins was nearly ready. Finally, the woman led them into a classroom that had been transformed into a makeshift courtroom. There was a bench for the judge and a stool nearby for witnesses. Several long tables were there for the attorneys and the accused. The only thing lacking was anything for observers to sit on.

The judge wandered in and sat down. He was about ten years older than Aiken, with a balding head and a large tuft of gray hair bushing out on one side. He was slightly heavy set and had a kindly face. King had heard that judges wore robes, but Judge Martins didn't. He was wearing loose fitting clothes that were much too casual in King's view.

Jasper began explaining the situation to the extent that he understood it. He told the judge about spotting King and Aiken racing across the bridge and then the guardsmen spotting the pursuers off in the distance. He even recounted some of their conversation that morning about the Pledge. "Yes, *that*," the judge had sniffed contemptuously. Finally, Jasper offered his own opinion, which was that he thought the two should be allowed to be citizens.

"And that naturally is for me to decide," Judge Martins winked. "So, no fan of the Pledge, is that it?"

"You could say that," Aiken smiled in return.

"Running away from them? Why to Oklahoma?" the judge asked

innocently. It was an innocent question, but they dared not reveal all. If the Pledge had been able to rally an army right there in a city in lockdown, they couldn't be confident that revealing their intentions wouldn't come back to haunt them. Their reticence was instantly noticed by the judge. "You're not going anywhere," Judge Martins reasoned with them, "So you may as well be honest."

King suddenly felt like honesty might be the best policy. "Judge Martins," he began, "I can see that you have no love for the Pledge. I see too that Jasper here does not either. Well, I bet that you have not hated them to the extent that I have! For, I was in the battle of Cairo, and I was there on the plains as the Pledge fired their heavy machine gun mercilessly into our defenseless ranks. I go to Oklahoma in order to bring about events to destroy the Pledge once and for all! If you detain us, I swear it will be to your loss! The Pledge will finish the task it has set before itself in Illinois, then it will consolidate its power, and then St. Louis will be a target. You know that St. Louis is not hidden from them, and of all people you would have wished to be hidden from it is them. So your decision today is not whether my friend and I live free in this town or as prisoners, but rather whether the people in this town will live or die, or themselves live as prisoners once the Pledge returns. Do not detain us, Judge Martins, I beseech you!"

There were gasps of awe from the judge, from Jasper, from the guards, from the woman who had escorted them in. Apparently word about the battle of Cairo had made it to St. Louis. And also some word of the outcome.

"The battle of Cairo ended poorly for the Pledge as I understand it. Mysterious circumstances are rumored to have bested them," the judge said.

"Bested their guns, yes," King replied, "but not their men. For Cairo was not their main objective—" King almost said that Peoria was, but then checked himself, "Rather Bloomington is their real goal. And right now some thirty or forty thousand Pledge soldiers are marching on that city. I say again, do not detain me! Do not delay me! I must ride to Oklahoma. Moreover, I say that you should immediately speak with the leaders of this town. Are there a million citizens in this city? End your foolish attempt to hide yourselves. You hide yourselves only from the good people of the region who need your assistance right now. You are fully exposed to the enemy. End the nonsense. Speak to your leaders. Raise an army. Go to the defense of your kindred!"

"You speak eloquently for a young man," the judge retorted somewhat annoyed. King himself had been surprised at the words that had come out of his mouth. The judge continued, "But I am only a judge. I am a thousand steps removed from the people in power in this town. I cannot do the things you speak of. Nor can I release you, for I am charged to uphold the law. That little thing I can do!"

"At your peril!" Aiken declared.

"Sometimes one does his duty in the face of danger. That is what doing one's duty is all about," Judge Martins snapped back. The judge had retorted as though annoyed, but both King and Aiken sensed that the judge was actually enjoying the exchange. It was the heat of battle talking.

"It is in your power to save all of St. Louis!" Aiken cried out.

"I can only exert the power that has been bestowed upon me. No man less than the mayor of the town himself can let people leave our city. Unless you can speak with a higher authority or bestow upon me authority higher than I presently have, we are at an impasse!" the judge exclaimed.

Aiken replied with something, but King didn't hear it. The lights were going dim and the sounds were going away, and suddenly he was alone. In the pitch blackness he felt rather than saw a great tearing asunder of something. The ripping grew more painful and pronounced until it seemed to him like mountains were being torn one from another, and the earth itself was falling away into the abyss. All this he felt: there was not yet anything he could see with his eyes.

Winds began howling around him. It was as though the sky was being sucked into whatever chasm had been breached. Now there was sound. A wailing. A wailing as if a person's very life was being snuffed out. King looked around in a vain attempt to fix his bearings. He didn't know where he was, or even if he was standing, or sitting. As the sorrowing cries subsided, King felt that he was now immersed in them, forced to swim in a current of pitiable agony. Hot tears fell down his cheek as he began sobbing and writhing. The tears washed down his face into his mouth and down his chin. He tasted the salt in them as they went by. A sharp cracking sound came to his ears, louder than thunder on the plains. Something had broken. There was at last a stillness and a chill about him. It came fast upon his mind what it all was: a broken heart and a fountain of grief beyond measure.

The coldness of the air around him helped him compose himself. He had tasted the grief of another, had drunk it deeply as though it were his own. He had his wits about him, though. With few exceptions his visions were of things that were occurring within his own experience of reality. This was different. He didn't think he could say that he was a *where*. Even as he thought it, he perceived a faint light on the horizon where once there had been none.

"Where am I?" King called out.

"Do you weep as I weep?" came an answer. Whether it was in his mind or outside it he did not know.

"I … don't know," King said.

"Here is one who grieves like the rest of men—at least as of yet."

"I see no one," King reasoned with the voice.

"That is because you are within the man himself. Within his mind; enmeshed in the fabric of his thought."

"Where am I, then?" King wondered.

"Not a place. You are glimpsing a reality that does not occupy space and time. It is an everlasting moment, sustained by a powerful word. This moment of grief, like every moment, including those of joy, bliss, love, sorrow, and more, are ones which are experienced in every respect by One who wills it so."

"Who would will such horrendous sorrow?" King raised his voice in anger.

"Not the sorrow is willed. Such things are *allowed*. It is experience which is willed. And see: every instant of every aspect of all things that exist are present everlastingly in the sustaining mind. You have had the smallest taste. Let no man say that He is distant. It is not so. It *cannot* be so."

"Who are you? What is your name?" King stammered.

"Do you not know? Why do you ask my name? It is beyond your understanding."

"For what purpose have you brought me here?" King demanded.

"Where is 'here?' Are you not listening? Yet I will tell you: You have been brought to See so that you may not wonder that you are loved. The sorrow you tasted on your lips is proof enough of his affection. Alas, it is shrouded in despair! But do you not see a glimpse of the light? The hard heart is now broken, and the warmth can slip through: if it is willed by the rendered heart. We shall see. But as for you, I tell you do not grieve as the rest of men, for you see that they do not pass ever out of the knowledge of the One who sustains all things and sets things right in His Good time. Go now and speak to Death with words that will be given."

"I don't understand!" King cried out.

"What will be well is even now well. And tell the judge that his sister Marian has gone further up and further in. He will listen to you then."

"Wait!" King exclaimed as the voice faded away. There was nothing he could do. As the voice faded away, the darkness melted back into the dusty light of the courtroom. He was lying down and people were gathered around him. He could see the judge standing up at the desk, peering at the commotion taking place in his courtroom.

"Is he ok?" Jasper was asking.

"He's fine. Back up, please!" Aiken told him.

"His eyes are opening!" Jasper pointed out.

"King! You're back! What did you see?" Aiken asked him.

"I'm alright," King said, struggling to his feet.

"You shouldn't be standing," Jasper told him.

"No, I must," King said, resisting efforts to lead him to a chair. He stood up and faced the judge who now sat down.

"Some sort of charade, perhaps? Maybe a rhetorical device?" the judge smirked. King looked sternly at the judge. It was clear what he had to do.

"Judge Martins, your sister lives!" King cried out. Judge Martins' face went white. He stood up in anger.

"What is this nonsense! How dare you!" the judge barked at him.

"Marian! She has gone further up and further in!" King replied boldly. At the naming of his sister the Judge's face regained its color, yet he trembled. He slowly sank back into his seat. The people in the room looked back and forth between the King and the Judge in awe.

"I never told anyone about her ... I was only eight and she twelve ..." the Judge was murmuring.

"He is a prophet, Judge Martins. Give heed to his word! Many lives hang in the balance, including the good people of St. Louis, though their troubles may be years off!" Aiken exclaimed.

"Yes ... a prophet ... that might explain it ..." the Judge continued to talk to himself. He looked dazed and unsure of what to do.

"Your honor," Jasper said, timidly approaching the Judge, "are you ok? Would you like us to come back?"

"No," said King, "Let's settle the matter here and now. Your honor, send out everyone except for Jasper, and I shall tell you what you need to hear."

The guards looked at King warily and seemed ready to oppose such a plan, but the Judge waved his hand and nodded. Against their will and best judgment the men left, leaving behind only the confused Jasper and bewildered Judge Martins.

When the room had cleared, King continued, "It is in my mind that you two will listen to what I have to say. Am I a prophet? I don't know what that means. Yet I did see something, and I was given the message about your sister to say to you. Do not ask me more about it, for I don't know. I do know, though, that you must let us leave, and soon. As we speak, there are tens of thousands of Pledge soldiers threatening to destroy the city of ... Bloomington. Their goal is the destruction of any rivals to power in this country so that they can rule it. I see in your eyes that you're opposed to them. You say that there is nothing you can do! Well, I go to Oklahoma where I will call upon my friends in the Cherokee Nation to take up arms and ride to the defense of the men and women in Illinois. They do not have pitchforks and baseball bats, but actual military style weapons. They will make the Pledge think twice about their plans. I do not know if they will agree to come, but you must let me go so that I can ask them."

"Unless I am mistaken, you have now twice paused at the mention of the city of Bloomington. You're trying to win my trust, yet you falter at naming the city," the Judge squinted at King.

King decided that honesty really was going to be the best policy, "I am sorry Judge Martins. I am telling you the truth when I say that Bloomington is a target of the Pledge. But the Pledge also seeks something in Peoria. They believe that they can lay hands on the Ark of the Covenant there." The Judge gasped. King continued, "Trustworthy voices have said that there is no such object in Peoria, but what is in Peoria is still of inestimable value and must be kept from the Pledge under all circumstances."

"I see that I have unwittingly found myself at the crux of a great matter," the Judge said to himself.

"What part you have to play in the affairs of this age I don't know," Aiken said, "But your part in this moment seems to me to be altogether clear."

"Hum hum! But letting you go is no easy thing to do even if I wanted to ..." said the Judge, falling silent. Judge Martins closed his eyes in thought. Jasper stood quietly awaiting the decision. He knew quite well what hurdles would need to be surmounted if the two were to go free. Sensing that the judge was deliberating, King and Aiken did not respond to his lingering statement.

A door creaked behind them. The woman who had led them to the room peeked in, but the judge waved her away impatiently.

"No one in this city knows about my sister. Not that I had one. Not her name. Nothing. Where did you come by this knowledge? A Pledge deception?" the judge opened one eye to gauge King's reaction (he was frowning) and then closed it again. "Mother died soon after. Old Kilney, he knew, that's true, but he was old. Blabbered, maybe? Yes, maybe he did, but the specificity involved ... someone would have known who I was ... where I grew up ... tracked down a person who had known a person who had known Kilney ... and why would they do that? Even if they'd gleaned that information by accident, how would they know to associate it with me? I've never mouthed a word about where I came from and how I arrived here ..." pondered the judge with eyes shut and fingers tapping, leaning back in his chair.

He continued, "Why not simply adopt the prima facie conclusion? It is straight forward and obvious. If it takes the construction of a Rube Goldberg explanation in order to otherwise account for it, have I really advanced my insight into the matter? I think not ..."

The judge clicked his fingers together a little longer. Finally, he opened his eyes, leaned forward in his chair, and smiled, "Jasper, it is no coincidence, I suppose, that he allowed you to stay. What do you think?"

"If he's telling the truth about you having a sister and knowing her name and you see no reason not to trust him, then I trust you ... and we'll do what is necessary," Jasper replied.

"Excellent. I thought as much. Well, it is quite clear isn't it? We have to get them out. How are we going to do that?" Judge Martins inquired.

"Easiest thing would be to declare them free citizens and then go from there," Jasper replied.

"Yes, but of course there is the naturalization process. Forced incarceration for a period of a month to ensure no signs of any contagious disease and a debriefing followed by some useful propaganda. I don't think these gentlemen want to wait a month, nor do I think they will want to share what they know in the debriefing," the judge countered.

"There is transit on the way to the naturalization center ..." Jasper thought aloud.

"Yes. But are you not the one who also oversees the stage two prison?" Judge Martins smiled at him.

"I don't mind smuggling them somehow, but I'd prefer not to do so in a way that might mean my own job," Jasper grimaced.

"I have some other ideas. At least if we go that way the two remain under our jurisdiction for awhile. I can sign the papers remanding them to your prison instead of another—I certainly have done that often enough—and we can go from there," the judge retorted.

"What about the rule of law and your duty?" Aiken put to the judge.

"A difficult ethical matter. Should the authorities who could take action on this affair hear this account with the type of confirmatory evidence which I have received, I have little doubt they would go along with it the way I plan to. As I said, though ... It is the mayor himself who reserves this power, and the next three judges up the chain are bloated blowhards who would never move the matter along. I will have to answer for it if I'm caught and will do so with dignity and courage. But I don't think I'll get caught. However, you will have to trust that Jasper and I will see to the matter. We will have to put you in jail at least for a day and maybe two. You'll have to trust me to act as soon as I believe I am able. Do you?" Judge Martins asked.

"Yes," said King.

"Very well. Jasper, get the guards and bring them in."

Jasper went to the door and motioned for the other guards to come back in. The judge was waiting for them.

"So that was a fine performance, my boy, and you nearly had me. Next time you try to concoct a story, make sure you cover all of your bases and not merely the obvious ones. I hereby remand you to the custody of Jasper Cunningham and the Eaton Hall facility until such time as paper work can be processed transferring you to the military division for debriefing, and from there to a level A prison camp for the duration of the self-embargo. Dismissed!" Judge Martins roared with contempt.

The guards smirked at King and Aiken as though they knew all along they had been frauds. They handled them a little roughly even, but Jasper let them. The cordial conversation from earlier in the day was gone. Jasper gave his guards orders to take them to the prison he administered, and then went to talk to the judge a little more. No one was suspicious, not even in the slightest.

After about an hour, King and Aiken found themselves locked in a jail cell. It was not nearly as comfortable as their first accommodations in St. Louis had been. The guards here didn't know about the courthouse fiasco, so their ill treatment ended. Later on that evening, Jasper came to the cell and gave them whispered encouragements and urged patience.

After having been in the outdoors sleeping under the stars for so long, sleeping on a hard bed in a dingy gray cement cell with bars adorned with peeling paint was quite depressing for King. Aiken kept his hopes high, however, and repeated Jasper's plea for patience. This became a difficult chore even for Aiken when the first night ended and then a second night came.

Lying there in the desolate cell, King and Aiken made small talk hoping that the following morning they would at least be set free. Their eyes became heavy as the night progressed and their conversation all but ceased, until at last, both men were sleeping as comfortably as they could manage.

*"I hear you again, phantom! Do you disturb me now that I have the rope in my hands?"*

*King's body tensed as he realized that he was in the cave again. He didn't know if, when he was having the vision of the cave all times previously, he was actually physically in the cave—but he had no doubt now. He was in the cave and perhaps only feet away from the speaker. Was he still in a St. Louis jail? The scientific question darted into his mind and then quickly out again as he came to grips with the situation. He remembered Aiken's advice to talk to the man but couldn't think of anything to say.*

*The man continued, "I go through all the trouble to find a rope, coil it up, hang it up, find a spot sure to be high enough. The minute I put it around my neck you arrive. You are a foul illusion, lifting me out of my madness by drenching me in more madness! As if you are really there!"*

*"I think I really am here," King assured the man. King felt the same sense of despair press down on his chest that he felt in his last vision of the cave.*

*"Madness! I am the only one alive in here! There is no way in—or out! Yet you sweep in and out at will. A trick of the mind ..."*

*King stretched out his hand in the dark towards the voice. His hand came to rest on the man's shoulder. His skin felt something like frayed rope near the man's neck. He felt the warmth of the man's body, and the man must have felt the warmth of his hand for he suddenly broke out in loud sobs.*

The next moment, there was no doubt that King was in, and only in, the St. Louis jail. Aiken was sleeping. The lights of the jail had been dimmed. King reflected on the incident until his eyes once again drew too heavy to stay open. He fell into a deep and dreamless sleep.

# == Chapter 17 ==

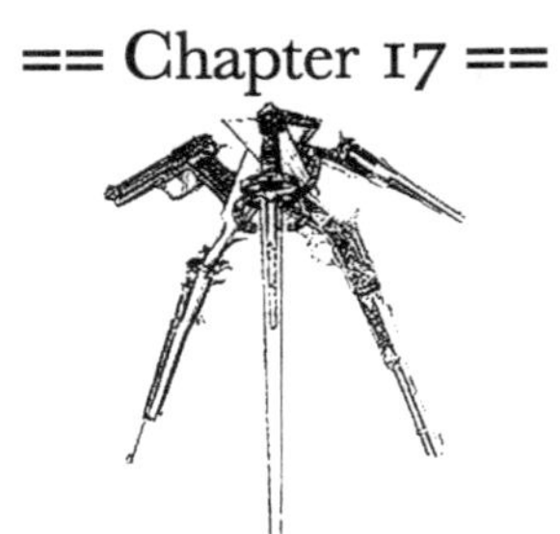

When morning arrived, a message of thanks and encouragement was sent from the judge through the mouth of Jasper. The wheels were now in motion. King and Aiken would never appreciate how difficult the operation actually was. The complexities were hidden from them, and for their part, all they had to do was sit in a horse drawn jail compartment for most of the day. Jasper checked on them when he locked them in and then, papers in hand, personally led the horses down the road. This leg of the trip took about two hours. It ended with Jasper parking the horses at some sort of way station and then departing.

After about thirty minutes, another man took the reins and pulled the cabin another hour. They stopped at another guard shack; that man also left them, while a third man took over pulling the reins. It was turned over to a fourth and a fifth man until finally the fifth man stopped the horses and opened the back of the compartment so that they could get out.

They were in a secluded grove of trees against a decrepit building. The man helped them out and then sat down on a stump of a tree, wordlessly. King and Aiken glanced at each other and then back at the man, wondering what to do. There didn't seem to be any other men about, either. Should they start walking away? Faintly they heard the sound of a horse clip-clopping their direction, and the man seemed to have been waiting for the same thing. After a few moments, a horseman entered their clearing. It was Jasper again.

"Hello guys!" Jasper called out to them. Then, spotting the man, Jasper said, "Simon. The judge sends his regards and thanks."

"It is my pleasure," Simon replied. "No doubt I still owe the man. I don't think my debt to him will ever be repaid for all he's done for me and my family."

"Many thanks anyway," Jasper said.

Simon pulled out some bags that were up in the coach and slid King's staff off as well. King's eyes widened when he saw it. He'd forgotten about it, but was very happy to see it again now that he'd been reminded of it. After he had given them their stuff, Simon climbed onto the coach and led it and its trailing compartment away. A few minutes more passed and it could no longer be heard.

"Alright. It is about two in the afternoon. You are in fact outside the walls of St. Louis. Not many come this way and there aren't many sentries. There is no wall here because there is a canal that does the job relatively well. On the other side of the canal you'll be almost completely safe. It's an old distribution center that has been razed to the ground to give the appearance to those traveling on I-44 that St. Louis has been leveled to the ground by a nuclear strike. I'll take you as far as I can, and then I have to get back before I'm missed," Jasper explained.

"Very well," said Aiken. "We are in your hands."

"Come, follow me. You will see the benefits of having Judge Martins as your friend," Jasper replied, leaping off his horse so that he could walk alongside them.

Jasper led them out of the grove and through some trees until they struck the canal that Jasper had mentioned. It didn't take long to find a shallow part to cross. In fact, it was barely a foot deep, and they were all able to walk across the canal with ease. On the other side of the canal were the remains of the distribution center. At one time, semi-trucks had come in by the hundreds each day carrying their cargo in and out. The buildings were now flattened, and occasionally they could see the remnants of one of the massive vehicles. After about an hour, Jasper stopped suddenly by one of the heaps of steel and wood. To their surprise, there was a door in the pile. Jasper had led them to a cinderblock shelter that had not been demolished and was still in good shape.

Jasper opened the door, strode into the dark, and emerged with an amazing prize: a motorcycle!

"Now that is generous indeed!" King declared.

"I was wondering about our horses, but I see that we've come ahead in the trade," mused Aiken.

"There is enough gasoline in it to get you as far as Springfield, perhaps Carthage. We don't know that area well enough to know which direction you'll want to go, but we know that there are motor vehicles operating out of Springfield, so perhaps you can get fuel there. Even if you can't, this baby will shave more than a few days off your travels," Jasper informed them.

"I am still amazed," King shook his head.

"Ok, but can you ride a motorcycle?" Jasper asked. King's face darkened as he realized that he couldn't, but Aiken came to his rescue.

"I know how. It has been years, of course, but I know how to do it," Aiken said. "What I want to know is where are all these people getting fuel? Where did you get gasoline for this?"

"For our own part, this city had been a center for the International Forces and they had plenty of fuel on hand for their purposes. After we overthrew them, naturally we retained their fuel supply. As for the vehicles operating out of Springfield, I have no idea where they get their fuel or how. A lot of our fuel has gone bad, so I don't know how they do it. This tank of gas has additives that have kept it good. Thank the Judge!" Jasper explained.

"We do!" said Aiken.

"And remind him about what I said about Bloomington!" interjected King. "If the city has as many people as you say it does, then you might be able to raise an army that could help Bloomington and you're much closer, too!"

"I'm sure it is on Martins' mind now, but the problem remains that he and I are basically underlings in this town. There is little chance of us gaining an audience with anyone who might care and it is not easy to leave on our own, though it might look like it to you since we've come this far without event. We shall see," Jasper said. "Now, you need to follow that road you see straight on until it veers to the left. Stay to the left as it curves around, and then you'll be able to see I-44. There is a checkpoint a mile or so ahead and it is pretty well manned, but if you hit it going sixty miles and hour I don't think you'll have any problem. If you do, we'll be sure to hear about it, and as long as you aren't dead, we'll see what we can do to help."

"Hit the checkpoint at sixty miles an hour. Got it," Aiken smirked.

"Alright. Ok, then, we should go!" King said, shaking Jasper's hand. Jasper shook Aiken's hand and patted them both on the back as they mounted the motorcycle. King struggled to situate his staff for the trip, but eventually succeeded. It was time to go. Aiken kick started the bike and it roared into life with fervor, as though it had been aching for a ride for many a year.

"Good bye!" they all shouted to one another. Then Aiken wound his way carefully through the rubble until the tires met the road. He went a little faster after that until, finally, they spotted the Interstate, just as Jasper had said. It wasn't difficult to get onto the Interstate. After ten minutes, they were speeding down the road as fast as they safely could. This usually meant forty miles and hour, but when the guard towers came into sight Aiken accelerated to seventy miles an hour. King yelped at the sensation of accelerating so quickly and squeezed Aiken's waist hard enough that Aiken started laughing.

The guard towers were looming ever closer, but Aiken only went faster. The men at the checkpoint started out as ants and grew bigger and bigger and some of them turned out to be fire ants. They were surprised, though, and didn't fire straight. People leaving the city was an uncommon experience for them—if they could remember it ever happening before.

Out of danger, Aiken slowed down to forty and fifty miles an hour. The road slipped away behind them. King reflected on the relative good fortune that had fallen on them. Yes, they had been arrested and incarcerated and put on trial, but they had made two new friends, and the investment of three days had probably saved ten days or more on foot. He commended himself at the realization that he had been right: St. Louis was passable after all! This would be news indeed in Tahlequah.

It didn't take long before the remnants of St. Louis's suburbs were behind them and they were coursing through forests and woodlands. They had seen no travelers. They had, however, seen people dressed to look like travelers. They knew that these men were sentries tasked to keep travelers from continuing on to St. Louis and maintain the story that the city had been decimated years back.

At forty miles an hour, the southwest journey through Missouri could be completed that very night. Aiken quickly judged that they would have to procure more fuel in order for that to happen. They took a break at a rest area a little past a city named Rolla. Rolla had been fairly well inhabited, but they were uncomfortable stopping so soon in a city they knew nothing about. The rest area was nice. It was sparsely populated with just a handful of vagabonds camped there. King took the opportunity to tell Aiken more about Chummy and his fleet. They had already passed a vehicle coming in the other direction. It appeared that Rolla was the furthest that Chummy's fleet would service, and also that Rolla was as close a town to St. Louis as its stewards would allow to be inhabited unhindered from harassment and rumor mongering.

They left the rest area after their brief conversation with the goal of making Springfield their next stop and Chummy's garages their priority destination. They needed fuel, though they had nothing to barter with except perhaps the good name and full faith and credit of the Cherokee nation. Unfortunately, Springfield was an outlying hub of Chummy's operations, and it wasn't likely that he would be there to directly negotiate with. It was equally unlikely that the name of the Cherokee Nation would have the same kind of weight with Springfield residents as it might have had with Tulsa residents. There was nothing to do but go on.

Around six-thirty in the evening, they reached the outskirts of Springfield. They spotted another vehicle ahead of them winding its way into the city. Not knowing a better way to find Chummy's garages, they followed it. Unlike the inhabitants of Rolla who had stared at them, Springfielders paid no mind to them. It didn't take very long before the rabbit vehicle had led them through the city and pulled into the depot. Their hunch had paid off and just in time: the gas tank was a shade over E.

King dismounted with staff in hand. The two walked over to the dingy station where men were loitering in the cool of the evening. Several old vehicles were parked in rows. It would take a mighty suspension of disbelief to imagine that they could still drive, but it was precisely one of those vehicles that they had followed in. The men looked up at them.

"What can I do ya for?" said one man.

"I'll come out with it," King replied, taking the initiative. "We're on our way to the Cherokee Nation with important news. We're out of fuel, though, and have no money or anything of value to trade for it. I know that Chummy is a businessman, so I will make sure that he is repaid with interest when we arrive in Tahlequah."

"If you know Chummy you know we don't part with anything on credit," another man said.

"I do know that, but this is an exceptional matter and I am sure he'd agree. He isn't in town is he?" King asked.

"Chummy don't come round this way very often. How about this? The next ride to Tulsa goes out tomorrow. For the price of that there bike of yours, we'll give you guys a seat," the first man offered, a smile playing at his lips knowing full well what an absurd deal that would make.

"Tulsa is not our destination. Tahlequah is our destination and we mean to leave tonight," King rejoined.

"I don't know what to say," the second man crossed his arms.

Aiken leaned over and whispered in King's ears, "Let's just bean'em and be done with it." King smiled but opted to pursue the diplomatic route a little farther.

"Let me put this in different terms," King said. "I come back to the area with important news about the doings of the Pledge. Nothing less than the safety of this area—including Springfield and including Tulsa—are at stake. If you don't help us with fuel, then who knows how much blood will be on your hands," King earnestly reasoned with them.

"No reason to believe you Indians," the first scowled.

"Oh for cripes sake," interjected a third man who had recently walked onto the scene. "The tank will only take five or six gallons anyway. Give them the fuel."

"You can't just give away Chummy's fuel," the first man cried out.

"I've seen you drive fifty miles out of the way because you didn't want to come home yet. How is that not 'giving away' Chummy's fuel? Since when are you his penny pinchers? When have you ever cared about his bottom line? But I'll pay it out of my own pocket just to shut your traps. Here is ten pieces of silver, and I know that is more than enough. You keep the change if it will make you happy," the third man scowled.

"Thanks a lot, mister," King said.

"You're such a downer, Leland," the first man smirked.

"Just get along with it," Leland snapped.

"We'll make sure you're compensated for this, sir," King said.

"That'll be alright if you do, but don't worry if you don't. Five gallons of Chummy's fuel isn't worth that much, I assure you," Leland stated. Before King could say anything else, Leland disappeared back into the shop.

Aiken shrugged, "Stout fellow."

"Seems that way," King agreed. They pushed the motorcycle over to the fuel pump and the men filled up the tank for them.

Not wishing to loiter any longer, they got back on the motorcycle again and sped back to I-44. It was already evening, but the days were getting longer so there was enough light to ride for another hour, if not two, although they had to slow down to ensure that they didn't end up in a huge pothole as the world dimmed. The signs informed them that Joplin was drawing near, and King remembered that somewhere around Joplin was a road that would take them to the Cherokee Nation. He just couldn't remember which road. He patted Aiken on the shoulder, and they pulled over.

"Somewhere here there is a road that will take us down by Tahlequah," King told him.

"Do you know where it is?" Aiken asked him.

King laughed, "Well, I used to. Things aren't looking quite like they used to."

"It is starting to get dark. Maybe we should stop for the night? Might not be a good idea to go road hunting in the pitch of night," Aiken suggested.

"Does the headlight work?" King asked. Aiken fidgeted with the instruments and finally found one that turned on the headlight.

"Yup."

"I really feel like we're right by it. Let's go a little ways farther since we have some light," King said.

"Alright. It's your territory!" Aiken smiled. King hopped back on the bike and re-situated his staff, and off they went.

"I think this is it!" King shouted when he spotted a sign that looked familiar. "We want to go south on 71!"

When they reached the exchange they saw the sign for 71 but couldn't figure out where to turn south on it. They followed 71 to the north hoping it would make sense.

"Where does it turn south?" Aiken called back over the noise.

"I thought we were going south! Maybe it does a jog," King shouted back.

"It's getting blooming dark!" Aiken yelled back irritably. They kept on 71 even after they spotted a sign that said Carthage. When they passed through what appeared to be a residential area, Aiken indicated to King that he was going to pull over. The night was now upon them, and the road was now nearly pitch black. Aiken was frustrated.

"I'm really sorry," King said.

"I knew it was too dark to go exploring," Aiken muttered.

"Well, I am sorry. 71 really should have turned southbound. I don't know what to say except that I apologize," King replied.

Aiken wasn't ready to let it go. "We're on a dangerous journey and you want to go by memory when you can't see and haven't been back in months and months? What were you thinking?" he snapped.

King was taken aback by how annoyed his friend was. Not knowing what else to say, he repeated his apology and offered to get firewood for the campfire. At last, Aiken relented.

"Let's get well off the road," Aiken said in a softer tone.

"The tree line looks to be pretty far off the road. I think we'll be safe from the eyes of random travelers that way, and there ought to be more wood for the fire there, too," King said.

"Sounds good," Aiken replied. The two of them each took a handle of the motorcycle and pushed it across the open spaces of the field. The trees loomed ahead of them like a tall, black curtain. Finally, they were under the outstretching branches.

"Let's lean it against a tree," King said.

"Yup," Aiken agreed. They heaved the motorcycle up out of the field. With a jerk they had it up against the tree nearest them. To their surprise, the tree trembled.

"That isn't normal," King said to himself.

"No, it Aaaaaaaaaaaaah!"

The ground fell out beneath their feet before Aiken could complete his sentence. Aiken, King, the motorcycle, and the tree, all fell into the earth. They tumbled unceremoniously into the dark for a second, and then two, and then with a resounding bang landed on something that gave away slightly beneath them. Echoes of their yelps and the clanging of the motorcycle resonated around them. They came to rest surrounded by groping branches. The tarry darkness of the pit yielded no insight about their predicament to their eyes.

"Ow." King said curtly.

"I'm fine. Anything broke?" Aiken's voice emanated from somewhere nearby.

King patted his body. "No, I don't think so. But I bet my body is going to ache for weeks."

There was an odd, hollow sound.

"What was that?"

"Darned if I know."

"It's the ground."

"This isn't dirt. It's metal."

The two used their hands to explore their environment. The branches of the tree hampered them, scratching at them in the dark. Eventually they were able to find edges around them, but beyond the edges could tell nothing. It might drop forever if one tried to brave a leap, for all they could tell in the dark. They shoved the tree over one of the edges with much effort, careful not to follow it unawares, and could tell that it didn't fall very far.

"I begin to form a hypothesis in my mind," Aiken offered.

"Do tell," King answered from the night.

"It is only eight feet or so from one edge to the other. The hollow metallic sound along with that measurement suggests to me that we are on top of a trailer. The ones that trucks used to pull," Aiken said.

"I have my own hypothesis."

"What is that?"

"That I have been here before—many a time!" King declared.

"The cave," Aiken murmured.

"The cave."

"Well, if I'm right, then we can carefully crawl along one of the edges and we will find one of the ends. Then we can climb down," Aiken said.

"I can't think of a better idea," said King. The two took opposite sides of the trailer and worked their way slowly in the same direction. At one point King yelped in pain: they had found the motorcycle. It had fallen halfway through the metal skin and King had put his hand on one of the sharp pieces of metal around the hole.

"That settles it in my mind. It is a trailer," Aiken said.

Finally, they reached the end. They began groping for something that seemed like a ladder, but couldn't find anything to put their feet on. They were beginning to contemplate what to do next when they heard something uncannily like someone "aheming" them.

"Ahem."

"What King?"

"Wasn't me."

"*Ahem.*"

"That isn't you Aiken?"

"Nope."

Now they heard an annoyed cough. The two crept back slowly away from the edge of the trailer. It was clear that they were not alone. It was less clear what to do next. They held their breaths, listening intently to the silence.

"Now I've got you!" the voice cried out. Suddenly there was loud banging and clanging and hooting and hollering. The man below was striking the trailer with abandon and shouting at them. He was saying things like "Treed like a fox!" and "Judgment Day!"

"He's mad," Aiken whispered to King. He didn't appreciate the way sound traveled in the deep caverns of Carthage, though, and the man heard him.

"Mad! Crazy! You would be too after how many years? Five years? Six? A hundred! I don't know, but you'll not get away this time you vicious apparition! Come and go as you please, but you're trapped now. No wall to dissolve into, no sir. Can't get down and run away, either. Just a matter of time!" the voice ranted.

"Do you remember me?" King called out over the edge of the trailer.

"I remember you! A ghoul to tempt me into despair, or out of it, at the most inopportune times!"

"But this time I am here to stay," King replied.

"We'll see about that soon enough! Made enough noise to stay. Sounds like you're making yourself at home. Quite the racket. I heard you a mile away, as they say," the man giggled.

"No. You don't understand. I'm really here this time," King reasoned with him.

"Here? You were 'really' here last time and then you were gone! You specter!" the man chattered.

"Look! …" King began.

"Look? Look he says! There is nothing to see! Nothing for years and years! No, nothing!"

King tried another approach, "See here!"

The man laughed uproariously, "See? You'll not play me for a fool this time!"

King was frustrated and humored at the same time. The man was running around below them on the ground, that much was clear. If he'd been down here for years as he said, he'd look a sight for sure, and King couldn't help but picture it. He tried again.

"Did you not hear two voices this time?" King asked him.

The man stopped yammering and stood still. "Yes, that is a point," he said.

"Yes, it is a point. This is no mere vision for me. I am really, truly, here. My name is King. My friend is named Aiken. We have no ill will for you, not even to disappear in a blink," King told him.

The man began crying softly.

"It passes, then. The long dark night passes at last … but perhaps they will go mad as the others did …" the voice trailed off.

Aiken dared to say something now. "How long have you been down here and how did you come to be here? Why not leave?"

The man regained his composure. It seemed as though he sat down in the dark for the voice came from a little farther away. He began to tell his story.

"It began years ago. I have never found a way to mark time, so I cannot say how many years ago it was. I worked here. It is an underground cold storage facility. Originally, trucks would come in and out with their trailers, and they didn't have to use their refrigeration units because the temperature was always perfect. When it happened there were few trucks, but it was still in use for the same reason. There was a tremendous earthquake. The entrances caved in, as did other parts of the cave. Many of us were trapped. There were perhaps thirty of us at one time, and we could hear others calling out from other parts of the cave—also trapped. It didn't take long for despair to set in ..."

The man stopped talking for awhile as though in deep contemplation. Sighing, he began again.

"No light. That was the problem. There was plenty of food and water. The trailers that had been left behind so many years before were now used for storage, and there were other chambers that we could find, too. Yet it was light that we longed for ... a single strand of sunlight would have fed us for weeks. Oh sure, we found some flashlights, but they didn't last. Some of the tractors still had working headlights, but after months none of these worked either. We had one another, true, but only our voices and the sound of our breathing. We could lend a shoulder as there was need, but as the first year wound down, it became too much.

"Some men simply curled up and died. We found them. You've heard about infants left all alone in their cribs in distant orphanages. The babies just waste away. For some it was like that. Others found different ways to end their lives. Others I wonder about: I never found their bodies. They are gone, though. They probably found a crack to pull themselves into and died there, and I have no light to see them. I cannot find them by smell, since the dry cold preserves their bodies. Yes, all the bodies are still here. We put them in an empty trailer, and they are there today. The last man faded away years ago, and it has been only me for time out of mind. Their bodies are there, calling me, beckoning me to join them and be done with this foul existence!

"And foul it has been. Apart from some aftershocks that came for a time after the first big earthquake, literally nothing else has occurred to interrupt the blankness of my existence. Nothing else except ... the arrival and sudden disappearance of someone ... In the stillness of the caves a single step can be heard, and likewise a breath, or the creaking of a man's joint ... and I would think I was going mad for hearing what I was hearing, but I knew I was hearing something. I *knew* it. One time the someone appeared very close to me and I spoke with him, and then he was gone. The last time, I felt his touch. It was you, King, and your going nearly broke me. I had it in my head that the brief visits were meant to maintain my sanity, but even as they grew more vivid you kept leaving—so that at the last I began to think that perhaps I was imagining it. I ... circled the morgue trailer with rope in hand... and wept ... but something inside me urged me to be strong and courageous in the face of utter despair. As maddening as it was to be exposed to a sane voice suddenly removed, I always felt a lighter heart afterwards, though it did not, *could* not last.

"Yet it was still so hard. All those I loved were dead to me and I to them. Completely alone with just my soul for company. That is hell: one's own company, and one's own company alone, forever and ever. I pray to God that if you're again just one vision, you will strike me dead before you go because I don't know if I could take it. You heard me ... I had cracked. I would break finally if you disappeared today ..." the man mourned.

"We are not leaving you," Aiken assured him, deeply moved.

"So you have been in these caves practically alone, in the dark, for years and years?" King asked incredulously.

"Yes, it is so. And now I don't know that circumstances have entirely improved, yet I hope more than ever. You have joined me now in my dark tomb. We are trapped together, but it is so good to be together with the living again, even if together trapped," the man said.

The man began weeping. He wailed into the dark as though smitten with whips. King and Aiken peered over the edge, but could not see the man in his sorrow. The convulsing sobs slowly turned into robust laughter, "I'm not alone any more! I live!" The man could be heard leaping for joy about the ground, dancing and whooping in glee. Finally, the man was spent.

"Would you permit us to come down?" Aiken asked the man.

"Yes, come down. I will help you," the man said, drawing closer. "Wait. I will open the doors of the trailer, and then I will stand inside it. You hang down and I will pull you in. It won't be a long drop that way." This seemed like a good plan. They heard the trailer doors creak and felt the ceiling of the trailer tremble beneath them. Finally he announced he was ready. In short order, both Aiken and King had their feet firmly on the floor of the cave. The man was shaking their hands and embracing them as if they were his long lost friends.

"Don't you think you should tell us your name now?" Aiken offered to the dark.

"Indeed!" he answered, and King noticed that the man's speech and demeanor had changed as he spoke, "My name is Sparrow. I am hard pressed on every side, but not crushed; perplexed, but not in despair; alone but not abandoned; struck down, but not destroyed. I am he who does not lose heart. I am Sparrow; guardian of the unseen. I am Sparrow; he who awaits what is to come with patience and perseverance; he who lives while others die. I am Sparrow: the son of Dokime, the son of Hupomone, the son of Thlipsis..." Sparrow's voice continued to swell with enthusiasm and dignity and power. He was hidden from their sight, yet they began to perceive the man ever more clearly as he spoke on, "I am Sparrow! Leader of the free tribes of the west! Chief of the Mighty Lakota, father of Fox Marion. I am Sparrow! Fierce in battle, tender in mercy, as just as a man today might be. I am Sparrow, the helmet of my people. Yes, I am Sparrow. That is my name!"

"Which part?" King joked.

"All of it," Sparrow replied seriously.

"Long name!" Aiken chuckled.

"All men have such names, though not all know it. I did not even give my name in full as I understand it, and, unquestioningly, even I do not know it to the final word. I know it enough, and that is enough," Sparrow said.

"You seem like a very noble man. It is a terrible shame that you have been interned in these caves all these years. The world outside is in peril," Aiken informed him, "and men such as you are sorely needed."

"Then I suppose it was appointed to you to find me at this time," Sparrow replied.

Aiken gasped, "If we hadn't gotten lost we wouldn't have found you at all!"

"Lost? Where were you going?" Sparrow asked.

"And I was so rude to you, King. I ought not have been, even if good hadn't come of it," Aiken spoke to King in the darkness.

"Think nothing of it. Perhaps I was overconfident. My mistake remains even if we are pleased with the result," King said.

"You may still be culpable for your error in judgment, but I am still responsible for my ill behavior, too," Aiken insisted.

"Alright, alright. You're all made up. Where were you going to?" Sparrow asked again.

"We are on our way to the Cherokee Nation. A great battle is forming up in Illinois, and I am going to Tahlequah to call upon the Cherokee to come to the aid of the city and towns there," King explained.

"Why? Who is attacking them?" Sparrow wanted to know.

It was clear that they would have to bring Sparrow up to speed about just about everything. They sat down on the cold floor and began telling the story of the Pledge and what its goals were. King told Sparrow about the meeting in Oklahoma City and the Cherokee's constant vigilance concerning the doings of the Pledge. Finally, he shared with him the less fantastic details of the battle of Cairo. At last he described in brief Fides' task in Peoria and the rush of the Rangers to defend Bloomington, and here Aiken was able to add comments.

"What makes you think the Cherokee will come?" Sparrow asked.

"I don't know that they will. But I know that against the great number of the Pledge, unless they do the whole region will fall," King replied.

"Yet the Cherokee is not all that great in number, either. You would send them to their destruction? Unless ..." and Sparrow gasped. "Ah, you know. You know about the Cherokee armory."

It was King's turn to gasp, "You know about that?"

"Of course." Even in the dark King could tell that Sparrow had shrugged dismissively as though everyone possessed this knowledge. Sparrow explained, "Would the leader of the Sioux and the leader of the Cherokee not speak about such things? And would not the Sioux and many other tribes have their own armory? Of course."

"Well, there were some battles between the Cherokee and the Lighter Sioux, and neither produced any such weapons," King said.

"Lighter? Talutah Lighter? I should have known that he would take command. But he does not know the details about the Cherokee armory. Come, tell me what my kinsman has done," Sparrow asked. King could only give bits and pieces of the answer. He knew that the Lighter Sioux had harassed many travelers and the residents of Oklahoma City, and thought he remembered that they played some role in the fall of Lincoln and Omaha, but he couldn't recall the details. Sparrow didn't seem to need them, nor did he seem surprised.

"Talutah wanted to rage against the International Forces. I sometimes wonder if Talutah would fight his left side if his right side could find nothing to strike. He was not easy to keep tamed," Sparrow sighed, remembering long past discussions and conferences.

They fell silent for a time, each to their own thoughts.

"Did you really think I was a ghost?" King asked Sparrow at last.

"No. I have no time for such things. A hallucination, perhaps. A dream, maybe," Sparrow said softly.

"Why did the others die? Why didn't they want to live?" King asked.

"Their hope failed them. Of course, some say wrongly that hope is wishing for something, no more, no less, but that isn't the case. You need hope to survive. In life outside the caves and in life within them. Only outside the caves it is easier to choose between things to hope in. Most of these prove false, yet it is no trouble to find another. Down here, though. No, there was merely hope laid bare and only one thing to place that hope in—all our efforts were dashed early on. So long as a man believes that there is something outside himself, he can hope. A man might live in the worst of circumstances so long as he has hope, all the more if it is a well-founded one. A man in a concentration camp without hope is dead even as he stands, while one with hope fights the good fight of the mind and so sustains himself for the future. This is no secret: it is why the first step in so many tyrannical systems is to crush hope and cultivate despair. It is only a secret to those who through sloth or ignorance—or both—believe that circumstances will not change. Yet circumstances do change. For this reason, one must train himself in hope before he is thrust into a darkened cave with only his own thoughts ... without light even to make shadows... for who knows how long. I ...," Sparrow trailed off.

"I don't want to speak too boldly. I was nearly crushed in the end," he concluded.

"How have you convinced yourself that you're not now in a dream?" Aiken wondered.

"The dream ... where does the dream come from?" Sparrow asked rhetorically, but Aiken offered an answer anyway.

"Out of your dark self, into the light of your consciousness," Aiken replied.

"But how did it get into my dark self?" Sparrow rejoined.

Aiken said, "The brain? Your brain was its mother, and the desire in your blood was its father."

"No, say rather," suggested Sparrow, "my brain was the violin upon which it issued, and the desire in my blood the bow that drew it forth. Man dreams and desires; God broods and wills and quickens. Here was my hope: When a man dreams his own dream, he is the sport of his dream; when Another gives it to him, that Other is able to fulfill it. So, the appearances of King were not as I would have dreamed, had I put flesh to hidden thoughts. No, I would have been speaking with him from the beginning. We should have been having coffee back in my house. No, it was still black as black. Then it was only at the end that we spoke. So, I felt that even if it was a dream it was not merely a dream: it came from without. And so long as there was a without I knew that circumstances could change. It is only when one believes they have only their own efforts to rely on, in ultimate terms, that despair is nearby, and death. At the last exchange with King, I knew that my deliverance was at hand. When it didn't come quickly I was nearly crushed, as I said. I should have known better," Sparrow sighed again.

"It is well reasoned and well said," Aiken said.

"But now I am exhausted," Sparrow told them. "Let's lie down here a little while in silence and sleep as we may. When we awake I will show you my lair, such as it is. My hope has flesh, now ... I have company to sustain me. Together we will hope for a way home. Together it might sustain us for years ahead."

"These are not comforting thoughts," King said.

"Then choose the thoughts that comfort you and sleep," Sparrow said.

With that, the three stopped talking. Each fell into a dark and dreamless sleep. How long they slept in that dull and damp place King could not say. He awoke slowly, as though beckoned by angels. Then he heard shouts of joy at their arrival. He opened one eye and then another, and beheld a blinding bright light shining hard upon him. Sparrow was leaping from place to place, exulting in the light. King glanced around for Aiken and found him sitting up, also looking at the light.

As King's eyes adjusted, he realized what it was. When they had fallen through into the cave they had opened a wide gap in the earth. Piercing shafts of sunlight now thrust their way into the opening. Sparrow leapt in and out of the light: this moment an arm could be seen, then he was lost again in the shadows; now this moment his whole body could be seen, with his face beaming, before passing back into the dark. Sparrow was dancing, dancing, dancing! Aiken began laughing, and King couldn't help joining him. It was the lifting of despair after the longest of nights, and it was impossible not to delight in it.

"We have to find a way up there!" Sparrow declared. He began talking to himself, planning how to do it. The trailer was about fifteen feet below the opening. Some improvisation would be required. He disappeared into the caverns, leaving behind only the echoes of his footsteps and catcalls. They grew ever more faint until at last nothing could be heard at all, and then they began to swell again until it was evident that he was on his way back.

"Rope!" he cried out to them. He mounted the trailer with perfect ease and positioned himself underneath the hole. Having tied an oblong chunk of heavy iron to one end, he began trying to swing the heavy end up through the opening. His clattering failures were loud enough to hurt King's ears. At last though, the iron went through the hole, and when Sparrow tugged it didn't come down. He grabbed the rope and was about to pull himself up when he suddenly paused. He gazed solemnly down at them, his body cloaked in the night of the cave but his face catching the glistening rays of the sun from above. After a moment he said, "This is the end - for me the beginning of life."

With that, he shimmied up the rope with joyous shouting and intermittent giggling.

"I suppose we should join him," Aiken chuckled.

"I'm not sure I can do that climb," King laughed.

"You're a young fellow. What about me?" Aiken retorted. But the two had no trouble pulling themselves out of the cave. The most difficult part was getting King's staff up. King had found it lying on the top of the trailer, perfectly intact, and refused to part with it. He tried to throw it a few times and, after having it fall to the cave floor, which required him to climb down the end of the trailer again, he finally settled on tying the staff to the end of the rope so that it could be pulled up once he had made it to the top.

Aiken and Sparrow were waiting for him. They were sharing laughs and breakfast and a good chuckle at King's expense. King blushed, but didn't defend himself. He did have his staff, after all.

The conversation turned to their next steps. The decisions were made quickly and easily. Sparrow would accompany them to the Cherokee Nation. He had no family in the area to seek out. The family he had was far off in Nebraska. Tahlequah, on the other hand, was relatively close. They lamented the fact that they couldn't extricate the motorcycle, but it had broken through the top of the trailer and wedged itself properly. It had a mangled look about it, anyway.

No matter. Sparrow was happy to walk. It was a perfect time to emerge into light. Spring was in full flower and beautiful—all the more if you've just endured the longest winter ever. Sparrow was not able to stop and smell the flowers, for in joining King and Aiken in their journey, he had joined them in their haste. They followed 71 south and after a couple of hours they reached I-44.

King marveled at Sparrow's fitness; he was at least fifteen years older than Aiken, perhaps more, with long, silvery hair that fell down to the middle of his back. He reminded King of an older Fermion. Sparrow sprang, he didn't walk. Ten miles they went, and the man didn't break a sweat or slow even once. In fact, it was they who struggled to keep up.

Ten miles later, heading west on I-44, they reached the town of Joplin. After the devastations most people in the area gravitated towards Springfield, but the exception was Joplin. Joplin was still well populated and well acquainted with travelers. Few had seen travelers like this, though. Sparrow's clothes were ragged. He appeared like a beggar, but carried himself like a king. He bounced along the streets as though insane, but issued witty rejoinders to any who addressed him. King and Aiken trailed along, bemused. Sparrow knew the way to Tahlequah. Sparrow led the way.

Aiken punched King in the arm.

"Ow! Why did you do that?" King demanded to know.

"Look at the sign!" Aiken pointed.

Before them was a big green sign indicating that they had stumbled upon south-bound 71. King smiled as he realized his mistake.

"Northbound and southbound are separated by ten miles! No wonder I didn't remember. What an absurd thing to do!" King laughed.

"You're off the hook for your 'mistake' a little more than you were already," Aiken beamed.

"Come on, you two! That is the road we are taking!" Sparrow called back to them.

That night they slept in the grasses on the northwestern edge of the city of Neosho. Sparrow fell asleep even before a fire was started. King and Aiken talked for awhile, but it had been a long day's journey—all on foot—and they submitted to exhaustion and soon fell asleep as well.

The next morning an alert Sparrow standing next to a jeep and a sheepish looking man, who apparently had been the driver of the vehicle, awakened them.

"We do not walk today!" Sparrow declared.

"What is the meaning of this?" Aiken rubbed his eyes.

"This young lad is Jim Merton. He was the driver of the third vehicle I stopped on the road ..."

"You stopped vehicles on the road?" King yawned.

"I knew if I stopped enough vehicles I would finally find someone I knew. Sure enough! Jim's grandfather worked with me when I worked in Kansas City. His granddad has passed on, but I shamed

Jim here into giving his kin's friends a ride to Tahlequah," Sparrow bellowed.

"Shamed? Threatened, rather," Jim smirked.

"A little arm twisting never hurt no one. Promised that we could get the Cherokee to repay Chummy for the lost revenue and fuel and that smoothed things over proper," Sparrow beamed. Sparrow glanced at Jim, "Anyone figure out how Chummy is getting his fuel yet, Jim?"

Jim laughed, "No, but we can guess: corn. Somehow he does it with corn."

"Not a bad guess, but you didn't hear it from me! That was a tight secret when I was about!" Sparrow smiled.

Jim and Sparrow let King and Aiken get their bearings and have a bite to eat before prodding them into the back of the jeep.

"We're only about eighty miles away, but she's a bumpy ride. Better hold on," Jim called back to them. Jim never said a truer word. The interstates were bad enough, but once the jeep hit the back roads the roads were treacherous. Jim drove them west into Oklahoma, and then wound his way south to Tahlequah. King and Aiken couldn't hear the conversation very well from up front, but it was animated—on one side anyway. Sparrow was constantly pointing and explaining what he was pointing at to Jim, who smiled knowingly.

Because of the condition of the roads, the eighty miles took a solid four hours. They arrived around 11 a.m., and heads turned to see why a vehicle was gunning through Tahlequah. Sparrow made Jim drop him off right at the entrance to the council building. Sparrow bounded out of the jeep with glee. Men and women began gathering around. Ramaen and Chief Thunderfist were late in arriving to see what the fuss was about, but the crowd cleared a path as the two walked forward.

"Sparrow, my friend!" Thunderfist shouted in happiness.

"Thunderfist! You've grown older than dirt!" Sparrow bellowed.

"When did you start calling yourself dirt?" Ramaen laughed, clapping his hands on Sparrow's back. The crowd backed away out of respect for the reunion, but most didn't recognize Sparrow for who he was. Clearly an old friend of Thunderfist and Ramaen, but beyond that the name wasn't ringing any bells. It wasn't until Charlie arrived and hooted that the rightful Sioux chief had arrived that people remembered. It was Sparrow, the leader of the free tribes of the west. It was Sparrow, he who had disappeared without a trace more than five years earlier as the devastations were beginning. For those who remembered when he left and what came of it, it seemed as though a long winter was coming to an end. Sparrow had come.

That day and the next, there were mad festivities throughout the city. Skirmishes with the Lighter Sioux had persisted and even gotten worse, though they had more recently disappeared from the area. With Sparrow back, it was firmly believed that the Sioux would be brought back under the control of more reasonable men. The Sioux had dealings with numerous other tribes seeking to reclaim the United States, so the taming of the Sioux was a useful first step. If the tribes of the plains could be united again, then also they might be able to throw off the groping hands of the Pledge.

In the course of the festivities, the Pledge was not forgotten, nor was King's tale. Early that afternoon, they escaped the clamor to a quiet council chamber to speak about great affairs. Sparrow was present, but at last silent, as King and Aiken shared with Charlie, Ramaen, and Chief Thunderfist what had transpired since King had left. It was a long tale, and Chief Thunderfist made him clarify a number of points about the Shadowmen, Fermion, and Fides' key. He heard about the mysterious aura and beatific Shadowmen and Fermion's courageous act in Cairo and Fides' quest. The story turned at last to the truth of St. Louis, a truth that the Cherokee council had long guessed, but never confirmed. Then, it was the discovery of Sparrow's Caves, and Sparrow himself. Here, Sparrow shared his account of the last half decade or so. It took three hours merely to hear it all.

"So, you have decided to See at last?" Chief Thunderfist eyed King.

"I have. It has been perplexing at times, but I have seen nothing as horrific as what drove me to reject the gift. I hope I do not," King answered.

"Perhaps not, but there is much more for you to See … in time. Not on your schedule, but in time," the Chief said.

Charlie interjected, "So, you come to rally the guns of Tulsa against the Pledge. We have noticed that the Pledge forces have thinned in Arkansas, though not so much that we thought their army dispatched. They have raised many more men than we anticipated. These must have come from the east, for we would have known about it if their numbers were drawn from elsewhere. This is no light request you make of us. We would leave the Cherokee Nation virtually defenseless to any other threats."

"But have we not also noticed," Ramaen said, "that the many bandit Indian tribes have disappeared as well? Perhaps they have already departed for Illinois, perhaps in concert with the Pledge? Our scouts have not encountered a reclaimer in weeks."

"If we could be sure that the Pledge army has sallied forth and that the Lighter Sioux and all the rest were no longer around, I would feel better," said Charlie.

"Then let's send out scouts. We shall double the amount and send them ranging far. Let's send them even as far as Little Rock to see what can be seen. We have never sent them so far, but if there is no one to resist them, then that tells the tale," the Chief suggested.

Sparrow spoke: "It is not enough that the Cherokee rides to Bloomington and the preservation of a treasure in Peoria. Many should go, each taking a hand in the establishment of liberty. A decisive blow against the Pledge by the combined forces of lovers of freedom will establish a new nation bound up in freedom and the sacrifice that makes freedom possible. Who do you know that could also go?"

Charlie thought aloud, "Oklahoma City. Joplin. Springfield. The Texans. Oh! If Chummy's vehicles would take us, we could move quickly and with a great tactical advantage. I bet he could transport a thousand if he wanted."

"Word must be sent also to Wichita," Ramaen said. "Fox would join us."

"Yes, my son must know that I live. He would join us indeed. And if you've gone as far as Wichita, why not reach out also to Omaha and Lincoln?" Sparrow asked.

Charlie's face grew dark, "Omaha and Lincoln fell to the reclaimers a long time ago. It was merciless. I don't think we could count on those cities for anything more than trouble."

"Ah, that is right. I have been informed that my kinsman was involved there," Sparrow said, remembering King's recounting of the world's affairs while they were still trapped in the cave.

Chief Thunderfist closed his eyes in thought, "At any rate, messengers must be sent and with great haste. We need not decide the question now. Let us call a great council and see if we will all go together. It would take many days for messengers to arrive at their destinations, however, and many days for them to return. If they are inclined for war, then they will need time also to assemble and prepare. Yet time is short."

"What do you propose?" Charlie asked.

"We must have Chummy's involvement. We must have access to his vehicles. Our messengers must ride to the Texan capital in Abilene. They must ride to Oklahoma City. They must ride to Wichita. In a word, we must call for Chummy's assistance today—ever so urgently, more urgently than we ever have before. Naturally, our Tulsa brethren must be made aware of events as well."

"What are you suggesting?" Charlie pressed the Chief.

"It is time to give Chummy a token of our appreciation. Let him have five of the weapons he has coveted for so long. We have them to spare. It is a small price to pay in order to have such quick messaging. When the council is convened, perhaps then we can persuade him to go beyond ferrying messengers, but join us in ridding this land of a mutual overpowering threat," the Chief concluded.

"It is good!" Sparrow declared.

"It is at least the best we can do. I wish I could know how much time we had to spare. Alas, I don't think we have much. We can do nothing, though, until we have Chummy's cooperation," Chief Thunderfist explained, "So, Charlie, make it worth the while of that jeep driver to take you and some scouts to Tulsa. Tell Philip to release five of the weapons as payment for Chummy's services, and then return as fast as you can with whatever vehicles you have been able to procure. How soon can you leave?"

"An hour," Charlie replied.

"Make it so. Sadly, you must miss the festivities celebrating the return of Sparrow, but that is as it must be. Tomorrow I will begin organizing the messengers and hopefully you will be back by then with vehicles," the Chief said.

It was agreed. Soon, Charlie was traveling towards Tulsa as fast as Jim would drive his jeep, and the Cherokee Nation feasted. Before Charlie left, King snuck in a word: "Tell Joan I am here!" Charlie had smiled, said nothing, and was gone. King was left to enjoy the feasting, as much as one could when one was so close to the woman he loved but could not yet be by her side.

The next day Charlie had returned from Tulsa. The negotiation with Chummy had clearly succeeded as evidenced by the fact that about ten vehicles had accompanied him. With vehicles procured, they proceeded to designate messengers and diplomats to dispatch. The cars and trucks were stocked with foodstuff and extra fuel.

Charlie took King aside and told him that he had delivered his message and had one back from Joan. The message was that she would be coming to Tahlequah several days later, when the Tulsan Cherokee traveled there for the council and the great mustering of the Cherokee army. To King it wasn't soon enough, but he would have to wait.

Ramaen came to King that evening and asked if he would be willing to join the delegation that was heading for Texas. He had nothing else to do but stew in the anticipation of seeing Joan, so he agreed. Aiken said he would go along as well. Frankly, he was looking forward to the trip. Texas sounded quite interesting.

King briefly saw his old friend, Luke. Luke was traveling to Wichita, though, and could not talk long. They exchanged warm greetings and then parted. Because the Texas party had the furthest to go—and because it was feared that the Texans would require the most discussion—they left that night. The other groups would fan out throughout the countryside the next morning.

Vehicles were going to Oklahoma City, Joplin, Springfield, Wichita, Abilene, and Shreveport. Scouts flooded into Arkansas and

Missouri to learn as much as could be learned about the Pledge. The Springfield delegation would continue as far east as Cairo in an attempt to fill in blanks in King's account and to try to determine the last movements of the Pledge within their region. The hope was that the leaders of all these towns would come to Tahlequah for a great Council of War, and that their muster would not be far behind them. If all went according to plan, they could march on to Bloomington within ten days, possibly sooner. King hoped it was soon enough.

## == Chapter 18 ==

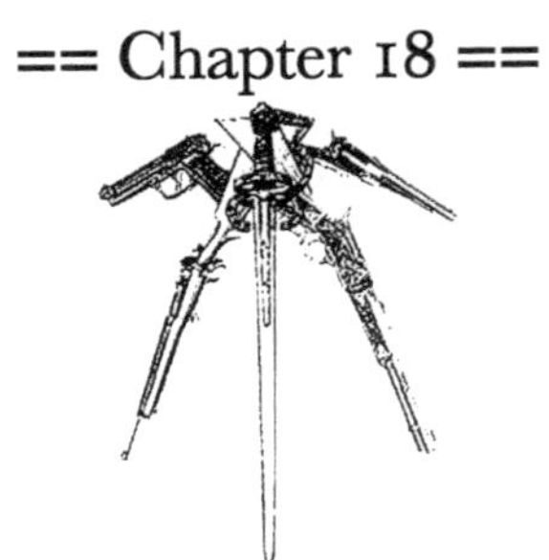

The Texas delegation consisted of eight men and two vehicles. They left before the sun went down and hoped to be in Abilene, the capital of the New Republic of Texas, as early as the next morning. Two of the members had made the trip before and vowed that they could guide them even in the dark. Still, it was a perilous trip. They would be forced to take back roads for almost the entire journey, and they would skirt the desolate remains of Dallas and Fort Worth.

King stayed awake for a time and chatted with Aiken and the other two men in his car, but as the sun went down, he couldn't keep his eyes open any longer. He fell into a deep sleep. Though jostled throughout the night, he awoke only once, slipping immediately back into sleep.

In the morning, the sun's rays were lighting up the Texan wilderness, and King woke up at last. Just in time! Abilene was before them. The Texans had done well to decorate the city in garments fit for a capital of a new nation. White columns and magnificent flags met their eyes in every direction. There were many people about and each was watching them in wonder.

It had been relatively cool in the morning wherever King had been in his travels, but it was hot in Abilene. Even rolling down the windows didn't help. The vehicles finally came to a stop outside a great rotunda. They took some time to stretch their legs and arms and yawn, and were shown the direction of the rest rooms by curious onlookers.

Finally, it was time to seek out the leadership of the New Republic. Apparently they were too early, though, and they had to wait. They waited until about ten in the morning but then complained loudly about the importance of their task, and word was sent to the leaders to come in haste—or more hastily, at any rate. It was nearly twelve before they'd all assembled in a large conference room.

They sat around a massively large, long table, and each had luxurious chairs to sit in. King felt out of place in those chairs. He was unkempt and dusty, but those chairs were immaculate. Indeed, no expense had been spared to make the conference room as comfortable as possible. It bore testimony to the wealth of their new nation.

King recognized some of them. Jerrod Hansley had been the ambassador whom King had seen in Tahlequah. He remembered him by name, as well as the Reverend Nolan White. He recognized three others, but had to be reminded of their names. They were senators now: Senator Stevens, Senator Felts, and Senator Buchwald. Sitting at the head of the table was a tall, grim-looking man who they learned was the president, Sam Guthrie. The Reverend was at Guthrie's left hand, and King felt that this didn't please the Reverend that much. There were many other Texans whom King didn't recognize at all.

President Guthrie initiated the proceedings.

"So, the Cherokee have taken the unusual step of obtaining vehicles so that they could drive overnight and be here this morning. It must be a pretty important matter. Would anyone care to explain?" Guthrie asked.

A man named Marty, whom King remembered as one of Charlie's right hand men, was the chief spokesperson for the Cherokee. He spoke now. It was necessary to explain what had happened in Cairo. Marty discoursed on the discovery that the Pledge army had grown massive. It was revealed that St. Louis was not desolated. The Key which Fides bore was alluded to, but little was said about that. The emphasis was on the fact that the city of Bloomington was about to come under siege by tens of thousands of Pledge warriors, and the time was now to stand up and resist the Pledge—hopefully once and for all.

The Texans listened attentively and respectfully as Marty concluded by inviting them to a Council of War to be held in Tahlequah, with Texan warriors following close behind. Then Marty said that they wanted to do this all in a matter of days, finally pausing to hear what they would have to say.

The Texans sat quietly for a few minutes. Guthrie clicked his fingers together in thought.

"We Texans have vowed not to involve ourselves in foreign wars. Sending our men to die in Illinois leaves our borders with Mexico greatly weakened. Though it is true that we have not seen any sign that there is a threat from the south, we should not like to be surprised. So, on principle and on pragmatics, we shall decline your request. I say that, but I will let those assembled speak if they like," Guthrie said, waving his hands at the assembled senators.

For a time no one spoke. It seemed as though all were in agreement. Marty wormed in his seat, fighting hard to hold his tongue. The other Cherokee held themselves in check better, but King could guess that they were not pleased with the president's reply. When it seemed as though the affair would end utterly in failure, a senator broke the silence.

It was Senator Felts. "It seems to me to be a poor way to start a friendship with our neighbors to the north. Imagine, if you will, that the northern territories fall to the Pledge. Do we want such a neighbor as the conquering Pledge? Now imagine that the Pledge is thrown down without our help. Will we be well regarded by our neighbors? Am I not right in thinking that they would hold us in contempt? So no matter who prevails to the north, if we do nothing, we will have at the very least a very cool relationship and at the most outright hostilities. Yet if we go to their aid and we prevail, then a common foe is defeated. If we fail, we would have also failed in time anyway, as it is unlikely that we could ourselves throw down the Pledge on our own if the great numbers of the north could not succeed. I say we go and fight!" he said.

Ambassador Hansley protested, "Then we will become entangled before the first decade of our existence has ended. What is the point of a principle if we never act on it?"

"Not every Texan believes that those to the north are 'foreigners,'" Felts retorted. "If the Mexicans or Chinese came again from the south, am I not right in believing that the valiant men and women of the north would come to our aid? Is that not clearly demonstrated in history?"

A Cherokee that King knew as Tooant now spoke, "You speak words of wisdom, sir. It is difficult to speak for the entirety of the 'northern territories' as you call them due to the fractured state of affairs, but I can speak for the Cherokee and assure you that we would indeed come to your aid. With only slight presumption I think I can say that Oklahoma City would come to your aid as well. Possibly the free tribes of the plains would come to your aid as well."

"Come now," Reverend White interjected, "the free tribes? That association has been long broken. Their agenda of reclaiming the United States is well known and clear, and we well know that it applies also to Texas."

"You speak a dark word that has truth," Tooant admitted, "And yet it might be that their minds could be changed."

"Do you know of something that could change their minds?" Guthrie asked inquisitively, cocking his head towards Tooant.

"I do. If Sparrow was alive, he could change their minds. He could cast a vision for a country united again on principle, rather than one on color or caste."

The Reverend White chuckled, "Ah yes, if only Sparrow was alive."

"He *is*. He is alive!" Tooant declared. Not everyone in the assembly knew who Sparrow was, but those who did gasped aloud in astonishment.

"What is the explanation for this?" Guthrie demanded to know. But Tooant nodded towards King, and King unexpectedly found himself speaking before all of those gray haired officials and leaders, telling them the story of what happened in Carthage. People nodded along and smiled as King told the story. This was news indeed.

After King had completed his account, Guthrie spoke again, "Some of you are yet too young to know who Sparrow is or what he has done. You have to go back to the Chinese-Mexican war. It was he who rallied so many of the Indian noblemen to come to our aid. Yes, we lost that war, and we lost many men, and the tribes did, too. Yet we won several battles, too, and Sparrow's accomplishments still trail behind him calling out for the praise of men. This is news. News indeed."

"So do you change your mind?" Marty asked.

"That I don't say," Guthrie cautioned him. "I appreciate what Senator Felts has said, though I disagree. I believe that Sparrow probably could unify the tribes of the plains and many others as well, but not in so short a time. And there is still the principle of the matter. When do you need an answer?"

Tooant answered for Marty, as those who knew Marty knew that he was presently irate beyond words. Tooant said, "We would like to know as soon as possible, but at the latest tomorrow morning. We must get back to the great council that is being convened. The Cherokee Nation, at least, will be riding to battle, and we must prepare."

"Then give us leave to discuss these questions alone and in private," Guthrie requested.

"We give it willingly," Tooant said.

"I will see to it that your needs are met through the day and night, and we shall deliver our answer as soon as we have it," Guthrie said.

"Thank you, Mr. President," Tooant replied. Then the Cherokee filed out of the room pensively, though it could be said more accurately that Marty stormed out.

They were met by staff members of the president who led them away to a comfortable room. Food and water was supplied to the delegation. There was little conversation between them. Marty made a joke at his own expense about his quality as a diplomat, but that was the extent of it.

An hour went by, and then two. Still no decision had been made. Afternoon was passing them by, as evidenced by the Texas sun bounding its way from one side of the windows to the other. When the senators and the president ordered dinner for themselves while they continued their discourse, they extended that provision to the delegates. The Cherokee decided after dinner that they would walk around the city. The room was comfortable enough, but they yearned to stretch their legs.

King and Aiken took to the streets of Abilene. It wasn't as hot out as it had been earlier, but it was still oppressive. They welcomed the shade of trees when they came to them. They quickly discovered that the Cherokee delegation were not the only ones waiting expectantly. Numerous Texan men and women were milling about the area seeking news. It was startling how much was known.

It was known that the Cherokee delegation had arrived in great haste. It was known that a call to war had been issued. It was known that the initial decision had been to decline the call, but that a few senators changed their mind and now the discussion had become quite prolonged. To King's amazement, many of the Texans also knew that Sparrow was alive. What amazed him most was that people had even heard of Sparrow.

All of the oldest men and women knew of Sparrow, and many of the people Aiken's age did. Only they very young didn't grasp the significance of the man and the fact that he was alive. The story unfolded, in ever greater detail, of Sparrow's heroic deeds in the defense of Texas and the then united United States. Not a few of those who knew the story were torn between their desire not to become "embroiled in foreign wars" and the moral pressure they felt to repay their debt to Sparrow personally, and the people of the north more generally.

The sun was beginning its descent when the deliberations ended for the night. The president and the senators filed out of the capital building and announced that deliberations would continue early the next morning. King and Aiken wandered over to learn what could be learned and found that many others were doing the same.

Marty, Tooant, and a woman King remembered as one of the Cherokee leaders, Adsila, were in conversation with Senator Felts. The senator had a grim expression on his face, and Marty was shaking his head in despair. King and Aiken joined them.

"In the end I persuaded a great many that we should ride north," Senator Felts was saying, "but not enough to win the vote."

"Why then did discussion continue?" Tooant wanted to know.

"I had convinced enough so that by our procedures I was able to compel another vote to be taken place after another round of discussion. Yet after three such rounds I only managed to convince one more person. As it stands, the lines are drawn in hardening concrete, and tomorrow morning it will be set at last. The final vote will be had, and the New Republic of Texas will not ride to war," Felts explained.

"Can't you perpetuate the conversation until at last they have been persuaded?" Marty asked.

"No, we are only permitted five such rounds, if there are enough votes to compel further conversation. Three are complete and in the morning there shall be two more, if I can help it, but I am afraid to say that unless some new information comes to light, the men of Texas will be staying put. Most of them, anyway," said the senator.

"Most of them?" Tooant asked, raising his eyebrows.

"It is a Republic, is it not? And we are yet free, are we not? The Republic may not go off to war, but I will. Others will join me. We will not go with the blessing of the president or the senatorial council, which means poorly armed and poorly equipped, but we *will* go," Felts asserted emphatically.

"That is a bright light in this dark matter," Tooant replied.

"Yes, but it is a matter of great haste, then, is it not? You hope to have your council within the week. Those of us who are going to go will need to leave no later than tomorrow night. Men will be gathering together to make the journey. Fortunately, it is the rare Texan who does not have a horse these days, so at least we need not be overly delayed, but we are still at least three hundred miles away. It took us six days to make that trip when I went to Tahlequah," Felts said.

"You might be able to do it in less if you went with haste. It should be said that the council begins in under a week, but we will not march to war until after the council is over. Even if the council decides quickly what to do, it will take a day or two before we set out. In eight days the last Texan could make it in time though he would not have a moment to rest before setting off with us," Marty informed him.

The senator was relieved, "that is good to know. Still, I intend to be there for the council, and at least several of the other senators will want to join me. We will not represent the Republic in any official capacity or have any authority over the mass of men who will be coming of their own free will, but I hope that we will be received as worthy representatives of those men—by your council and by the men themselves."

"That can be arranged most certainly," Marty said.

At that moment a messenger from the president found them.

"Hello! I have come to direct you to your sleeping accommodations for the night and give you further word on where matters stand. May I speak?" the messenger asked.

"You may," Marty said, following the messenger off to a more private location.

"I must go now," Felts said, "I must prepare for this trip and spread the word as I am able. It may not be that the tens of thousands of Texas warriors we have will come to battle, but I would not be surprised if you don't gain five thousand stubborn men who act out on their own principles. We shall see!"

With that the senator was gone. Soon, Marty returned to them with the news. They were to drive to a large house on the edge of Abilene. They would be sheltered there. They were to remain there until after the last vote. After the last vote, which was expected to go against going to war, word would be sent to them of the final decision. They would then be free to leave at once for the Cherokee Nation. It was well known that the delegation didn't want to loiter and that any decision, especially a decision which meant that the Texan army would not be coming to their aid, would need to be made known to the organizers in Tahlequah.

That night, King and Aiken sat on the house's front porch, enjoying the quiet of the Texas night. Little was said, though King wondered why he hadn't had any kind of vision throughout the whole event.

In the morning, Aiken roused King out of bed shortly after the sun had come up. Breakfast was served to them, and Marty wanted to share with the delegation the news he had heard in the middle of the night. It was good news, so far as it went: an outcry had gone up throughout the Republic whenever a man had learned about the impending decision, and men in droves were vowing to ride north. Even at that moment, in fact, they were preparing.

"Yes, Felts said that there will be a thousand Texans at least who leave this very day, with more to follow. So many are staying who would have been a great help, but even four or five thousand is a respectable contribution," Marty said.

"I fear most of all that their refusal will have a bitter taste in all the mouths at the council of war. If ever war opens again on Texas, I wonder if they will receive the help from the 'northern territories,'" Tooant grumbled.

"I for one will remember the deeds of the men who leave of their own free will and not at the commands of their generals or their president," Aiken interjected.

"Well said," Marty agreed. "We will not forget them, at least."

The breakfast ended as more messengers arrived from various people. When King went outside this morning, there weren't only representatives from the president or Senator Felts. Men and women had gathered to seek information on their own from the delegation as they began to make their own plans.

King joined the rest in explaining the general timeframe. They briefly explained the situation as it was understood. Many people expressed their sympathy, but after hearing the full story stated that they would abide the judgment of the leadership. Still others were confirmed in their conviction to head north. These left hastily to make the necessary arrangements.

Indeed, as the morning wore on, men, and occasionally women, could be seen trekking east out of Abilene en route to Tahlequah. Apparently, word was spreading throughout all of Texas and warriors were expected to begin trickling in from cities, both big and small. King and Aiken wanted to see more closely the strength of the exodus, so they told Marty what they were doing and marched off to find the major thoroughfares.

They walked through beautiful treed neighborhoods and well kept houses. Abilene had suffered a great deal during the Chinese-Mexican war, but it had recovered nicely. Eventually they found themselves standing on a main road that seemed to be the road of choice for those marching off to war. Horsemen were traveling in groups of two and three with larger groups occasionally spotted, too. On occasion a man might have a rifle slung over his shoulder. Others had makeshift swords. Most had sharpened axes or clubs or weapons improvised from more ordinary items such as shovels or baseball bats. They marveled at the passing stream of men. It renewed them in their conviction that whatever the Republic said or did, there were good men and women of Texas who still warranted their respect and thanks.

Most of the travelers were on horses, though not all. Certainly there were no vehicles. Some in fact were on foot. These had a long road ahead of them, but none seemed prepared to complain. King and Aiken found themselves walking with two individuals who were giving their horses a break. The two were remarkable.

Besides both being much older—the woman much too old to fight, one would suppose—they appeared to be foreigners. The woman was a shriveled up Asian woman whom King guessed was of Chinese origin. That in itself was something to marvel at, given the recent history of events in Texas. The man appeared to be from Eastern Europe, though King reminded himself that he had little knowledge upon which to form such a conclusion.

They were a pleasant couple, but lurking beneath the surface was a steady and certain fierceness. When Aiken questioned them about whether or not they were really planning on going to war, the woman unleashed a tirade on him, lashing out at him as only matriarchs can do, and telling him to mind his manners and not presume to tell and old lady what she could or couldn't do—or be able to do. The man merely smiled. They were quite a pair. After a little while, the two climbed onto their horses and rode off, leaving King and Aiken behind.

Now the road they were on intersected with the remains of I-20. People were coming from both directions on the interstate and exiting onto the road that they travelled. Apparently, they were currently treading on the most direct route out of the city and towards Tahlequah. They were joined now with others who were also on foot and heading to the battles of Illinois. King and Aiken walked with them, answering their questions the best they could, and asking some of their own. Over the years, farmhouses had sprung up along the road and now men, women, and children were standing outside them waving. Some had even come out to the road to wish them well, and King found a loaf of fresh bread stuffed into his hands by one attractive young woman. He blushed and hurried along.

"I think we've about seen enough, don't you think?" Aiken asked him.

"Yes, it seems like no other roads are joining this one, so we could probably go back to the Interstate and see anything there is to see from there," King agreed. The intersection of their road and the Interstate was only about a twenty-minute walk from the house they slept in, too. It would not have been wise to get too far away, they reasoned. So they bid farewell to the walking travelers around them, turned around and started back.

They made their way past the farmhouses they had only recently passed by. They decided to stop and rest and talk with one family who had come out to greet those setting out on the journey. Across the street, another family was walking down their driveway to the road.

"I knew Matt would go," the woman who King and Aiken were standing with said to her husband.

"Yep," her husband agreed.

Matt was holding his horse by the reins and leading it to the street. His wife was close behind and was carrying a toddler. A slightly older child waddled closely alongside her. Packs were stowed on the back of his horse. Matt appeared to be among the few Texans to own a rifle. It was slung over the horse's back, too. Matt and his wife didn't seem to notice the four of them standing just within earshot. It was impossible not to see that the woman had been crying and was likely to start again at any moment. When Matt had gotten to the end of the drive, his wife put the toddler down and the two children, a boy and a girl, began playing in the weeds just shy of the ditch. Matt swooped down to kiss them goodbye, but they paid him little attention. Their father had to leave on horse often enough—what was different about this time?

"Please stay," the young woman pleaded with her husband.

"Lillian, please. I must go. I have told you that I must go," Matt said.

"But it is not *must*. Nobody is making you," she sniffed.

"The voice of my father compels me, love. I told you," he said, adjusting the belongings on the horse.

"Your father is dead. I don't believe he would want you to spend yourself in this way," Lillian retorted.

"Spend? You assume I go to my death. I have no intention of dying. Why don't you understand? My father would have died if it were not for the brave men of the Midwest who came down here to fight for us. It is on account of the debt owed to a certain Chris Ranthem that I am alive to leave you today, and I must repay that debt. My father's life was saved by Mr. Ranthem," Matt insisted.

"That was so long ago. This Ranthem is certainly dead now, and your father is dead. But your family lives here and now, and we are here, *here*," Lillian replied, tears welling up in her eyes.

"Then I will find his son, if he has one, and I will fight for him," Matt stated firmly.

"He probably died, too! There was a Disease, don't you remember?" she implored him.

"Then I will find the son of his son, and you if you loved me you would be grateful that I go to thank them. If not for them, you would not have had me at all, not even for a little while. Don't deprive me of this moment … and stop … making it so … difficult," he choked.

"No!" she cried out, beginning to sob, "I will make it as hard for you to leave as it is for me to see you go!" She clutched at him, pulling him back towards the homestead.

He pulled away, "Woman! My love, do not do this to me. You know I must go. My friends wait for me. You would have them go alone. If it came to it, you would have their wives widowed, and me alive here, the one who abandoned them?"

"Yes, I would have it!" she declared fiercely.

"Perhaps you would, but I could not," he sighed. "My children … what kind of father would they take me to be if I hid from danger and duty while friends went to fight and past debts went unpaid?"

"But you would be a live father," she argued.

"A live father, but a dead man. I cannot yield, Lillian. You must let me go … the kind of man I would be if I stayed would not be the kind of man you'd want, nor the man you married …"

It had become increasingly difficult to watch the exchange, and King was uncomfortable beyond words. The two hadn't yet noticed that they were being watched from a mere thirty feet away, but even as King and Aiken pulled themselves away Matt pulled his wife into an embrace and he spoke tenderly into her ear. In his last glance over his shoulder, Matt was perched upon his horse and it was slowly heading east down the road. Lillian was sitting in a heap while the children played, unawares.

"I hope that Matt comes home alive," King said.

"As do I. We can hope that they all come home; they are all loved by someone, but it is a fell truth that some certainly will come to grief," Aiken said.

"It must be a hard thing for a man to say goodbye to wife and children," King said, trying to imagine it.

"It is … but at least he has hope that he will see them again soon …" Aiken said softly, and then King remembered and felt terrible, and they went back in introspective silence. King never forgot that scene, but when he replayed it in his head it always seemed as though there was something else besides mere drama that burned within him.

When they arrived back at their house the final message from the senatorial council had been delivered: The Republic would *not* ride to war. The vehicles were being packed, and Senator Felts was there with several other men having a last conference with Marty and Tooant. The street was filled with curious Texans. At last, it was time to begin the journey back to the Cherokee Nation.

Unlike the trip down, the trip back was by day. Aiken was unusually pensive and in no mood for conversation, so King watched the passing terrain through the window of the car. The vehicles caught up to the stream of Texas volunteers; they honked their horns in salute to them, and the volunteers raised their hands in response. They would see one another again relatively soon. King didn't notice Matt, but did not doubt he was still on his way. The old man and woman he did notice. They had taken a break along the side of the road and nodded their heads as the vehicles went past.

A couple of hours later, the signs for Dallas and Fort Worth appeared alongside the road. The first thing King noticed was that the signs were often scorched on the side facing the cities. The closer they came to the cities, the more signs, trees, and buildings were observed to have been knocked over. They all lay away from the city. It seemed clear enough that, unlike St. Louis, these cities really were desolate. However, they did not venture close enough to the cities to see for certain. The vehicles turned north and went around the cities, even cutting across the barren wilderness at one point in order to make the straightest path.

It was not an eventful trip. King found himself falling asleep for a time and waking up to be informed that they had passed into Oklahoma. One thing that King did notice was that there were plenty of folks on the road who seemed like they, too, were on their way to Tahlequah for battle. They were on horseback or on foot and carried staffs, clubs, hatchets, and axes. It bolstered King to know that the word had spread. Though it may arrive too late for Bloomington, they might yet assemble an army capable of overthrowing the strength of the combined Pledge armies.

They arrived in Tahlequah late in the afternoon. The town was frantically busy. Hundreds of tents dotted the parks and lanes and hundreds of men roamed the streets. These were volunteers from the countryside who had heard about the muster, but otherwise answered to no man. They too, wanted to fight. More would arrive.

Chief Thunderfist had standing orders that any returning delegations should come to him immediately and be debriefed. Charlie quickly herded them to the council halls after they arrived, and the Chief joined them in short order. There was disappointment, but not surprise, in the Chief's eyes as he heard about how the matter had played out in Texas. He was heartened, though, to learn that volunteers from the Texan countryside would still be coming, and impressed by Senator Felt's communicated request not to think ill of all Texans on account of this one event.

Now it was a matter of waiting. With nothing else to do, King and Aiken sat at the crossroads and watched warriors enter the city seeking direction. That night, the Oklahoma City delegation returned with good news, though it had never been in doubt that Oklahoma City would come. The next morning the Shreveport delegation arrived. After lunch, the Wichita delegation drove in. All the while, the city and its environs swelled with citizen-soldiers. By that evening, all the dispatched delegations had returned, and the Cherokee council had a good idea of where things stood. The main thing that remained was to agree on strategy, tactics, and chain of command. The Council of War would begin after the leaders of each of the free cities had arrived. Coming as to war, however, they had much to do before coming to Tahlequah. They were not expected for several days.

There was one group of people that King continually craned his neck in search of: the Tulsan Cherokees and his beloved Joan. Charlie must have noticed, because he casually mentioned that they would not come until the last minute, which meant that it would still be days before they arrived. Though disheartened, he was not dissuaded from continuing to look to the northwest.

After a couple of days, the first delegations of the free cities began to arrive. President Neff from Oklahoma City and a host of soldiers and advisors were the first. Then it was Shreveport. Wichita arrived. Joplin and Springfield arrived the following morning. Still Tahlequah continued to grow in population as men and the occasional woman arrived for war. There were probably four or five thousand tents peppering the hills when at last the first volunteers from Texas arrived. That night, Senator Felts arrived with his contingent, and to King's great pleasure, the Tulsans arrived. He watched Philip and Mary and others that he remembered escort Chummy into the council hall where the Cherokee leadership had taken pains to show hospitality to the various delegations.

He did not, however, see Joan.

The next morning, the Council of War began. It was about a week after King had arrived with Aiken and Sparrow. It was an impressive logistical accomplishment and yet many days of travel remained for any army that was dispatched to Illinois. King despaired that they would make it in time.

King was delighted to be personally invited by Chief Thunderfist to observe in the council. He knew that the Chief hoped to gain something if King had a vision, but it was still an honor. Besides that, there was surely no other place in the entire region that would be more interesting than that council chamber. When he arrived, he saw that Aiken had been invited as well. This made perfect sense as Aiken was the only person with intimate knowledge of Illinois. King sat near the Chief, and Aiken sat down by his side. Now, the chambers began to fill up as officials from far and wide filed in.

After everyone had time to come into the hall and sit down, the Chief ordered that refreshments be served. Once everyone had smoked meat, bread, and drink, the ancient man rose to address the assembly. When he stood, the hundred or so men and women in the room became silent.

"My friends!" the Chief cried out, "What a privilege it is to have you all in these halls to discuss a matter of such great importance. Yes, it is an honor to have you, and the question we have to decide is also a question of honor. We need not go over everything again; you know why we are here. It is a moment of great decision, though it pleases me greatly to know that, in fact, we have already agreed on the most important decision: we will come to the defense—or rescue—of the people of Bloomington, Illinois. These people are likely under siege by the armies of the Pledge as we speak. All of us know the Pledge. The Pledge has been engorged with volunteers from your cities and towns. The Pledge has sent delegations far and wide offering peace and security for those who ally with them, and wrath for those who don't. No town within communication range of the Cherokee has fallen for their crafty offers, but who knows how they have fared east of Little Rock, and south to New Orleans. So, we are all agreed that we must go. Now we must decide the manner of our going. It would be good if the leaders of the various cities began by advising us of their estimated strengths. President Neff, would you please begin?"

"Gladly," said Neff, rising from where he sat. "We have five thousand men departing from the city on the morrow. The day after that, another two thousand or so men will come. We are armed mainly with sharpened farm instruments. The Pledge, as we hear it, has guns. Still, we are brave enough; if wisely led, you will find our soldiers valiant enough. I must add, though, that most of my men will be on foot."

"I am Fox Marion, from Wichita!" declared a man from the other side of the room. King recognized him, though it had been many years since he had seen him. When he saw Sparrow sitting near him,

King remembered that Sparrow had claimed him as his son. Marion continued, "We have no more than two thousand men from the city of Wichita to send, and they are even now on their way. However, Sioux warriors who remain true number another thousand or so, and they will join us on the road. They are otherwise engaged at this moment on a matter that I shall mention for the council's deliberation at the proper time."

"I am Senator Felts, from the New Republic of Texas," the senator said, standing after Marion had said his piece. "To my dismay, the Republic of Texas has declined to come. We are a free people, though, and I am here on my own, not speaking for my country. I will try to represent those from Texas who, like me, have journeyed here or are on their way. They come without a leader, but I at least will try to speak for their interests and try to convey the conclusions of this council to those who will listen. I should mention that the New Republic does have representatives here who do speak for the New Republic ..."

At this, to King's surprise, Ambassador Hansley and Reverend White both stood up. The Ambassador spoke, "The decision not to fight in Bloomington was made after long and careful deliberation and via the democratic process. President Guthrie is aware of how that will appear to this council—" there were catcalls and boos and the Ambassador waved his hands to calm them, "—so he has sent me to listen and observe and offer what assistances we can despite not going to war. I will be available ..."

Felts cut him off, "Alright, Hansley. You can start listening and observing. As I was about to say, if I were to estimate the number of Texans on their way, I should put it at about four thousand. There are probably four or five hundred rifles among them. Some will be coming on foot, but we have many horseman. They come to settle their debt to the families of those who died in the Chinese-Mexican war. These have not forgotten, and I hope that this council will not forget that they have not forgotten. In future need, please do not hold Texas in contempt, but aid us as you see fit."

A woman rose. She proudly declared, "I am Alyssa Mortimer, and I am the mayor of Shreveport. We have long had dealings with the Cherokee Nation, but I am delighted to meet the representatives of so many other cities. I am comforted knowing that this country is not broken beyond repair. We know the Pledge better than most. They have already declared war on us for not accepting the terms of their 'treaty.' They declared war, but have evidently delayed it. The armies of the Pledge that were in Little Rock departed suddenly not too long ago and headed north, away from us. Now it seems that we know a little of the reason why: something about Bloomington, Illinois has drawn their thought. I hope that in this council I might learn what was so important about Bloomington, which is so far, that it distracted them from Shreveport, which was so near. About numbers. Not many, I'm afraid. Three thousand, half on horses, none with guns. They are marching north together, as we speak. They will meet us on the way, at the request of Chief Thunderfist, who has presently asked that they defend the flanks of our journey east."

Chief Thunderfist nodded and smiled at her in an expression of gratitude.

Another man stood up, "My name is Roger Kraft. I will speak for both the towns of Joplin and Springfield, though we have representatives present from each. Our men are not on their way—at the Chief's request they remain in our cities awaiting our arrival. We are little horsed and little armed, but there are four thousand of us ready to travel to Illinois to prove our mettle."

Roger Kraft sat down and Chief Thunderfist stood up.

"Charlie, our general, has counted the volunteers who have straggled in from the countryside after they heard that Sparrow was alive and what we planned to do. Before the Texans began to arrive we counted about four thousand five hundred of them. Now that the Texans are arriving we have lost track of who is from nearby and who is from Texas, but we might suppose an even five thousand. Tulsa is here, but represented by the Cherokee Nation and myself. There are about eight thousand Cherokee warriors between the two cities, and we anticipate two thousand patriotic, non-Cherokee citizens from Tulsa, for a total of ten thousand fighters. As for our armament and our traveling capabilities, that will be discussed shortly. As for our assembled strength including all the cities here present, if we do the math ..." and the Chief paused to do the calculation in his head, "Thirty-six thousand. The estimated strength of the Pledge armies in Illinois is forty thousand. Not a bad match, though admittedly the full army of the New Republic of Texas would have made for a much better advantage."

"Thirty-six thousand, but only half with horses and very few with guns," objected Neff, "Isn't it now known that the Pledge is well armed? I am concerned that at best we'll be able to send half our number, and that half to their doom, as they will be greatly outnumbered."

"It is a point worth considering," the chief agreed.

"If I understand what I have been told," Marion stood and answered, "many of the Pledge guns have been silenced. How, I don't know, but I have the feeling that it has something to do with their change of mind regarding Shreveport. If the chief would be so kind, could he expound on the remarkable story I have been told by your messengers?"

"It would be better if heard by someone who was there," the chief said, nodding to King. King jerked his head in surprise. He didn't think he would be speaking! But he couldn't refuse the chief. He rose slowly.

"My name is King. President Neff, you might remember me … I set out with the two swordsmen who came during our meeting with you in Oklahoma City, at which the Pledge was present. We traveled in the company of those men with Bloomington as our objective, if you will recall. There was a family registry there, and Fides and I wished to track down our families. In the course of that journey, we were waylaid by a Pledge army. I suppose it was the one from Little Rock. And then—my, the Shadowmen! I forgot about them!"

"The Shadowmen?" more than one person asked at once. King paused to reflect. How does one explain the Shadowmen?

"There is yet another army that stands opposed to the Pledge. They call themselves the Shadowmen, but they are mighty warriors. They have horses, swords, and bows and arrows. They were routed, I am afraid, by the Pledge guns, but they number about ten thousand themselves, though I don't know if that number should include the men of Cairo who fought with them. As I understand it, when I was heading north to Bloomington with the Rangers, the Shadowmen were in pursuit of the Pledge army," King explained.

"The Rangers?" more voices called out in confusion.

"Yes, the Rangers have horses and guns, and number about three hundred. They helped save the Shadowmen army before Fermion silenced the Pledge guns. They were escorting the Key to Bloomington …" King said.

"The Key?" even more people wanted to know.

"How were the guns silenced?" others called out.

King grew frustrated and began to stammer, "Uh, I can see how this is confusing … let me try to explain …"

Ramaen stood up from nearby and interrupted him, "King. I think you had just better tell the story. Tell the whole story from when you first traveled this way with Tasha through to your arrival here with Sparrow a week ago. Take your time. I think that will help things a great deal."

So King did. When he came to the part where Fox Marion had met them, Fox leapt up and shouted "Yes! Seer!" and King laughed and continued his story. He even mentioned the fact that the Shadowmen seemed glorious. While he related the account of Fermion's charge on the plains of Cairo, there were gasps, and incredulous mutterings. As he was getting to the part where he was about to explain the Ranger's theory that the Pledge was seeking the Ark of the Covenant, his eyes went dim and he Saw something …

He saw Reverend White, then White's son, then his son's son. He could see the Reverend gloating over his election as president, but in an instant he saw White's grandson engaged in cruelties as the Despot of Texas. The vision faded away and King opened his eyes and saw that people were staring at him, waiting for him to speak again.

"Go on, King," Thunderfist said, encouraging him.

King decided to skip mentioning the Ark of the Covenant, but told the account of the treasure presumably in Peoria without referencing some of the theories about that treasure. The story soon turned to the discovery of another Pledge army and word about even more, and the first strong hint that St. Louis was not a nuclear wasteland. There was clapping and more gasping when King recounted his experience in St. Louis. Finally, he was in Carthage, and in a cave, and face to face with Sparrow. At last, the story ended with their arrival in Tahlequah and the summoning of the free cities.

"Astonishing," Kraft declared.

"Amazing," Mortimer exclaimed.

"Hogwash," said Reverend White.

"Yet all true," Chief Thunderfist said. Then the Chief began sharing with them some of the corroborative facts that had been generated over the last few days. Cherokee scouts had reached Cairo and learned that King's story there was accurate. Other scouts located the cave where Sparrow had been found. Yet other scouts had infiltrated into St. Louis and learned definitively that it was inhabited.

The Chief said, "Perhaps you may struggle to believe King's account at one or two points that strike you as particularly extraordinary, but my men can vouch for his veracity on nearly every other point that we have been able to check. Within such a pattern of truthfulness it is true that he may deceive you just on those points, but I can find no reason not to believe him. I should note that the scouts in Cairo uncovered the story of Fermion's charge, so that particular extraordinary element comes to us through more than one witness. And Aiken, here, can attest to the strength of the Pledge army seen coming from St. Louis and the information gained there. I do not think it wise to disregard this account because certain parts are fantastic."

"This thing about St. Louis," Fox Marion said, "They said that there were a million inhabitants. That is a very large number and certainly we could muster a sizable army from there. I bet it would be bigger than our armies and the Pledge armies combined. Also, they are relatively close. Why not seek the help of St. Louis?"

King answered, "If they will admit you to the city they will not release you. I don't know how you would make contact with them without facing that hurdle. But the people I interacted with told me little about how things were run. Also, they themselves were distantly removed from high power. It seems to me that an attempt would be worthwhile, though, because the citizens of St. Louis, though private, seemed quite decent and generally opposed to the Pledge."

"Fascinating," said Neff.

"I must now share another bit of news," Marion said slowly. "I said that my Sioux warriors were currently indisposed. Well, that is because they are trying to seek out the reclaiming Indians. All of them, including all of the Lighter Sioux, are gone, and have left no traces behind. Through some very expert tracking we have determined that they too have ridden to war ... in Illinois. They are gone. The Lighter Sioux, the Dakota, the Cherokee reclaimers that we are aware of, the Blackhawk ... gone. I cannot say that they have joined with the Pledge, but we have collected enough information to conclude that they have gone east. Through careful questioning, we have learned that Illinois was their goal. If we had to put a number to them, we must suppose there are ten to fifteen thousand of them, though possibly more."

"That is an interesting piece of news," Ramaen said.

"Yet it is encouraging in its own way," Chief Thunderfist declared, "for it means that our region is emptied of its threats. The Pledge is in Illinois, the Reclaiming Indians are in Illinois. We need not worry so much about our flanks, nor concern ourselves so much about the defense of our cities. We can commit ourselves more fully to meeting the strength that is being exerted in Illinois."

"A fair point," Charlie agreed.

"I should like to mention again my concern about how we are going to get there and how we are going to fight against the Pledge guns," President Neff interjected.

Thunderfist answered, "If King's account is accurate, we can suppose that many of their guns are now inoperable. As for how we are going to get there ... well ... I have invited Chummy to this council. Chummy, as many of you know, runs a transportation outfit out of Tulsa. I have asked Chummy if he would be willing to lend his fleet to the service of our armies. If he agrees, we may settle that part of your question. Since Chummy will no doubt mention this if I am remiss, let me address the Pledge guns in another way: the Cherokee have guns, too. A thousand of them. These are military issue weapons which were stored in safe keeping long ago. This is a fine moment to produce them, and it is my hope that revealing them at last will assure Chummy that his fleet will be well protected, and persuade him to give his consent."

Chummy stood up. He was a large man, much larger than anyone else in the room. He wore coveralls and smelled like earth. "That is a fine bargaining chip," Chummy declared, "but my fleet has only one hundred and fifty vehicles, and I bet thirty of those don't even work right now. In terms of capacity ... figure seven or eight hundred people at a go. I should mention that I'm short a number of vehicles after the last trip—and those I sent to escort them ..." he glanced pointedly at King, "have never returned."

"So, if we guessed that you could handle seven hundred and fifty foot soldiers at a go, if we had fifteen thousand men that we wanted to drop off in Illinois, that would be twenty trips," Charlie counted.

Chummy growled, "If every vehicle worked and if we were carrying ordinary travelers and not men with packs and bags and weapons. Twenty trips? We're talking about hundreds and hundreds of miles. It would take weeks to ferry them. Also we must think about fuel."

"There is no question that you have enough fuel," Charlie retorted. "If you're worried about compensation, there is of course the fact that the Pledge will no longer pose a threat to you, and I suppose you could expand your operation if you didn't have to fear them. Also, I have looked at the maps, and it is only three hundred miles or so if we went through St. Louis rather than through Cairo. If the armies marched while you ferried, constantly cutting down the distance between your fleet and them, then I think you could complete the task in a week of hard and earnest driving. Provided you're well compensated, I don't see why you should complain."

"Oh, I can still think of plenty of reasons. I'm not saying no. Compensation is on my mind, but we're talking about a logistical nightmare. Having the walking armies close the distance sounds like a good idea, but then the fuel has to go with them," Chummy grumbled.

"Well, this is progress, at any rate," Chief Thunderfist said, clapping his hands. "Now, though, I think we should take a break. Let us pause and come back in an hour. There are many things to decide, but I trust you all begin to see the general picture."

With that, the council was dismissed, and many of the people left the chambers to walk around for awhile. Everywhere there were clutches of conversations, but King and Aiken went outside to wander in the open air.

If the first couple of hours had made it seem as though the council of war would settle all its issues quickly, the next couple of hours revealed what disagreements still remained. For example, while some general agreement with Chummy had been reached, there was dissension regarding who would compensate him and with what. Another problem that arose concerned the disappearance of the Reclaiming Indians. President Neff was loathe to leave his city undefended when the Reclaimers were unaccounted for, and Fox Marion was strongly sympathetic. The clues and intelligence that had led Marion's scouts to conclude they had crossed into Illinois was presented and re-presented, analyzed and re-analyzed. Yet a full half day was invested in disputing whether or not their first move should not be towards Illinois, but rather to St. Louis. Various stratagems were proposed. Some thought that a small party should extend an olive branch to St. Louis. Others argued that such a party would be captured and interred. These argued that the full collected armies ought to approach the walls of St. Louis in order to immediately win the respect of the city. Others countered that this might result in open war, which clearly was not their purpose.

At least it was agreed by all present that they should go to war; that settled the most important matter. While the leaders and diplomats were in consultation with one another, the captains and generals organized their men and met with one another to discuss how their various units were going to cooperate. Very few of the warriors that had arrived were part of any regular army. Few of the cities had anything like that. Ordering men who were mere volunteers around was a delicate business, and there was a steady trickle of men leaving Tahlequah because receiving orders, especially orders from complete strangers, seriously rankled them.

The Council of War dragged on into the second day. King lost his stomach for the deliberations, and Chief Thunderfist graciously allowed him to excuse himself from the council. King paced the fields and encampments impatiently, wondering if it was going to be all for naught. Late that afternoon, the Council of War was officially concluded. The whole city of Tahlequah breathed a sigh of relief. Overflowing with men and beasts, everyone was looking forward to at last mobilizing.

## == Chapter 19 ==

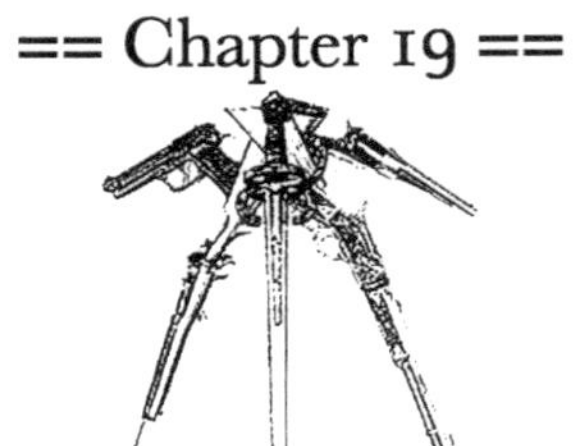

The next morning, preparations began in earnest. Regiments of horsemen were dispatched to serve as advanced units, scouting ahead and guarding against surprise attacks. King watched them go and felt a certain longing to have gone with them. Meanwhile, Chummy's fleet drove in en masse from the other side of the city. Chummy managed to drum up one hundred and forty working vehicles, not including six tankers. Charlie was apparently quite right in believing that Chummy had the fuel situation well in hand.

Messengers were sent out to the Shreveport men who had encamped in Fort Smith, Arkansas, urging them northward into Joplin; once there, they were to turn east and continue on until the rest of the army caught up with them. Meanwhile, messengers were sent to Joplin and Springfield, to the bands of men forming into an army in those locations, instructing them to join the Shreveport men. Thus, to King's comfort, at least six thousand men were already on their way.

That day, Joan arrived. The Tulsan Cherokee had been quite busy. All of the military hardware that had been stored in hidden places had to be brought out, organized, and packed into the vehicles that Chummy provided for that purpose. Residents of Tulsa who never suspected that such an arsenal existed right beneath their noses gathered to watch the affair, forcing the Tulsa Cherokees to set guards and further slowing down matters. The rumor persisted for years afterwards that the Cherokee there still retained plenty of weaponry, but Philip would never confirm nor deny those rumors. At any rate, after the council had made it plain that there would be war, the weapons were prepared for movement, and late on the day after the council concluded, the weapons were moved.

King had heard that the Tulsans were coming and watched eagerly for their arrival. It had required twenty of Chummy's vehicles to ferry the weapons and another thirty to carry the Cherokee to guard them. Joan was among those sent, though she herself had effectively stowed away. She would not be going to war, and her father saw no reason for her to come to Tahlequah; she, of course, could think of one good one. When she stepped out of the car, King's heart leapt up, and his body quickly followed suit.

She spotted him just as quickly. Soon, they were embracing. Her black hair fell softly around his arms which pulled her as close to him as they could. There they stood for a few minutes, swaying gently, while Cherokee worked around them to unload the vehicles. Finally, they looked each other in the eyes and walked away hand in hand. Each thought they saw in the other some change since the last time that they could not put their fingers on.

It was impossible to be alone with so many thousands of men and women in the city, but they did their best to steal quiet moments alone, even if they were never more than moments. He introduced her to Aiken, who approved of her and then respectfully gave them their distance. He ignored Charlie, who he had heard had orders for him. That night they sat on a park bench and pretended they were the only ones there. They parted for the evening, but with great reluctance. When King went to bed, sleep came only after an hour of contemplation and repeated savoring of the memory of Joan in his arms.

The next morning, King could not evade Charlie, who found King in the park where he was sitting close to Joan. The park had been filled with tents the night before, but now warriors were taking them down and packing them and organizing their gear. Clearly, the day of departure was on hand.

"I think you've been trying to hide from me, King," Charlie said, smiling at him broadly. King smiled in return, but it was half-hearted.

"I think you would find that hard to prove," King tried to joke. Joan glanced at the two uncomfortably, worried that she had gotten King in trouble.

"Well, I will deliver my message, and then you have a little time. So, listen up," Charlie said, "Chief Thunderfist and Ramaen desire that you ride tomorrow with Aiken in one of Chummy's vehicles. I will come with you. Much of the army has already set out and many more will set out tomorrow, including many that will be transported in waves by Chummy's fleet. It is deemed that people who are somewhat familiar with the area should be as far front as possible. That would be you and Aiken. But Thunderfist says that he will not order you, rather, he emphasized with me that this is his desire and request to you. You must decide soon, though. We will meet tonight to plan, and then early tomorrow morning we shall go."

"A request and not an order?" King mused. "Leave it to Chief Thunderfist to find a way to make a request irresistible and yet not be an order."

Charlie smiled, "And yet others he orders. I must go. I suppose you have heard that I am the general of the entire force. I have much to do."

Charlie left them. Joan squeezed King's hand and said, "you have to go …"

He looked at her. Her statement was certain enough, but in her dark and misty eyes he knew that it also contained a question. He sat in silence and thought. He remembered his friend Aiken who had accompanied him thus far and would feel betrayed if he did not join him in the return trip. He remembered that he had not yet achieved what he had hoped to in his trip to Illinois in the first place. Then he remembered the exchange he had witnessed between Matt and his wife, Lillian. His resolve stiffened. At last he ventured an answer.

"Yes, I do have to go. I could stay … I see that now … the offer is there … but I cannot bind myself to you while I am yet bound up with the affairs of the world. I … am not yet whole …" he said.

"Will you ever be whole?" she asked, a hint of frustration in her throat.

"I don't know. But it seems to me that although I learned nothing directly about my family in Illinois, I have somehow sensed that I do know something about them. They would not choose the luxuries of peace while the tides of war washed around their friends, drowning them. I don't know how I know that … a sense seems to have recently come upon me …" he tried to explain.

"I don't hate you for this," Joan comforted him. "I know that you must go. My father is going as well. My uncles leave, too. I know that they leave—and that you leave—and that your deeds are not merely to the benefit of those you come to assist and defend, but that they also protect me, and those you leave behind. If you do nothing now, if the might of the plains was not sent to rescue those in Illinois, the Pledge would stretch out its hands against us after its victory. Yes, I know it …" Joan began crying, and King brushed the tears from her cheek with one hand and caressed her face with the other. "I know that it would come to blows no matter what. Either we fight them there or we fight them here, but in fighting them there you serve not only your blood kindred, but also your brothers and sisters in the human race. So, I don't despise you for your decision, but my heart … it … I …"

She could not complete her thought. Nor did she have to. King also began crying, unashamedly weeping in her arms. They held each other close. At last, spent, they pulled apart, and she looked him in the eyes with a sternness that he had seen before.

"You must go now. I will pray that you return to me alive and whole, and then we shall see. But I will only distract you if I stay … be resolved in your heart, King. Don't forget me, but don't look behind you as you march. As for me, my duty is to aid the defense of

Tulsa with so many men gone. I have been away for too long already ..." she said.

"A couple more hours ..." King protested.

"No!" she cried out, putting two fingers to his lips. "What you must do, you must do with all your heart and energy. Mourn as though you do not, be happy as though you were not, buy things but do not think they are yours to keep ..."

Then they kissed. Salty streams fell from each eye and mingled together on their hard pressed cheeks; passion mixed with grief, a sweet agony oppressed by bitter despair. They broke away—rather, she pushed him away—and she took him by the hand, and they looked at each other.

"I love you," she said plaintively.

"I love you," he said softly. Then she pulled away, and their hands touched to the last moment as their fingertips brushed together. Before anyone said another word, she turned away from him and strode out of the park. She did not look back, not even once, though King watched her until at last she disappeared from sight, one more black-haired person in a convulsing ocean of dark haired warriors preparing for battle and coursing through the streets.

There in the park he wept for another hour. He was left alone, and for that he was glad. But the day was pressing on and he knew he now had no reason to stay. He turned his thought to battles to the east. He felt a fire begin to burn in his soul as he remembered what it was all about: his friends, Fermion, Fides, Tasha, Jonathan, and the Rangers; also possibly his very own family, though he knew them not; the Shadowmen, noble and valiant; the nameless, defenseless men and women of Bloomington; and the Treasure in Peoria. Woe to the one who would stand against him in his wrath!

By the time he found where Charlie was organizing the advanced units, including the ones that he would be joining, King had completely regained his composure. He had packed his clothes and grabbed his staff. He tied his boots and put on his hat. King was ready to ride to war. Charlie had been ready for some time, and so had Aiken. They awaited him along with a fair number of other men, most of whom King didn't recognize. The time was nigh.

"So, just to bring you up to speed, King," Charlie explained, "A careful schedule of pickups and dropoffs has been arranged with Chummy to get as many of the foot soldiers to Illinois as quickly as possible. Already, there are thousands of riders treading the roads to the northeast. The goal is for the entire army to assemble and stage at Hannibal, Missouri. Recently gained information tells us that the bridge there is still up. A delegation of some two hundred fifty men will venture to St. Louis, but our part is not with them. Our part is to rush to Bloomington as quickly as possible and gather as much information as possible. So, as I said, we will leave sooner than the rest. I want to be in the staging areas personally before the masses arrive. So, we will leave tomorrow morning by vehicle. Seven hundred of us will go, and Chummy has equipped half his vehicles with horse trailers, so that many of us will have our horses with us. The fleet will take us to the Missouri town of Columbia, which is a bit past Jefferson City. Both towns hold the remnants of refugees who fled from Kansas City so many years back. From our drop-off, we will make all haste to be in Hannibal the next night. If all goes well, almost the entire army, foot soldiers and cavalry, will have arrived within four days, and then we'll be able to proceed to Bloomington. Those who would not yet have arrived in Hannibal when we leave will be our rear guard. Such is the plan through Hannibal. What follows after that I suppose depends on what we find there."

"Sounds fine to me. I don't mind traveling by vehicle, I'll tell you," King said. "It will be nice, though, to be back on a horse again."

"Aye," said Aiken.

"Excellent. Well unless you have questions, King, that really settles things. We leave at the break of dawn, so be at the staging grounds while it is still dark!" Charlie said, dismissing him.

King walked out into the streets with Aiken.

"How are you doing, buddy?" Aiken asked, sending a sidelong glance in his direction.

"I've had better. Yet I feel more sturdy than I've felt in a long while. I wish this to end, and I am burning to end it well," King answered.

"I am glad you're coming with me," Aiken said. "You didn't tell me how beautiful Joan was. It must have broken your heart to leave her."

"Yet I would have disappointed her if I had stayed, ultimately, I think," King said.

"Then her beauty runs deep, beneath even sight," Aiken remarked.

"Yes," King agreed, but then fell silent, and grew distant, and Aiken understood and said no more.

The next morning the sounds of hundreds of engines shattered the early morning stillness. The dew on the grass collected on the feet of men and beasts as they assembled at the first muster. In the fields east of Tahlequah, the Cherokee Nation was girding itself for war.

King and Aiken found Charlie and received instructions. Eventually they found the vehicle that they had been assigned to. They loitered outside it as Chummy's employees worked frantically to resolve last minute mechanical issues. Vans and trucks towed horse trailers of various sizes. Cherokee riders were carefully loading their mounts into the trailers. King observed a handful of farewells between men and wives, but by and large such details had been seen to already.

The fleet did not depart at sunrise as Charlie had hoped, but it didn't leave too late. By about seven in the morning, word was passed along to get into the vehicles. This was put off to the last minute on account of the plain fact that they were going to be stuffing warriors into every last nook and crevice that could be found. Indeed, some industrious warriors had strapped themselves to the tops of some of the vehicles. Some of the horse trailers had ladders. Men were clinging to these, attempting to balance their safety with the securing of their weapons and belongings. After all horses had been delivered east, the horse trailers would carry men.

The signal was given, and the vehicles began flowing out of the city. The horns of all the vehicles began a noisy salute to Tahlequah, and as they turned onto the road that would take them east, many hundreds of Cherokee citizens returned the salute with cheers and clapping. The line of admirers was passed in moments: they were on the open road, now.

Each vehicle was far too packed for pleasant conversation. King's vehicle, for example, was a four door car. Four grown men were crammed in the back seat which would have only ever comfortably held two. The front seat had three men. Windows were rolled down to fight against the stifling heat of seven men breathing, and judging from the sight of other vehicles doing the same, the discomfort appeared to be universal.

After a couple of hours, Joplin was reached. An hour after that it was Springfield. The fleet passed by thousands of men on horseback right outside Springfield. They waved at the fleet and saluted, and those in the fleet hung their heads out and cheered back.

King had fond memories of his last trip this direction, heading east to Cairo. Then the scenery changed. They were not heading due west, to Cairo, but rather towards Hannibal. That meant that they now followed I-44 northeast. For King and Aiken, this was retracing their journey by motorcycle out of St. Louis. Memories were short lived, however. In Lebanon, the fleet turned north. Curious citizens of Lebanon gazed at them in surprise. Chummy's vehicles had often been seen in Lebanon, but never this many, and never before filled to the brim with so many men that they were hanging off the backs of trailers or tied to the tops of trucks.

An hour after changing direction at Lebanon, the town limits of Jefferson City were reached. Again amazed onlookers gathered to look at them. King supposed that at some point these towns would learn what was going on. When the horsemen arrived, they would surely explain.

To every man's intense relief, the journey by vehicle came to an end. They had arrived at a small town called Kingdom City. It was at the intersection of the road they were on and I-70, a few miles east of Columbia. The fleet deposited its wearied sardines. Kingdom City consisted of old truck stops, which now stood empty and desolate. There were few inhabitants, but King and Aiken suspected that the ones who were there were border scouts for St. Louis. While the horses were unloaded the fleet refueled, making use of the several fuel tanker trucks that had been sent along.

By previous arrangement, some two hundred and fifty men took positions in the small city. It would be a critical part of their supply line, and it was to be held at all costs. Many of these men had some of the guns of Tulsa. Few were left with horses. Most of the horses were going to carry the remaining men to Hannibal. King hadn't thought about procuring a horse for himself, but Aiken had thought for the two of them. Soon, the two were horsed. Now sitting high up off the ground as in days of old, King felt a new thrill, and a new expectancy. Perhaps it was only glee at being out of the stuffy car.

Charlie did not dawdle. Soon the horsemen were traveling along the back roads of Missouri. Some riders were sent ahead as an advanced team and others were held back as a rear guard, but King and Aiken rode with Charlie in the main group.

"I thought Sparrow would be with us," King said to Charlie.

"Sparrow will be in the next group," Charlie said. "We've spread our leaders out appropriately. Sparrow will just be a day behind."

"I know he could not be stopped, but he seems a bit old to be warring," Aiken said.

"Sparrow springs eternal," Charlie said. "If you ask me, Sparrow intends to die in Illinois. He doesn't expect to return. Fox will assume his father's mantle. Officially, that is. When Sparrow disappeared, authority gradually came to fall on Fox's shoulders anyway. But he received half-hearted support, and even in his own mind he doubted. Should Fox live, he will unite the tribes that remain in the plains of the west and Midwest," Charlie said.

"I thought we would have more guns with us," King said.

"These too must be spread evenly between the groups. We have enough, I think. We are still skilled in bow, and some of us have taken up the sword. You see that I have a sidearm?" Charlie said, pulling up his coat so that King could see it.

"Nice!" King exhaled.

Charlie laughed, "It is the same one that I had that time you and Luke got crazy. You're lucky you weren't shot with this gun!"

"Well, here I am. Water under the bridge," King smiled.

"Yes, here you are. And you're not merely a young man or a boy anymore. You are a man at last, so I say. However you spend your life now, I expect you'll do it with wisdom, care, and ferocity," Charlie said, eyeing him.

"Thank you," King replied, honored.

"Nothing to thank me for. I merely report what I observe," Charlie said. Aiken was nodding his head.

"Well, let's not say more about it. You'll make me blush!" King joked.

"Very well. And I see that scouts from the advanced party are coming, so I have to go for now. Peace!" Charlie said, sprinting out of their group to meet the messengers.

As it began to grow dark, they decided to camp for the night. They reckoned that they had another twenty or thirty miles to go; with another early morning start, they were certain they could reach Hannibal early in the evening the following day. Men huddled around campfires and sang songs and told stories. Except for the fact that they all carried weapons, you could not have guessed that they were marching off to war. Charlie roamed the camp taking men to task for their carefree attitude. He pointed out that they were camped without the cover of city or wood, and that their fires would be visible far and wide, but even he could not bring himself to order them to put them out.

The next morning, riders were in the saddle as the sun kissed the lip of the horizon. Desolate farm field after farm field marched past them. On very rare occasions, they came across a farm that was being worked. Nonetheless, they saw very few people. They were not on a major thoroughfare.

Route 61 was a major thoroughfare, however. It paralleled the Mississippi. Those who wanted to cross the river were bound to take it in search of the rare crossings spanning the great river. When they turned onto Route 61 there were dozens of travelers heading both north and south. These had already seen the advance guard, but now, seeing the main body, they stopped in their tracks and gawked at the passing of so many riders—clearly Indian—heading north. Some south bound travelers even turned around to follow them with their eyes, they were so curious.

Their time on Route 61 was brief, however, as there was just a short leg between where they met it and Hannibal. It was late afternoon when finally they stepped inside the borders of the town. It was a beautiful town, with streets lined with tall trees. One might have thought the calamities of the past had skipped over the town altogether if it weren't for the fact that there were so many travelers about and businesses arrayed to meet their needs.

Hannibal appeared to have an intact government as well. Shortly after the riders arrived in the city, representatives from the government came out to greet them … and seek out their intentions.

What Charlie told them both pleased them and frightened them. It pleased them to hear that they had no ill will against the city, as five hundred armed horsemen could have done a lot of damage. It frightened them to learn that some thirty thousand warriors were expected to amass there before heading out to war. They wisely saw that they could not dissuade them and gingerly offered to accommodate them to the best of their ability, but you can be sure that their leaders were up late that night in tense and confused meetings. Businessmen were of a different mind. So many men surely meant a windfall for them. Word spread quickly. Even that night, though no more men were expected, some businessmen had set up booths where 61 entered the city, or otherwise staked out territory to do so soon.

Charlie led the riders immediately to the bridge. Holding the bridge was imperative, and taking it in hand was one of the objectives they had been assigned. The bridge fell to the Cherokee without a fight. The bridge had toll collectors who had made themselves rich, but these were escorted off without incident. Then, half the riders stayed on one the Missouri side of the bridge, while Charlie took the other half across to Illinois.

King and Aiken went across with Charlie. There was a dramatic difference in the terrain between Illinois and Missouri at this point. The Missouri side was wooded and homely. After you got away from the river, the Illinois side was flat, with farms sprawled in all directions. At least it would be easy to spot an enemy approaching from the east.

Their first objective accomplished and the remaining ones out of reach until more elements of the army arrived, the riders set up camp. Charlie established a rotation on both sides of the river, so that the bridge would be well guarded at all times, and set a watch and dispatched scouts. After all this, most of the men were able to water their horses and begin cooking their dinners.

Cherokee songs were sung around the fires, and Charlie recounted to Aiken the story of Luke and King's adventures against the Lighter Sioux where Charlie had nearly shot them himself. Aiken hadn't heard the story before and marveled at the spunky courage of King. The sun was completing its arc through the sky in search of its nightly resting place as they mused over the past. It had just dropped below the roof of the earth when something remarkable happened.

The horses noticed it first. They began whining and stomping their feet. The men looked about, and some of them reached for their weapons. Not more than a half moment later the sky came alive around them: a silvery light past by and through them, like a frothy wave overtaking a boulder in an ocean bay. Their cooking utensils rattled and their skin tingled and their hair stood on end.

As quickly as it had come, it had gone. Men looked about in wonder and laughed nervously. But not King.

When he opened his eyes at last, he saw Aiken and Charlie both staring at him intently.

"What did you see?" Aiken asked him.

"I saw the passing of Fermion. He is no more!" King cried out in sorrow.

"What? How?" Aiken prodded.

"I didn't see the event … it is hard to explain … but I saw him … extinguished …" King moaned.

"Fermion was stout," Charlie said, raising a cup in honor, "I don't doubt that he left this orb in power and mighty exertion, and achieved a great good in doing so."

But King whispered, "He spoke to me. The wave brought his thought to me, and I heard him …" Charlie sat with his cup raised high, frozen with anticipation, waiting for King to complete his thought.

"What did he say, son?" Aiken asked him tenderly.

"He said, 'Behold thy name: thou art Keane! Keane, for now, and then the white stone!'" King said softly.

"He has renamed you?" Charlie wondered, incredulous.

But King shook his head. "No, I think … I think that has always been my name, only I have just now remembered it. In Fermion's last thought, he dealt a blow to the enemy, but he included me in the affairs of his mind, too. I … am Keane."

When no one said anything, King added, "And unless I am mistaken, our guns will no longer work, and there is a good chance that most of Chummy's fleet is incapacitated, too."

Charlie leapt up, astonished. "What do you mean? What is this about?"

King reminded Charlie of the story of Fermion at Cairo. The effect of Fermion's charge had been that most of the Pledge guns and some of the Ranger's guns ceased working. The Pledge vehicles no longer worked, either. "So you see," King said, "Fermion's thought has stretched out quite far, and I think it will have the same effect."

"This would be a dire situation indeed if that were the case!" Charlie exclaimed.

"I have to believe that Fermion did what seemed best to him and meant us no harm," Aiken defended Fermion.

"Meant? Perhaps he meant not, but if he did, then we are in a bind! We are days ahead of the men coming by horseback, and if Chummy's fleet is disabled we are weeks ahead of those who were coming by foot. It will be just the five hundred of us exposed to whatever dangers are present around us, without hope for relief!" Charlie shouted.

"Let us not despair," Aiken counseled, "We might suppose our enemies have been similarly afflicted."

"Yes, we may hope, but we cannot know, and so we must assume that they haven't. It would be irresponsible to assume they have," Charlie muttered.

"You should do a test while you can," King said.

"A test?"

"Yes, spread the word to have the men see if their weapons will fire. At least you will gain sure knowledge of whether or not you have lost the use of your arms," King explained.

It was ordered. The men were confused by the order to fire their weapons into the woods, but were astonished to discover that nearly all of them no longer worked. When they tried to examine the mechanisms they discovered that the innards of the weapons had melted. The ammunition was even impotent: much of the powder was as useless as sand. The fading sunlight was completely gone when men came from the other side of the bridge with the results of their testing. Out of all their guns, only ten still worked.

Startled at this turn of events, Charlie brought the leaders to him to discuss what to do next. King and Aiken sat around the campfire, but said nothing. The men were frantic. They talked on into the night, but settled nothing. King fell asleep with the sound of Charlie's flustered voice in his ear, and the heated arguments and ringing suggestions that the men produced. In the end, all they could do is wait to see what the morning would bring.

# == Chapter 20 ==

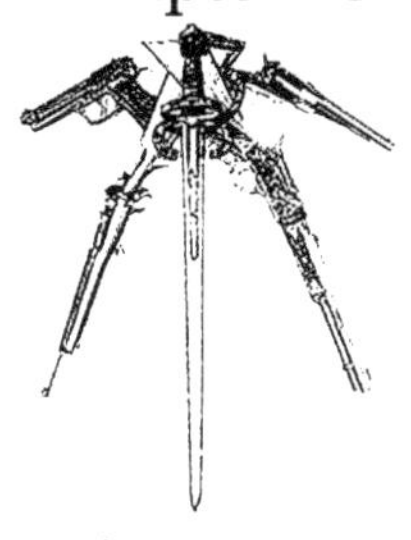

When King awoke he found Charlie and Aiken together with many of the leaders arguing about what to do next. The loss of their guns was a tremendous blow, but it could not compare to the loss of the entire army. If the fleet could not function, then they would be alone in Hannibal for several days. The thousands of riders that they had passed outside Springfield weren't due for another two to three days. If by some wind of fate a Pledge army happened their way while they were waiting for allies, they would not be able to withstand them.

That was the unsettling, but that was not what the arguments were about. Many of the men did not wish to remain outstretched and exposed with no hope for reinforcements. They wanted to withdraw until they met the main cavalry, which they guessed would be right about in Kingdom City. Others expressed the concern that the whole campaign was being called off even at that moment, and the cavalry had turned around. Establishing lines of communication seemed to be paramount.

But Aiken said, "*Oft hope is born, when all is forlorn.*"

He was on the other side of the argument along with one or two of the other leaders, and to some degree Charlie. Charlie saw the merit to points made by both sides, but leaned against retreat. They had come this far in order to offer a hand of help to the people of Bloomington. To withdraw completely and forsake all of the plans that had been drawn up to this point meant to leave the people of central Illinois to fend off their foes on their own. Aiken did not counsel sending all the men ahead without thought to those who were supposed to come behind, but he reasoned that if they were now to be considered an isolated party which could choose either to go back or go forward, they may as well go forward. Leave some men behind to convey their decision and press on to Bloomington on their own. Perhaps five hundred worthy riders might not be worthless?

King walked into the conversation at this point. He listened carefully as the men argued back and forth. He saw the danger of advancing forward or even of waiting when no one had even an inkling of the status of their armies behind them, like for example, were they even still coming? On the other hand, he felt in his bones that coming this far and accomplishing nothing was abhorrent. As the conversation progressed, King came to this realization: whatever was decided, he at least would be going on to Bloomington.

With that decision firm in mind, King didn't feel like it was his place to try to persuade the captains to his view. It was a difficult decision. Also, Aiken was marshalling the arguments well. Yet it was that Charlie beheld King standing there by the fire and put the question to him.

"What would you have us do, King?" Charlie asked him.

"I see all sides of this argument. I feel that all I can say within my rights is that whatever is decided, honor and loyalty drive me on. Do what you must; I will go to my friends, who even now must be in the teeth of peril. It must be so, or else Fermion would not have reduced himself to ash. I will go forward," King asserted.

"And I will go with him," Aiken declared.

"It would likely be for naught if only the two of you went," one of the soldiers remarked.

"Possibly. But that is not known. I simply must go on," King stated with finality.

The men were moved by his commitment to those in Bloomington. It helped remind them that they were engaged in a noble task. As King turned away from the campfire, compromises were being struck. After a time, Aiken found King sitting under some trees, his staff resting in his lap.

"Well, I wouldn't say we've carried the day, but at the least we'll be able to get word to Bloomington that they are not forgotten in the world," Aiken said.

"What did they decide?" King asked.

"Three hundred will go forward. One hundred will stay in Hannibal. The remaining hundred will begin the journey back in an attempt to establish communication with the army behind. I think it is a decent compromise. Three hundred riders from Tahlequah will make the average Pledge soldier's heart quail, I warrant," Aiken said.

"What about timing?" King wondered. "I think I should set off already this morning if we are not going to be waiting around."

"Charlie thought the same. The three hundred will leave around noon today. Charlie is currently organizing the men and issuing orders. He asked if I would take command of those going forward, or if you would be interested in the job, but I declined and thought you would not want it either. I hope I didn't misjudge?" Aiken asked him.

"You're right. That is a duty that I don't want right now. But why isn't he coming?"

"He feels that he must remain in Hannibal in case the armies do finally arrive."

King scratched his head, "Why wait until noon? That is hours from now. We could leave in an hour, easily!"

"It is simply this: according to the time table, the fleet was to arrive with the next wave of troops around ten or eleven this morning. By noon it will be plain, or at least reasonable to infer, that the fleet has been stopped. So, we wait for a little longer to ensure that we are not acting rashly. I thought it was a fair compromise. Some wanted to wait until six this evening," Aiken explained.

"I suppose I can make myself wait until noon," King sighed.

"Now, I had a question for you, King. You said that Fermion spoke to you somehow and said your name is Keane. What do you make of that? Should I now be calling you Keane?" Aiken inquired.

"I don't know yet. It seems strange. For now 'King' is fine. I will think about it, and perhaps it will become plainer in the next few days," King answered.

"Fair enough. But come! Let's go and see where things stand and get something to eat. Also, I should like to get a look at the river in the daylight, and not running for my life to get over it!" Aiken said, remembering the nine riders that had last driven them over the Mississippi. King laughed and the two made their way back to where the other riders were eating and talking. After a time, they made their way to the bridge. The Mississippi was beautiful, and they lingered long there.

It was not long, however, until noon had come.

King and Aiken joined the other riders assembling east of the river. There were final agreements made about the distribution of the remaining working guns and the ways in which they would leave messages behind them for those who would come after them. A Cherokee rider named Manfred was the leader of the three hundred. King knew of him and thought highly of him, though he had never became more than a passing acquaintance with him.

With no sign of any vehicle coming from the west, the order was issued at last to depart. Charlie stood by the side of the road and nodded to King as he passed. Other Cherokee watched them go as well. It was a quiet, solemn moment. Though it was known that the three hundred were marching into danger, it was feared that all the others were on the brink of calamity as well.

They marked Bloomington as being about one hundred fifty miles away. Manfred was resolved to make the trip in three days, less if possible. There was no question that the horses were capable of making the trip in that time—even two days was possible—but no one knew what obstacles lay before them. Even with Aiken as their guide, they couldn't guarantee that they wouldn't get lost.

The horses were set on a quick gait, and the miles began to slough off their journey. They passed quickly through numerous small towns. As in other places, people came out to gawk at them. No one lingered to explain to the residents what was transpiring. They were following I-72, which meant that there were also a fair number of travelers on the road. The Cherokee paid them no mind.

Starting off at noon meant that they did not have as many hours of daylight to travel by. After about thirty miles, it had begun to get dark. Manfred found a road breaking off to the north and directed the riders to follow it. He left markings near the road so that later allies could follow their path. If they had been in Oklahoma, they would have continued on, even into the dark. As they were in foreign territory, however, they chose to camp for the night as the sun was waiting to drop the final distance beneath the arc of the earth. They set up camp in the outskirts of a tiny, abandoned town, called New Salem.

Sentries were dispatched and watches were set. King and Aiken were part of the twenty or so men in the first watch. As the stars sparkled and the night deepened, King inhaled the heady breath of the earth at rest and felt … as though on the verge of some great adventure. Perhaps Aiken sensed it, too. Both were quiet. They passed the hours of their watch in silence, and when it was their turn to sleep, they slept deeply.

The riders were up before dawn. Horses were fed and watered and then mounted. Manfred gave the word, and even before the first blades of sunlight pierced the morning, the riders were off. The roads didn't seem as though they were going to cooperate, so with a general sense of their position relative to Bloomington in mind, Manfred led them off the roads, heading as close to northeast as they could. When the sun came up they were already miles more into their journey.

After about an hour they found a river. They followed it north in search for a bridge to cross or a shallow section to ford. Within a half-hour, they found a bridge. Signs informed them that the river was the Illinois River, and that the city was Meredosia. The bridge seemed to be intact as they approached it and there was no indication that the city was populated. They cautiously stepped out onto the bridge, scanning the region around them.

They were halfway across the bridge when a shot rang out. A rider fell off his horse, dead. Other horses went into a panic, but most were well mastered. It was not known which direction the shot came from, so Manfred ordered them across. Weapons were out. The four guns that they had brought were ready for action. The riders were galloping across the bridge, and nearly over, when fifty men rushed at them from their hiding places in the broken buildings of Meredosia.

"Straight on!" Manfred shouted, ordering the riders forward into battle.

Already two thirds of the riders were across. More gunshots had rung out, but these had not hit anyone. Though the gunmen couldn't be located, the men rushing them were easy enough to see, and the Cherokee gunmen fired into them. It did not take long for the attackers to realize their danger. The Cherokee riders were upon them, and they were only on foot. Moreover, the Cherokee had more than one gun, and each was effective, while they seemingly had only one. No sooner did their ambush begin did call for retreat ring out.

The sounds of horses stampeding in the city filled the morning air. For his part, King had been near the back of the column when the action broke out, and did not have an opportunity to engage anyone in combat. Manfred was giving orders, now.

"You there, check our flanks south!" Manfred called out to one squad, which turned quickly in that direction. To King's squad, he said, "Follow them, but then turn north and encircle the city!"

King and Aiken drove their heels into their steeds and joined the other twenty or so riders following Manfred's commands.

The city wasn't very large, but it was large enough for their attackers to hide in. The Cherokee riders stormed down streets and alleys hunting for their prey, especially the sniper. King's squad had the task of shutting the back gate to the city, keeping their attackers hemmed in. Another encircling party had been sent north around the city, and the two squads would meet on the other side and make for a formidable blocking party.

When they made it around to the other side, however, they were startled to see three horsemen escaping the city, riding wildly to the east. These were not Cherokee riders: and one had a gun.

"The sniper!" King cried out.

"Gettem!" Aiken shouted.

Aiken and King, joined by three other Cherokee riders, followed in hot pursuit. The terrain was open and flat. The well-trained Cherokee horses were rapidly catching up to the fleeing foes, but they had had a decent head start. The thundering of the hooves on the dirt filled King's ears. His staff was extended like a javelin, and next to him Aiken and the other riders were leaning forward in their saddles, the wind whipping their hair back.

The sniper team turned to the north. The mad pursuit continued. They had closed within thirty yards as the fleeing men reached a tree line that paralleled the road. Another road broke off to the right and the enemy followed it. King caught a glimpse of name of the road as they turned down it: Trinity Church. No sooner did he read the road sign did he turn his gaze down that very road and see that he was in an awful lot of trouble.

A hundred men on foot were facing him, not more than forty yards away. About thirty of them had taken a knee and were aiming rifles at them. There was no time. The sniper team got out of the way and these new foes unleashed a fusillade upon the five of them. Horse and man fell to the ground. King's horse crumpled and rolled over its neck. They came at rest with the horse lying still between him and the riflemen. The horse's body shielded King, but King's right leg was throbbing. He was sure he had broken something. Still, he nodded with grim glee that at least he had not been shot.

Aiken was also on the ground. His horse was dead, too. Shots rang over his head as he clambered over his horse for shelter. They exchanged glances; the fifteen feet separating them might as well have been a hundred.

Now King surveyed the other three men. Two were dead. One of their horses was alive, but was streaking back towards the city in panic. The third rider lay on the ground, disabled by a gunshot wound. He was in plain sight of the riflemen, but as he was lying still, he drew no fire. Since Aiken had been seen alive, however, there were still bullets coursing over his mount, and sometimes into it.

The shots slowed. King peeked between the shattered legs of the horse and saw that half of the troop was jogging in their direction, while several riflemen remained on their knees, firing over Aiken's horse to remind him to stay down. There was nothing to do.

The men finally arrived, and Aiken quickly surrendered. Then they discovered that King was still alive and alert, and they tossed aside his staff and prodded him to his feet. He winced as he tried to walk. Aiken and King were forced to put their hands on their head. The foes checked the other fallen riders. The third man was deemed to be mortally wounded. He was checked for weapons and then left alone, presumably to die.

A man stepped forward. He wore military fatigues and had bars pinned to his shirt. His lips were drawn tight across his face. It was impossible to gauge the man's emotions. He was clearly the leader.

"Put them down on their knees!" the man ordered. King and Aiken were roughly shoved to their knees. King cried out in agony. Certainly, something was broke.

"Now," the man continued, "You will tell me all you know. The sooner you do, the sooner you die, and the better for it you will be."

Another man stepped forward. He spoke to the leader, "Sir, there are many more men. Hundreds of them. They crossed the bridge at great speed, all on horseback. We killed one or two on the bridge and then a few more in the streets, but they've got rifles as well. We had to give way. There can be no question that we are overrun in the city and that the riders will be upon us any minute!"

The leader now cast an evil sneer at King and Aiken. "Who are you? Where are you from? Where are you going? Quick!"

But they gave only silence in answer.

The man scowled at them, "You will answer me quickly, or you will die slowly. That is the truth of it!"

"We can question them later after we deal with the threat in the city ..." the sniper suggested.

"You fool! I want to know more about that threat before I go trotting into it. There will be others to question if these won't cooperate," the leader snarled.

"Very well," the sniper said, falling back in with the other men who were gathered about them.

"Now, as to you two, here now is your final opportunity. I will count to three. If I get to three and one of you hasn't started talking, you'll pay."

King and Aiken stared at the man with hot contempt in their eyes.

"One. Two. Three."

The leader slid a long knife out of a sheath and stepped forward and thrust it into Aiken's chest. Aiken fell backwards, writhing in pain.

"You ...!" King shouted in rage, leaping to his feet, ignoring the pain in his leg. But even as he reached to throttle the man he learned that the man had anticipated this response. He stepped back and stabbed at King. The knife blade fell deeply into his abdomen. With a frightful gurgling noise, King collapsed to the ground. His hands reached for his belly instinctively, and blood seeped through his fingers and poured out onto the ground.

"As I said. Die slowly. But I think we can make it hurt a little more," the leader said, stooping down to inflict more damage.

But lo! A sudden stamping of horse's feet filled the clearing followed by a sustained volley of rifle fire. Shrieking filled the air as bullets met their mark. Panic filled the rest. The leader began shouting at his men to try to instill order, but he was only barely successful. The most he achieved was that he and his men began falling steadily away from their assailants in the direction of the city.

After that, the ninety or so men (for ten lay dead in the clearing) made a mad rush for the city, heedless of the fact that the sniper had warned them that it was occupied by the riders from the west.

Silence fell upon the clearing in which King and Aiken lay. King kicked his legs rhythmically in response to his agony, moaning. Aiken pulled himself to sitting as the rescuers came close. Even King saw them. He had merely assumed that Manfred and the other riders had saved them. It was not so.

King beheld wild looking men. They were dressed in thick leather hides. The hides overlapped and were stained with different colors, valiant hues of red and black. The leather was thick and clearly heavy, and would probably turn a blade and might possibly absorb a bullet, if the bullet was of more recent vintage when craft had grown inferior. Their hair was long and scraggly. It fell down to the middle of their backs. For a moment King thought they were Rangers. Indeed, there was some resemblance, but these men were still different. For one thing, most of the wild men had beards that hung down well below their chins. Each was armed with a rifle and a long blade. Their horses were similarly adorned with leather armor. By King's count there were only thirty of them. Thirty, yet they had routed a hundred.

Several of the men leapt from their horses and began tending to King and Aiken.

"You will be fine," one said to Aiken. "It missed your lung, though I don't doubt it hurts greatly. But your friend ..."

Two of the venison smelling men were tending to King. One was digging into the knife wound with his fingers while the other held King's hands and arms to keep them out of the way. The man worked frantically on him. Aiken pushed his way through.

"Water!" the man called out. The wild looking men gathered around them in a wide circle. Some had their heads bowed as though in prayer. Others rushed forward with canteens. The man who had been working on King poured water over the wound so that he could see better what he needed to do. He brushed Aiken's hands away and then began working again. King blinked up at the man as he told Aiken to put pressure on a particular spot. Then the man said, "I don't know. I have slowed the bleeding I am sure. I don't have the skill to do better. We must wait, pray, and hope."

"Am I going to die?" King asked the man, squinting with pain.

"Yes, of course. But as for today, that I do not know. I have stopped the bleeding as well as I can, but I see that you still bleed. I do not wish to speak a word that is not mine to declare. You may live, but it will not be by the skill of man. You see we are in prayer," the man said, nodding towards the wild men who had encircled them. Many eyes were closed and heads were slightly bowed, and their lips worked silently.

Aiken continued to press on the spot where the man had directed him, but now he began to weep. With no hands to brush the tears away, they fell down his tired and careworn face, falling in the rivulets time had carved into his flesh. King reached up with his bloody hands and took Aiken's head in them, though Aiken did not abandon his duty and kept his hands upon King's belly. The man who had been working on King nodded solemnly and backed away in respect.

"Your affection is certain and moving. See! Our captain arrives. Perhaps there is hope for you," the man said.

King's body shuddered.

Boom!

BOOM.

Tum Bum-Bum-Badil Tum Badil Bum Bum

"I think he is fading away, my friend ..." King heard someone saying.

"No! It is something else! King ... what do you see?"

Ratta-tat-tat-tat. Boom-Boom-Boom Ratta-tat-ratta-tat-ratta-TAT. Boom-ratta-Boom-ratta-BOOM. Ratta-Ratta-TAT-Ratta-tat-tat-tat.

"A cascade of diamonds falls upon the earth with great power ... the earth gives way as they strike! Out of the blackened craters come ... thousands ... hundreds of thousands ... no ... countless ... they are countless on the plains!"

Ratta-tat-tat-tat BOOM BOOM BOOM
Ratta-tat-ratta-tat-ratta-TAT TAT TAT.

King realized he had once seen them amassed in the sky, but now he saw them upon the earth.

Drums! The Drums of War! He trembled in the rhythm.

Bum BOOM BOOM Bum Bum BOOM Bum
BOOM BOOM Bum Bum BOOM

BOOM BOOM BOOM Ratta-tat-tat-TAT Tat Ratta-tat Tat Ratta TAT!

BOOM Bum bu-Bum-bu-Bum BAM BAM!

Tum Bum-Bum-Badil Tum Badil Bum Bum

BOOM BOOM BAM!

"What else do you see, King?" Aiken's voice wafted into his ears from some distant place.

"It is beautiful! Fell warriors with shields and swords, and they shout! The world around them is dark, but the fires of their coming light up the field! They shout! They yell! The swelling roar of their proud cries moves river and mountain! Their faces stretch to yell all the louder, one sustained and mighty call to arms! And still the drums! My God, still the drums!"

"What is this?" a distant voice said aloud.

"I think he is a prophet," Aiken's voice came back as in a dream.

"A prophet? But prophecy is sealed," the other said.

"Perhaps, yet here he is."

The distant voice drew nearer, "What do you see, my son?"

Great welling tears were falling down King's face, but it was not from pain—rather from some terrible joy inspired by touching some dreadful goodness. He searched for words to communicate what he saw and failed. He offered these, instead, "The knights from the sky seem so young and yet old, like their time was cutoff, but not their being ... each has a glint in his eyes, mischievous, maybe devilish, I cannot say! They ... know they've thwarted some great stratagem ... they bang, they bang on their shields ... the sound of it ... the sound of their voices combined ... and still the drums!"

"Whose side do they fight for?" someone near his ear asked.

"I ... cannot say ..."

"Some dark magic, I say ..."

"Speak no such nonsense!"

"There is nothing dark about him!" Aiken snapped.

King spoke again, "I see something else ... Iurwain Ben-atar advances with sword in hand and a glint in his eye. The sword flashes in the crimson fires that dot the darkened horizon ... behind him strides Jacob, Reborn, and Clever Sunshine. They are followed by a host of those like them ... they ... are different than the first ... Lord, who are these?"

From within the vision a voice near at hand replied, "Look!"

"And I beheld that from some of them skin fell off them, like a snake shedding its skin, but the skin seemed mechanical and metal, yet tied to their being. Their skeleton had been on the outside and now it fell away leaving pink skin, lo! Men came forth and robed them and then other men came forward with armor, shield, and sword, with shiny helms which glistened in the light of others, and I said, Lord, tell me, who are these and why are they different than the others?"

And the Lord replied, "Love's unborn is with the others who came not at all, but these came for a little while but were scorned by fate. To them now comes the greatest gift ever proffered. See, they come."

"Who are you Lord?" I asked.

"A messenger, that is all. He who has ears let him hear. He who has eyes let him see. But now! I too go to fight!"

With that King blinked and before him was the clearing, and many men gathered around him. The pain in his stomach came back and with vengeance. Indeed, the pain seemed to widen.

"His bleeding is internal," the man told Aiken. "You can move your hand. See, he no longer bleeds out of the wound."

Aiken moved his hand. King looked at him. Tears were still falling down Aiken's face and King was moved, he spoke, "Grieve not like the rest of men."

One of the Wild Men drew forth and said, "Nay, there is nothing dark in him, but even now light is breaking through. I will not say do not weep; for not all tears are an evil. Yet weep not like men who have no hope, for here is one who is filled with it."

"My *God*," came a voice close to the last speaker.

"What is it?" the Wild Man said.

"I know this boy!"

Aiken glanced up at him, "What are you talking about?"

"I know his father!" the man said, stooping low to look more closely at him. He knelt down next to King and studied him carefully. "Yes, I'm sure of it! He has his father's features! My name is Ed. Keane, I knew your father from long ago. I have come west as the guide to the Wild Men. The call to battle rung out throughout the land, and when they came I deemed that helping them arrive in Bloomington would be good. But your father! Keane, he is in Bloomington, too! Gideon, we must transport this boy to Bloomington! They have not set eyes on each other for years!"

"My name is Keane," King said. And Keane he became there in a clearing, with blood drenching the grass. He said, "I am not a boy."

"My apologies!" Ed said, laughing, "You're your father's son for making that observation!"

The Wild Man named Gideon said, "We were going to Bloomington eventually, anyway, though to go there now is to abandon our current mission."

"A mission purely of our making and choosing. We can choose and make another," Ed said.

"You speak truly," Gideon said. Suddenly there were shouts from some of the other wild men and Gideon jerked his head to see what was the matter. He left Keane's side to investigate.

Keane clenched his fists and winced as a wave of pain washed over him. His eyes fluttered open. A smile crossed his face and he began attending to the invisible spaces around him as though listening intently to some messenger. A look of recognition crossed over his face as Aiken watched him carefully.

"I remember you ..." Keane said.

"Yes, of course, Keane. I am your friend, Aiken!" Aiken cried out. But Keane was not talking to Aiken.

The sound of thunder rumbled through the woods. Men leapt up and horses jerked their heads in agitation. In the echoing clamor of the thunder came the words "The Wound is Healed." Men looked at one another in awe and wonder.

Keane closed his eyes again to give ear to the voice speaking to him. He listened for a while, and then he pulled Aiken close to him. It was growing hard for Keane to speak; a voice just above a whisper was all he could manage, so he spoke right into Aiken's ear. The other men stood around in respectful silence, sensing that Keane's final moments were at hand. The thudding sound of hooves on the plain made them all turn their heads. Gideon was standing with some of his men, gazing back and forth between the thundering sky and the direction of the city, from whence the thundering horses were coming.

When the horses arrived, Keane was dead.

Aiken wept.

The riders dismounted to find three of their kindred lying dead in the midst of some fallen of the enemy, as well as some horses. Gideon led them over to the body of Keane. Aiken was sitting near it, stunned. He was crying, but softly. He had already been crying for so long. Ed was there, too, deep in thought, yet in his eyes too, salt water gathered. Aiken looked up to see who had come.

"Sparrow!" Aiken shouted, leaping to his feet, ignoring his pain.

"Yes, I have come, but that is not good news. We must go!" Sparrow cried out.

"What do you mean we must go? Of course we are going!" Aiken said.

"No. Now, we must go in with haste and all speed! We are in peril!" Sparrow exclaimed.

"We cannot leave Keane, for that is now his name, here. At least let's bury him!"

"Let the dead bury the dead," Sparrow said. "We will go to them, but they will not come to us. But let's not abandon this present duty in order to hasten our meeting, for we are in deathly danger."

Even as Sparrow spoke the clearing was filling up with even more horsemen. Manfred's riders were there, but also countless new riders. It was, possibly, the next wave of horsemen due in Hannibal, but if so, they had made great time. Aiken looked and saw that there were thousands of horsemen. Few were stopping; most were sprinting by on the road, following it to the northeast. A look of panic was in the eyes of the riders and Aiken could taste their fear.

"I cannot leave him to rot on the ground!" Aiken shouted in anger.

Gideon came and put his hand on Aiken's shoulders, "If you do not, then your body will rot on the ground as well. There is little time, not even for a burial. Such is the tragedy of our time, when not even grief is allowed its proper expression. Come, ride with my sons and be comforted."

"Can we not carry him?" Ed protested. "At the least his father should see his son, even if he has passed, when he has not seen him in ever so long?"

"I am sorry, sir," Sparrow said. "These other men you see lying around have fathers too, and these also will not see their sons. We must ride in haste, though, and cannot be encumbered by the dead."

"Maybe I will just lie here and rot, if danger is so imminent. My honor seems at stake," Aiken grumbled.

Sparrow replied, "Set aside your honor. King would not want you to sacrifice your life for his corpse. Don't you know that we will all be changed? In the twinkling of an eye! If you fix your eyes on this world, you will accomplish nothing. If you fix your eyes on the next, you will do much. It is because so many have ceased to think of the other world that they have become so ineffective in this one: or worse, their efforts create more harm than good. Let hope drive you on. Your 'honor' merely holds you back!"

Charlie came forward through the men who were gathered, "Come, Aiken. He was a son to me long before he was to you. Let me say goodbye to him in the stead of his real father, and then let us go. It is imperative."

When Aiken saw the grief mingled with fear in the eyes of those around him, and the tender compassion yet earnest conviction in the eyes of Gideon and his Wild Sons, he saw that he was defeated. He nodded. One of the Wild men produced a horse for Aiken, and he climbed onto it. Aiken sent a fleeting glance back to the clearing as it emptied of the living. The bodies of men and beast and son lie still and un-offended by their leaving.

Horsemen were sprinting in panic around them, but Sparrow and the Wild Men and those from the clearing departed in a more moderate speed. They were looking to form the rear, so waited for the others to pass.

"Did Keane have any last words?" Sparrow asked Aiken.

"Many," Aiken said. "And many of those need to be written down as soon as a moment can be spared."

"Say them aloud now so that we can remember them together and get them down correctly when time is given," Gideon said, riding closer so as to hear better.

"He said, '*He who has ears, let him hear. Let him who has eyes, let him see*,'" Aiken said, and then added, "And then he said, as though asking me specifically, but perhaps it was meant for all, 'What do *you* see?'"

"A prophet he seems to me," Gideon said, telling Sparrow about the voice from the sky.

"What else?" Sparrow asked reverently.

"Of the last, he said, '*Hope comes from the west, yet despair in those who have been ...*'" Aiken recounted.

"These words seem on the verge of fulfillment to me," said Sparrow with cold recognition. "Yes, we see clearly now that we cannot put our hope in the strength of men. How could we have ever done so? We ride to meet the enemy to the east, but find ourselves outmatched by a new enemy, biting at our heels. Yet, we will not despair, for despair is only for those who see the end beyond all doubt. Come, give me the next words. I know they will tell me where we ought to put our hope, and it will be of sterner stuff."

With that, Aiken proceeded to speak of many things that King said and saw in his final moments, taking his final breaths. Men wept at their hearing, and yet found in the words a stiffening of their resolve.

The clearing of the dead was now silent and still. The horsemen were far off. Even the drum beat of the hooves could not be heard. So it was that there was no one to see the shimmering of light that suddenly filled the space. Droplets of light splayed the grass and green, and there stood two men, splashing radiant colors in all directions. Shields were on their backs and swords were in their sheaths.

They stooped first to carry off the dead Cherokee riders, finding low places in the woods to put them. They covered the bodies with branches and leaves, and nodded in respect. Then they did the same with the horses. At last, only the lifeless body of Keane was in the clearing. Gay colors fell about his body as the two now bore him off to the edge of the forest. With their swords they dug a hole in the earth; it did not take them as long as you might think. Then they placed the body of Keane into the hole and covered it.

The two Men of Light nodded their heads in reverence, and then walked to where the roads intersected. Now they spoke to each other in crystal clear voices.

"Go, A-dah-Mah. Another of thy children hast thou wept upon and tasted of his despair. Thy task is to do the same elsewhere and oft' more. Do not tarry here. Here lies the one whom I touched, and here will I stand for a time to see to it that the carrion-eaters touch it not."

"It is grievous, but thou art right in your counsel. I depart."

With that, A-dah-Mah disappeared in a flash, in a twinkling of an eye, and in a thundering clash, as though the drums of war had issued its final dare.

The remaining man seemed to dissolve into the air, but his flaming sword could be seen to the last, and then it was gone. Yet he was not gone. Many a man would pass that way, but none would dare to enter the clearing, defended as it seemed by a swaying white fire. A fierce warning would pierce their hearts, and though they understood it not, a voice seemed to emanate from the clearing, crying out,

*"The saying that is written will come true:*
*Where, O death, is your victory?*
*Where, O death, is your sting?*
*Marana tha!"*

And the faint sound of drums ... growing in their ears if they lingered too long ...

*Tum Bum-Bum-Badil Tum Badil Bum Bum*

Ratta-tat-tat-tat. Boom-Boom-Boom Ratta-tat-ratta-tat-ratta-TAT.

Boom-ratta-Boom-ratta-BOOM.

Ratta-Ratta-TAT-Ratta-tat-tat-tat.

Ratta-tat-tat-tat BOOM BOOM BOOM

Ratta-tat-ratta-tat-ratta-TAT TAT TAT.

Bum BOOM BOOM Bum

Bum BOOM Bum BOOM BOOM Bum Bum BOOM

BOOM BOOM BOOM

Ratta-tat-tat-TAT

Tat Ratta-tat Tat Ratta TAT!

BOOM Bum bu-Bum-bu-Bum BAM BAM!

*Tum Bum-Bum-Badil Tum Badil Bum Bum*

BOOM BOOM BAM

B

O

O

M

B

O

O

M

Though few did, those who lingered long enough to hear the final thunderous beat heard on the breeze the distant echo of a voice saying, "What do *you* see?"

*Nudisnudum Christi sequi*

TO BE CONTINUED IN ANOTHER BOOK

## About the Author:

A.R. Horvath is married and the father of four children. He is a graduate from Concordia University Wisconsin with a pastoral ministry degree. Having nearly abandoned Christianity in college, he credits C.S. Lewis and J.R.R. Tolkien as baptizing his intellect and his imagination. Anthony has been active on the Internet as an apologist and evangelist for more than a decade. He enjoys writing both fiction and non-fiction.

The first book in the Birth Pangs Series, Fidelis, was released in 2006. You may purchase it or contact the author at www.birthpangs.com.

The Birth Pangs website is also the home of a fantasy role playing game based on the series.

## Concise Index of Names

**Aiken** – a traveling companion to King who becomes a father figure to him.

**Charlie** – one of the Cherokee Nation's finest soldiers and scouts, he befriends King and Tasha. Also known as Tsali.

**Charis** – A traveler with the Rangers, and briefly one of King's companions.

**Chief Thunderfist** – the aging chief of the Cherokee Nation.

**Chummy** – owner and operator of a ferry service out of Tulsa, Oklahoma. It is unknown how he acquires his fuel.

the **Copperheads** – a group evidently bent on creating a racially pure country.

**Dolam** – a member of the Shadowmen council and a fan of a good smoke. Though he does not fight, he is valued for his wisdom..

**Ed** – A man who appears at King's death claiming to know King's father.

**Emory** – one of the leaders of the Rangers. He is cool headed and strategically minded.

**Falda** – a member of the Shadowmen council and like Dolam, a fan of a good smoke. Though he does not fight, he is valued for his wisdom.
**Fermion** – One of the 'Nephilim,' whatever they are. He accompanies Fides on his journeys as both Fides' master and his servant.
**Fides** – the man burdened by the key to a mysterious bunker. He is separated from his family by thousands of miles and journeys home.
**Fox Marion** – the leader of an honorable Sioux tribe.
**Gol** – a giant among the Shadowmen who rescued Fermion from the plains of Cairo.
**Gongral** – she is a member of the Shadowmen council. Like Dolam and Falda, she is valued for her wisdom.
**Harold Felts** – a senator in the New Republic of Texas.
**Henryetta** – she is a member of the Shadowmen council.
**Jim Parson** – Pastor Parson is a belligerent traveler who King identifies as a scoundrel through one of his visions.
**Joan** – a childhood friend of King who becomes increasingly dear to him as time goes on. Her father's name is Bardia.
**Jonathan** – a traveling companion who Fides rescued on the journey to Bloomington. He swears loyalty to Fides and refuses to leave his side even after he has fulfilled his vow.
**Joshua** – the leader of a band of old friends who help Tasha and King when they first become refugees. Joshua saves them all, giving his life to warn about attacking slave traders.
**Judge Martins** – the judge in charge of King's fate while in St. Louis.
**King** – rescued as a young boy by Tasha, King finds that he can receive visions. Given shelter by the Cherokee, he eventually sets out to Illinois to discover the fate of his family.
**Leredo** – a member of the Shadowmen council.
**Luke** – the son of Chief Thunderfist, Luke becomes King's closest friends while he resides in Tahlequah.
**Melody** – a friend of Charis and the Rangers and briefly a traveling companion to King..
**Misaluva** – a member of the Rangers who eventually becomes close friends with Charis and Melody, and briefly forms part of King's company.
**Nagro** – a member of the Shadowmen council, and apparently the second in command. Yuri Ryson insists that Nagro should have command.
**Neff** – the president of Oklahoma City.

**Perry** – one of the leaders of the Rangers. He is blunt and gruff, but well-meaning. He loves to tell a good story, and you don't want him fighting against you.

**Philip** – the leader of the Cherokee council in Tulsa.

the **Pledge** – an organization that has formed an army to install its own ideas about government on the country. It is composed mostly of average citizens who have nothing else to do and are looking for a cause to rally around. Its leaders are a mixed bag.

**Ramaen** – a chief of the Cherokee, Ramaen assists Chief Thunderfist in the administration of the Cherokee Nation.

the **Rangers** – a group of men and some women who rallied together informally to resist various groups angling for control of the country. Their fathers hid their guns where no one could find them, so of all groups they are often the most well armed.

**Redemptus** – an apparent exception to the rule that the Shadowmen are a wonderful sight to behold.

**Rich Mullings** – a type of Elijah who appears briefly to give King insight into his visions.

**Sam Guthrie** – the first president of the newly established New Republic of Texas.

the **Shadowmen** – a mysterious group that also appears to have a beautiful radiance about them, at least initially. It is determined that they are not Nephilim, but that they serve the same master.

**Simus** – the Rangers' acting general, though he defers to Perry and Emory for decision making. Simus is an excellent tactician.

**Sparrow** – the leader of the free tribes of the west, Sparrow was rescued by King and Aiken.

**Tasha** – King's rescuer and guide. She leads King to safety in the Cherokee nation and accompanies him on his trip to Illinois in search of his family.

**Tom** – Chummy's appointed man to escort Fides and his company to Bloomington.

**Trots** – the leader of the Pledge delegation to Oklahoma City.

**Yuri Ryson** – the apparent leader of the Shadowmen.

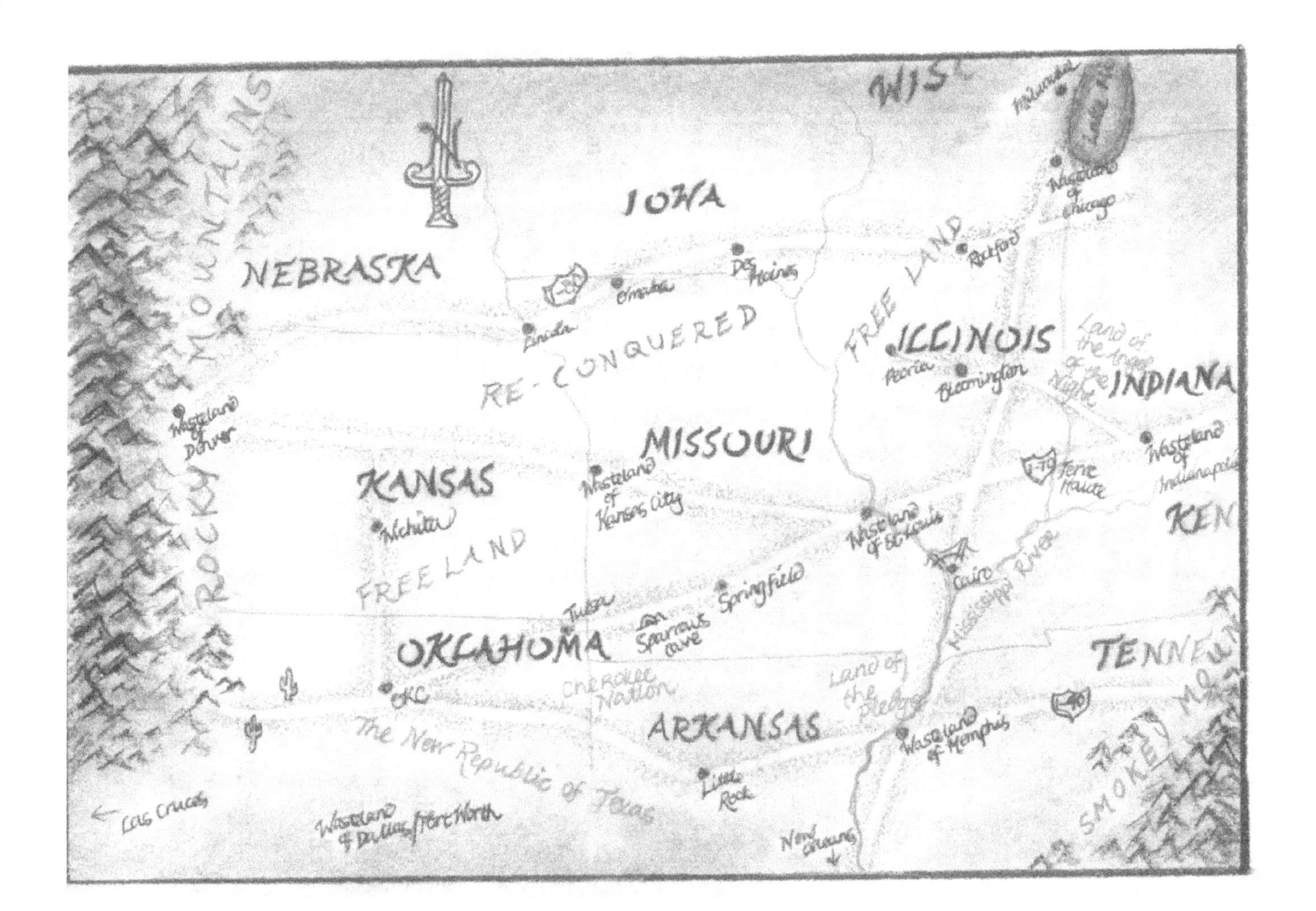
ROCKY MOUNTAINS
NEBRASKA
IOWA
WIS
Milwaukee
Wasteland of Chicago
Rockford
Omaha
Des Moines
Lincoln
RE-CONQUERED
FREE LAND
ILLINOIS
Peoria
Bloomington
Land of the Angels of the Night
INDIANA
Wasteland of Denver
MISSOURI
KANSAS
Wichita
Wasteland of Kansas City
I-70
Terre Haute
Wasteland of Indianapolis
KEN
Wasteland of St. Louis
FREE LAND
Cairo
Mississippi River
Tulsa
Springfield
Sparrow's cave
OKLAHOMA
TENNE
Cherokee Nation
OKC
Land of the Plebs
ARKANSAS
Wasteland of Memphis
I-40
The New Republic of Texas
Little Rock
SMOKEY MOUN
Las Cruces
Wasteland of Dallas/Fort Worth
New Orleans

www.ingramcontent.com/pod-product-compliance
Lightning Source LLC
Chambersburg PA
CBHW060607310726
48982CB00008B/1262/J
* 9 7 8 0 9 7 9 1 2 7 6 3 2 *